BACK FOREVER

KAREN BOOTH

Copyright © 2014 by Karen Booth

All rights reserved.

No part of this book may be reproduced in any form or by any electronic or mechanical means, including information storage and retrieval systems, without written permission from the author, except for the use of brief quotations in a book review.

This is a work of fiction. Names, characters, places, and incidents either are the product of the author's imagination or are used fictitiously, and any resemblance to actual persons, living or dead, business establishments, events or locales is purely coincidental.

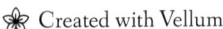 Created with Vellum

*For every reader who fell in love
with Christopher and wished to be Claire.*

CHAPTER ONE

CLAIRE'S SIDEWAYS "What are you up to Penman?" grin was always at the ready. "Looking for something?" She rolled to her stomach, draping an arm across the pillow.

Her bottomless blue eyes stopped me in my tracks. They captivated me in a way that I'd tried like hell to put into words, but I always fell short. As well as I'd done in my music career, turning tales of women and love into song lyrics, attempting to distill anything about Claire into a few lines of poetry only reminded me that I had a lot to learn.

Still in boxer shorts after unearthing my trousers from the clothes slung over a chair, I traipsed across the aging hardwoods of her bedroom. At some point, she'd need to admit that her house was no longer quaint—it was bursting at the seams. It had been nearly four months of cohabitation and I was still living out of two sticky, stubborn drawers she'd emptied in her bureau.

"I'm sorry I woke you." I plopped down on the mattress, scratching my head. My hair was thankfully returning after I'd had the not-so-brilliant idea of shaving it. "I was trying to be quiet."

"You're sweet, but you're not quiet." She eased back to her side and stretched. "What time is it anyway?"

"Nearly six. Your dad wanted to run some supplies to the recording studio before I take you to the airport."

"Why am I not surprised?"

I circled my finger on the creamy bare skin of her arm. Without fail, it thrilled me to see that my touch gave her goose bumps. "How are you feeling this morning? Still no sign of your monthly visitor?"

"My monthly visitor? You sound like my grandmother."

"Come on. I'm just excited." I smiled and peeled the covers back. "Scoot over."

"Isn't my dad waiting for you?" She slid to the middle of the bed and I cozied up next to her. She giggled as I nosed around in her neck, a musical sound that produced welcome tremors in my body.

"Your father can wait fifteen minutes."

"Is that all I get?"

"Unfortunately, my dear, I doubt I can give you the full business this morning. Richard is far too punctual for that to happen." I propped myself up on my elbow and combed my fingers through her tangled, flaxen hair. "I was just hoping for a bit of a morning snog."

"I'm sure I have the worst breath." She quickly clasped her fingers over her lips.

"I'll take my chances." I pried her hand away and pressed my mouth against hers. Even the subtlest sense of surrender had me eager to take her. *Damn her father and his schedule.* I reluctantly put on the brakes and kissed her forehead. "How many days late are we?"

"We?" She grinned, as sunlight filtered into the room and cast her in an unearthly, angelic light.

"Yes. We."

"Only two."

"Two days is better than none."

"I could take a test when I get back from New York tomorrow if you want."

"I don't want to wait that long. Let's do it now."

"It's pretty soon. It might be a waste of a pregnancy test."

"Do you honestly think I care about that?" Delayed gratification had never been my strong suit, and my impatience was much worse with this matter. A lifetime was a terribly long time to wait.

Claire tugged on my earlobe with her fingers, a seemingly innocent move that zipped electricity along my spine. "No. I don't suppose you care about that." Her forehead crinkled as she studied my face. "If we're going to do it, it has to be now. It's more accurate right when you wake up, when your pee is concentrated."

"Mmm. I love it when you talk about things like tests and urine."

"You have to promise not to get too excited. The test could very easily be negative and then you'll only be disappointed."

I skimmed my finger along the contours of her collarbone. "I don't think it's possible for me to be too excited. And of course, I'll be disappointed. I'd be lying if I said I wouldn't be, but we just keep on trying. I like that part."

"I know. I do too. I just don't want you to get your hopes up."

"We've been trying for four months. It's got to happen soon." I caught uncertainty in her eyes. "You aren't worried that something's wrong, are you?"

"No, not really." She shook her head. "But you're going to be forty-five this year and I'm already forty. It could take some time."

"It's not going to take me long to get you pregnant. I was bloody accurate the first time."

She twisted her plump, raspberry-pink lips. "I'm not a carnival game. You aren't swinging a mallet to ring the bell. Maybe the first time was a fluke. A lot of women have fertility issues at my age."

"As far as I'm concerned, we're a couple of kids." I gently lifted her tank top and kissed her stomach. "Hopefully there's a little nipper already in the oven, and if not, we try again." I circled my finger on her belly. "I vote that we take the test." I rolled out of the bed and pulled the covers back. "M'lady."

Claire scooted across the mattress. "Here goes nothing." She ran her hands through her messy blonde bedhead, shuffling into the bathroom. The cabinet door creaked when she opened it and took one of the pregnancy tests from our small stockpile.

"Do you really want to be in here for this?" She broke the seal on the box and unwrapped the test stick.

My brow furrowed. "Of course. I've been in the loo while you peed, darling. This is hardly new territory."

"Okay. If you say so."

I searched in the medicine cabinet for a distraction. Claire already felt enough pressure. I didn't want to make it any worse. *Band-aids? No. Pain reliever? I don't have a headache. Ah, yes, dental floss.*

She placed the cap on the test stick and set it on the side of the sink. "Get your watch. It takes five minutes."

I stumbled into the bedroom. Much like the rest of the house, the top of the bureau was a mess of her things and mine, co-mingling. Under a few t-shirts, I found my watch. "Do we do four minutes since it took me a minute to find it?"

"No, just do five," she called back above the sound of rushing water in the sink. "It's the same difference."

I returned to the bathroom and tried not to steal a peek at the dreaded stick. She lowered the toilet lid and sat, so I took a spot on the edge of the tub.

My mind was a torrent of nervous anticipation. Something felt different, but perhaps that was wishful thinking. *Is she? She really could be. Our baby could be inside her right now.*

Claire crossed her legs and ran her hand along the bare skin of her calf. "I need to shave."

"I didn't want to say anything last night, but you are getting to be a bit scratchy."

She frowned in an entirely adorable way. "Gee. Thanks."

"Honestly? I hadn't noticed at all." I glanced at the watch. Only two minutes into this exercise in mental torture. *Bloody hell.* "You're perfect just the way you are."

Her chin dropped. "That's very sweet."

There it was—the look on her face, the early morning sun streaming through the bathroom window, seconds ticking away at a snail's pace—a moment captured in my consciousness. Something monumental was about to happen. It made the hair on my arms stand on end.

My vision dropped to the watch again. "One more minute. Can we look?"

She shook her head vehemently. "No. Just wait."

"But I don't like to wait."

She smiled. "I know you don't. It's adorable. And a little annoying."

I consulted my nemesis, the watch, again. "Ten seconds."

"Hold my hand." She reached for me, her fingers wagging. "We close our eyes and open them on three."

"Deal." I stood as she did, enveloping her hand with mine. My eyes clamped shut as ordered, she began to count.

"One...Two...Two and a half..."

"Very funny."

She giggled. "Three. Open."

I blinked. I focused.

There it was.

One blue line.

Bugger.

I caught the sigh before it left my throat. Sharing my disappointment would only make her feel worse. I tugged her into an embrace, pressing my cheek to the side of her head. My fingers trailed through her silky hair. "Weren't we just saying how much we like trying?"

She managed a quiet laugh, but trembled beneath my touch. "I didn't want to say anything, but I actually thought I was pregnant."

The admission only made me hold on tighter, never wanting to let her go. She wanted this as badly as I did and I'd talked her into taking the test. "It's okay, darling. Really. And it's still early, right? We could do another test in a few days if you're still late." I choked back intruding tears. "I love you so much, Claire. That's all that matters."

"I love you too. I'm just ready for this to happen. I don't like feeling like our life is on hold."

"Do you really feel that way?" *You know she's right. Our life is on hold.*

"Yes. I hate seeing that look of disappointment on your face. I want to give this to you and it hasn't happened."

"I don't want it to be more important than us." *You're all that matters.*

"You can't deny that you want this very, very badly."

"I don't want it as much as I want you." *Am I the most daft man on the face of the planet?* Without another moment wasted, I dropped to my knee, which hurt like hell when it thudded against the tile floor. "Ow."

"Chris, what are you..." She looked down at me with

genuine puzzlement, certainly warranted as she was in her pajamas, me in my boxer shorts, both of us in the bloody bathroom for God's sake. *Not the most glamorous of settings, but I think it works.* Her lips were lovely and pouty. *Get on with it so you can kiss her.*

I took one of her hands, but failed to catch the other before it flew to her mouth. Her deep blue eyes were wide with wonder.

I cleared my throat and took a deep breath. I had one shot at getting this perfect. "Claire Abby, I love you more than I have ever loved another human being." The words left me feeling as though my heart might burst out of my chest. "You are the most extraordinary and wonderful and frustrating woman I have ever met and I want you to be mine forever."

She gasped. A giggle leaked out of her.

"Did you squeak, darling?"

"Maybe." Her shoulders shook, her eyes watered. "Please, go on."

"I want you to be mine. Forever. Even if we never get to have a child together, I'm never letting you go. That is, if you'll have me. Claire, will you marry me?"

Her other hand dropped and she smiled in a way that left her cheeks as full as ripe peaches on a summer day, mine for the picking. Her face was such a distraction that for a heartbeat or two, I didn't realize she hadn't yet answered the question. I wagged an eyebrow, hoping she had no defense for that.

"Well?" I asked.

"Shhh." Her smile returned as soon as she relaxed her lips.

"Shhh?"

"I'm savoring the moment."

"Why don't we savor the moment after you give me an answer?"

CHAPTER TWO

MY FACE ACHED FROM GRINNING. I loved Chris, adored him, and he'd just asked me *the* question, but the temptation to toy with him was too great. "Okay. I'm sorry." Not a breath could leave my lungs. He deserved his answer first. "Yes. A million times yes. Yes, Christopher James Penman, I will marry you. Now get off the bathroom floor and kiss me."

He stood, peering down at me with eyes that were extra sparkly, full of the mystical green light I prized. He would be mine. I would be his, for real, forever. His strong hands gripped my shoulders and I rose to my tiptoes, closing my eyes, even when I wanted to watch every millisecond of his reaction. His lips were so tender and perfect, kissing me with a softness that felt more sincere, more real, than any kiss we'd ever shared.

He rested his forehead against mine and smiled. "Don't cry," he whispered, lowering his head and kissing a tear from my cheek.

"I can't help it." I sniffled. "I'm happy."

"Good. Because that's all I want." His lips went to my jaw then inched down my neck. "I mean, in addition to this."

He held on to me tighter. I leaned into him. The brush of

his skin, his body heat, was so enticing it made me dizzy. "I know. I want that too." I was so ready to give in, fling my pajamas across the room and rid him of his boxer shorts, except that I couldn't. *My flight. The interview.* "You have no idea how badly I want you right now." I sucked in a deep breath. "But I have to finish packing."

He stopped every wonderful thing he was doing to me, sighing deeply. "Your father is waiting for me downstairs."

"My dad. Right." My shoulders slumped. *Back to reality.* "Sam's probably up too. Are we telling people?"

"We have to tell Samantha and your dad."

"Of course." I nodded.

"We should do that this morning." He hoisted my suitcase from the chair in the corner and plopped it down onto the bed. "Otherwise, they'll feel left out. After that, Graham and Angie."

Right. Chris's best friend and his wife would need to be told right away.

"My mum," he continued. "My sisters. Your sister."

One simple question, one suitably simple answer, and two minutes later the weight was on the accelerator from sheer inertia. *We're getting married.* "Wow. It's a lot of people to think about."

"The rest of the world can wait for a little while. I don't want this turning into a circus, although we can't keep people from finding out forever. It'll get out eventually. Very soon if we aren't careful."

"You know I'm not comfortable being in those magazines. I hate the feeling of not having any privacy."

"We can't control what people decide to write about or take a picture of. It's only a matter of time before your dad slips and tells one of the guys at the hardware store. That'll be the end of it."

"I know. You're right." I flipped through the clothes in my

closet until I found the two tops I wanted to take to New York. "I shouldn't be such a control freak." I turned and looked up at him. His hair was so adorably squirrelly in the morning, so drop-dead sexy. "You know what my dad's going to say about this?"

"Run, Claire, before it's too late?"

I slugged him in the arm, prompting an irresistible smile. "Stop it. My dad loves you."

"Richard is warming to me. I'll give him that much."

"He's going to ask where the ring is, Penman." I smirked. "He's an old fashioned guy."

"This is awful, but I don't have a ring for you yet." He grasped my elbow. His eyebrows drew together. "Or do I?"

He bounded to the dresser and tugged open the sticky bottom drawer and began rifling through a stack of t-shirts. When he turned, he held a wooden box, the size of a paperback book. He flipped the lid, revealing a green felt-lined compartment.

"These are some of my dad's things. His dog tags from when he was in the British army, a few photos of him when he was a boy, and...here we go. This is what I was looking for." With a flip of his fingers, a man's gold wedding band appeared in his palm. He reached for the hem of my t-shirt, giving the ring a quick polish. "May I?"

I watched as he took my left hand in his and slipped the ring on to my finger. My entire body tingled. "It's a little big, but I love it." I held out my hand, fingers splayed.

"It's just a placeholder, darling, until we can buy you a proper ring."

"So it was your dad's?"

"It was. My mum couldn't bear to let it go when he died. She gave it to me to wear when I got married."

My stomach sank, thinking about eight-year-old Chris losing his dad to a heart attack. It still haunted him and was a big part of why he was desperate to have a child. That wasn't the only thing that dulled the shine of the moment.

"You wore this when you were married to Elise?"

"Oh, no." He shook his head. "Absolutely not."

"You never wore a wedding band when you were married?"

"I did. Just not this one. I bought something. Something generic and expensive."

"Huh."

"It never felt right. I can't really explain it any more than that." He took my hand and twirled the ring on my finger. "Perhaps some part of me knew I was waiting for you."

Goosebumps crept along my arms. "You always find the perfect thing to say."

"That's why you love me."

"That's part of it." I kissed him on the cheek. "We should probably head downstairs before my dad has a heart attack about the fact that you're making him wait."

One of Chris's looks crossed his face. "What in the world am I doing?"

I cocked my head. "Flirting with disaster if you put my dad off his schedule."

"I asked you to marry me, there's no time for proper post-proposal sex, and I'm letting you get on a plane to New York with a man's wedding band that's three sizes too big." He plucked his jeans from the floor. "I'm coming with you."

"Today? Now?"

"Yes." He finished the button-fly on his jeans, an act that made me inexplicably hot and bothered. "You and I are going to Tiffany's to buy you a ring."

"Really?" I rattled the Tiffany bracelet around my wrist, the one he'd given me soon after we'd started our romance.

"Yeah, of course." He wrestled on his favorite gray t-shirt. "Let's go tell your dad and Sam."

Hand in hand, we traipsed down the hall. The sound of Sam and my dad chattering away became clearer as we reached the top of the stairs and started down. No wonder my dad hadn't noticed Chris had put him behind. He could get lost in conversation with his beloved granddaughter for hours.

"Morning," Chris quipped, patting Samantha's shoulder. "What are you lot up to?"

"Breakfast," Sam answered. "Sorry, but we're out of bacon."

"Bloody hell. A bacon famine."

My dad tapped his watch. "Geez, Louise, Chris. We're going to be late to make that run to the lumber yard before you take Claire to the airport."

Chris looked at me conspiratorially. "About that. Claire and I have news." With a wag of his fingers, he beckoned me, although I was drawn to him anyway, so the gesture was superfluous.

I took his hand and looked at Sam. The questions on her face caused a lump in my throat. It had been the two of us for her entire life, seventeen years. Now everything was about to change—a good change, a happy change, but change nonetheless.

"News?" Dad asked.

I couldn't tear my sights from Sam. *She knows. I know she knows.* Her lip jutted out and I saw her as a three year-old, running around this very kitchen in footy pajamas, giggling, me in hot pursuit and laughing just as hard.

"Chris and I are getting married."

The waterworks came for both Sam and I at the same time.

Her cheeks pinked. "Oh my God. You guys." She smiled through tears, swiping them away. "You're getting married?"

I threw my arms around her, holding her tight, rocking her back and forth. "You're happy?"

"Are you kidding? I've been waiting for Chris to get off his butt and ask you."

"Off my butt?" There was a hand on my back and I knew immediately that it was Chris. "Listen you two, can I get in on the group hug?" He didn't wait for an answer as he pulled Sam and I snug against his chest.

My dad cleared his throat loudly across the room.

"Dad." I freed my head from Chris's embrace. "You haven't said anything."

He stood up from the kitchen table with something he rarely showed the world—unguarded happiness. "Ladybug, the only thing that would make this news any better would be if your mom was here to witness it."

Just when I'd managed to stop crying after hugging Sam, my dad had to pry it back out of me. "I know." I nodded, easing closer to him, watching him fight the tears that he never, ever, allowed himself to shed, at least not in front of anyone. "But I think she's here. In spirit."

I actually felt her there, could hear her telling me that she was happy and how I shouldn't pick out a wedding dress that made me look like a lemon meringue pie. To this day, my dad didn't know that my mom and I carried on a conversation in my head. No one knew.

He took my hand. "I'm as happy as a fly at a picnic. And I'm pleased that you and Chris finally got some sense and realized this was the only way to do it."

"Do what, exactly?" Chris asked.

"Well, life, of course. I don't know what you two were thinking when you decided you'd have a baby before you got married."

I BUCKLED the dark blue seat belt across my lap. "I can't believe you spent two grand on a plane ticket so you could take me shopping for an engagement ring."

Chris patted my hand, flipping through the in-flight magazine. "It was for more than that. Don't forget the hotel sex."

The flight attendant had impeccable timing, arriving in time for "hotel sex". "Anything to drink before we take off?" she asked, screwing up her lips while she waited for an answer.

"Just water." I stifled a giggle.

"Perfect," Chris added, layering his British accent with extra sexiness.

"How do you manage to do that and not get the slightest bit embarrassed?"

He snickered. "Years of sticking my foot in my mouth. I'm a professional."

I shook my head. "You're a professional all right. A professional goof."

"And very soon, my darling, you will be Mrs. Goof."

Mrs. Goof. I smiled so hard that my cheeks hurt again. *There's something really fun about being a giddy twit.* "I can't wait for that."

The flight attendant brought miniature bottles of water. After a short delay, we were airborne.

I turned Chris's dad's ring on my finger. I'd wrapped some bandage tape around one part of it to keep it from falling off, but it was still loose. "I was wondering, what did you do with your ring when you got divorced?"

"I went to the house in St. Barts and threw it in the ocean."

"Never to be seen again?"

"That was the idea. It seemed like a fitting end to that chapter of my life."

I pictured Chris on a pristine white sand beach near his villa in St. Barts, possibly the beach at Colombier, which can only be reached on foot or by boat. With his long arms and a motion much like the one you make skipping a rock, I could see him flinging that ring into the waves. When his marriage to Elise had finally ended, he was as eager to rid himself of all evidence of the hell she'd put him through—her drug addiction, infidelity, and unwillingness to have a child with him. The loss of the pregnancy that came from their marriage had been the worst of it. There was no coming back from that.

Chris took my hand, rubbing the tips of my fingers in tiny circles with his thumb. He'd done it hundreds of times, but something about it always felt so reassuring, like an inside joke, something we didn't need to talk about.

"Did you ever come close to getting married?" he asked. "Was there a guy who you thought you would end up with? I mean, before me, of course." He focused on our joined hands, not making eye contact.

Chris's love life, his checkered romantic past, was common knowledge to anyone who'd read any 80s teen-idol magazine or grocery store tabloid. My history in that department was likewise rarely discussed. I didn't like to think about him with other women and he'd proven more than once that he had a jealous streak that was sometimes difficult to control.

"If you're wondering if anyone ever asked me, then no. I was never engaged." I cleared my throat, bracing to bring up the ex-boyfriend of mine that Chris abhorred. "I thought Kevin might ask me, but that never happened."

His eyes were quickly drawn to mine, the green that always stole at least a little of my breath. "Kevin? Tosser Kevin? Would you have said yes if he'd asked?"

A rush of air escaped my lips. As much as I'd been stubborn when it came to men, it had never occurred to me that saying "no" to a marriage proposal was an option. "I don't know what I would've said. I was in love with him at one point. At least I thought I was."

His eyes narrowed, his endlessly expressive eyebrows drew together. "In love. With Kevin."

"I said I thought I was. It's not like it is with you. Not even close. But at the time, it felt more real than any other relationship I'd ever been in."

"So you would have said yes." His eyes held a rare sadness.

"I don't know why it matters. He didn't ask me, and now I wish that he'd move to Borneo or at least lose my phone number." I dropped my head, wanting eye contact. "Chris, honey, don't let this bother you. It's ancient history and nothing ever came of it. Really."

He smiled and squeezed my hand harder. "I know. I just, well..." His lips seemed to struggle for the words. "I think about fate, about the circumstances that brought us together. I still haven't completely gotten past the idea that I could've lost you a few months ago and it would've been my fault. Hell, I could've lost you to Kevin and not even known it. I would've just been left feeling empty, without a clue how to fix it."

"But that didn't happen. We're together. Forever. I'm going to be Mrs. Goof soon."

He grinned and leaned over for a kiss, a soft and tender meeting of our lips that made my knees feel like jelly. "I love you Mrs. Goof. I really, really love you."

I leaned on the armrest and snuggled closer to him. The only downside of being in First Class was the massive console between the seats, an obstacle good for nothing more than drawing my ire. Still, things weren't going to get much better than this—cozied up with my dream man, my prince, on my way to New York to interview Amanda Carlton, the sort of assignment I'd long dreamt of.

Ms. Carlton was more than one of the most beautiful

women in the world; she was the Hollywood starlet who could demand any salary, director, and leading man. She'd left for Hollywood at seventeen and waitressed until her big break, which, as luck would have it, came for her after only four months. Surely aided by her beauty, she caught the eye of an executive producer and landed a supporting role in the action film franchise "Fightin' Army V: The Battle for Planet Earth", the highest grossing installment.

My personal stakes with the Amanda interview were high. Sure, the *Rolling Stone* article I'd written about Chris had landed me other high profile assignments, but now that our relationship was public knowledge, I needed to prove to every skeptical editor than my journalistic chops were real.

"You okay?" Chris asked.

I nodded, looking up at him and catching a glimpse of his stunning green eyes. "Yep. Just thinking about the interview."

"Don't worry, darling. You'll do great."

CHAPTER THREE

STROLLING through the lobby of the Hotel Rivington on the Lower East Side of Manhattan, hand in hand, it was impossible not to think about the last time Claire and I had been here together, more than six months ago. How time changes everything.

"Reservation for Penman," I said to the chubby chap at the registration desk. Claire sniggered. "I called and changed the reservation that was originally under the name Abby."

The bloke began tapping away at his keyboard.

"What's so bloody funny, darling?" I asked.

"Nothing." She shook her head and smiled, lips pressed together. "There's just something really, really awesome about checking into a hotel with you."

"Ah, yes, Mr. Penman. That particular suite won't be ready for a few more hours. The bell staff will gladly stow your bags and bring them up this afternoon."

I leaned against the front desk. "Well? Shall I have Lou take you to your interview and then I'll get on with my errands?"

"What are you doing today, anyway?"

I took her hand and stepped away from the prying ears of

the man at the front desk. "I'm going to visit a studio or two, chat up a few guys about gear and layout. Try to learn from their mistakes if I can. I'm actually going to Avatar Studios, which used to be the Power Station. That'll be fun. Haven't been there in years."

"Wow. Cool." She glanced at her watch, crinkled her forehead. "Sounds good."

The nervousness was plain on her face. Even her hand was a bit clammy. She'd been in virtually the same state the day we met, wound as tight as a spring. Even now, it was adorable. Every moment of unguarded vulnerability was endearing. "Just so you know, you'll do great today."

We walked back outside to the town car. "Lou, we're going to drop Claire at the Four Seasons and then on to Avatar."

"Absolutely, Mr. Penman. No problem," he said, in his distinct Brooklyn accent. He pulled away from the curb and into traffic. "You have dinner plans this evening I should be aware of?"

"Uh, no. I think we're staying in tonight, Lou. Claire and I have some celebrating to do." *Hours and hours of naked celebration.*

Claire smacked my leg. "I thought we were keeping this quiet," she mumbled under her breath.

"Oh, yeah, Mr. Penman? What's that?"

"It's fine," I whispered to Claire. "Believe it or not, Ms. Abby has agreed to marry me."

He looked at me through the rear-view mirror, his face lighting up. "Congratulations. Really. That's wonderful." He shook his head. "And just think, I drove you two the day you met. I feel honored. I'm sure you'll be very happy."

Claire's cheeks flushed with pink.

"That's just between us for right now, Lou. We want to keep things out of the papers for as long as possible."

"Of course, Mr. Penman. Your secret is safe with me."

"See?" I said to her. "I'm going to call Graham today, too. I can't wait to tell him."

"Make sure you send him and Angie my best."

"I will. Are you going to call Julie today?" I'd never even met Claire's sister. That would surely come to pass this year, as well as Claire meeting my mum and sisters. The importance of family was absent when I was married to Elise. She never spoke to her parents, wanted nothing to do with mine. Looking back, it was difficult to imagine how I'd ever thought Elise was right for me.

Claire nodded. "Yes. If I have time. Otherwise, I'll do it tomorrow."

Lou pulled up to the curb. "The Four Seasons."

She took a deep breath. "Just when I thought there was time, we're here."

"Let me walk you in," I said.

Amanda Carlton and her entourage were readily apparent when we entered the lobby. Two hulking men stood as a physical barricade, bulging arms folded across beefy chests. Behind them, Amanda and another woman sat in high-backed chairs. Amanda wore oversized sunglasses and was tapping away at her phone, but her trademark wavy brown hair gave her away.

Claire came to a halt before we reached Amanda's muscle. "I can do this, right? I can interview anybody, right?"

I laughed. "You convinced me to spill my guts. Amanda Carlton is a cake walk."

She frantically nodded. "Okay. You're right."

A girlish squeal came from the corner of the room. I turned as Ms. Carlton pushed past her bodyguard, removing her sunglasses.

"Oh, my God. You're Christopher Penman."

Bloody hell. "Guilty," I replied, holding out my hand.

"I'm such a huge fan." Her eyes grew impossibly larger. "I loved Banks Forest when I was in high school. My friends and I were all into retro, you know the 80s and stuff like that. Obviously I'm way too young to have been a fan when you guys had your heyday."

Obviously way too young. "Lovely. Thank you." I felt Claire's presence at my elbow. "You need to meet my fiancée, Claire Abby. That's why I'm here. She's interviewing you today."

Claire's face had gone pale. Not only had the moment she'd worried about become all about me, I'd said the f-word—fiancée. *So much for secrets.* "Amanda. Hi. It's great to meet you." She remained calm and collected, but I could tell that beneath the surface was a rattled Claire.

Amanda's eyes darted back and forth. "Oh, my God. That is so weird. Well, this must be meant to be or something."

Amanda's companion, a smart-looking woman in a suit jacket and skirt, teetering on sky-high heels, broke through the wall of bodyguards. "Hello. I'm Valerie Stanwick. I'm Ms. Carlton's publicist." She zeroed in on Claire and I'd never been so thankful to have someone Type-A and on the clock take over. "You must be Ms. Abby. It's nice to meet you." She turned to me, but Amanda started chattering again.

"Val, do you have any idea who this is? It's Christopher Freaking Penman, from Banks Forest. Can you believe it? I loved him when I was in high school and now I get to meet him because he's engaged to the woman who's interviewing me. How weird is that?"

I held back a powerful groan. *The woman who's interviewing me? Did she really have to put it that way?* Luckily, Valerie seemed non-plussed by the idea of meeting me. "Pleased to make your acquaintance, Mr. Penman." She turned to Amanda, who was still staring at me. There was a time when I would've found such behavior enchanting, but in this situation, it grated. "Amanda, we should get you settled with Ms. Abby. We want to make sure you two have as much time as possible."

"Please, call me Claire..." Claire interjected, but Amanda had other things on her mind.

"I have to get a picture with Christopher before we go." She situated herself next to me, threw her arm around my waist and leaned in, holding her phone out in front of us. *Click.* "Oh my God. This is so adorable."

"Amanda, please," Valerie added.

Amanda hooked Claire's arm with hers. "Come on, Claire. I want to hear all of the dirt on your hunky fiancé."

"Oh, um, sure." Claire looked at me with anxious befuddlement. "I'll see you later, Chris?"

"Yes, darling. At the hotel. Have a good interview." I kissed her on the cheek. "Nice to meet you, Amanda."

Amanda let go of Claire and held her arms open wide for me. "Don't I at least get a hug?"

I suppose it'd be poor form if I strangled you. "Of course, you get a hug."

THE DRIVE from dropping Claire at the Four Seasons to Avatar Studios afforded me just enough time to share the big news. I fished my phone from my back pocket and hit the speed dial for Graham Whiting, my oldest friend and front man for Banks Forest.

Graham picked up in uncharacteristic quick fashion. He usually derived great pleasure from making people wait. "P-man. I was literally just about to call you. I have huge news."

Bugger. "Hello to you, too. I have my own news."

"Fantastic. Can't wait. Listen, I spoke to Terence and Nigel last night. They're on board for doing these reunion shows. I spoke to the booking agent and he says we can do three nights at Radio City Music Hall. Maybe more if the tickets go quickly."

"So you were serious about this. When?"

"Of course I was serious. November. As soon as I get the rubber stamp from you, we'll put tickets on sale."

Are you kidding me? I sank back in the seat. Graham had asked me a week ago if I was amenable to reuniting the band for a handful of shows in New York. I'd said sure, thinking it'd be great if it happened and no great tragedy if it didn't.

"P-man. You there?"

"Yeah, I'm here. This is just, wow. Guess I didn't know you were so gung-ho."

"It's hard not to be when everyone is so bloody excited. Terence and Nigel are right chuffed. I just need you to give me the high sign and we'll get everything going."

"A few nights and that's it, right? Because I haven't even had a chance to mention this to Claire."

"Don't worry about Claire. She's going to love it. Go tell her now. I'll stay on the line."

I pulled a notepad and pen out of my messenger bag and began taking notes. "She isn't here right now. We're in New York so she can do an interview."

"Is that your news?"

"No—"

"Wait. Hold on. Let me guess. You've asked Claire to marry you and she said she'll think about it?"

"Bloody hell, Graham. Why in the world do you have to be such a tosser about these things?"

He laughed heartily. "I'm sorry, man. I saw an opening and I had to take it. Is that what's really going on?"

"You're taking all of the fun out of this." *Every last bit.*

"Don't be a girl about it. Tell me."

"Okay. Fine. I've asked Claire to marry me and she bloody well said yes, so you can sod off about that part of your fabrication."

"Why didn't you tell me in the first place?"

"You didn't exactly—"

"This is fantastic. Congratulations. That makes me so happy. Hold on one second. Hey, Ang, guess what? Chris is on the phone. He asked Claire to marry him and she said yes." A delighted squeal rang out. "Angie says congrats as well. She says she can't wait to talk to Claire."

"I know she'd love to hear from Ang, but tell her to call her later. Claire's in the middle of her big interview, with Amanda Carlton, the American actress."

"She's quite a lovely lass, that one."

"I guess. Claire's really nervous about the interview."

"And what are you doing? Along for the ride?"

"I only asked Claire this morning and I wasn't exactly planning to do it, so I didn't have a ring. I'm taking her to Tiffany's tomorrow so we can get that sorted."

"That was the right call anyway. You don't want to pick a ring on your own. You'll never make it out alive."

I chuckled and shook my head. "That's definitely the case with Claire. She needs to make this call."

"So, what brought all this on? If you weren't planning on asking her?"

Do I jinx it if I tell him? "Uh, between you and me, we're trying to get pregnant too."

"Oh, I know about that. Claire told Ang and Ang told me. I didn't want to ask you about it because I figured you'd tell me when you wanted me to know."

I can never surprise him with anything. "It occurred to me this morning that I'm doing all of this backwards. I don't just want to have a child with her, I want her to be mine. I had to sew that part of it up."

"I gotta tell you, P-man. I'm a bit surprised it took you this long to figure that out. Claire's amazing."

I grumbled under my breath. "Of course she is. I just wasn't sure she'd actually say yes. She's not the most predictable woman on the planet."

"This is true. Likes to keep you on your toes."

"In a good way."

"Where are you at with baby-making? Giving it your full and undivided attention?"

"No luck this month. Soon, hopefully."

"There's always adoption, Chris. Lots of older couples go that route."

Older couples? "We're a good year away from needing to explore that option."

"Oh, of course, man. I'm sure it'll be fine. Have you two set a date?"

Set a date. Right. This is starting to feel like a swift-moving freight train. "Not yet. Claire and I both have a lot going on right now. I've got the studio project with her dad and she's writing like crazy these days. Sam's about to start her last year of secondary school. If we're doing these New York shows, I have to set aside time for that. We need to sit down and figure out what's going to work best."

"Make sure you keep us in the loop so I get it on the calendar."

"You're assuming you're invited."

"Of course I'm invited. It won't be any fun without me. I'm also assuming I'm the best man."

Jesus. Decisions. "Not the way you're acting today, you aren't."

"Don't be such a spoiled sport. If I'd known you were going

to tell me you got engaged, I would've let you tell me first. I was just excited about these shows and don't say *if* we're doing them, it's *when* we're doing them. I know you want to."

Of course I want to. "Yeah, okay. Go for it."

"Excellent. I talked to Terence last night and he's got some song ideas he's working on. Maybe we can play around during rehearsals. See what we come up with."

"Maybe you need to find a hobby. Have you considered whittling? Perhaps knitting."

"Have you considered comedy?" Graham's dismissive laugh came over the line. "Look, I'm serious about this. We start off with the shows. We see how things go, maybe write some new songs, record some demos, shop around for a new record label."

Lou pulled up outside Avatar. Having recorded everyone from Madonna to Iggy Pop and Chic to Bon Jovi, it was the perfect place for me to do research for my own recording studio, the project I was pulling together in Chapel Hill.

"Shit, Graham. That's not just a few shows. You're talking about getting the band back together."

"What the hell else do we have to do?"

I don't know...get married, have a baby, start a new life with the woman I love. "I have a lot on my plate with Claire and Sam and the recording studio project. That alone is a huge job. There's construction to do, all of the electrical in the building has to be re-done. I have an unbelievable amount of gear to order."

"Sounds like fun to me."

"It is, but it's work too."

"I don't think you realize how lucky you are. I'm starting to feel like an old retired man and I'm far from being old," he continued. "Don't forget, I'm not Christopher Penman. I can't do a solo thing. I need a band behind me. I need this."

I took a deep breath. "Okay. I get it."

"I just sprung this on you," he softened the tone of his voice. "I say we go ahead with the shows. You take some time to think about the rest of it."

"Sounds reasonable."

"But let me just say that if we don't do it now, we'll never do it and I'm not sure I'm ready to say that chapter of my life is over. I'm not willing to say that Banks Forest will never exist again. Are you?"

I kneaded my forehead. *Getting the band back together?* "No. No, I suppose not."

CHAPTER FOUR

AND I THOUGHT my dad was bad. I stared out the taxi window on the way back to the Rivington, mindlessly watching the city whiz by, struggling to grasp the enormity of the bomb Amanda Carlton had dropped in my lap. If I were the writer who ignored the emotion of a person's story, I might have felt as though I'd hit pay dirt. But there was no feeling good about the secret she'd shared, that her dad was blackmailing her with potentially career-ending photographs, even if it might sell a shitload of magazines and cement my position on the map.

I really wanted to call my dad and tell him how much I loved him, even if the gesture would have likely prompted the question of whether I'd been drinking. However contentious our relationship has been over the years, however misguided either of us might have been at times, he always loved me. I always loved him.

My cellphone beeped with a text. *Chris.*

At the hotel yet?

I smiled at my phone. I couldn't help it. *Almost there. Five minutes.*

A few minutes behind. Be there ASAP.

I went straight to the registration desk once I reached the Rivington.

"I'm very sorry, Mrs. Penman, but it will be another fifteen or twenty minutes until your room is ready."

The woman behind the desk must've thought I was nuts. At the very least, she had to be wondering what about her apology had pasted a huge grin on my face. *Mrs. Penman.*

"That's okay. I'm still waiting for Mr. Penman. I'll hang out in the lobby until he gets here."

"I can send out a cup of coffee or tea if you'd like."

"A bottle of water would be great."

I'd found a quiet corner to work when my cellphone rang. "Hello?"

"Claire, hi. It's Laura Simmons. From *Vanity Fair*."

"Laura. Hey." *Holy shit.* Laura had given me the second prestigious writing assignment of my career, based solely on the merits of the tell-all piece I'd written about Chris earlier in the year. "How are you? It's nice to hear from you." I eased into a chair, hoping she'd say she had another assignment.

"Actually, I probably shouldn't say that I'm with *Vanity Fair* anymore. Bad habit."

So much for that. "Did you change jobs?"

"I'm transitioning to something new. That's actually why I'm calling. I'm starting a new magazine."

"Oh, wow. Cool." *Maybe she does have something.* I settled back in the chair. "Tell me about it."

"Same publisher. That much hasn't changed. We're still finalizing the magazine's name. It'll be a combination fashion and entertainment magazine, a lifestyle publication. It'll be targeted at women in their thirties and forties. It will be smart and a bit irreverent. I want to push the boundaries of what's in a women's magazine. The features will be very in-depth. Absolutely none of the fluff you typically see. I want to be on the cutting edge. Politics, sex, the works. Nothing will be out of bounds."

"That sounds amazing. Do you have a story for me?"

"Actually, I'm calling about more than a story. I want you to be my entertainment editor. I want you to come and work for me."

My mind didn't race. It did back-handsprings. *Editor?*

"You'd have your pick of stories. Full-rein. Of course, as executive editor, I'd have the final say, but I totally trust your taste and your instincts. You're the first person I thought of when the publisher and I began discussions about the magazine. I've been waiting for the green light to start hiring. I want the executive staff to be as tapped into our audience as possible."

"But I'm in North Carolina. You must want someone in New York." *Chris would never go for a move, not after the stink I made about staying in North Carolina for Sam's senior year of high school.*

"That's the beauty of it. With the technology available, you wouldn't have to move. I'd need you up in New York once a month, two tops. It's a quick flight and you're in the same time zone. Don't worry. I'll work with you. I promise. That part of it shouldn't be a concern. Frankly, I just want you to think about whether or not you're interested in the job."

"Of course I'm interested."

"You're perfect for it. Your writing, your music background, your smarts, your tenacity. I need all of it, Claire. You're the whole package."

"I suppose we'll have to talk about money." As if money was of any real concern now that Chris and I were getting married. Ironic, after years of scraping by as a single mom, I might earn a guaranteed salary the minute I didn't have to stress over finances.

"Of course. I can email you the details if you promise me

you'll seriously consider it. I have a lot of people who'd be great, but you're the one I really want. I know you'll do a fabulous job."

The one I really want. The inflection and enthusiasm in her voice reminded me of the lunch she and I'd had in LA before she gave me the *Vanity Fair* assignment. After only a few hours, we were getting along like old friends.

"Seriously, Claire. Think about it. You'd have the elite interviews and you wouldn't be fighting for them because it'd be your call. I'm willing to give you a lot of autonomy."

I'd have to be an idiot to not consider it.

"And keep in mind," she continued, "You'll make contacts doing this job that you simply wouldn't be able to make as a freelancer. Even if you only stay with the magazine for a few years, it could lead to bigger and better things. If nothing else, think of it as a launching pad for the next phase of your career."

"It sounds incredible and I'm really, really flattered, but I should probably discuss this with, uh..." I didn't want to spill the beans about the engagement. Chris had done enough of that for both of us. "Discuss it with my family."

"Yes, of course. I understand. So, tell me, what are you working on these days?"

"I'm in New York right now. I interviewed Amanda Carlton this morning."

"Holy shit, Claire. That's incredible. How'd it go?"

"It went great." I wasn't about to tell her that it had been far more than I could wrap my head around. "I'm really excited about the story. She gave me so much to work with, I'm hoping it'll turn into a bigger feature."

"See? This is exactly why I need you. Can I at least send you the offer?"

"Yes, of course."

"I need an answer in a day or two. Three, tops. My schedule

to pull these things together is ridiculously tight. We're hoping to launch in March."

The lobby doors opened and my eyes flew to a sight that still sucked the breath right out of me—Chris, making his entrance, in his silvery aviators. He smiled the instant he saw me, his strides becoming impossibly long. There were no words to describe the sudden lightness in me. *How does he do that?*

"Claire? Are you there?" Laura asked.

I stood and he pulled me close, pressing his warm lips to my temple. Every nerve ending in my body went on high alert.

"Yes, Laura, I'm here. Sorry." *Just barely. Jesus.*

"May I send you the offer?"

Chris swiped off his sunglasses and cocked an eyebrow, asking me to hurry up and get off the phone, all without uttering a word.

"Yes. Please."

―――

CHRIS QUICKLY SWEPT me into the elevator and ultimately down the hall to our room.

"Christopher James, Penman. You shouldn't have." I dropped my bag on one of the modern black sitting chairs in our suite, scooting past it to admire the splendid arrangement of red and purple tulips atop the coffee table. Early evening light filtered through the floor-to-ceiling windows.

"You're kidding, right?" he answered. "I ask you to marry me, you have the nerve to say yes, and then I don't buy you flowers? I don't see any world in which that's the right thing to do." His hand was on my shoulder as I turned.

"You are the most romantic man." I poked the center of his chest and flattened my hand, feeling the steady rise and fall with each breath. "Nobody else even comes close."

His eyelids closed halfway and he gave me the look, the one that always made me wish the rest of the world would go away. "It's all instinct when it comes to you."

I sighed. "There you go again. You're so sweet."

His arms closed around my waist, he kissed my neck, delicate closed-mouth kisses that quickly included welcoming flicks of his tongue. His words, ringing through my head, made me tingle from head to toe. My heart thumped wildly as the moment sank in—our first chance to make love since he'd popped the question.

He toed off his black Chuck Taylors and went to work on the buttons of my blouse, freeing them from their holes. "I promise you, there will be nothing sweet about what I'm about to do you." He snickered into my neck as he pushed my top past my shoulders and deftly unhooked my bra. "Okay, there'll be a few sweet moments. You're about to be my wife. I can't go about this as a complete animal, as much as that might be my tendency."

I smiled, threading my hands underneath his shirt, up across the flat plane of his stomach, until it was over his head and gone. He never failed to take my breath away when he wasn't wearing a shirt—the tiny patch of coppery brown hair in the middle of his chest, broad, wonderfully bony shoulders, his trim waist from countless laps in the pool. The sight still made me feel like a hormonal teenage girl.

He unzipped my black dress pants, leaving them to slide to the floor, while I unbuttoned the fly of his jeans. The instant he was down to his blue and white striped boxers and I down to my lacy black boy-shorts, his arms quickly reined me in, causing me to arch my back. I rose up onto my tiptoes and he kissed me hungrily, his tongue sweeping along my lower lip as I matched the intensity of his kisses. His hands dipped lower and pulled my hips into his.

"I need to get you horizontal," he huffed against my ear.

I grabbed his hand and led him to the bed, placing one knee on the mattress edge. With a firm hand, he flipped me over. The soft and silky fluffy white comforter puffed up around me like a cloud. I walked back on my elbows to the center of the bed, watching him move in on me. Chris followed like a tiger on the prowl, purposefully planting his hands on either side of my hips when he reached his destination.

He pressed his lips against the base of my throat and started a red-blooded descent, blazing a trail down my chest. There he settled in the flat spot between my breasts, which he knew drove me crazy—take-me-now crazy. He dropped down onto his side next to me, and kissed my shoulder. "There's no way we're going out tonight. I want to make every inch of my bride happy." He circled his finger on my belly and slipped his hand down the front of my panties.

My eyes were about to roll up into my head as he rotated his nimble fingers, good for so much more than just guitar playing. "Oh, God." I smashed my face into his chest. It took everything not to sink my teeth into him out of pure need. "Whatever," my voice quaked, "you want."

I hitched my leg over his hip and he settled his chin on the top of my head. The pressure wasn't merely building with the precision of each pass—I felt like a shaken soda bottle about to explode. "Chris, honey. Slow down a sec."

"Just relax, Claire. I want to make you feel good."

I dropped my shoulders, my eyes fluttered shut, and he went faster and harder—sending the top right off that soda bottle. My breaths became deeper, ragged, hitching every few seconds as wave after wave broke through and faded, slowly bringing me back to earth, except that being in bed with Chris never felt as though it was on earth.

"Kiss me," I said, my breaths now delivering fuller doses of oxygen.

His mouth was on mine, soft and giving, tender and wet, his hands otherwise occupied, shimmying my boy-shorts down my hips. I reached over and hooked my fingers over the waistband of his boxer shorts, doing the same for him.

"I love you so much," I cooed into his ear as he eased me to my back again.

He hovered over me. "You have no idea how happy you made me when you said yes this morning." His words and lovely green eyes stoked the fire inside me.

"You have no idea how happy you made me when you asked." I raised my torso and rested on my elbows, stretching my neck to bring my mouth closer to his. As our lips met and tongues tangled, he seemed to follow my every cue, or perhaps we were perfectly in sync. I could have kissed him for a lifetime —all of it perfect, but never enough.

With gentle pressure on my lips and some strategic placement of body weight, he urged me to recline back down on the bed. I hooked my ankle around the back of his leg, caressing his thigh while I tilted my hips to make it plain how badly I wanted him. He rocked against me and kissed my neck, stopping short of giving me the gratification I craved.

I groaned when he hit an especially frustrating spot. "Chris, I need you."

"Mmm. I love hearing you say that." He nudged my ear with his nose. His breath came in hot puffs against my neck. "But I don't like to leave you waiting for too long."

He positioned himself between my legs and it felt as if the world fell away. Together, we had something that would never be duplicated, a love unlike anything I'd thought possible. It was ours, a singular experience.

His lips traveled down my chest to my breast as he began to

rotate his hips at the end of each thrust. It didn't merely feel good, it felt as if my brain was turning to sticky toffee pudding and couldn't have been happier about it. His tongue wound circles on my skin and sent electricity zipping through me. I responded by wrapping my legs around him tighter, digging my feet into the backs of his thighs. When that wasn't enough, I reached down and grabbed his incredible ass, with both hands. He got the message. Big time.

With new force, his thrusts became more insistent and I did my best to keep up. We kissed—hungry, passionate, staggering kisses that left me light-headed. It felt as if the peak was circling around me, sometimes perilously close, other times teasing and elusive. Once it barreled into me, I was gone.

Every wave of physical pleasure bloomed in my mind, dots of color dropped on to a canvas, spiraling and changing of their own will. He groaned and buried his face in my neck. His body tensed in my embrace and let go, his familiar bodyweight gradually coming to rest on mine.

I wasn't sure where I stopped and Chris began and it was of zero consequence. He was mine. All mine.

CHAPTER FIVE

"THAT WAS RING-WORTHY, MRS. PENMAN," I said, kissing Claire softly and taking in her appealing post-lovemaking scent. *Honestly, I'll buy you ten rings after that.*

"I don't even know what that means, but I agree," she muttered, rolling her neck.

"I'm buying you a Tiffany ring tomorrow and however beautiful and stunning it might be, it won't come close to matching that."

"Poor little jewelry store. They never stood a chance."

"Not with us, they didn't." I pecked her on the forehead, just as my stomach growled with a vengeance. "We need food." I rolled out of bed, fetching the room service menu from the bureau.

Claire peeled back the covers, granting me an unobstructed view of her pert breasts and smooth stomach. The hollows of her collarbone were stunning—I wanted to pour champagne into them and drink them dry. She swished her hand seductively across the mattress. "You sure? I think I can exist on you alone."

Everything below the waist tightened and not because I was

hungry. I eased into bed next to her. "I need the chance to gather my strength." I thumbed through the pages. "What do you want?"

She scooted next to me and wormed her head into the crook of my armpit. "Whatever we get, it has to involve dessert." Her delicate fingers stretched across my bare stomach, sending cues to my groin.

It'll be a miracle if I don't have a stiffy by the time room service gets here. "I like where you're going with this. So you want me to decide?"

"Just promise you'll order something green."

"Got it. One something green and one something sweet."

I picked up the phone receiver and pressed the button for room service. "I'd like to place an order, please." The woman who'd answered put me on hold, but I had to get Claire. "My fiancée has worn me out and I need sustenance."

She popped up on to her elbow and narrowed her stare, admonishing me with a headshake that made her hair fall into her face. *So hot.*

I stifled a smile. "Yes. Great. We'll take a Porterhouse, medium-rare, with fries, the roast chicken and I guess you'd better give me the vegetable medley with that one. Oh, and chocolate mousse. Two spoons." I looked down at her sparkling blue eyes and winked at her. "And a bottle of the Prosecco." Claire nodded. "A half hour? Perfect. I'll be sure to put on some clothes by then." I hung up the receiver and tossed the menu onto the nightstand.

She giggled. "You're so bad."

"That's not what you said earlier." I inched down far enough for her to rest her head on my chest. "This is perfect." I combed my fingers through her mussed hair. "I don't think I could want much more than you, naked of course, and a steak."

"I vote that we never leave this hotel room."

"That can be arranged."

"We might start to miss our family and friends. Speaking of, did you talk to Graham?"

"I did. He and Ang both are both ecstatic." My heart felt as though it had taken off in a gallop. How long had it been since I'd had something so happy to share with my oldest friend? Too damn long. "They both send their best, although I think Graham sends more than his best."

She laughed, her tittering, musical laugh. "Sounds like him."

"He also had a bit of a proposition for me." *Let's see how this goes.*

"Oh yeah?"

"He wants the band to do some shows, in New York. Radio City Music Hall. He's already spoken to our booking agent."

She bolted upright, clutching the sheet to her chest. "A Banks Forest reunion? Seriously?"

I scanned her face, somewhat taken by surprise. "He thought you'd be happy."

"Are you kidding? I'm ready to start jumping up and down on the bed."

I laid back and folded my arms behind my head. "Don't let me stop you. I'll watch."

She kneeled next to me, earnestness painted on her face. Her eyes were bright and eager, a total turn-on. "I'm serious. This is really exciting."

"I have to say, this is more enthusiasm than you show for most things."

She crinkled her forehead and pursed her lips. "That's not true."

"It's not a criticism, darling. I'm merely saying that you aren't easily impressed." I cleared my throat. "If things go well, Graham wants to go into the studio and record a new album, possibly tour after that."

She took my hand. "Wow. Really? What did you say to that?"

"I told him I'd think about it. Not sure I'm ready to commit to all of that. I've said yes to the shows and we'll see how it goes."

"It's certainly a lot to think about. There are a lot of moving parts to our life right now." She gnawed on her fingernail. "I actually have my own wrench to throw into the this. I got a job offer today."

"New writing assignment?" I got up and plucked my boxer shorts from the floor. "Water?" I reached into the minibar for a bottle.

"Yes. Please. And while you're up, can you grab my pajamas from my suitcase?"

I unzipped her case and rifled through her clothes. "How long did you think we'd be gone? There are enough clothes in here for a Trans-Atlantic cruise."

"A woman needs options. You should know that by now."

I located a tank top and lounge pants, and tossed them to her. "Tell me about this new writing assignment." I wandered over to the towering windows. The night sky had taken a rich, inky blue turn after a murky gray start.

"When I said job, I mean a job. A full-time writing job." She threaded her arms through the tank top. "As an editor. But I'd also write features and do interviews."

"There's a job like that in Chapel Hill?"

"Will you please come here and sit down?"

I smirked and traipsed over to her, slugging down my water. "Sorry."

"Let me start over. Laura Simmons, from *Vanity Fair* called. You met her in LA, remember?"

I nodded. "Yes."

"She's starting a new magazine and wants me for entertainment editor. The offices would be here in New York, but she said I could stay in Chapel Hill. She'd only need me up here one or two days a month."

Guilt washed over me. My enthusiasm for her news in no way matched hers for mine. "That sounds brilliant. Really, Claire. You've worked so hard." *She's worked harder than hard. She's worked her ass off.*

"So you think I should take it?"

Bloody hell. How do I know? "You should consider it. I guess my only concern is that part of the genius of being a freelance writer is that we'd have flexibility when the baby comes along. You'd be giving that up. We'd be giving that up."

There was a knock at the door—room service, with the world's worst timing. Or perhaps it was the best timing, giving me a moment to regroup. I got up to let them in, trying to get past the feeling that I was being a selfish prat. Granted, there was a big difference between a handful of shows and taking a new job, but it still made me wonder why I couldn't simply shut up and be happy for her.

The bloke from room service wheeled in our food, but I declined to have him set things up for us. I signed the bill and showed him the door.

"If you think about it." She climbed out of bed and joined me on the couch. "This will at least be more predictable work. I'll know exactly what the expectations and workload is like from the beginning."

"Being an editor is a big responsibility." I set down our plates and removed the metal domes. "Damn. This steak looks good."

"I know it's a lot of work, but it's an amazing opportunity."

"I'm not discounting that at all, darling. Really, I'm not. But I don't want you to get so wrapped up in the opportunity that you lose sight of how it will change our life." I popped a french fry into my mouth and opened the Prosecco.

"I don't even know what that means. Do I not get to be excited about this?" She stabbed a piece of broccoli with her fork, but didn't eat it. Instead, she looked at me with disappointment.

"It's no different than the Banks reunion. I could get swept away with the excitement that comes with being on the road and recording an album." *Pour the Prosecco, Penman.* "I love doing those things, but they'll take away from our time together. We need to be realistic about what our life is going to be like with a baby."

"I worked full-time when Sam was a baby and I didn't have a husband to help me. Rosie next door babysat her on weekends when I took a waitressing job to make ends meet." She watched as I filled the glasses. "I can juggle this. I've done it before."

CHAPTER SIX

WELL, that's it. I tossed the wrapper in the trashcan and washed my hands. We'd already had time to deal with the disappointment. The confirmation was merely a somber dose of reality. *Why does this have to happen on the day we go to pick out my engagement ring?*

I emerged from the bathroom. "It's official. I got my period." I forced a smile, and it took even more effort than I thought it would.

"It's okay, darling. We already knew that, didn't we?" He pulled me close and I sank against his chest, taking in his warm and musky smell.

"We did. I'm just bummed. The tests can be wrong sometimes."

"Let's focus on the positive. We're going to buy you a big fat diamond ring today."

"Big and fat are two words I definitely would not use when describing jewelry. That doesn't really seem like me, does it?" I'd had this discussion with Chris about dozens of things since I'd met him—cars, vacations, dessert.

"I want to buy you the ring you deserve."

"I have a feeling that if I had the ring you want to buy me, you'd need to hire someone to hold up my wrist for me." Chris lacked very few things, but he did lack restraint.

He chuckled, zipping his overnight bag shut. "I'm sure Lou would love to move to Chapel Hill and make some extra money."

In the elevator on the way down to the lobby, I had to broach the subject that I'd been waffling about since our talk. "I checked my email while you were in the shower. The offer from Laura came. The money is really good." *Better than good.* There was a time, not particularly long ago, when I would've fainted at the notion of the starting salary. The problem with impressing Chris was perspective—it probably wouldn't seem like more than a pittance to him.

"I knew I should've made you take a shower with me this morning."

"What does that mean?" I asked, as the elevator doors slid open.

"It means that I wanted to take a shower with you. It has nothing to do with the job."

"Are you sure? Because I need you to be honest with me."

He took my hand and we walked to the front desk, where he dropped off our room key. "Checking out. The room is under Penman." He turned to me. "I want you to be happy, so that means I want what you want. If you want the job, take it."

"That's not really the answer I want. I was hoping you'd be excited for me." His unwillingness to tell me that everything would indeed be okay if I took the job, left me that much more uncertain.

"You're all set, Mr. Penman."

Chris unhooked his aviators from his t-shirt. "Claire, I'm extremely excited for you. Truly. I just want you to know that you don't have to take it."

The doorman opened the door and Chris placed his hand on my lower back. I glanced up at him as the sun glinted off his sunglasses and had the most bizarre flashback to the day we met. More specifically, to five minutes after we'd met—when every last thing out of his mouth was infinitely fascinating and he could fluster me just by uttering words that began with "p".

I scooted across the backseat of the waiting town car. Chris took my hand. That was all I really wanted—the two of us, together. Everything else was gravy, even if I'd worked my ass off to get this far in my career, and even if not writing wasn't an option for me.

We zipped along Sixth Avenue, hitting small pockets of traffic along the way. Lou pulled up in front of Tiffany & Co. on Fifth Avenue, and Chris squeezed my hand, hard, before we climbed out of the car. The Manhattan air was thick with inescapable summer heat and yet I couldn't have cared less as we strolled past the engraved stone facade, through the glass front doors, into the most famous jewelry store in the world.

The maze of glass cases, stocked with shiny, magical things amidst shocks of Tiffany blue sent a flutter of excitement through me. A hum of quiet talking amongst the scores of salespeople in black blazers and greater numbers of eager shoppers filled the room. Jobs and career choices seemed so insignificant. *We're getting married.*

"I made an appointment with a personal shopper. I didn't want to risk them being too busy to take care of us," Chris said.

"Of course you did. That's thinking."

"Claire, you should know by now that I don't toy with this sort of thing. If we're going to do it, we're going to do it right."

Chris spoke to a woman behind the counter and she directed us to a gray-haired gentleman tending the long glass case across the aisle.

The man tilted his head back, peering through tiny-framed

glasses teetering on the end of his nose. "You must be Mr. Penman." His regal British accent caught me completely off guard. He offered his hand before Chris had the chance to introduce us. "I'm Mr. Russell. You must be the future Mrs. Penman." He looked at me with a knowing twinkle in his eye that made me smile and blush. He was like the Santa Claus of Tiffany's. Mr. Russell had likely gone through this routine thousands of times if he'd been with Tiffany's a long time, and by the way he carried himself, my guess was that he had.

"I am the future Mrs. Penman, but you may call me Claire." *The future Mrs. Penman. Holy shit.*

"I understand we have an important purchase to make today."

"That we do." Chris planted a soft kiss on my temple.

"Excellent. Let's get on with it then. No more mucking about." Mr. Russell reached beneath the counter and put on a pair of white gloves.

"Did you ask them for a Brit?" I whispered into his ear.

"Luck of the draw, my dear," he quipped.

"Now," Mr. Russell started. "The first thing we must address is the shape of the diamond." A velvet presentation board held a row of rings. "Tiffany offers ten choices."

Chris picked up an Emerald-cut, but I already knew what I wanted.

"I prefer round." I pointed to the ring in the middle.

"You sure?" Chris asked. "What about this one?"

"Round." I nodded. "I'm sure."

"Round is classic. Timeless," Mr. Russell said, showing polite neutrality about my decision. "Now, have we put any thought into the type of metal for the setting and band? Platinum?"

"Yes, platinum," I answered.

Chris cleared his throat as if annoyed that I hadn't consulted with him.

"Perfect." Mr. Russell whisked away the presentation board and turned to unlock a cabinet behind him.

Chris elbowed me. "I find it interesting that the woman who made such a stink about not wanting a big fancy ring had clearly put some serious thought into wanting a round diamond with a platinum band."

I shook my head. "These are things I determined at a very young age."

Mr. Russell turned back with a new presentation board filled with wonderful, twinkly diamond rings. "We have twenty-one settings to choose from. Of course, we will hand-select the stones."

Chris pointed out a three-stone setting with a diamond band. "What about this one?" He then set his sights on an even larger ring closer to him. "Or this?"

I, however, was drawn to a simpler, more modern design. "I like this one."

"Ah, the Etoile." Mr. Russell removed the ring. "Simple. Elegant."

Without a word, Chris put his arm around me as Mr. Russell slipped the ring onto my finger. The wide, shiny band had a single diamond surrounded by a raised ring of platinum.

"This is a bezel setting. It protects the diamond."

It was beautiful. Stunning, not flashy. Probably quite far from what Chris had envisioned as the ring he'd put on my finger. He didn't utter a word though as I admired it, turning my hand and watching it catch the light. His silence made me love him in a new way—he seemed to sense that it was the ring for me, just as he was the man.

"I love it," I whispered. "I really, really love it."

Chris kissed the top of my head. "Then that's the one we'll get."

"May I?" Mr. Russell asked, reaching for the ring.

"Of course." Taking it off was the last thing I wanted to do.

"This stone is just under one carat in weight. This setting won't accommodate much larger than one and a half carats."

"One is fine with me," I said.

"Claire, come on," Chris pled. "Let me buy you the one and a half. Just so I can feel like I played some role in this."

"Allow me to fetch the matching bands while you discuss it." Mr. Russell again retreated to the cabinet behind him.

I grasped Chris's elbow. "Isn't one carat big enough?"

He shook his head. "This is a very public symbol of my love for you. There's a very good chance that photos of that ring on your hand will turn up in magazines."

"If it means that much to you, okay. We'll go with one and a half."

His face lit up like a Christmas tree, but then he narrowed his eyes. "I can't believe I'm saying thank you for your allowing me to spend more money, but thank you."

Mr. Russell brought a third presentation tray, this one with two bands—one plain and one studded with diamonds. "The choice here is pretty straightforward."

I didn't even get a word out of my mouth before Chris weighed in. "Diamonds. Definitely the diamonds."

It was a showstopper—sparkly and twinkly and totally over-the-top. *The man's trying to buy me more diamonds. Who am I to stand in his way?* "It's perfect."

An hour later, we'd chosen a stone, I'd been sized for the rings, and Chris put an absurd amount of money on his American Express. It would be a week until I would receive the finished product. It would've taken longer if Chris hadn't paid to expedite the process.

As we strolled through the door holding hands, flashes of light hit my eyes. *What the hell?* I averted my eyes, struggled for my sunglasses in my purse. An arm around my waist jerked me forward. The lights persisted. *Bam. Bam. Bam.* I turned my head to escape the flashes, but they were everywhere. Voices called out.

"Over here."

"What kind of a ring did you buy?"

"Chris, is it true you're getting married?"

I was blinded. I stumbled. A strong arm that I assumed belonged to Chris tugged me ahead. I landed in the backseat of the town car. Lou screeched away from the curb.

"Are you okay?" Chris looked down at me, his sunglasses on.

I nodded. *So this is my new life.* "Uh, yeah. I'm fine." I blinked, computing what had just happened. I sat up straight and grabbed his hand.

"Well, that was a successful shopping trip."

I was still catching my breath. "Except for that last part."

"I'm sorry darling."

"It's okay. Guess I'd better call my sister before that ends up on newsstands, huh?"

"I'm afraid you're right," Chris said. "So much for secrets."

CHAPTER SEVEN

I'D THOUGHT it would be fun, but as I flipped through a catalog of studio gear, I quickly realized it was work. *And why is the print so ridiculously small?* Frustrated with having to squint to read the specs on a mixing board, I nicked Claire's reading glasses from the bedside table. "Much better," I mumbled, settling back into bed.

Claire flicked off the bathroom light and approached, rubbing her hands and forearms, presumably with lotion. She was constantly moisturizing, not that I would ever complain. There was nothing better than running my hands all over her silky soft skin. She climbed onto the bed and took me by surprise, straddling my lap and plucking the catalog from my hands. *Now we're talking.*

I gripped her hips, watching her eyes flicker with flirtatious amusement. "Is there some reason you so rudely interrupted me?" Her fidgety body weight against my crotch was about to make ordering studio equipment the best amusement ever.

"You look insanely cute in my reading glasses, but why won't you admit that you're getting old and get your own?"

I removed them, rubbing the indentations that had formed

on the sides of my nose. "I don't really need them. They just help me see better."

She leaned forward, kissing me softly. "I'm pretty sure that's the definition of needing glasses."

I pulled her flat against my chest and she began to play with my earlobe as we kissed, tugging, running her finger along the sensitive skin below it. Blood flow was beginning to circulate below the waist when there was a knock at the bedroom door.

"If it's my dad, I'm going to kill him," she whispered, rolling to her side.

"It's ten-thirty. No way your dad is still up."

"Yes?" she asked.

Sam stuck in her head, a mass of blonde curls hanging about her face. "Hey, guys. I'm sorry. The power is out in my bedroom again."

I threw back the quilt. "It's the fuse. I'll take care of it."

Claire sighed and climbed under the covers. "Try to get to sleep at a decent hour tonight," she said to Sam. "Only two more nights until you're back at school."

"I'll try," Sam replied.

I walked past Sam and started down the hall. "It will only take a second."

"I don't get why this keeps happening." She trailed me down the stairs.

"Because this house is ancient. These circuits weren't meant to handle the number of gadgets we use nowadays." I flipped on the light switch in the laundry room and opened the fuse box. For the second time in as many weeks, the one for Sam's room had a dark center, telling me that it was indeed blown. Above the box sat a neat row of fuses, fully stocked thanks to Claire's dad.

"Why don't you just teach me how to do this?" Sam asked,

pushing up the sleeves of her sweatshirt. "Then you don't need to worry about coming down here the next time."

I unscrewed the old fuse and replaced it. "Absolutely not." I popped the stubborn metal door into place with the side of my fist. "I don't trust this thing at all. I don't want you getting hurt."

"I have to learn how to do this stuff at some point."

With a wave of my hand, I shooed her from the laundry room, and followed her into the kitchen. "Not this you don't. There's no way I'm letting you live somewhere with this sort of antiquated wiring. I can't believe we all sleep in this house every night the way it is."

"Are you going on about the electrical thing again?" Claire came down the stairs.

Much like an animal desperate for sustenance, Sam rummaged through the freezer. "Who wants ice cream?"

"You know I do," I answered.

"I'm good." Claire filled her water glass at the sink.

"Electrical thing?" I asked. "It's what's commonly referred to as a fire hazard."

Claire said nothing, downing her water, but I could see in her eyes how much she deplored this topic.

"I'm only going on about the electrical because it's a problem," I continued, placing my hand on her back. I sucked in a deep breath. "I think we need to look for a new house."

She clunked her glass on the kitchen counter. "What's wrong with my house?"

"Would you like me to make you a list?" I keep my voice even and measured, knowing full well that I'd struck an unpleasant chord. "I love the house, but we're at maximum capacity with your dad staying in the guest room."

"It is sorta cramped, Mom." Sam loaded massive scoops of ice cream into two bowls.

"The plumbing is bad, the electrical is old," I added. "The

air conditioning struggles to keep the upstairs cool and the driveway is crumbling. There's more. Do you want me to keep going?"

Claire folded her arms across her chest. "What if we just fix things up?"

"That doesn't remedy the space issue." Sam slid a bowl of ice cream across the counter to me. "Thank you." I took a bite of mint chocolate-chip, not my favorite, but Sam lived on the stuff. "What happens if we get pregnant? It's a year until Samantha leaves for college, which means her room isn't a possibility for a nursery. And it would be great if we could find a place with a pool."

"I thought you only wanted to stay in Chapel Hill for a year."

"That seems silly now. The studio could be a new phase of my career, and I love the idea of having it somewhere that isn't LA."

She gnawed on her thumbnail, likely still processing everything I'd said.

"We could keep two houses and we can go back and forth, but stay based in North Carolina."

"Really?" Her voice squeaked.

"I thought this would make you happy." I took another bite of ice cream.

"Maybe I should go upstairs," Sam said.

"No, Sam, this involves you too," I said. "We're a family. You should stay."

She twisted her lips. "It's kind of getting tense."

"I know. Your mother's having a hard time with the idea, but we have to talk about it."

"Mom? Aren't you happy Chris wants to stay in Chapel Hill?"

"I am." Her face became pinched with stress, an expression

I'd seen from her hundreds of times. "It makes me really happy. There's just a lot going on right now."

"So you and Chris are getting married. Big whoop. That's awesome. That doesn't have to be a big deal if you don't want it to be. Although it'd be cool if you guys had a really fancy wedding."

"There's a little more than that, Sam," I said. "Your mother got a big job offer while we were in New York."

"You did?"

Claire nodded. "Entertainment editor with a new magazine. But don't tell your grandfather. I haven't made a decision yet and he'll just want to offer his opinion."

"It's a big thing to consider." I sensed that Claire had made up her mind to take the job. I wasn't convinced it was a great idea, but I wouldn't hold her back.

"And Chris has his own excitement. Banks Forest is reuniting to do some shows in New York."

"You are?" Sam asked, placing her ice cream bowl in the sink. "That's so cool. Can I come up for the shows?"

"We'll have to see how your school schedule shakes out." Claire shook her head. "See? There's a lot going on. Do you really want to move in the midst of all of this? We haven't even set a date for the wedding yet."

"So set a date," Sam said flatly. "How about December? Christmas weddings are cool."

Hmm. "I love that idea."

"Would that give us enough time to plan it?" Claire asked.

Sam flipped up the miniature pages of a bank calendar stuck to the fridge. "It's August now. If you get married in December, that gives you more than three months."

"Perfect," I said. If she felt as if this was just a pesky loose end, perhaps we should scratch it off the to-do list. "We both said we didn't want this to be a big affair. No reason it'll take much time to plan it. If we find a new house, we can have it there."

Claire stared at the calendar. "I do like the idea of not taking forever to do it. What about the Saturday before Christmas?"

Sam tapped the date. "The 20th."

"Claire Abby and Christopher Penman cordially invite you to witness their betrothal, Saturday, the 20th of December."

"Betrothal?" Claire cocked her head and gave in to a small grin. "Let's do it. One less thing to worry about."

Exactly my thinking.

"And are we really going to try to find a new house before then?"

"I know it seems like a lot, but this is just part of merging our lives." I took her hand, squeezing hard. "The new house will be a chance for us to build something. Something that's truly ours."

"Now I really think I need to go upstairs. This is getting a little too lovey dovey."

"Goodnight, honey," Claire said.

"Night, Mom. Night, Chris." Seconds later, Sam was thundering up the stairs.

I set my hand on Claire's stomach and wrapped my other arm around her as she peered up at me. The worry on her face was starting to fade.

"I know there's a lot to think about," I said. "It's going to be like this for a while." I stroked her warm, pink-tinged cheek with my thumb.

"I'm sorry if it seems like I'm stressing out. I have a hard time letting go of things. It'll be sad to say goodbye to this house." She dug her head into my chest and I pulled her even closer, inhaling her sweet scent.

"Don't think of it as saying goodbye. You can drive by as much as you want until it's condemned by the city."

She exhaled and fully relaxed in my embrace. "Very funny."

"It's all good, darling. I love you and we're going to get married and have a baby and a wonderful life together. Absolutely nothing to worry about."

She looked back up at me, showing me one of her magical, unguarded smiles. "You're amazing. You know that, right?"

"I may have been told that a few times here and there, yes. Still doesn't mean I don't like to hear it." I kissed her on the forehead then tilted her chin for a straight shot at her lips. "And you're the one who's amazing. I'm just a lot of hot air."

CHAPTER EIGHT

I'D PERFECTED the art of inconspicuously flattening my hand and splaying my fingers. Or so I thought.

"Admiring your ring again?" Sam asked, hunched over a bowl of cereal.

I shrugged—one of those "I am so, so guilty" shrugs, where your shoulders touch your ears. "I can't help it. I want to stare at it all day long." I turned my hand so the diamond could catch the morning light and sparkle. "I love it."

She smiled for an instant then frowned. "What happened to summer? I can't believe there's only one day of vacation left."

"You should be excited." I produced a big smile, trying to sell it. "Your senior year of high school."

"I like sleeping in too much to be excited."

"I've noticed." I poured myself a third cup of coffee. I would've enjoyed the chance to sleep in that morning. Instead, I'd had another of Chris's unintentional six am wake-up calls when he'd knocked the alarm clock off the bedside table while attempting to quiet the snooze. "Are you coming with me this morning? Chris is dying to show off the studio space."

Her spoon clanged in the bowl. "I'll go for Chris, but it'd better not turn into a big long thing. I can't listen to Grandpa talk about tools and nails."

"We'll swing by Leah's afterward and pick her up. You can take my car and go to the mall or whatever it is that you two do."

Her face lit up. "Deal."

I parked in front of the building when Sam and I arrived an hour later, less than bowled over, like every other time Chris had driven me past it. A good decade beyond run-down, it's most memorable design features were multi-colored layers of paint peeling from the bricks and a rusty loading dock door, smack dab next to the main entrance. The dirt and gravel parking lot meant everything was covered with dust—windows, sidewalk, and my still-new Volvo. I found it curious that Chris would purchase a building where his own new car, a decked-out black Ford F-150, would be exposed to so much grime.

"This place is a dump," Sam said.

"It's not that bad." I sighed. By all reports, Chris's little project was going to be a much bigger job than first anticipated. I hadn't had the heart to tell Sam that by the look of things, her grandfather would be staying with us for at least six months, rather than the original three he and Chris had estimated. Some people might call that denial. "Don't say anything to Chris. He's very excited."

I pushed the door open with a single finger to keep from getting my white shorts dirty. The room we entered was claustrophobic with chipped, speckled brown linoleum tiles and wood paneling. The sun strained through filthy windows, making it difficult to see much more than that. The distinct smell of stale cigarettes lingered. It was comparable to being inside a toaster oven, stuffy and much hotter than the sweltering day outside.

"Hello? Chris?" I called out.

"In here," he yelled, as if I was supposed to have a built in homing device, his British accent echoing throughout the building.

Sam and I made our way through a towering doorway into a massive warehouse space. A mountain of building supplies sat inside the loading dock door.

"There you are." Chris pulled me into a half-hug. "What do you think? Isn't it great?" His excitement was exactly like that of a little boy who'd caught the biggest fish of his life.

"You weren't kidding when you said it was a blank slate. Tell me what you're thinking about doing."

"Your dad and I were going over measurements, talking about where things are going to go, the control room, the isolation rooms. I think we're going to be able to put in a pretty big rehearsal space."

Sam looked completely miserable—like me, she'd never been big on dirt or heat.

"Grandpa, what is the deal with your face?"

My dad strode toward us from the far side of the room with a measuring tape, writing down notes in the darkness. "Why? Do you like it?" As he became more visible, I realized that Sam was on to something—he hadn't shaved. He ran a hand over his graying stubble. "Chris suggested it. I'm trying something new."

The only thing that kept me from fainting was the idea of collapsing onto the disgusting floor. Chris gave me one of his sly looks and winked. I took his arm and we walked to the other side of the room. "A beard?"

"I thought Rich needed to mix things up a bit." He smiled—talk about mixing things up, no person had ever called my father Rich, but my dad seemed to like it coming from Chris and thankfully, Chris had never attempted to call him Dick. "I think Rosie from next door will like it too."

I shook my head. "You're still working on that too, huh?"

"Why not? Your dad deserves a little romance in his life."

Romance wasn't the first thing that sprang to mind when thinking about Rosie, the sweet yet sometimes ornery gray-haired lady next door. "I suppose. Although she might not be happy when she finds out we're moving."

"Maybe we leave your dad behind."

"I like where you're going with this." I grasped his arm, leaning against him. "How much longer will you two be here?"

"We're going to finish measuring everything out, but we can't do much else until they switch the power on tomorrow and we get some lights and air conditioning going. Your dad's electrician friend should be here in about an hour. The electrical is a big job, so we need to tackle that first."

"I'm going to go home to get some more work done on the Amanda story."

"How's that going?"

"I don't know. I got a message from Amanda's publicist saying she needs to talk to me. I have the feeling she might recant some of the things she told me in the interview."

"Sounds dodgy to me."

I twisted my lips. Maybe it really was all too good to be true. Or maybe it was better if the things she'd told me never saw the light of day. "Tell me about it. I need to call Laura too and tell her I'm taking the job."

"Did you call your sister? You keep forgetting to do that."

Fuck. "No. I gotta do that too." *Call Julie. Don't forget to call Julie.* "Home by dinner?"

Chris put a hand at my waist and gave me a kiss. "Do you know how much I love the sound of that? Home and dinner?"

"Perfectly ordinary for the vast majority of people."

"And extra special for me." He reached around and parked his hand on my butt, pulling me closer.

I blushed. "You're lucky it's so dark in here. You know my dad doesn't like seeing that." He squeezed my ass and I felt like I might faint.

He whispered in my ear, "He's lucky I can keep my hands to myself at all around his daughter."

CHAPTER NINE

RICHARD AND HIS FRIEND MARTY, each with clipboard in hand, shuffled through the dusty, open expanse of the former auto parts shop that would one day house my recording studio. It was hot as blazes outside, making the air indoors impossible to breathe.

"We won't know exactly what we're looking at until we get the specs on the equipment. This is my first time doing a recording studio." Marty tapped his clipboard with a pen incessantly.

"Of course." I pulled my t-shirt away from my sweaty, growling stomach. "I have one more engineer friend to consult with and then I'll order everything. You'll have your specifications soon." Thoughts of a wedding, babies, and electrical specifications had me foggy. *Lunch. I need lunch.*

"You know, I could coordinate this Chris," Richard offered.

"That'd be brilliant." Richard was always happier with his own domain and he'd undoubtedly been paying greater attention than I had. "Thanks for taking that off my hands." He stood taller, straightened his glasses with new purpose. He and Marty ambled off, discussing watts and amperage.

My phone buzzed with a text. *Samantha*.

Hey Chris. Ran into Bryce at the mall. Don't worry about me for dinner.

I shook my head, knowing precisely what Claire's reaction to this scenario would be. Sam had been quick to figure out that I was a good buffer between her and her mother.

Ask your mum?

She's writing. Don't want to bug her. Xoxo

Smart girl. Very smart girl. *No problem. Be safe.*

Richard and Marty returned, Marty removing his sunglasses from their perch atop his head. "We can start as soon as you make the decisions about the equipment."

"I guess I have my marching orders then."

While Richard bid his farewell to Marty, I started up my truck and got the air conditioning going, taking a reprieve from the modern country station Richard favored by turning down the radio.

"We should run by the lumber yard since we're on this end of town." Richard hoisted himself into the car. "We can grab some lunch at the taco truck."

"A man after my own heart." My stomach agreed. The wheels of my truck kicked up dust as I pulled out of the gravel car park.

"You okay today, Chris? You seem a bit preoccupied."

I glanced into the side mirror and changed lanes. "Oh, you know. Just thinking about the studio and the wedding. It's a lot of excitement."

"Don't forget a new house." He reached over and turned up the volume on the radio.

"So Claire told you?"

"No. Sam did. I'd noticed there was a fuse missing so I asked her if the power had gone out in her room."

"I don't think Claire's totally sold on it."

"As long as you get something solid, it's a great investment. You have to be careful with some of this new construction. They don't make houses the way they used to." It seemed in Richard's mind that they didn't make anything the way they used to—cars, houses, relationships.

I found a parking space near the taco truck and we took our place at the end of the queue, behind a mix of laborers and office workers. "What are you in the mood for today, Rich? My treat."

He made a cursory survey of the specials board. "The usual."

Of course. The man never strayed from plan if he could help it. "What about the shrimp? The sign says it came up from the coast this morning."

"Chicken will be just fine."

"Carne asada? It's delicious."

"I think I'll stick to chicken, thanks."

"Got it." We stepped forward, getting respite from the afternoon sun under the truck's awning. "I'm going for the shrimp." I placed our order and we found a seat at one of the picnic tables along the side of the dilapidated lumberyard building. "So, Rich, I was thinking it might be nice if you invited Rosie over for dinner one night."

"Seems like you or Claire should be the ones extending invitations. It's not my place." He tucked a paper napkin into the collar of his neatly pressed, short-sleeved dress shirt.

I finished a bite of shrimp taco. "Well, I'm giving you the go-ahead." I coughed, realizing I'd gone overboard with the hot sauce. "She must be lonely over in that big house, all by herself."

"She seems to get along okay. Always out there puttering in that garden of hers, filling her bird feeders."

I grumbled under my breath. "Of course, but she's got to eat. Must get lonely cooking for one all of the time. You know what that's like."

He looked at me quizzically. "I suppose I do. I get awfully tired of bologna sandwiches, I'll tell you that much."

"Of course you do. We can't leave poor Rosie next door eating sandwiches all by herself."

Richard dabbed at the corners of his mouth. "Chris, I didn't fall off the turnip truck yesterday. I can see what you're trying to do and I don't think it's a good idea."

"Why not? Rosie's a lovely lady. Everyone can use some company. Maybe a little romance?"

"Romance? For goodness sake. I am not about to sully the memory of my wife by romancing another woman."

"I wasn't suggesting you sully anything." *You'd think I'd suggested he ravage Rosie on her front stoop.* "We're talking about dinner. Claire and I'd be there to make sure you two keep both feet on the floor."

"Now you're being crude."

I closed my eyes and pinched the bridge of my nose. *No, you need to lighten up.* "I only thought you might be happier if you had some female companionship. That's all."

"I'm plenty happy."

Except that your entire life revolves around your daughter and granddaughter. "Of course you are. I'm sorry." I swiped my thumb across the beads of water on my Coke bottle. "Will you do me one favor, though?"

"What's that?"

"Will you help her with the big bird feeder in her front yard? She asked me for help, but I don't know the first thing about it." Nothing of the sort had happened, but Richard never turned down a project.

"What's wrong with it?"

You would have to ask for specifics, wouldn't you? "Oh, I don't know exactly. She was struggling with it yesterday morning when I went out to get the newspaper. She just needs someone who knows what he's doing."

The annoyance on his face faded. "Claire's mother Sara loved birds. I was always repairing the feeders at the house. Darned squirrels break everything."

"You know the squirrels in North Carolina. Bunch of meddlesome troublemakers."

"I'll go over there this afternoon after I call Marty and ask him when he's coming down to look at the studio."

I cleared my throat, giving him a chance to catch his own mistake, but he didn't. He just kept eating. "Rich, we saw Marty an hour ago. Do you mean you're going to call him to go over the plans? Because he won't be back in Asheville until at least five."

His face flushed. "Yes, of course that's what I meant. I got off track when you wouldn't stop talking about Rosie."

Maybe he really does like her. "Don't worry. I'll try to keep my thoughts about you and Rosie to myself."

CHAPTER TEN

THE STORY on Amanda Carlton was to hinge on her new movie, a screen adaptation of the blockbuster, sappy-sweet romance *Lonely Coast*. She'd managed the impossible, landing a role that dozens of top actresses had vied for, while stepping beyond the action genre that had launched her career. There was already talk of an Oscar nod. Amanda's publicist wanted to stand on a mountain and shout it to the world. I was to be the megaphone.

From the beginning of the interview, Amanda had been as difficult to keep on task as a toddler at Disneyland. Over and over again, she returned to the topic of her dad and her adolescence. It wasn't news that Amanda's father was a piece of work, but something told me to let her talk. That was when things got interesting.

Her dad hadn't been in her life since she'd moved to Los Angeles. As far as he was concerned, she was worse than dead, she was an ungrateful whore. Lovely words from the man who'd lived off her waitressing money for the previous two years. Little did he know that a year later, the so-called ungrateful whore would be one of the highest paid actresses in Hollywood.

Behind quiet tears, Amanda admitted to me that her father had betrayed her. "It was stupid," she said. "I was drunk. At a party. Some guys from school were egging me and another girl on. First they wanted us to take our tops off. They kept pouring shots." Amanda's hands trembled to unwrap a piece of gum she'd dug out of her purse.

"Do you want me to stop the tape?" I asked, but she never answered. She merely went on.

"They got us to kiss. I don't remember much after that, but one of the guys took photos of everything. She and I both had our clothes off. We were all over each other." She shook her head. "Somebody gave the photos to my dad. That was horrifying enough. Then he..." She choked back tears. Her pale blue eyes had gone glassy.

I'd leaned forward, placed my hand on her knee, but she never looked at me. It was the oddest situation—the talk we'd had before the interview started, the one where she'd wanted to hear all about Chris, had created a familiarity that might not have been fair to Amanda.

"He blackmails me," she continued, with a bite to her voice. "He threatens to send the pictures to the highest bidder unless I buy them from him. At first it was one picture. Then another one. I always think I've bought them all, but he always has more."

She could forget her dreams of positioning herself as a true leading lady if those pictures ever saw the light of day. I'd sat in silence, scrambling for the right thing to say. All I'd been able to come up with was, "I'm so sorry. That's terrible."

"Do you have a good relationship with your dad?"

Under any other circumstances, that question might have solicited sarcastic laughter. "He's a very sweet man. I love him very much."

"You're lucky."

"I am."

Then she'd started to cry again. "It really makes me miss my mom. I miss her every day."

I knew exactly how she felt. I missed my mom every day too. I hadn't felt so torn while conducting an interview since the day I met Chris and learned the secrets of his failed marriage. "I'm sure this has been difficult."

Now that I was more than halfway done with the story, which was due to my editor in forty-eight hours, I had a voicemail from Amanda's publicist Valerie. I tapped my pen against my creaky old desk, not deliberating so much as delaying.

"Valerie? This is Claire Abby returning your call."

"Yes, Claire. Thank you for getting back to me. Do you have a minute?"

"Of course."

"I didn't realize that Amanda had told you about everything with her father. That's very delicate information. Information I would prefer was not in the story. I'd really like this piece to be about the positives in her career right now. She's poised to take off. I don't think she realizes the ramifications of what she shared with you."

"I asked her more than once if she wanted me to turn off the recorder. She seemed very cognizant of what she was telling me. She volunteered all of it."

"I understand, completely. Believe me, I know the situation Amanda has put herself into. I think she thought that she could end the blackmailing if she publicly revealed what her father has been doing. The problem is that it will also force her father's hand, and I have no doubt that he will fight back and the only ammunition he has is those pictures."

"You're putting me in a really tough position here."

"Look, Claire, Amanda is a young woman. She's still learning the ropes and this was a huge misstep on her part. You have a daughter, don't you? You wouldn't want her to destroy everything she's worked so hard for just because she misspoke in an interview, would you?"

Fuck. Do I even have a choice? There's no way I can be cutthroat about this. "Okay. I understand. I will respect her privacy, but is she available to do another thirty minutes over the phone later today? I'm on deadline and I'm not sure I have enough material to flesh this out. She wouldn't stay on the topic of the movie."

Paper rustled on the line. "Yeah, that is going to be tough. Amanda's on set until midnight tonight and she has an early call tomorrow."

Great. My editor is going to flip. "I can't write about nothing and I have virtually nothing right now."

"Tell you what. Email me any questions you have and I'll make sure Amanda answers them. She can do it on her phone from the set between takes."

I sighed. "Okay. Fine. I'll send it right over."

"Thank you so much, Claire. You're a real doll for helping me out with this. I owe you one. If there's ever anything at all that I can do for you, please let me know."

I hung up and seconds later, my phone rang again.

My sister. "Hey, Jules. What's up?"

"You're getting married and nobody calls me? Thanks a lot."

Oh shit. "I was going to call you today."

"I'm floored. I can't believe Dad wouldn't think to call. We both know how adept he is at spilling the beans."

"Jules, I'm really sorry."

"I mean, this is kind of a big deal, Claire, and I have to find out from my babysitter because she read it in a tabloid?"

I dug my hand into my hair, slumping back in my squeaky office chair. "I said I was sorry."

"You were one of the first people I called when Matt asked me to marry him. Am I going to be your matron of honor?"

I was actually thinking Sam would be maid of honor. "I, uh—"

"If I am, this is a really shitty way to ask me."

CHAPTER ELEVEN

"IF THIS WORKS, YOU'RE A GENIUS." Claire finished setting the tiny kitchen dining table. It would be a miracle if we were able to squeeze everyone into the cramped quarters.

"That hardly seems fair. I shouldn't lose my status as genius, even if your father wants to punch me at the end of the night." I seasoned the last of six steaks with salt and pepper.

"What are you going to tell him when Rosie shows up?" she whispered.

There were footfalls on the stairs, a measured pace that could only be her father. "Not sure yet." I washed my hands at the sink.

Claire came up behind me, popping up on to her toes and whispering in my ear. "Good luck, genius. I'm staying out of the line of fire."

"Something smells good." Richard snatched a baby carrot from a platter of veggies and hummus. "Six steaks? I thought there were five of us."

Claire planted her hand on her hip, slyly smiling. Her dress was a deep marine blue, making her eyes even more intense and beautiful, but since she almost always wore jeans, her dad should've been able to figure out we were up to something.

"Yes. I stupidly bought one too many at the market, so I invited Rosie over," I said. "Wouldn't want the extra food to go to waste." *Like that ever happened with me around.*

"Chris, we've been over this. I'm perfectly happy being a bachelor."

The doorbell rang. *Showtime.* "Its just dinner." I breezed past Richard and opened the door before he had a chance to make a stink. "Rosie. Don't you look lovely?"

She smiled through shockingly pink lipstick, wearing a white blouse and a flowery skirt. "Christopher. You'll have to keep the flirting in check when you two exchange the I do's."

"He's terrible, isn't he?" Claire hooked one arm in mine, hugging Rosie with the other. "So glad it worked out for you to come tonight. Sam and her boyfriend Bryce will be joining us."

I closed the door and trailed behind them into the kitchen.

"Hello, Rosie," Richard said gruffly, extending his hand as if he was attending a stockholder's meeting.

"Hello, Richard." She glanced at me, then back at Claire's dad. "Or is it Rich? I never know which one to use."

"It's Richard," he answered. Awkward silence followed.

"How are your bird feeders holding up?" I asked. Spending time with Richard was a regular lesson in small talk, and I'd mastered the art.

"Good as new since Richard fixed them a few weeks ago." She smiled at him but he didn't take notice. "Did you enjoy the oatmeal raisin cookies I brought by? Claire told me they were your favorite."

"Oh, I did." He removed his glasses and closed his eyes, scrunching up his nose as if he was in pain. "I guess I should have come by and thanked you. Must've slipped my mind."

"Dad, I reminded you at least once to thank her for the cookies." Claire's voice was edged with disappointment.

Slipped his mind? I shook my head. Richard rarely passed up a formality. A thank you note was a given.

Samantha and Bryce came downstairs from her room.

Richard made an audible, "Tsk". He regularly gave Claire a hard time about allowing Samantha to have a boy in her room, but the house was so small, there weren't many places for them to go.

"Dad, stop. We talked about that." Claire felt that trust was paramount in her mother-daughter relationship, even when she'd been burned a few times. "Sam, why don't you get Bryce and yourself something to drink? Rosie? Dad? Wine? Beer?"

"Do you have any of that hard lemonade?" Rosie asked.

Rosie. A wild woman. I like it.

"Sorry." Claire smiled sheepishly.

"Oh, don't worry about it. I'll have white wine," said Rosie. "With a few ice cubes, please."

"I'll stick to water," Richard said.

Water. Great. I'd been counting on a beer to loosen him up, get him to talk. "Rich, why don't you and I get these steaks on the grill? We'll let the ladies talk."

Richard and I went out to the backyard and the postage stamp of concrete that Claire referred to as the patio. It was scorching and sticky as hell, even though it was already late September. I lifted the grill lid and got a rush of dry, hot air to the face.

"What in blue blazes are you doing?" Richard asked. "You got that thing set to five hundred degrees?"

The grill was my new domain, even though the learning curve had been more than I'd anticipated. I'd been watching the Food Network to gain a foothold. Claire was ecstatic if someone helped with the cooking, so I'd heard zero complaints from her. Richard was another story.

"The grill's got to be ripping hot for steak." With a long set of tongs, I wiped the grill grates with paper towels soaked in vegetable oil, which sizzled and steamed.

"It's too hot. You need to cook beef low and slow."

"We want a good sear. We can only get that with high heat." Despite his protestations, I slapped the steaks on the grill. "Then we'll back down the heat, finish them off, and have a perfect pink center."

"I want mine well done."

Of course you do. "It's not a problem. Actually, can you go and ask Rosie how she likes her steak?"

Sam and Bryce came outside with the bocce ball set. "Grandpa, you wanna play?"

"I'm helping Chris. Can you ask Rosie how she likes her steak?"

Sam rolled her eyes. I followed suit. "Sure."

Bryce heaved the balls out of the carrying case. It struck me that Bryce was far more buttoned-up than Sam's old boyfriend, Andrew. Bryce wore polo shirts and khakis much of the time, unlike Andrew who'd been a skinny jeans and ratty t-shirt sort. Sam didn't seem to care. Perhaps she liked being the fashion maven of the relationship.

"Rosie wants medium-rare." Sam skipped over to Bryce, pecking him on the cheek before picking up the dark green bocce balls and knocking them together.

"Okay, then. Five medium-rare and one well-done."

Richard watched as I turned the steaks. "Sara and the girls always liked their steak pink in the middle. Guess I'm the oddball."

"Did you cook out a lot when the girls were growing up?"

"We did. Nothing more beautiful than a Minnesota summer

and my Sara loved to spend time outside, loved to get her hands dirty in the garden. Those were good days." He watched Sam and Bryce with a wistfulness I'd never seen. "Very good days."

"It sounds brilliant. Can't imagine anything better." Claire and Julie, Sara and Richard—the quintessential Nuclear Family, out in the back yard enjoying their slice of the American dream. I'd seen pictures, which were funny and embarrassing at times for Claire, depending on her hairstyle or clothing choices. Richard had carved out quite a life, much like my parents had.

Of course, Richard hadn't counted on losing his Sara. My mum, Harriet, never dreamed she'd lose my dad, Alistair. *Nothing more painful.*

Sam tossed her final bocce ball and it landed smack dab next to the *pallino*. "Yes!" She jumped up in the air and tore off for the other end of the makeshift bocce court, Bryce in hot pursuit. "Ha. Two for me."

Bryce wrapped his arm around Sam's waist and kissed her.

"Hey, you two," Richard yelled. "That's enough of that."

Sam giggled and smacked Bryce on the arm.

"Oh, come on, Rich. They're having fun." I moved the first five steaks to a platter and closed the grill lid to finish off Richard's. "I thought you liked Bryce." *You two certainly share the same fashion sense.*

"He's a fine boy. He just doesn't need to kiss my granddaughter in front of me. For that matter, he doesn't need to kiss her at all. She's still only seventeen."

And going off to college in ten months. "Samantha, we're about ready to eat. Five minutes." I removed Richard's steak from the grill and plunked it down on the platter. I followed him into the house, wondering if I should've lectured him about good behavior around Rosie.

"Smells amazing." Claire toted a large salad bowl to the table, which was already perilously crammed with glasses, dishes, and platters. "Dad, Rosie, why don't you two go ahead and take a seat? Down at the end by the window would be good."

Rosie poured a splash of wine into her glass and took her seat, but Richard was clearly biding his time, milling about the kitchen, doing nothing at all but being in the way.

"Can you do me a favor and serve the steaks, Rich? The well-done is on top."

Sam and Bryce filed into the kitchen. "I kicked Bryce's butt at bocce. Anybody want to play with us after dinner?"

"I'm in." I stood behind my chair waiting for Claire. I grasped Sam's arm as she wiggled past me. "Leave the spot next to Rosie for your grandfather," I whispered.

Claire's hand was on my back. "Sit."

Richard served the last steak, placing the platter on the kitchen counter. Claire dished me far more salad than I would ever want, a sweet smile painted on her face. Richard turned and grumbled, yanking the ladder-back chair next to Rosie.

With one look, Claire and I held a conversation about her father and his disposition. She broke the silence. "Rosie, you look lovely. Are you doing something new with your hair?"

Rosie patted it then took the salad bowl from Sam. "Oh, goodness, no. It's the same old thing."

"It looks really nice, doesn't it, Grandpa?" Sam asked.

I nearly choked on my steak. Claire knocked her knee into mine under the table.

"Samantha, I don't find this to be acceptable subject matter for the dinner table. Why don't you tell us about the bocce ball game?" Head down, he cut his steak, several bites at one time, each identical in size.

"I kicked Bryce's butt. End of story."

"Samantha. Language."

"What? Butt?"

"That's quite enough, young lady."

Bryce cleared his throat and hunkered down on his steak. Claire and I did nothing but watch. This was far too entertaining to stop to eat.

"Grandpa, I'm having fun. You should try it some time. You might like it." She shrugged, as if talking to her grandfather in that tone would never raise an eyebrow. "Plus, I'm pretty sure that Mom does not consider butt to be a bad word."

"Don't pull me into this," Claire said.

"I have fun all the time." Richard pursed his lips.

"You aren't having fun right now and you should be. Mom is starting a new job and they're getting married. Chris's band is going to play in New York. We should be celebrating."

Claire beamed. I was equally proud of Sam's willingness to point it out when someone was behaving like an ass. Without this aspect of her personality, Claire and I might never have reconciled after our break-up.

Richard gathered himself, but his temper had clearly been at the boiling point. "You're right, Samantha. We should be celebrating." He took his water glass in hand. "Cheers to my ladybug, Claire, and her fellow, Christopher."

We raised our glasses to toast and the tension in the room ebbed. With a clatter of silverware against plates, we all returned to the meal—everyone but Sam.

"Sorry, Grandpa. Sorry, Rosie. I hope I didn't ruin your first date."

CHAPTER TWELVE

CHRIS ROUNDED a corner in the truck, heading down one of the steepest hills in town, nestled deep in a residential area. His hand landed on my knee and squeezed. "I really hope this is a good one. This business of looking at houses is starting to drain on me." He stopped at the intersection and waited for a lawn service truck then continued onto Lakeside Rd.

"It's only been two weeks. These things take time." I glanced out the window at the lovely older homes of Lakeside, one of my favorite neighborhoods in Chapel Hill, generous parcels of land on a heavily wooded tract surrounding a small lake. There was a time when I'd drive past these houses and wonder about the people who could afford such an idyllic way of living. Now it might be Chris and me moving into this neighborhood.

He slowed down. "It must be that one. I see Bob's car." He pulled in behind our real estate agent's white Prius.

I'd been careful not to express to Chris how much I hoped this house was the one. We'd already gotten into quite an argument about the last house we'd seen, in a gated community outside the city limits. He loved it. There was a huge pool, seven bedrooms, kitchen the size of a bowling alley, wine cellar, and a media room with stadium seating for twelve. Totally over-the-top.

"Morning." Bob bumped his car door closed with his hip as he juggled his sunglasses and a handful of paperwork. "How's the best-looking couple in town today?"

"I don't know, Bob," Chris said. "Why don't you tell me how you and Walter are getting on?"

"Flattery will get you everywhere, Christopher." Bob shook Chris's hand. "It's a good thing Claire has a firm hold on you."

"That she does," Chris said as we ambled down the driveway, hand in hand. I nudged him with my shoulder and he smiled down at me.

The thicket of trees opened up once we reached the end of the narrow driveway. The secluded setting was a deal maker. The house, at least from the outside, was a deal-breaker.

The design was right—mid-century modern, Chris's preference. Unlike his home in Los Angeles, modern construction with a mid-century feel, this was an original and considerably less glamorous incarnation. The cedar-clad exterior had grayed, the nearly flat gabled roof looked as though it needed to be replaced. There were wonderful large windows on the front of the house, but as we approached, those showed their age, too. It was the Brady Bunch house, minus the Technicolor splendor.

"No garage?" Chris pointed to the covered carport. "We can't have a house without a garage.

Bob worked on the lock box hanging from the brick-orange front door. "Afraid not, but the property is plenty big to build one."

Strike one. "The yard is amazing, don't you think? Very private."

"There's a huge vegetable garden out back." Bob opened the

door and handed me a sales sheet. "The house was built in 1954. You can't put a price tag on original architecture."

The entry to the house was much like Chris's house in LA—an open landing with two steps down into an expansive, central living area.

"The house has had one owner," Bob continued. "Lovely couple according to the neighbors. He passed away and she was moved to a retirement community. Her kids live out of state and are handling the sale."

"It's spacious." I cringed at the sea of avocado green carpet. *No wonder they didn't have many pictures on the website.* "I love the light fixture." The vaulted, wood-beamed ceiling had a satellite chandelier with shiny gold-tone arms in all directions.

Chris turned a full circle in the center of the room, rubbing his chin.

"The fireplace is amazing." I pointed at the floor-to-ceiling slate surround. "We could put a big sectional in front of it, curl up on winter nights. It's the perfect place for a big flat-screen."

"Any chance there are hardwoods?" Chris asked. "This carpet has to go."

"We can ask the owners if we can pull up a corner and take a look," Bob said.

"Chris, look at the lake. Isn't it beautiful?" The windows were filthy. Still, they were tall and there were a lot of them. The room would be stunning once they were clean and you could really see down to the water.

"No pool, right?" Chris peered out at the backyard.

"No pool, but there's a sizable patio off the kitchen and it's a large, flat lot. I'm sure you could find the room, but you'd likely have to tear down some trees." Bob consulted his folder. "You'll have to get approval from the homeowners association for any exterior changes, including building a garage."

Strike Two.

I took Chris's hand. "I think there's plenty of room for a pool. And I love the lake. It's so peaceful."

He put his arm around me and squeezed my shoulder, but didn't say a thing.

"Let's see the rest of it," I chirped, trying to keep things upbeat.

"The kitchen is this way," Bob said.

My stomach lurched again. More avocado green—range and wall oven, although the fridge was a more updated white, which still would never cut it with Chris. He would want all stainless, all new, no questions.

"This is a gut job." Chris shook his head. "The appliances, the sink, the floor."

Good God, the floor. Yellow-and-white linoleum. "The cabinets might be salvageable. They're solid." I strode into the breakfast area. A sliding glass door lead out to the patio, with another view of the lake. "Look. Ducks." *Good, Claire. Like wildlife will help.*

Chris joined me. "Cute." It was the most positive thing he'd said since we'd walked through the front door. "I suppose a pool might fit."

"We can get you a big new grill." There I was, throwing man toys at him—grills, televisions.

He kneaded his forehead and wrapped his other arm around me. "That'd be nice. Not sure it makes up for the disastrous state of the rest of the house." He granted me half of a smile. "Do you want to keep looking?"

"I do. Don't you?"

He pursed his lips. "Let's have a look at the bedrooms and the bathrooms before we talk anymore about it."

Bob had played the seasoned real-estate agent, staying silent during our discussion. "There are four bedrooms and two and a half baths. And a home office."

"Don't forget the home office. We need that," I said. "Four bedrooms. The perfect amount."

"Yes, darling, I know."

Bob lead the way down the hall, past a half bath that was serviceable, but out of date. The same could be said for the home office, although it was on the back corner of the house and overlooked the backyard. Beautiful. Upstairs, the first two bedrooms were just off the landing, both a good size, with a Jack-and-Jill bathroom between.

"Hardwoods up here." I tapped my heel on the floor.

Chris poked his head into the bathroom. "This is in surprisingly good shape."

He was right—attractive ceramic tile in a sage green that had managed to come back into vogue since the house had been built.

"I believe the tile is hand-glazed. Very desirable," Bob said.

Even better, the fixtures were white. *Aha. No avocado green.* "Is the Master down here?" I asked, starting down the wide hall. A single step into the room, I ground to a halt.

Chris nearly ran right into me, grasping my shoulders from behind. "Wow."

"I know."

"Is this the same house?"

Bob laughed. "It is. Some mid-century design has aged better than others."

Stunning was the only way to describe it—a wall of windows with an unobstructed view to the lake, divided only by a black slate fireplace dead center. There was ample space for a King bed, which would mean a big upgrade. As much as I loved cuddling close to Chris, sleeping in a Queen with a six-foot-four man with wandering limbs had sometimes left me wishing for a pillow wall between us.

Tall ceilings gave the room a spacious feel. It was hard to

believe how perfect it was. I kept waiting for something avocado green to leap out at me.

"There's a large walk-in closet." Bob opened a door and flipped a light switch.

Chris ducked his head in. "Unreal. This is as big as my closet in LA."

"And that's a big freaking closet," I quipped.

"Let's see how the master bath suits you," Bob said.

I braced for Strike Three. Instead, my breath was taken away again. The bathroom had a gorgeous double vanity, made from an exotic-looking wood. The countertop was done in a beautiful aqua mosaic tile in near-perfect condition. The glaze was varied, exactly like the hand-glazed tile in the Jack-and-Jill bath.

"Is that bamboo?" I asked.

"I believe that's walnut." Bob ran his hand along the rich wood drawer fronts adorned with chrome pulls. "Shows off the vertical grain. You can't even buy cabinetry like this anymore."

"The profile is a little low." Chris stood before one of the two round vanity mirrors. The countertop reached his crotch.

Bob laughed. "Not the best spot for you, is it? That's easily fixed by a good carpenter."

I noted two windows with splendid wooded views. "No tub?"

"Afraid not," Bob said. "But in exchange, you got a huge shower. This was unusual for the time, but apparently the original owner spent a lot of time in the shower."

Chris snickered and stepped into the oversized glass enclosure, which had the same aqua tile. "People in the 50s were short." The showerhead hit him square in the neck.

"That can also be fixed," Bob said.

Chris cocked an eyebrow at me. "Lots and lots of room in here, darling."

My face flushed with heat when I saw the look in his eye. "I see that." I had to glance away so as not to embarrass myself by blurting out that now would be a good time for Bob to go away.

"I hope I'm not interrupting anything." Bob flipped through papers in his folder.

I poked my head into the shower. "One more bedroom to see?"

Bob led us to the end of the hall. "It's a small room, but perfect for a little one."

The light streamed in from a window that looked into the backyard.

A smile crossed Chris's face when I sat on the built-in window seat and patted the spot next to me. "Bob, may we have a moment?"

"I'll be in the kitchen if you need me."

Chris joined me, sitting nice and close. He took my left hand, pulling it in to his lap. "You like it. I can tell you do. I just —" He squinted and looked around the room. "I'm not sure. The whole point of getting a new house was to get a new house. As in new."

"I know, but I can't see us living in some massive house with a home theater. It doesn't feel like us."

"That was a beautiful house in a very safe neighborhood. More importantly, a gated neighborhood, where we wouldn't have to worry about fans or photographers or other invasions of our privacy."

True. "That hasn't been insurmountable so far."

"Things could very well change. You never know when people will figure out that I'm living here full-time."

Also true. "All I can wonder is where our child will learn to ride a bike in a neighborhood like that. Who will there be to play with? A bunch of wealthy old people?" I turned and gripped his other arm. "Families live in this neighborhood. It's the whole reason to live in Chapel Hill."

He nodded and scratched his head. "We'd have to find a contractor. Somebody who can work fast."

Does that mean yes? I pointed to the other side of the room. "I can see a crib right there."

He squeezed my hand. "You can?"

"And I can see a rocking chair in front of the other window. I can see reading books on this window seat on a dreary day, watching the raindrops on the lake."

He squeezed again. Harder. His eyes found mine, and the pictures in my head of our future came to life. "Tell me more."

"I can see us in the back yard, in our new pool, you teaching the baby to swim."

"You really love it, don't you?"

"I really do." *Please say yes. Please say yes.*

"Then let's do it. Let's take this one part of our lives off hold. No more looking."

"You mean it?" Without question, I hadn't smiled that hard since he'd asked me to marry him.

"Come on." He held out his hand. "Let's tell Bob. I'm sure we'll make his day."

I twined my fingers with his and he pulled me quickly into a hug. "You make me so happy." Leaning in, I pressed my lips against his.

"You make me so happy." He kissed me softly. "And now that we have the house situation settled, we can start planning the wedding."

CHAPTER THIRTEEN

I HUNG UP THE PHONE. *Bloody hell. Amazing when things go the way you want them to.* "We're all set," I called out to Claire from her office. "Bob wants us at his office at nine tomorrow morning to sign the papers."

"I can't believe it went that fast." She filed into the room wearing a purple workout top that showed off her incredible shoulders and a pair of perfectly snug yoga pants. Shame that the amount of privacy in the house with Richard around was nil unless he was fast asleep.

"It significantly speeds up the process when you pay cash."

"Yeah, well, I never bought a house that way, so I wouldn't know." She perched herself on one end of her desk. "So, um..." She twisted her lips into an adorable bundle. "Now that we're getting married and buying a house, I feel like I have to ask if everything is okay money-wise."

Cute. "Yes. Everything's fine. I don't want you to worry about that."

"You really want to hold on to this house? I might be sentimental, but we don't have to do that."

I rolled the office chair closer. "That's not sentimentality. That's simplification and self-preservation."

"I have no clue what that means." She took down her ponytail, then gathered her hair in her hand and pulled it back in place.

"Selling a house is a pain in the ass and we have five hundred balls in the air right now. I don't want to deal with it."

"Five hundred is a bit of an exaggeration."

"Not really. As far as self-preservation goes, I have a sneaking suspicion that your father is going to want to spend more and more time in Chapel Hill once we have a baby. It's silly that he lives four hours away." I watched as the lights went on behind her deep blue eyes, but she still made a bit of a face. "This way we keep him at arm's length and we give him a project. He could work on this house all day long every day and never finish."

"You know my dad will never accept a gift like that. He'll want to pay you for it."

"Either I'll tell him it's payment for his project management on the studio or I'll come up with something else. You know, if we wanted, we could have him stay here and not come to live in the guest room of the new house."

"I like where you're going with this."

My email beeped and I rolled the chair back to check. Two new messages, one from Graham: *Are we psyched for the tickets to go on sale today?* "I'd just like to see your father happy. He's got a lot of years left in him and it'd be nice if he was a little less underfoot."

She craned her neck, looking into the living room. "Did you notice he was super moody again this morning?" she whispered.

"How could I not? How long can the man possibly hold a grudge? It's been nearly three weeks since the Rosie dinner."

Claire hopped down from the desk and closed the French doors on her office, cringing as one of the hinges squeaked. "If my dad is holding a grudge, he doesn't let it out like that. He holds it inside until it burns a hole through his stomach. I don't think its Rosie."

"Maybe it's old age. Does senility run in your family?"

She leaned into me when I snaked a hand around her hips. "Not that I know of. Maybe I should get him to see the doctor. Knowing him, he hasn't had a check-up since my mother died."

"It's not a bad idea." *Speaking of check-ups and medical things...* "Are we still clear to take a test tomorrow morning?"

"We are." She smiled and crouched down next to me. "Fingers crossed." With a delicate touch, she drew a short line down my thigh and punctuated it with a dot.

I cleared my throat. *I have work to do, darling.* "Going for a run?"

"Yep." She stood and twisted from side to side, then pulled one foot back behind her butt to stretch. "I'm way too amped up about the Amanda story coming out today. I need to take the edge off. Will you be here when I get back?"

"I should be. The tickets for Radio City Music Hall just went on sale at ten. I'm sure I'll be getting up-to-the-minute updates from Graham." I returned to my laptop. "Otherwise, I'm trying to see if I can get the contractor to meet us at the house tomorrow. Your dad and I are off to the studio later."

"Sam is actually going to grace us with her presence at dinner tonight. Are you confident enough in your grilling abilities to tackle some fish? I was thinking Snapper. It's her favorite and I wanted to officially ask her to be my maid of honor."

"Am I confident?" I shook my head. "At this point, there's nothing I can't handle."

"Okay, Mr. Grillmaster. I'm putting you to the test tonight." She kissed me and was out the door.

My fingers were poised above the computer keyboard when my phone rang. *Speak of the devil.* "Please tell me you and Angie are in London right now. I can't even fathom the idea of you being awake at seven am West coast time."

"LA, baby. And I get up early."

"Since when?"

"Since I became a grown-up."

"So you're a week into it?"

"Very funny. Will you shut the hell up so I can tell you the news? The first night is sold out. Eleven minutes, P-man. Eleven minutes."

The time on my laptop said 10:19. *He's certainly on top of this.* "Brilliant. Good to know the die-hards are anxious to see us."

"I'm getting updates from the agent. Second and third nights are already 80% sold. He wants the green light to add the other two nights."

And Claire just ran out the door. "Can't we wait a day? If people want the tickets, won't they want them just as much tomorrow?"

"Hold on. I've got a text." From the sound of it, Graham fumbled his phone. "Second night is sold out. Two hundred seats left for night three."

"Bloody hell." *The theater holds 6,000 people.* "I guess the fans really do want to see us, huh?"

"Of course they do, and no, we can't wait. We need to announce them right away, when people are in a frenzy to get seats."

I blew out a deep breath.

"It's two nights, Chris. Just say yes."

"Can your voice hold out for five nights in a row? I don't think we did that more than once or twice in our heyday."

"Don't you worry about my voice. I'll take care of that."

"Terence and Nigel are on board?"

"They want to do as many shows as possible."

"Okay. Yeah. Do it. Pull the trigger."

THE SILENCE WASN'T DEAFENING—IT was insufferable. The new issue of *Entertainment Weekly* had gone online that afternoon and Claire hadn't wanted to talk about it, at all. No, she declined to discuss how crushed she was that her long-awaited story on Amanda Carlton had been cut down to a three-question sidebar.

And Sam was late for dinner. Again.

"Claire, come on. Say something." My voice seemed to boom through the near-silent kitchen.

"There's nothing to say." She chucked cherry tomatoes one-by-one onto a heap of spinach in the salad bowl. "They turned my story into something a trained monkey could've written. The biggest actress on the planet told me a huge secret, with the tape rolling no less, and I couldn't write about it." She jerked open the refrigerator door and pulled out a bottle of salad dressing. "Of course, like an idiot, I bragged to Laura Simmons about it. That'll sure boost my credibility with her."

"You don't need to worry about your credibility with Laura. She adores you." I carried a pitcher of iced tea to the table and returned. "Perhaps you need to speak to your editor."

"And say what?" She threw up her hands. "I can't blame him. After Amanda's publicist begged me to pull the stuff about her dad, I had very little left to write about. She answered some other questions for me, but it was all a bunch of fluff." She picked up the salad and headed for the table, but I blocked her path.

"Give me that." I took the bowl from her hands, set it on the counter, and corralled her into my arms. "Come here." I rubbed her back, which was so tight I could feel exactly how wound up she was about this. "I'm sorry. I know this is hard."

"Thank you." She sighed so deeply that her shoulders rose and dropped several inches. "What's done is done. I'm just looking forward to starting this new job and not having to be at the mercy of editors anymore. I'll finally have some control."

"Control over what?" Richard asked, traipsing into the kitchen.

Claire grumbled and let go of me, picking up the salad bowl and making a beeline for the table. "Nothing, Dad."

"For all of the stuff that's going on around here, I sure do get a lot of nothing answers to my questions." He took his seat at the table and poured himself a glass of tea.

"Claire's disappointed with her *Entertainment Weekly* story," I said. "Her editor cut it pretty significantly."

"Chris—" Claire said.

"What? It's true."

"Well, Jellybean, you win some, you lose some. I'm sure you tried your hardest and that's all that matters."

I brought the Red Snapper to the table on a beautiful platter Claire had garnished with fresh herbs from the garden and slices of lemon.

"It looks incredible, Chris." Claire took seat next to me.

"Thank you."

She consulted her watch. "Too bad Sam isn't on time to see it like that."

"You know, Ladybug, I think you need to lay down the law with her." Richard reached for a dinner roll without making eye contact with Claire. Eye contact was too personal, especially when doling out unwanted parenting advice.

"Dad, please." Claire unfolded her napkin and placed it in her lap. Her eyes pled with me for something—a rescue from her dad, my opinion, a pat on the back. It was hard to know what she wanted when it came to her writing and even more so when it came to Sam. "I'm trying to find the right balance between letting her have her independence and keeping her in check. This is part of that."

I doubted I was dreading next September as much as Claire, but it was close. It would be very difficult to watch Sam walk out the door. "I think you're doing a splendid job, darling. So she's late for dinner. There will be other dinners."

Richard cleared his throat and swiped the butter with his knife, slathering his roll.

Claire stabbed at her salad, loading the fork and then setting it down on the plate. "She knew we were having fish tonight. It's one of her favorites. And you can't just grill a fish and let it sit around until somebody decides to show up for dinner."

"She did send you a text to tell you that Bryce would be late bringing her home," I said.

"Ten minutes before she was supposed to be here. She had to know we were in the middle of cooking."

"Not every teenager thinks like that," I said. "I doubt I did at her age."

"Regardless, she's late." She closed her eyes and took a deep breath through her nose. "It's okay. This is not a big deal." When she opened her eyes, she looked unconvinced.

On cue, strains of Sam and Bryce's laughter filtered into the kitchen.

"Hello, everyone," Bryce said, trailing through the side door behind Sam.

Sam dropped her backpack on the floor next to the door. "Sorry I'm late. We decided to stop and get a coffee. Is it cool if Bryce has dinner with us?"

I could swear Richard held his breath while we waited for Claire to answer. I know I did.

"Of course," Claire said, in a sweet voice with a very sarcastic edge. A loud scrape peeled out when she pushed her chair from the table. She abruptly turned and stalked to the kitchen cabinet, pulling out a plate and closing the door with a thud. Silverware clanged as she dug through the drawer.

Richard scooted his chair toward me, making room for Bryce between himself and Sam. I had the sense to snatch an extra placemat from the kitchen counter.

Sam and Bryce took their seats. A new, more ominous silence loomed. I passed the fish to the other end of the table and Richard followed suit with the rice and salad.

Sam stole a bite of the fish from the platter with her fingers. "Wow, Chris, this is really good."

"Thank you. Your mother deserves the credit though. She did all of the preparation. I merely cooked it."

"Mom, I'm sorry we're late. It won't happen again."

"How do I know that? Ever since school has started, this sort of thing is happening with greater frequency."

What Claire really meant to say was that it had been happening ever since Sam and Bryce had started going out over the summer.

"I said I was sorry. I'll try harder."

"It's my fault, Ms. Abby," Bryce said. "I had to do a few things for my dad before we left my house. You can blame it all on me."

Claire pressed her lips into a thin line. "Thank you. I appreciate that, but I'm not trying to blame anybody. Sam, honey, I only wish this wasn't happening so often. There's a lot going on right now and I want us to have this time together as a family."

CHAPTER FOURTEEN

HOWEVER LONG A WINK WAS, I knew for sure that I hadn't slept one. Instead, I tossed and turned, re-hashing my argument with Sam at dinner, serenaded by occasional bouts of Chris's snoring.

He was back at it at seven, prying me from the fitful sleep I'd managed to slip into. I stared at the clock until it reached 7:10 and I knew Sam would be up. I couldn't let her go to school without talking to her.

I stood outside her room for a moment before I knocked. The shadow of the hand-painted sign that had said, "Samantha's Room" in pink and purple was still there on the white wood door, even though it'd been more than a year since she'd begged me to take it down. *Stay positive.*

I rapped my knuckles quietly and opened the door. "Hey. Can we talk?"

She was wrestling on a t-shirt. "Is this about dinner last night? I said I was sorry."

I sat at the end of her bed, patting the empty space next to me. "Wanna sit?"

"I'm good." She put on earrings then fished a pair of knee-high socks from her dresser.

It felt like I'd been cut off at the knees when she kept her distance. "Okay. I'm sorry I got upset at dinner. It's just that you're spending a lot less time at home and when you are here, either Bryce is here too or you're busy doing homework, which is great, but I feel like I never see you anymore."

She studied me, clearly thinking. "I don't know what you want from me. I'm killing myself at school right now and I like spending time with Bryce. He makes me laugh. It feels like that's my only downtime." Her head dropped and she picked at her fingernail. "You and Chris are off doing your own stuff all the time. Sorry, but I don't feel like hanging out with Grandpa."

"Do you really feel like that? About me and Chris?"

She folded her arms across her chest, saying volumes with body language. "It's true, isn't it? You're either up in New York or you're writing or talking about the new house. Chris is always at the studio with Grandpa. I just feel like everything that's going on doesn't involve me."

At least she hadn't brought this up at dinner. My dad wouldn't have hesitated to chime in and cloud the issue. "Maybe you'd feel more like you're a part of it if you did more with us. If you were here more."

"Mom, think about it. You and Chris are starting a whole new life together. That's just about you two. You're getting married. You're buying a new house."

"A new house that you will live in. A new house that has an awesome bedroom for you and will have a pool eventually."

"And that'll be cool, but I'll live there for a few months and then I'll leave for college. This house has been the only home I've ever had." She sat in her office chair and pulled her leg up, planting her foot on the edge of the seat, wrapping her arms around her knee. "It's sad for me to leave that behind and you never even asked how I felt about it."

I sighed. I hadn't taken the time to consult with her. "I'm sorry. I thought you'd be excited to have a bigger house."

"I am. But before Chris came along, you used to ask my opinion. Now you don't do that anymore."

This was the price of single parenthood, a price among many. It'd been me and Sam for seventeen years and out of my need for a sounding board, I'd involved her in as much as I could, from as early an age as possible. It'd never occurred to me that finally finding the right man meant Sam felt as though she was being elbowed out of the picture.

The door opened a sliver and Chris poked his head into the room. "Sorry, ladies, just me." He looked so adorable with the pillow crease across his cheek, but his timing left something to be desired.

"What's up?" I asked.

He leaned into the doorframe. "Remember, we were going to take care of that thing this morning. You know. In the bathroom."

Sam looked as confused as I felt.

The bathroom? Oh, shit. The pregnancy test. "Two minutes? Is that okay? We're just finishing up."

"Yes. Of course. I'll get coffee on." He closed the door behind him.

"Fixing something in the bathroom? Is that some code for sex that I don't know about?"

"What?" I squinted at her. "No. It's the faucet. It's leaking and we were going to try and fix it."

"Isn't that Grandpa's job?"

"Chris wants to be the man of the house, honey. It's important to him." *New subject.* "Look, I'm sorry, honey. I really am.

You're right about a lot of this. I need to try harder to make sure that you feel included."

She scooped up her Converse high-tops from their perch atop a pile of laundry. "Mom. It's okay. I know you're trying." Her blue eyes twinkled. "I just felt like I had to say some of that. Because I do feel left out sometimes. Not all the time."

How many more of these talks would Sam and I ever have? Not many in this house. A mainstay of our life together would soon be gone, which left an indescribable emptiness inside me. "Part of the reason I got so ticked off last night is because I'd planned to ask if you'll be my maid of honor."

"Grandpa told me it was going to be Aunt Julie."

"He did? Seriously? When did he say that?"

She shrugged. "I don't know. A few weeks ago. After you got back from New York. That's kind of why I was feeling left out. I figured that if you already knew she was going to be your maid of honor, then you would've asked me if you wanted me in the wedding at all."

"Oh, honey. That's so not true." I shook my head. "Remind me to strangle your grandfather."

"Won't Aunt Julie get mad?"

"About which part? Your grandfather not being around anymore or the maid of honor bit?"

She laughed. "Both. Either."

"I don't really care what your Aunt Julie wants. I want you to be my maid of honor."

She smiled. "Do I get to pick out my own dress? I promise to pick something unusual, but not so unusual that I outshine the bride."

Outshine the bride? "Oh, crap. I need to start thinking about a dress, don't I?"

"Uh, hello? Yes. Now."

"You're coming with me. There's no way I'm doing this on

my own. Plus, it's the maid of honor's job." I kissed her on the forehead. "Now hurry up. You don't want to be late for school."

I left Sam and hurried back to my bedroom, where Chris was waiting with the pregnancy test, box open. "Sam said yes to being maid of honor."

"That's fabulous news. I'm so glad." He pulled the wrapped text stick from the box. "Ready? I brought the timer up from the kitchen so we don't have to rely on my watch."

"I'm a little worried this might not work. I got up and peed at five when I couldn't sleep."

He shooed me into the bathroom. "No worries. We'll try it and see what happens."

I pulled down my pajama pants and sat on the toilet. Chris tore open the foil pouch and removed the test stick, but it might have been the most ungraceful thing I'd ever seen him do and Chris was not clumsy, however big he was. He popped off the protective cap and it fell to the tile.

"You okay, honey?" I took the test from him and tried to relax.

He nodded—short, fast, choppy nods. "Yeah. I'm great. Just seems like the chances of you being late two months in a row are slim. I'm feeling good about it."

I was too, but again, I'd chosen not to share that with him. If he thought he was on pins and needles every month, I might have been worse. Every twinge in my pelvic region reminded me of what we were waiting for. I'd endured day after day of wondering if my breasts were sore when I put on my bra. Same routine every night when getting ready for bed. Several afternoon bouts of drowsiness had left me convinced last month, only to be disappointed. I'd tried to save him from that. I'd been waiting six months. He'd been waiting much longer.

"I might be late because my cycle is wonky."

"Whatever the reason, here we are." He watched me,

intently, and I watched him back. "Aren't you supposed to pee? I don't hear anything."

I closed my eyes. "You're making me nervous. I can't get it to go." My body tensed with every word, even when I was screaming at it in my head. Just. Relax. *Right. Shut up. You relax.*

"Just relax."

"Gee, thanks. That's really helpful. Go do something for a minute and come back."

He gave me a look that said he hated missing even a second of this. "I'll be right outside the door if you need anything."

"You're sweet. Now go away."

I took a deep breath. It felt as if the pressure was even more immense than it had been a minute ago. *Seriously, Claire. Relax.* I took another deep breath and finally let go. It was the most relieved I'd ever been to pee and that included many last-minute dashes to the bathroom when I'd been pregnant with Sam.

"The coast is clear—" I said, as he materialized in the doorway. "Oh. You're here."

He pointed over his shoulder. "I was only hiding around the corner."

I shook my head and pulled up my pajama pants. Chris tapped away at the digital kitchen timer then waited with a towel while I washed my hands. He pulled me into a hug when I finished.

"Now we wait." I pressed myself against him. His smell was so wonderfully heady in the morning, when there was only the slightest trace of his cologne.

"How does five minutes end up seeming so impossibly long?"

"I know. It's ridiculous."

"We could slow dance to pass the time." He began shifting

his weight from foot to foot and I followed. Taking his time, he turned us in a circle.

"Perfect." I ran my hand up and down his back, familiar and enticing contours through the worn cotton of his t-shirt. *If I'm not already pregnant, I will be after this dance.* "Why don't we dance in the bathroom more often?"

"No idea." He teased my hair back over my shoulder and hummed a tune in my ear, sending all kinds of warm tingles along my spine. "It's probably the tight quarters."

My fingers wove into his hair, which was now back to the length I loved—sloppy and messy and perfect for hands. "We can dance all we want in our new bathroom."

"Mmm. That's not all we can do." His stubble scratched at my jaw when he placed kiss after kiss on my neck. "No more squeezing into a tiny bath to take a shower together." He stopped and reared back his head. "That reminds me. The contractor is meeting us at the house at noon."

My shoulders dropped. "Chris. You're ruining the moment."

He furrowed his brow. "Sorry, love. I just had it on my mind."

The kitchen timer sounded behind me. *Beep. Beep. Beep.* My heart was off to the races, pounding frantically in my ears. "Here we go."

"Same routine as last time? Close our eyes, count to three?"

"I don't know. Is it bad luck if we do the same thing again?"

"No. I call it tradition."

"Okay, yes. Tradition." My eyelids fluttered shut as we squeezed each other's hands. "One...two...three. Open."

A gasp left my mouth. "It's—"

"Positive."

Two blue lines. "I'm pregnant." My body lightened, worries vanished, lost to that moment.

"You're pregnant." The smile on his face was half jubilance, half dumbstruck.

"We're pregnant."

He picked up the stick and swept his hair from his forehead, regarding the piece of plastic as if it was the solid gold key to a lost city. "We did it. We're actually pregnant."

"I know." My voice wobbled. I bounced on my toes. "I can't believe it."

"No more waiting."

"No more waiting." I nodded like a little kid who'd been offered a second scoop of ice cream. "No more taking tests."

"No more scheduling sex. We still get to have lots of sex, right?"

"Until I'm the size of a barn, yes. Then it might become more sporadic. It just depends."

He kneeled on the bathroom floor, just as he had when he'd proposed, lifted up my tank top, pressing a tender kiss to my belly. "Hello in there." His other hand slid around to the small of my back. All I could see was the top of his head—I would've paid good money to see the look on his face as he spoke his first words to our baby. "We are so happy you're here. Now, be good. No giving your mum a hard time."

Mum. I'm going to be a mum. Again. "I wish we could tell Sam. I really want to tell her."

"Isn't it bad luck?"

There was a thundering knock at the bedroom door. "Mom? Can I come in?"

I pushed down my tank top and bounded into our room. "Yeah, honey. What's up?"

She poked her head in. "If you guys are done with your plumbing project, I need a ride to school. I missed the bus."

CHAPTER FIFTEEN

"WHEN CAN WE MOVE IN?" Sam climbed out of the Volvo in front of our new-to-us, but actually quite old, house. Three different contractor vans sat in the driveway—the electrician, the painters, and the floor company. Much had been set in motion in a few short weeks. Cash and a highly motivated contractor helped.

Claire closed her car door. "It looks so much better now that they did the pressure washing. It's like a new house."

"I don't know about new, but it does look pretty good, doesn't it?"

"I know how to run a pressure washer," Richard said. "I don't see why you had to hire someone."

He and Sam started down the long driveway, walking several yards ahead of Claire and me. "He takes it as a personal insult every time we don't include him on something, even menial labor," I muttered.

"I know it's a pain, but he wants to feel useful."

"I've given him more than enough work to do at the studio and I still feel like I'm pestering him about things. I have to say, he's not quite as on top of things as I thought he'd be."

"He's getting older. I need to bug him about the check-up again. Every time I ask him about it, he changes the subject."

Inside, we found a bustle of noise and workers milling about.

"Looks like they're done sanding the hardwoods." Claire swept her foot across the pale wood floor. "When do they refinish them?"

"This weekend. When the other workers are out of here. Takes a few days for the finish to cure and then they'll put down paper until everything else is done."

"Are you going to be here to supervise?" Richard asked. "If not, I could do it."

"You know, I'm going to trust that the floor people know what they're doing."

His forehead crinkled. "If you say so."

"Mom, you're going to do the ceremony right here? In the living room?"

Claire's face lit up with pure delight. "We are. The contractor says we can move in ten days before the wedding. We'll just delay the furniture delivery for the living room."

"We'll put chairs for the guests here and here," I said, indicating two swaths of floor that ran diagonally from the entry. "The aisle will go up the center. Haven't quite sorted where everyone will go when the caterers set up tables for the reception, but we'll figure something out. The weather could be dodgy that late in December, so we can't count on sending everyone outside." I took several long steps to the far corner of the room. "We'll exchange vows right here. Then we have a party."

Claire sidled up to me and grabbed my hand. "Right after the I-do's."

I grinned from ear to ear. "I do."

"I do," she echoed, pecking me on the lips.

"Oh brother," Sam said. "You guys are so gross sometimes."

"That's what happens when you're in love and incredibly happy, Sam." I didn't take my eyes off Claire or her lovely smile. "You'll find that out for yourself one day." I noticed that Richard had wandered off and was now staring out a window. "Anyway, there's plenty of space in here. It'll be perfect."

"There is?" Sam asked, looking around.

"There will only be about twenty people," I said. "Family, a few close friends, that's it. Any more and you risk the word getting out and that could turn into a circus."

"I guess that's what happens when you're a rock star," Sam quipped.

I shook my head. "I think we need to put a ban on that term. I'm a musician, not a rock star."

"I guess." Sam shrugged and checked her phone, tapped off a text and put it back in her jacket pocket. "I don't understand why you don't get married in St. Barts. Then we can all just hang out on the beach when it's over."

"We thought about that," I said. "But we don't want all of you underfoot after we get married. We need our alone time." *Do we ever.*

"So, we get to move in the beginning of December?"

"That's the plan," Claire said. "We didn't want to push for November. The Banks Forest shows in New York are that month and I really wanted to have one last Thanksgiving at the old house."

"Cool," Sam quipped "Can we see the kitchen?"

"Dad? You coming?"

He turned, seeming puzzled. "Oh, uh. Yes."

Claire approached him. "Are you okay?"

He nodded, his jaw set firmly. "Just fine. Maybe a little tired."

"Come on." Claire patted his back and led him to the kitchen.

An electrician was at work, fishing lines through the wall. Otherwise, the room was empty, a complete gut job, by far the biggest part of this first wave of renovation.

The house would see a second wave and possibly a third, but for now, everything was about the first floor. With our tight timeline for the wedding, we weren't able to address anything more than fresh paint upstairs.

Sam traipsed off to the sliding glass doors and looked out. "The pool is going to go out here?"

"That probably won't happen until the spring," I said.

"Good timing, guys. Just in time for me to go to college."

"You'll get a few months of use before you leave us." Claire took my hand. "My dad is acting so weird," she whispered. "I think we should do a quick pass upstairs and take him home. A nap would do him good."

Richard had again wandered off, being unusually quiet. "Sure thing." I cleared my throat. "Who wants to check out the bedrooms?"

The four of us scaled the stairs, Claire and I both seeming to notice how slowly Richard was taking the steps. "You sure you're okay, Dad?" Claire asked. "We don't have to do this today if you're tired."

He stopped at the landing and turned. "Will you please stop asking me if I'm okay, Samantha? I'm fine."

"Grandpa—" Sam started.

He shut his eyes, removed his glasses, and pinched the bridge of his nose. "Dag nabbit. I meant to say Claire. Don't go thinking there's something wrong with me. I'm fine. Can't a guy be tired without it being a big deal?"

Claire patted him on the back. "Okay. I'm sorry. We'll be

done in a few minutes anyway." Her face told me exactly how concerned she was.

Sam walked into her room. "It looks good in here." Claire and I followed, while Richard went into what would be the guest room. "So, what's the deal, mom?" Sam asked under her breath. "Is Grandpa going to move in with us here or is he going to stay at the old house?"

I looked down at Claire. Much of this was her call. We hadn't discussed it with Richard, so that was another situation altogether.

"I don't know," she whispered. "If you asked me today, I'd say he's coming with us. He's just not himself. I hate the idea of him being alone."

I put my arm around Claire's shoulders and squeezed. "We'll get him to see the doctor, make sure he's okay."

"I'm calling to make an appointment myself. If we wait for him to do it, it'll never happen."

"We've had an awful lot of activity lately, far more than he's used to when he's at home by himself in Asheville. Maybe it's too much."

Richard came into Sam's room via the Jack-and-Jill bath. "My room looks good. They goofed on the trim in a few spots, but otherwise they did a good job."

My room. Suddenly, it looked like all four of us would be making the move unless Claire could figure out a way to convince him otherwise. Richard wandered out of the room before we could take the subject any further.

"Mom," Sam said, with a distinct look of horror. "Would Grandpa and I be sharing a bathroom?"

"Well...yes." Claire shrugged. "Just like at home."

"It's not the same." Sam winced. "Our rooms aren't connected at home. It's sort of creepy."

Claire kneaded her forehead. "Unless we can convince him to stay at the other house, you two will just have to work it out." She blew out a breath. "Should we check out the other bedroom?"

Sam was at it with her phone again, smiling to herself and tapping away. Claire and I sneaked down the hall to the baby's room.

"Oh, wow." Claire turned in the center of the room. "The color looks nice. I like the pale green."

"It's perfect." Now that the room was repainted, I could better imagine everything she'd suggested—where the crib would go, a rocking chair. I put my arm around her, settling one hand on her belly. "How are you feeling?"

"Fine after that bout of morning sickness. I'll probably need a nap later, but so does Dad."

I kissed her forehead, but couldn't bring myself to pull away. "I wish we could tell the whole world."

"I know. Me too." She wrapped her arms around my waist and I pulled her close.

"Are you two at it again?" Sam asked, interrupting our moment.

I snickered into Claire's ear. "Can we help you with something?"

"Yeah, you guys better come downstairs. It's Grandpa."

"Oh, no." Claire hitched her purse over her shoulder and rushed out the door.

"Mom, stop." Sam hurried after her. They ground to a halt in the middle of the hall. "He's fine. Really. He's fine."

"Don't scare me like that." Claire held her hand to her chest.

"Sorry. It's just kinda weird. He's sitting on the bottom of the stairs dipping his finger into Splenda packets."

CHAPTER SIXTEEN

I TURNED off the car in the parking lot of the bridal boutique, waiting for Sam to finish her hot cocoa. The coffee shop visit had tested my talent for on-the-fly excuses. I always got a coffee, especially in October when the pumpkin spice latte was available, but now that I was expecting, I'd cut back to one cup a day. I chose water, told her I was thirsty. She gave me a sideways look, but let it go.

"Done." She popped her paper cup into the holder.

A bell jingled when we entered through the black-framed bridal boutique door. A thin, sophisticated woman greeted us, wearing a tweed jacket and pencil skirt in pale blue and gray. It looked to be vintage Chanel. "You must be Ms. Abby. I'm Georgia McIntyre." She teetered on block heels, her jet-black hair pulled back in a high bun.

"Please, call me Claire. This is my daughter, Samantha."

Sam was thumbing through bridesmaid dresses. "What do you think about this one, Mom?" She pulled out a strapless black satin number with a flared skirt.

"Hmm." I stepped closer and ran my hands across the

fabric. "I'm not sure about black. I was thinking a softer color like lavender."

"Lavender?" Sam grimaced.

"I'm sure we can find something that will make both mother and daughter happy." Georgia faltered every few steps, making her way to a black velvet curtain that spanned the width of the boutique. With a flourish, she pulled it back to reveal a room brimming with wedding gowns. A white-carpeted platform stood in the middle of the room, with an expanse of multi-way mirrors behind it.

"Wow, Mom. Cool."

I'd never once thought about where in town I might shop for a wedding dress, but if I'd had to guess, it wouldn't have been this place. It was almost too nice, carrying big designers and requiring an appointment. Chris had insisted that I at least take the time to look. My mom, per her usual, had sided with him.

I went to the rack nearest me and looked at the first dress. Hideous. Ruffles, ruffles, and more ruffles. It had the most profuse bustle I could imagine. *Like I want a bigger ass when I'm four months pregnant.*

Georgia stood behind me. "Did you bring photos of dresses that you like? From brides' magazines?"

Shit. "No, I'm sorry. I didn't." I'd only purchased one magazine and dog-eared two things in it, neither of which I loved.

"It's not a problem. If you want to give me an idea of what you're looking for, I can start pulling some gowns as you look."

The second dress on the rack was as bad as the first. "I want something very simple. No sequins or bows. I'd like to keep the lace and ruffles to a minimum."

"What about fabric?" Georgia took a clipboard from a small antique writing desk in the corner. Slipping on a pair of reading glasses, she began taking notes.

"Matte satin? Organza? Nothing shiny." *Nobody wants to see a shiny pregnant bride.*

"Neckline? Sleeves? Sleeveless?"

Shopping for a wedding dress made sending a man to the store to buy tampons a piece of cake. "Strapless. I think. Maybe a halter? Sam? What do you think?"

"You don't really have the boobs for strapless, Mom. A halter might be better."

If this pregnancy is like the first, I should have some lovely boobs by the wedding day. The blood drained from my face as I realized that I would need to accommodate my growing size in whatever dress I picked. Why it hadn't occurred to me earlier was a mystery. "Yes. A halter. And I'd like something with a high waist and a skirt with a little fullness, but not poofy." *I gotta hide that baby bump, but I don't need an airplane hangar for it.*

Georgia's glasses slid to the end of her nose. "Allow me to pull a few things."

"Any luck?" Sam asked, joining me.

"Nope." I flipped past dress after dress. "This is really stupid. I should've been better prepared. I guess I didn't realize there would be so many choices in a boutique this small."

"The whole thing is sort of silly, isn't it? You're going to wear it for a few hours and then you'll put it in a box forever."

"You never know. I might pick something so great that even you want to wear it."

"That's assuming I'm going to get married."

"Don't you want to get married?" I continued to flip past dress after dress.

She shrugged. "I don't know. You did okay without a husband."

"I guess."

Georgia had placed a few dresses on a small rack near the

mirrors. "Would you like to see what I've already chosen? You might like one of these and if not, you can tell me where I'm missing the mark."

"Sure." I considered the first batch. None of them were close. "The first two are almost too plain. This one is fitted in the waist and hips. That won't work."

"You have a lovely trim figure," Georgia said. "No need to hide it."

Sam eyed the gown. "I like it, Mom. You'll look like a mermaid."

A pregnant mermaid? "Sorry. It's not me."

Georgia nodded, her lips pressed in a thin line. "I will continue to look. We might need to consult some catalogs."

I retreated to the spot where I'd last been looking, feeling defeated. The three of us continued with our quest for another twenty or thirty minutes. Sam had moved to the other side of the room, seemingly frustrated with my near-perfect dislike rate of the things she showed me.

I'll know it when I see it. No. No. Ugly. Frumpy. Poofy. Slutty. Eww. Yeah, right. Maybe when I was eighteen and had zero cellulite. No. Hmm. Maybe. Why do they have to put ruffles on everything? No. No.

I flipped past another. *Yes. Oh, wow. God, yes.* "I found something."

"You did?" Sam rushed over.

Georgia did her own version of rushing, far slower than Sam.

"Mom, that's strapless. You said you didn't want strapless."

"The skirt has a very wide lace trim. With hand-beading," Georgia added. "You'd said you didn't want lace."

It's perfect. "May I?" I asked, reaching for the hanger.

"Certainly. Let's bring it over here so we can see it better." Georgia draped the dress over her arm, sidling to the staging rack in her odd gait. "It's an exquisite gown, sheer silk organza over an underskirt of matte silk satin. The beaded lace at the hem is in a style that was popular in England in the 1800s and is part of the organza. It's not applied. It's a painstaking process. If the skirt needs to be hemmed at all, it has to be done from the waist."

"Sam? What do you think?" I asked.

"Try it on."

"Smart girl," Georgia said. "You can change behind this screen."

I set my purse on the writing desk and stepped into the changing area, where Georgia held the dress, averting her eyes. I undressed, and when I turned, Georgia had it unzipped and waiting for me to step in. I held the bodice to my chest and she zipped it up.

"As I expected." Georgia tugged on the back of the dress. "It's roomy in the bust. It'll need to be taken in. Let's take a look in front of the mirror."

Sam gasped when I stepped out from behind the screen. "Mom." In uncharacteristic Sam fashion, instead of spouting her opinion, her hand clasped over her mouth.

I lifted the skirt and stepped up onto the circular, carpeted platform in front of the mirrors. It felt as if my heart was talking to me. *I'm beating. I'm still beating. Believe it or not, I'm still here.* The bodice had gorgeous layers of ivory organza, twisted in the front like a bandeau bathing suit, with skinny straps. The skirt was gathered, but without crinoline, it gracefully swept to the floor. The lace trim was weighty, giving the dress an elegant drape.

"Mom, it's so pretty. Do you love it?"

I nodded, staring at myself in the mirror. I almost didn't recognize the woman before me. This wasn't where I'd pictured myself five years ago. Not even a year ago. Part of me had become resigned to the idea that this might not ever happen. Fairytales can't happen to everyone, can they?

"I do love it. I really love it."

Georgia stepped up on to the platform and tugged at the back again. "The seamstress isn't here today, but you could come back for the initial fitting next week."

I wiggled back and forth, discreetly holding up the dress by pressing my arms to my side. "I don't know. Seems like it fits great."

Georgia lifted one of my arms. The bodice drooped. "You don't want this. It'll need to come in."

"What happens if they take it in and I gain weight?" *Because I'm definitely going to gain weight.*

"Well," Georgia said in her oddly nasal drawl. "The tailor can leave some wiggle room, but not much. Don't worry though. I doubt you'll gain weight."

"Mom." Sam blew out an exasperated breath. "You're not going to gain weight. You run six days a week."

"What if I get nervous? I might start to eat a lot."

Georgia looked at my reflection in the mirror, still holding up the bodice in the back. "Every bride has to suck it in to get into their dress, darling."

"I can't suck it in. I already have a hard enough time breathing when I get excited."

My phone rang and Sam grabbed it from my purse. "It's Chris. Do you want to talk to him?"

"Yes." I took the phone from her. "Hey. Is everything okay?"

"If you mean with your dad, he's fine. I was calling to see how it's going. Any luck?"

The combination of Chris's buttery accent and a glimpse of my reflection in the dress made my face flush with heat. "Actually, yes. I have it on right now."

"Oh, really?" His voice took an even lower, sexier tone.

I closed my eyes, steadying myself. "Yes, really."

"Can you tell me anything?"

Every syllable out of his mouth tempted me into telling all. "You know I can't."

"How about a hint? I want to picture you in it."

Sam plopped down on the edge of the platform.

"That will ruin the surprise." I smoothed my hand over the dress, turning in the mirror.

"Are you going to get this one?"

"I have to ask how much it costs."

"Don't worry about that. Just get it if you like it."

This was an idea with which I wasn't remotely comfortable.

Georgia approached with a large, three-ring binder open in her hands. "It's fifty-nine hundred," she said, matter-of-fact. "Plus alterations."

I'd guessed half that. "It's more expensive than I thought. I should keep looking."

"Absolutely not. I gave in on a smaller ring. If you think a penny of that matters to me more than your happiness, you haven't figured me out."

I smiled. Like there was any defense from him when he was being generous and romantic. "Okay, then. Sounds like I found a dress." My hand swished across the fabric one more time, prompting another smile.

Forty-five minutes later, I'd committed to the dress, with my first fitting appointment to come in three weeks, despite Georgia's protests that I was pushing the timing.

"Mom. What is your problem?" Sam asked, closing her car door. "I bet your weight hasn't changed more than two pounds up or down in ten years.

I jammed the key into the ignition. *This is so stupid. I should just tell her. She deserves to know.* "I'm nervous. That's all."

"Are you having second thoughts about getting married? Because Chris is awesome."

I looked in the rearview mirror. "No, it's not that."

"Then what is it?"

Tell her. I cut the engine. The confusion on her face didn't portend the immensity of the coming announcement. She was more annoyed with me than anything. "If I tell you, you have to keep it a secret."

"Okay."

"I mean it. Not Bryce. Not Leah. Especially not your grandfather."

"Now you're freaking me out. Is everything okay?"

I sucked in a deep breath. "I'm pregnant."

"Oh, my God." Her eyes scanned my face, and I did the same to her, hoping for some sign of elation. I could've been content with a blip of plain old happy. "I guess I knew this was coming. I just didn't think it would happen now."

CHAPTER SEVENTEEN

CLAIRE WAS TWELVE WEEKS ALONG, with a due date of May 27th, and aside from Sam, nobody knew. It was torture.

Being quiet made very little of it real. Claire wasn't showing. I kept waiting for her belly to pooch out. No such luck. This wait was almost as bad as waiting to actually be pregnant.

I pulled up to the clinic for our second prenatal appointment, hurrying to open Claire's car door. The early November air held only a hint of autumn crispness. The weather had otherwise stayed stubbornly warm.

"Chris, honey. I'm fine. You don't need to get my door."

"I like doing these things for you. I feel blooming useless otherwise." The truth was that these appointments had me at sixes and sevens. I was so paranoid that something would go wrong. Today, we were to hear the baby's heartbeat, a thrilling and terrifying proposition.

"Don't worry. There will be plenty of time to do stuff for me." She whisked past me as I held open the clinic door.

I followed and she took her place in line.

"Next," a plump, dark-haired woman at the desk said.

"Claire Abby. I have an 11:30 appointment with Dr. Miller."

I bristled at the mention of her maiden name. *Abby. My bloody fault for not asking her to marry me sooner.*

"I'll need your hospital card." She took the paperwork from Claire and seconds later, placed the card on the counter. "The nurse will call you back in a minute."

We took a seat in the waiting area. One woman's belly was so rounded and protruding that it looked as if she might soon burst. I didn't want to stare, but it was hard not to, out of sheer fascination more than anything. Imagining Claire that big, that shape, was such a foreign idea and yet, it would happen. Soon.

"Ms. Abby?" the nurse called, clipboard in hand, holding open the door. Wispy red hair framed her face, freckles dotted her cheeks. "I hope Mom and Dad are doing well today."

Mom and Dad. I'll never tire of hearing that. I took Claire's hand, holding on tight.

"I have to tell you, this is a little funny, but my first name is Abby." She directed us down the hall. "We're in the first room on your right. We'll take your vitals real quick."

"Wow, Abby," Claire said as she entered the tiny room, which had a scale, chair, and miscellaneous medical equipment. "Isn't that funny, Chris?"

"Good thing I didn't marry this guy." The nurse pointed at me. "Or my name would be Abby Abby."

Claire laughed. "Actually, Abby is my maiden name."

I folded my arms across my chest, watching as she had Claire stand on the scale. I shifted my weight, trying to ignore how annoyed I was with myself. *She should have been Claire Penman from her very first appointment.*

"Ah, a modern woman," Abby said. She flicked back the counterweight on the scale. "Got that. Let's get your blood pressure." She placed the cuff on Claire's arm and turned on the machine. "You look so familiar." She narrowed a stare at me. "I just can't figure out from where. I don't think I know any Brits."

Claire snickered.

"I get that a lot."

"Oh, okay." She looked unconvinced. "Just a familiar-looking face, I guess." A few minutes later, Abby was done collecting data and led us back to the exam room. She handed Claire a plastic cup. "You know the routine. When you come back, undress from the waist down and use the drape." She pointed to a thick, folded piece of pale blue paper on the counter.

I waited for Claire to return, studying the posters of a fetus as it develops. At twelve weeks, there were fingers and toes, spindly little legs and arms and quite a large head. *A baby. Miraculous stuff.*

"I'm back." Claire set the specimen cup on the counter and kicked off her shoes. She removed her pants and underwear and set them neatly on a chair, then climbed up on to the exam table.

I unfolded the paper blanket and laid it across her lap. "Doctor Miller hasn't been in yet. Thank goodness. She might've put me up in these things." I pulled out the metal footrest near Claire's hip and fiddled with it.

"The stirrups," Doctor Miller said from the doorway. "Trust me. I don't think you could handle it."

My face went hot. "Sorry about that."

"Oh, I'm just giving you a hard time." She closed the door and shook hands with Claire. "How are we today?" She shook my hand and winked at me. Her eyes were crinkled at the corners, her dark blonde showing gray at the roots.

I let out a breath and forced myself to relax.

"We're listening to the heartbeat today," Dr. Miller said. "How exciting. Claire, we'll do a quick pelvic exam first."

I grasped Claire's hand as Doctor Miller approached.

"We're not quite in labor yet, Dad, but I like that you dote on her. Don't forget to do that for all nine months." She held a stethoscope to Claire's chest. "Take a deep breath."

Claire and I locked eyes, both of us as quiet as could be, grinning like happy fools. She mouthed, "I love you" and I did the same. *I love you.*

"Your heart sounds perfect. We're going to take a quick look down below." With a metallic clatter, the doctor pulled out the foot contraptions. "Make sure your cervix is doing what it's supposed to."

That was a lot of uncomfortable verbiage, but I stayed at Claire's side, holding her hand and ignoring the doctor who was about to take a look-see between my fiancée's legs.

"Just a little pressure and some cold," the doctor said.

"You okay?" I asked when Claire grimaced.

"Yep." She nodded and squinted. "Not my favorite part."

"Everything looks perfect. Now let's see if we can find that heartbeat."

Yes. Please do. My own heart felt as if it might crawl out of my body via my throat.

Doctor Miller pulled out a device about the size of a handheld video game, with a curly cord and a wand attached. "This is a fetal Doppler. It uses sound waves to detect the baby's heartbeat." She flipped a switch and squeezed some gel on to the end of the device before placing it on Claire's belly. Slowly, she moved it over her skin, rocking the wand back and forth and changing the angles. It made crackly noises like an old radio. Seconds ticked by as we waited. "Sometimes it takes a minute." The expression on her face was impossible to read, stoic, almost blank. "Seems like someone is hiding from us today." She frowned and readjusted the position of the wand.

Doctor Miller's comments only put me more on edge. My hand was sweating. So was Claire's.

A frantic rhythmic whoosh rang out. Claire squeezed my hand.

"Is that it?" I asked.

"It is." The doctor consulted the Doppler. "160 beats per minute. A little fast, but not outside the range of normal."

Claire and I stared at each other, the wonderful alien sound of life coming at us at lightning speed. *Whoosh. Whoosh. Whoosh. Whoosh. Whoosh.* For the second time today, we smiled as if we'd won the lottery. It certainly felt as though we had.

Doctor Miller flipped off the Doppler. "It all sounds good. You can go ahead and sit back." She wheeled her stool to where Claire's chart was and opened it up.

"Doctor, what's the big label on my chart?" Claire pointed to the front cover of the folder, a red sticker obscured by the doctor's hand.

"Advanced Maternal Age."

Claire's face paled and her forehead crinkled with worry. "I'm only forty."

"In the world of Obstetrics, that's advanced. Sorry to tell you."

"Is that a big deal?"

"Remember we discussed the genetic testing at your last appointment? That's all because of your age."

My stomach knotted. Advanced Maternal Age. *Why do they have to put it that way?*

"Oh," Claire said. "I thought that was just the routine these days."

"It is when you're over thirty-five." Dr. Miller scribbled a signature on a sheet of paper and handed it to me. "You can give this to them when you check out."

I stood straighter. Didn't matter, this was what I'd signed up for. I smiled and kissed Claire's forehead. "Don't worry, darling. It'll be fine."

CHAPTER EIGHTEEN

I WRAPPED my wet hair in a towel and swiped at the fogged-up bathroom mirror with a washcloth. "Hey, Chris? What time is it?" With a damp cotton ball, I wiped mascara residue from beneath my eyes. "Hey. Penman. I know you're tired from packing boxes all day, but we need to get this show on the road." I took my mom's old bathrobe from the hook on the back of the bathroom door and started into the bedroom. "No fair falling asleep—"

Chris was in the middle of the bed, in the grubby Clash t-shirt and khaki shorts he'd worn all day while we'd gone through the attic and a few closets. He looked at me with a playful grin. "Sorry, love. I was just completely engrossed with this bit of reading I found." He teased me with a wag of a spiral-bound school notebook, decorated with my handwriting. My teenage handwriting. Next to him sat an open cardboard box with girly lettering on the side: *High School Memories* with a heart for the dots above the "i" in "High" and "Memories".

Oh my God. I buried my face in my hands then lunged for the notebook.

He anticipated my move and jerked it away.

"Give me that."

"I know I shouldn't have looked."

"But you did." I tightened the tie on my robe as he held the tome against his chest.

"Where did you find that?" My vision narrowed as he smiled. "More importantly, when did you find that?"

"I came across it when we were up in the attic today. I nicked it when we came down to get ready for dinner."

"That's so not cool."

"I know. I'm bad. You can punish me later." He wagged his eyebrow. "The thing is, you never talk about your teenage days."

"You mean when I was obsessed with you and your band? Do you really want to listen to me talk about that?"

"Well, sure. Why not?"

"Because you already have a pretty high opinion of yourself?" I ruffled his already messy hair.

"Oh, stop. You can't blame me for wanting to read it. It says my name right here on the cover." He pointed to the place where indeed, it made mention of Christopher Penman. "I figured I was entitled to at least take a peek."

I slumped down on the bed next to him. "How much did you read?"

The bed wobbled when he inched closer and put his arm around me. "Oh, I don't know, a few pages, twenty, tops. I'd never read the whole thing without your permission, so I skimmed for my name."

"Of course you did."

"Well, with a title like this, how can you blame me?" He ran his finger along the rambling string of words on the cover. "Claire's Diary, My Random Thoughts On Life, Love, (Or Lack Thereof) and Everything Possible Pertaining to My Future Husband Christopher Penman and Banks Forest." Fortunately, his accent made what had seemed like a good title at age sixteen, a bit more distinguished sounding. "Although you needed an editor, I can see your writing ability was strong from a young age."

"Very funny."

He flipped it open and began thumbing through the pages. "I loved the part about putting the poster of me near your bed so it looked like I was in bed with you. So adorable. I never knew girls did that."

"I seriously feel like dying right now."

"I could spend hours going through it. It seems to be quite the treasure trove of Claire Abby secrets."

"It mostly just shows you pathetic I was as a teenager. I'm glad you find that so entertaining."

"Don't say that, darling. It's very sweet. Plus you thought of me as your future husband. Doesn't that strike you as the most remarkable bit of fate?"

"Millions of girls thought of you as their future husband. You had a very large pool to draw from."

"But I chose you. That's all that really matters." He leaned forward and kissed me softly. "I think I did incredibly well for myself. And think about it. The roles could have just as easily been reversed."

"I don't understand." I settled against his chest, partly because I was tired after hours of menial labor and he made a great pillow, partly because I was eager to wrestle the notebook from his grasp.

"What if you'd been the famous one? An actress or a rock star in your own right? A Debbie Harry or Patti Smith or Pat Benatar."

I snickered. "Yeah, right. That's hilarious. You've heard me sing in the shower. It's not pretty."

"You could've been famous for writing. What if you'd

written the great American novel?"

"Hey. You never know. I still might."

"All I'm saying is that the way life turns out is so far out of our control. I could've just as easily been a miserable flop as I was a success."

The hem of his shorts was fraying and I pulled at the threads. "I'm not sure if I believe that completely. Everyone plays a part in their successes and failures."

"Well, sure, but even then, just because you work hard at something, doesn't mean it'll happen. Just because you want something more than anything, doesn't mean it'll work out the way you want it to."

"I guess you're right, but it still seems like you're trying to distract me from the fact that this particular moment of nosiness might rival The Snooper."

"Not your dad."

"Yep, Penman. You're getting to be as bad as Richard."

———

DRESSED FOR DINNER, I went downstairs to sneak a snack before we left. Morning sickness was a misnomer—my nausea always seemed to hit late afternoon. Now that today's was gone, I was starving. I found an apple in the fridge and washed it at the sink.

"What are you up to, Ladybug?"

I whipped around. "Dad. You scared me. I didn't hear you." I grabbed a paper towel and dried off the apple before sinking my teeth in. *Hmmm. Needs peanut butter. Or Nutella.*

"I was in the living room, taking a little snooze on the couch." He took a glass from the kitchen cabinet and filled it with water from the tap. "I talked to your sister today. I gotta tell you. She isn't too pleased with you. Can't you at least make her a bridesmaid? She asked you to be in her wedding."

"Dad, Julie and Matt had nearly a hundred guests at their wedding. It's not the same thing at all. I don't need a wedding party. Sam is my maid of honor and that's all I need."

"Well, she feels slighted."

I grumbled to myself and crunched down on the apple. Even my mom had been rambling on in my head lately, giving me a hard time about not including Julie in the wedding party. *Why does Julie have to make such a big deal out of this stuff? It's not like we're even that close.* "It wouldn't be the first time I did something that made Julie mad."

"Why are you eating now? Isn't our reservation for six-thirty?" He consulted his watch. "It's six-ten. We'll be leaving any minute."

I nodded and finished chewing, wishing Chris would hurry up and get his butt downstairs and create a distraction so I could stop lying about the recent changes in my sleeping and eating habits. Without that luxury, I resorted to changing subjects. "Did the test results come back today from your visit to see Dr. Stevens?"

He stuffed his hands into the pockets of his khakis. "Yep. Gave me a clean bill of health. I'm fit as a fiddle."

Such a relief. "Cholesterol and all of that is good?" I took another bite of my apple, studying his reaction. He'd seemed much more on the ball over the past few weeks. His moodiness had turned to regular Richard-ness, although I couldn't escape the feeling that there was an edge of sadness about him that hadn't been there before. Regardless, I was happy he'd taken my plea seriously and finally seen a doctor.

"Yes, ma'am. No problems." He pushed his frameless glasses further up on to his nose. "Hate to disappoint you."

I dropped my head to the side. "Dad. Don't say that. I worry about you." I placed my arm around his shoulder and he tensed the way he always did. "Isn't it okay if I worry about you at least a little bit?"

"Well, Jellybean. No need to worry anymore."

Chris came clomping down the stairs with Sam behind him. "Everyone ready?"

I took one last bite of the apple and tossed the core into the compost container under the sink. "I think we should share our news before we go to the restaurant. In the interest of privacy."

"News?" Sam asked, with an unconvincing squeak. She'd been practicing for this moment for a few days—the moment when she pretended that she was learning about the pregnancy at the same time as my dad.

Chris rolled his eyes and took my hand. "Yes, Samantha, news." He cleared his throat, which made it seem that much more like theater. "Claire and I are happy to announce that we are expecting a baby." His hand went to my belly and gently patted.

"Oh my God!" Sam exclaimed. "Grandpa, can you believe it?" She bugged out her eyes in dramatic fashion and clapped frantically. "You're going to be a grandpa again. I'm going to be a big sister."

I started to laugh. If it hadn't been right to tell Sam before anyone else, at least it made it a hell of a lot more fun. Of course, I had to wonder how much of Sam's reaction was an act and how much of it was real.

"My goodness, Ladybug. How wonderful. I don't know how many more happy events you and Christopher can cram into one year, but I'm not complaining. I'm only glad I'm around to witness it."

"Dad, you aren't just witnessing it. You're a part of this."

Chris pulled me closer and pressed a kiss to the top of my head. "She's right, Richard. You too, Sam. It's important to us both that you know that you're a part of everything that's going on in our lives right now. The wedding, the house, and most importantly, the baby."

My dad put his hands back in his pockets. This much open talk about feelings and happiness was a lot for him to take. It was surprising he hadn't initiated talk of renovation projects for the nursery. "We should go or we'll be late."

We piled into the Volvo and headed into Carrboro, a once-tiny mill town surrounded by Chapel Hill on three sides. When I'd moved to North Carolina, there wasn't much happening there, but nearly twenty years later, it was bursting at the seams and home to lots of very happening restaurants.

Chris pulled into the parking lot where the farmer's market had once been and we entered through the restaurant's back patio. The four of us went to the hostess stand, which was a little silly, since all she did was grab menus and the wine list before marching us back outside to our table.

"Lovely evening, but I'm glad they have heaters out here." I took my seat on the metal bistro chair next to Chris. A woman across the patio had pointed at him and was now taking a picture with her phone. *Can't get away from it anywhere.*

Chris perused his menu, oblivious to it. "I guess wine is out of the question since you can't drink." He put his arm around me. "Unless you want something, Rich."

"Water is good for me," Dad answered.

"You should get a cocktail or a beer," I said to Chris.

"No. It's all right. I don't need the extra calories anyway. I need to stay in fighting shape for the shows coming up in New York." He patted his stomach. "Can't wait until we're in the new house and have a pool. I've started to develop a paunch."

"No, you haven't," I said. "But you can always come running with me if you want."

"I might have to take you up on that, however abhorrent I find the idea."

"Ladybug, is it safe for you to exercise like that while you've got a little one on the way?"

My eyes darted around the patio, wondering if anyone else had recognized Chris, if anyone was listening to our conversation. *You're being paranoid.* "Yes, Dad. It's fine. Lots of women run right up until their due date." I closed my menu. "Where's the waiter? I'm starving."

"You're always starving."

"Now you know what it's like to be around you all the time." I squeezed his knee under the table.

"Between the two of us, we're eating for four." Chris flagged down our waiter. "We have an emergency eating situation on our hands. Pregnant woman. Very hungry. We need an order of the hushpuppies, the pork belly, and four house salads to start."

"Bring some bread too," I said. "Extra butter."

"You have no idea how excited I am to hear you say things like extra butter." Chris handed his menu to the waiter.

"So. When's the due date?" my dad asked.

"Late May," I answered. "Right around Sam's graduation."

He shook his head and sat back in his chair. "Goodness. A baby, a new house, renovations, a wedding, a studio project, a new job, high school graduation. It's a wonder we can all keep up."

Chris sat back in his chair. "I'll be glad when it's next May and we can finally breathe."

"Tell me about it." Sam grabbed a hunk of bread from the basket and slathered it with butter. "I can't wait to be done with high school."

"I bet." I nodded in agreement, admiring Sam as candlelight flickered, casting shadows across her rosy skin. Her blonde ringlets were extra bouncy today, her eyes somehow an even prettier shade of blue. *Done with high school.* My nodding stopped, the corners of my mouth turned down. May would be anything but a time to breathe.

CHAPTER NINETEEN

I'D SHRUGGED off this reunion business as nothing more than a return to old hat, but the truth was that I was as excited as the day my dad first let me have at his beloved acoustic guitar. We'd managed to sell out Radio City Music Hall for five nights, in record time no less. It was thrilling, even if I did my best to play it cool.

It felt like it'd been a lifetime since Banks Forest had done this—played proper shows. My life was so different then, an unholy tangle of drama and discontent. Now things were on track. I was about to marry the woman I never thought I'd find. We had a baby on the way, another milestone I'd once convinced myself wasn't meant for me, no matter how badly I'd wanted it. The band itself was on excellent terms, all of us happy to be back in the saddle, grateful that the fans had embraced the reunion rather than balking at it. If ever there'd been a time for me to reclaim a bit of the past without becoming mired in nostalgia, this was it.

The three rehearsals, all in New York, went much better than expected. It was evident that Nigel and Terence had both been practicing quite a lot on their own. I certainly had, although that was more of an ongoing proposition. A day or two without the guitar in my hand and I started to get antsy, or as Claire would call it, "dickish". In a similar vein, Graham's entire existence was practice for this, so he was "on" from the minute he had the microphone back in his hand. Angie's most persistent complaint in their marriage had long been that he was always behaving as though he'd never stepped off the stage. For her, it was a trial in patience. Hell, I could only take it in small doses unless I had a pint or two in me. For the fans, it was pure gold.

On the first day, mere bars into *What Do I Say?*, which was the second song we decided to tackle, any worries I'd had about us being a bunch of old farts evaporated. Terence pummeled the drums, pounding away as he had when we'd been in our twenties. Nigel's bass lines locked in, thumping and boosting the music to the sweet spot that sustained the urgency of the songs in their original form.

"Bloody brilliant." Graham bounced up and down behind the mic, grinning ear-to-ear when we'd wrapped up the first go-through on that song. "The fans are going to go bonkers."

"I hope so." On the inside, I wholeheartedly agreed, but no sense blowing Graham's ego out of proportion. Keeping him hungry was the best way to make this happen. For me, the blood was pumping through my body in a way it hadn't in a long time. If this was a comeback, we'd taken complete control—we owned it. The media had panned our live performances endlessly over our long career, but if they decided to slag this incarnation, fuck them. If I knew one thing mid-way through the first rehearsal, it was that we'd never sounded better. Not even close. "Let's take another run at that one."

The only bump in the road was coming up with a set list, a task we dove into at the end of day one. Graham and I argued like brothers, so badly that Terence and Nigel begged out of the discussion entirely saying that as long as we played *Love,*

Destroyed, it didn't matter. By the end of day three, Graham and I were still bickering over the track listing, never mind the sequence of songs for the shows.

"Come on, Chris, we're leaving out half of the hits."

"If we play all of the hits, it'll be a three hour show."

"Oh, so that's it." Graham scribbled two more songs at the bottom of the list. "Don't think you can last that long."

"Piss off." My phone rang, Claire to the rescue. I dug it out of the back pocket of my jeans. "Hello, darling." I plucked the pen from Graham's hand. He scowled in response, but I didn't want him tinkering without my supervision. "How are you?"

"Hello, Claire!" Graham yelled as I walked away. "Can't wait to see you tomorrow, even if your future husband is a pain in my arse."

"Is that Graham?" she asked.

"Yes. Annoying, isn't he?" I found a quiet corner and perched on one of the hard equipment cases.

"Sounds like somebody has some extra energy. Poor Angie."

Poor Angie? How about poor me? "Tell me about it. How did your meeting with Laura go? Are the magazine's offices nice?" I spied Graham talking to Terence, gesturing wildly and pointing at the set list we'd been working on. Luckily, Nigel was having none of it, shaking his head "no" when Graham tried to wave him over.

"The offices aren't much now. They have Laura in a temporary space while the up-fit is finished. I didn't get to see any of it."

"Did you tell her that you're pregnant?"

"I did." The line was so quiet it sounded as if the call had dropped. "I can't say she had the best reaction."

"What did she say?"

Her hesitation with my question was again, unsettling. "Nothing bad, it was just that it seemed like she was forcing herself to act excited. She was definitely shocked when I first told her."

"Do you think you could've misread her reaction?"

"I don't think so. She was pretty clear about her concerns. You know, whether I'm going to be able to focus and balance life at home with a new job, especially since I won't be working out of the New York offices."

"How do you feel about all of that?"

"I get it. She has a lot riding on this. She wants it to be a home run. She isn't interested in wading into these waters. She wants to blow everybody away, right away. That means she needs an editorial staff that's top-notch and totally committed. I already worry that I might not be in the category of top-notch, so that scares me."

"Don't say that. You know you're better than top-notch."

"As a writer, maybe, but I've never been an editor before. She's taking a big chance on me. I'm probably even more of a gamble now than I was before and that has to make her nervous. I mean, let's face it. I'm going to be distracted with a new baby. It doesn't matter how much help we have. It's going to be tough."

"I don't plan to be one of those dads who doesn't change diapers or walk the floor in the middle of the night."

"Oh, I know. But I'm going to be nursing and I can't just sit back and hand the baby over to you all the time. Plus, we're both going to be tired and stressed. Add in the fact that I'm already going to feel a little out of the loop with work by virtue of not working out of that office. It'll be tricky."

"You know you don't have to take this job. You can tell her no. Even though you already agreed to it." I rubbed my forehead. I wanted her to be happy, I wanted whatever she wanted for herself, but I couldn't deny that what I really wanted, more than anything, was for *us* to be happy. Together, one unit, as harmonious as possible.

Again, she was quiet. I really wished we weren't having this conversation on the phone, so I could gain a better sense of how she was feeling. It was far too easy for her to hide behind words, and if Claire had any weakness, it was getting wrapped up in what she thought the world wanted from her, rather than what she knew in her gut was right. "But I really want it," she said, in a breathy, almost desperate tone that told me how dead-set she was on this. "It's a challenge and I like the idea of pushing myself professionally. After the whole *Entertainment Weekly* fiasco, I want to have more control of my destiny as a writer."

I had to admire her motives. She saw something better for her career and wasn't afraid to try it, however daunting the prospect might seem. "Then we have to find a way to make it work, so you can prove to Laura that you were absolutely the right woman for the job. We'll find a way. Together."

"You're so amazing," she said, in a sweet lilt. "Oh, I almost forgot to tell you. There was a photographer waiting for me outside Laura's office when I left. He asked if I was pregnant."

I closed my eyes. "He wasn't aggressive with you, was he?"

"No. He just took some pictures and talked to me while he followed me down the sidewalk. I ended up hopping in a cab."

"We may need to get you your own driver when we're in New York."

"Yeah, there were a lot of fans outside the hotel, too. They had to put them behind a barricade."

The same thing had happened outside the rehearsal space. It always amazed me the bits of information the fans were able to dig up. *Here we go.* "I'm sorry. I hope that didn't bother you."

"No, it was fine, but you'd better be careful when you get back here. When are you coming back? I miss you."

I smiled and shook my head as I caught another glimpse of

Graham berating Terence. "I miss you too, darling. I'll be there as soon as I give in to Graham's demands."

"How long is that going to take?"

"Not long, if I can help it."

"Okay. Hurry back. Love you."

"Love you, too."

I hung up and sidled up to Graham and Terence. "How many thousands of times have we done this?"

Graham shrugged. "I don't know. Too many to count, I suppose. Why?"

"Did it ever really end up mattering? Did we ever once walk off the stage and say that the show would have been better if we'd played this song or that?"

"Maybe once or twice," Terence said, always the most even-tempered member of the band. "Not many."

"Exactly." I patted Graham on the shoulder and handed him the pen. "Consider this the white flag. You two sort it out. Ask Nigel if he cares to chime in."

"What's that?" Nigel pushed his now-thinning long hair off his face as he fiddled with an effects pedal. "You talking about me?"

"Just putting your name in the mix for the set list conundrum. If you want in," I answered.

"You're serious." Graham stared at the ballpoint as if it was the gift he'd always wanted. "You're giving in. To me." His eyes narrowed. "What's the catch?"

"Believe it or not, there is none. I would simply prefer to spend my time with Claire. And we had such an excellent rehearsal today. I don't want to spoil the mood with an argument. I'll see you lot tomorrow."

CHAPTER TWENTY

"YOU ARE SO GORGEOUS." Chris pressed the elevator button for the lobby and kissed my temple with his temptingly soft lips. The compliment didn't go unappreciated. It'd taken considerable effort to squeeze my pregnant ass into my jeans. "I don't really want to take you anywhere, but I suppose people would be upset if I didn't show up to the gig tonight."

"Your adoring fans might stage a riot." I admired him with a sideways glance. He'd already dressed for the show—black leather pants that made his butt look ridiculously good and a black dress shirt that had never once been buttoned all the way. While getting ready, he'd asked for help with his hair, which made for a very surreal moment as I combed gel into it with my fingers, watching him scrutinize his own reflection in the mirror.

"Speaking of adoring fans, as the head of the International Banks Forest fan club, do you need to stop out in front of the hotel and lead the die-hards in some sort of pre-show ritual?" He smirked and cocked an eyebrow.

"Very funny."

"I try."

The elevator doors slid open. The man at the front desk

caught sight of Chris and rushed over. "Mr. Penman, your driver has asked me to have you wait for a moment. He's on his way inside."

Chris slipped on his aviators, a move few mortals can pull off indoors.

Lou stormed through the lobby doors and made a beeline for us. "Mr. Penman, things have gotten a little hairy outside. We'll need to be quick."

"My primary concern is Claire."

"Absolutely. NYPD has everyone behind a barricade, but the fans are anxious to see you. An officer will lead us to the car. You follow him, then Ms. Abby, and I'll bring up the rear."

"Ready, darling?" Chris asked. "Will you be okay with this?"

I nodded, having flashbacks to the scene outside Tiffany's. "I'll be fine."

We were inundated with shrieks and flashes of light the instant the lobby door opened.

"It's him."

"Christopher, over here."

"I love you."

I huddled behind Chris as we dashed across the sidewalk. The car door opened, we were swept inside, and the noises muffled when the door was closed.

"Are you okay?" Chris asked, as the crowd noises filtered into the car again when Lou climbed into the driver's seat.

My heart raced, and so did the car, away from the hotel. I had to admit that it was exhilarating. "I'm great."

He took my hand. "Of course you are. You'll be an old pro at this before long."

I looked at Chris for what felt like the one-hundredth time in a few short hours, studying his strong profile, that perfect jawline. It was so wonderfully strange to see him in his element, basking in the spotlight he so deserved, all while taking me along for the ride.

He caught me staring and swiped off his sunglasses. His eyes were so brilliant it was as if they were on fire. "You're sure you're okay?"

"I just can't believe this is happening."

He leaned over and kissed my ear, taking a gentle nibble of the lobe. "I can pinch you if that will help." The waft of his cologne left me light-headed.

I giggled breathlessly, his lips hovering near mine, thankful that Lou was likely accustomed to bearing witness to private displays of affection in the backseat.

"Darling, you aren't the only one having a hard time believing this." His face was so close to mine that his breath warmed my cheek. He tucked his fingers beneath my chin, running his thumb along my jaw. "I feel like the luckiest bastard on the planet."

"Mr. Penman?" Lou asked. "Excuse me for interrupting, but do you want me to find another route? Traffic up ahead only looks like it's getting worse." I then realized that the town car hadn't moved in minutes.

Chris leaned his head against the car window. "Yeah, I guess so. I can't afford to be late." He took my left hand and wiggled my engagement ring back and forth.

We arrived at Radio City Music Hall a good twenty minutes behind schedule. Chris had spent the last several blocks of the car ride frantically bobbing his leg up and down. "I have a bunch of things I need to do before we go on. Will you be okay hanging out with Angie if I need to leave you for a few minutes?"

I nodded. "Yes, of course."

"Hey, Reggie," Chris called out.

A bald, rotund man pointing to a lighting rig overhead

answered. "Yeah, Chris?" He ambled over to us, smiling at me, his bulky arms covered in a tangle of tattoos. "This must be the future Mrs. Penman." His thick British accent suited his happy, yet blustery disposition. He held out his pudgy hand to shake mine.

"Please, Claire."

"All right, then. Very nice to meet you, Claire." He reached into a black fanny-pack and pulled out an all-access laminate, attached a black lanyard, and looped it around my neck. "You're going to need this, love."

"Perfect, Reggie. Exactly what I was looking for." Chris clapped him on the back. "Is his royal highness anywhere to be found?"

"Graham? In the dressing room eating up all of the catering." He gestured to the end of the hall with a head toss. "You best get back there before he polishes off your peanut M&Ms."

"Take care of Claire tonight, all right? Absolutely anything she needs." He put his arm around me protectively. "She's pregnant, so make sure the coolers are stocked with plenty of water, okay?"

"Are you joking? She's going to want to run off with me by the time the night's over. Claire will be just fine. Don't you worry your pretty head about that."

The corridor outside the band's dressing room was bustling with people, mostly crew. Chris greeted many of them with a nod, but otherwise kept us moving.

My heart did a flip as Chris gave the dressing room door a single knock and opened it. It was far from the conventional scuzzy band room, a straight, narrow shot with dressing tables, director's chairs, and mirrors. There was one sofa and a table off to the side stocked with deli trays and snack foods. I recognized Nigel, the bass player, in the corner. I could only presume that the woman he was talking with was his new wife, Heather, who also happened to be his third. Terence was standing with them and he waved, seeming to recognize me from our brief meeting after the band's second rehearsal.

Angie walked in right behind us. "Claire, Christopher." She and I embraced. "Big night, huh? Pretty exciting."

Graham traipsed over with a beer in his hand. "Taking the edge off. You want one?" He raised the can to Chris.

"No, thanks. I'm good." Chris shook his head. "Can we grab Terence and Nigel and go over the encore real quick?"

"Yeah. No problem. We'll leave the girls to their gossip."

Angie gestured to the couch. "Want to sit? We're going to be standing all night."

I squeezed in between Angie and a remarkably busty woman sitting at the other end.

"I'm Angela." The other woman shook my hand. Her voice, steeped in Southern charm, was comically fast. "People really call me Angie, but I don't want to get mixed up with you." She nodded in Angie's direction. "I'm Terence's new girlfriend. Well, it's only been a few weeks. I suppose I'm his girlfriend. I don't know. He doesn't really call me anything." She closed her eyes and rattled her head back and forth. "I'm sorry. I start talking and I can't stop myself."

"Nice to meet you. I'm Claire."

"I know." Her deep brown eyes flickered with recognition. "You're Chris's fiancée. I wondered if I'd meet you tonight." Her eyes grew wide. "I read about your pregnancy in *People* magazine. I hate that they took that photo of you from that awful angle. Nobody looks good from that angle."

I laughed nervously. "Yeah. I know." *This is all so weird.*

The door swung open and Reggie entered. "'Ello, ladies. The band is going on in ten minutes. If you like, I can escort you to the side of the stage."

We followed Reggie down the hall, around a maze of equipment cases, backstage doors, nooks and crannies in the historic theater. The sounds of the audience got louder and more distinct with every step. Once we were to our viewing area, right behind the on-stage soundboard, I could hear the instrumental version of *Living in Infamy*. My pulse raced. It was the same intro they'd played the only other time I'd seen Banks Forest live, when I was seventeen. I found myself again wondering if I was dreaming all of this—being backstage, part of the inner circle, the future Claire Louise Penman. *Damn. I should have let Chris pinch me in the car.*

The crowd suddenly erupted and the massive stage curtain slowly began to draw back. Stage lights flickered and someone tugged on my elbow. *Chris.* He kissed me on the temple without a word. He only smiled that melt-me-into-a-puddle smile.

Next thing I knew, the four of them had taken their places. Every atom in my body became charged with electricity. Angie beamed. Angela screamed at the top of her lungs. Graham uttered something impossible to hear over the roar of the crowd. Chris stomped on an effects pedal. A single strum of his guitar and the audience went berserk. The hair stood up on my arms. *It's happening.*

The show was such sensory overload that I learned to focus on one thing at a time, sight or sound, not both. Sight—Chris as if he was performing beneath a magnifying glass, every attribute now larger-than-life. *God. He is so fucking hot. I can't wait to get him out of those damn leather pants.* Sound—the music I'd spent a lifetime worshipping, lyrics etched in my brain, all of it right here, in my face.

It was so intoxicating that butterflies literally fluttered in my stomach, becoming more active when the music became more intense. *Wait a minute. Those aren't butterflies.* I pressed my hand against my belly. *That's the baby.* Another flutter. *Hi, baby. Daddy's on stage right now. He sounds amazing, doesn't he?*

Contentment spread over me from head to toe. *How could this possible get any better?*

The band played for a full two hours plus a twenty-minute encore. At one point, I simply gave in to the roller coaster and stopped trying to remember every remarkable thing. I had four more nights of this to look forward to, the fifth night with Sam. I could sit back and let it all happen, take it in and enjoy the ride.

Angela and I chatted out in the hall after the show, while the guys were changing out of their sweaty clothes in another dressing room. Angie had gone off in search of a bathroom.

Chris joined us wearing a Rolling Stones t-shirt. Luckily, he'd left the leather pants for me. "How'd I do?" His tone said that he knew full well what the answer was.

"You were spectacular." I pressed my lips against his. "Unbelievable." He'd given an incredible performance, deserved every accolade. "Guess what?" I took his hand, flattening it against my stomach. "I felt the baby move during the show."

"You did?" His eyes were wide with fascination. "I don't feel anything."

"Don't worry. You will." We walked back to the dressing room hand in hand.

Graham had planted himself on the arm of the couch and Angie sat next to him at the end. She nodded and smiled tentatively at me, but didn't get up. They were both in conversation with a petite woman with long brown hair, wearing a gauzy, flowing dress with a bold black and white pattern. Her back was turned to the door.

Graham made eye contact with Chris and then his sights flew to me. He bolted from the sofa, pulling me into one of his all-encompassing hugs. "Claire. How much did you love the show? I was better than Chris, wasn't I?" He loosened his hold. "I won't make you answer. It'll only make him mad." He smiled at me in the most confounding way. "Uh, I have someone I need you to meet."

The woman turned, her long locks whipping at the air. Her beautiful face was camera-ready, stunning and eye-catching, but an even more compelling feature was impossible to ignore—her massive, protruding belly. *Oh my God. It's Elise. And she's pregnant.*

CHAPTER TWENTY-ONE

ELISE TURNED TO ME. "CHRISTOPHER." The familiarity in my ex-wife's voice felt like two fat hands around my throat.

"What are you doing here?" I was shocked I'd said something so benign with evil incarnate standing before me.

"I was in New York. I thought I should come to the show. Wish you well." She smiled, shrugging as if it was of little consequence that this was our first meeting since she'd written the memoir that'd dragged me through the mud. Never before had I had such a deep-seated desire to erase all history between myself and another human being.

Claire grabbed my hand, holding on for dear life as Elise came in for a hug from me. One half of me pulled back, the other half forced forward by some horribly odd sense of politeness. I gave Elise a fleeting pat on the back and quickly retreated. Claire's tension was palpable, it radiated from her. "This is my fiancée, Claire Abby."

The most bizarre curiosity came over Elise's face as she took stock of Claire. She didn't smile, it was more a look of smug amusement, which stirred up an intense need to protect Claire, step in front of her and keep her and our baby from the soul-sucking force of Elise. "Yes, I recognize you from the tabloids." Elise held out her bony hand and I shuddered when she and Claire touched. "She's cute, Christopher."

I tightly balled up my free hand. *Cute? She's cute? And you fucking talk about her in the third person like she's not even here?* "Claire's an incredible music journalist. Insanely talented. Brilliant, really. She just took a job as entertainment editor for a brand new magazine." I was prattling on like a complete wanker, trying to illustrate that I'd found the perfect woman, someone who was her complete opposite.

Graham pulled me aside. "Are you okay?"

"How in the hell did she get back here?" I hissed.

"It's her bloody new husband, the singer from Mission Mad. Practically the biggest rock star on the planet right now. His management called Reggie. He had no bloody idea the passes were for her."

I glanced over my shoulder to see Elise watching us closely.

Graham must've seen it too. "How about your new hubby's band, Elise?" he asked. "They're on a bloody roll right now."

I shook my head at Graham. He wasn't doing any better than me. *What's next? Why not offer her a spot of tea?*

Elise smiled slyly. "They're playing Wembley in January. He really wanted to come tonight, but he's in the studio doing some remixes. He sends his best."

Graham shook his head in disbelief. "Can you imagine? Wembley? Ninety thousand blooming people."

He looked at me as if I might actually care to converse about this subject. I couldn't have cared less about her new husband. His band was bollocks, their music a steaming pile of rubbish, and he'd had the good fortune of marrying the most miserable woman on the planet. He could sell out fucking Wembley stadium fifty times and it would've made no difference. I was free of the misery of Elise.

I slung my arm around Claire's shoulder and pulled her close, subliminally encouraging her to stop holding her breath, but she was trembling. *It'll be okay, darling.* "Claire and I are getting married next month and we have a child due at the end of May. We're very excited. I've never been happier."

Elise rubbed her belly. "You're not the only one with a little one on the way. I'm due at the end of February."

A confounding mix of anger, envy, and irrational sadness washed over me, but just as quickly, it faded back into the recesses of my mind when Claire turned her head and kissed my hand on her shoulder. This whole business of one-upping each other was ridiculous, and I was pissed at myself for giving into it.

"Congratulations," Claire said, only when there'd been so much awkward silence after Elise's announcement that someone had to say something. It just wasn't going to be me.

"Claire's an amazing mother. She has the most incredible teenage daughter." S*top bloody talking*. I couldn't believe that I'd again taken the bait. *I don't even want to deal with this. I don't want to deal with her. I'm supposed to be happy right now. We just played the best show in a decade and Claire felt the baby move.*

Elise cleared her throat and directed her eyes at me. "Do you have a moment? I was hoping you and I could speak alone."

"What? Why?"

She glared at me as if the questions were preposterous. "Christopher, please."

"Whatever you have to say, Claire can hear it. There are no secrets between her and I. She knows about everything." Of course, this wasn't completely true. There were horrors from my marriage to Elise that were best kept buried.

"No, Chris, it's fine." Claire shook her head. "If this is private." She tried to turn away, but I held on to her tightly.

"See, Chris? Claire understands," Elise said.

I had to grit my teeth to control my temper. Her manipulation was far too familiar. "Nothing between you and me is private. You saw to that when you decided to make a public spectacle of our past."

"Christopher. Please. Don't be an asshole. It doesn't do any good to be so angry."

Angry? Anger is for a far less complicated situation. The lies that she'd told about me, about our marriage, about the baby we'd lost—each untruth ate at me. Everything she'd chosen to put in print, for money, for her own personal gain, it was all done with complete disregard for me. *I won't hesitate to be an asshole.*

"Whatever you have to say, should be said out loud," I said. "It's too bad we didn't take advantage of the sold out house tonight and put you on as the opening act. You could've apologized to our fans for making me look like the biggest bloody jerk on the planet."

Elise wrapped her arms around her ribcage, resting them atop her belly. She looked at me, a tear rolling down her cheek.

I had once loved those eyes. They had meant everything to me. Now I didn't recognize the person behind them. Still, she had a child growing inside her, an innocent being who had no choice but to have her for a mother. I couldn't bear the thought that every cross word I spoke might somehow affect the baby, even when I was quite aware that I had little control over my emotions. "Tell me what you came here to say."

She swallowed and swiped away the tear. Her face tensed with a familiar expression.

I couldn't escape the feeling that this was all a show to her. She was, after all, standing backstage, with dozens of people silent and hanging on her every word. "Please say what you need to say so that we can both get on with our lives."

"This is probably more than one conversation," she said.

I closed my eyes to conjure a calm response. "No. I'm sorry, but you and I are not speaking again after this."

"Fine." She nodded. "I understand that you're angry, but I'm here to tell you that I'm sorry. I've been sober for seven months and this is part of beating addiction. I have to go through the steps."

At least she got sober before she got pregnant. I took a deep breath. "It's good to know that you're sorry. You can go now."

"That doesn't sound particularly sincere. I need to know that you really understand how sorry I am."

"Forgive me if you aren't selling it very well. Or perhaps it's just that I'm not buying it."

"Will you stop being such an asshole? I'm trying to apologize and you're just pissing me off. This is so typical of you. You know, I didn't have this problem with anyone else." She jabbed her finger at me. "Everyone else I talked to was generous and forgiving. Angie and Graham both seemed happy to see me."

In my periphery, Graham was shaking his head "no".

"I don't know why you're being such a goddamned jerk about this," Elise continued.

"Guess I can't help it." I shrugged. "I'm a natural asshole. So much so, that it was the subject of an entire book. Please be sure to talk about what an asshole I am at your next Narcotics Anonymous meeting."

She laughed dismissively. "You have got to be kidding. I don't go to those meetings. I read a book. Those meetings are for normal people. Not me."

I opened my mouth, but Claire's voice stopped me.

"Okay. Hold on one second here." She waved her hands in the air like a referee stopping the play. "You don't go to the meetings? You read about this in a book?" She turned and looked at me with astonishment. "Uh, no, this is not happening. I love you and you are not an asshole," she said firmly.

"Excuse me?" Elise asked, her angry eyes darting to Claire. "I don't think anyone asked your opinion. This doesn't concern you. This is about me and Christopher."

"You know what?" Claire took a step closer to Elise, leaving me paralyzed with awe. I'd seen Claire angry before, with her dad or Sam or with me, but this was something different—very different. "This does concern me because I love him and you made him miserable. He's worked insanely hard to put this behind him and you're bringing everything back up when he should be on top of the world."

"This is part of sobriety, so I'm sorry if the timing is inconvenient."

Claire shook her head. "I'm guessing that since you're pregnant, nobody in this room feels like they can say any of this to you." She cocked an eyebrow. "But I've got you there, because I'm pregnant too, so I guess it's going to have to be me. I had a boyfriend who went through the steps. This isn't how you make amends. You don't ambush someone with your apology and you certainly don't just read a book and start checking things off a list." She shook her head. "No, the real reason you're here is to ruin his night or to get some glimpse of what you used to have. Whatever it is, I think you need to leave. Chris shouldn't have to put up with this."

I blinked, still disbelieving this version of Claire. It was as if she'd bottled all of this up inside her and damn if Elise didn't end up being on the wrong end of it.

"You don't know anything about me. At all." Elise's voice was cold and steely.

"Believe me, I know enough." Claire's voice was just as steady and measured as Elise's, perhaps more so. "All I ever needed to know was that you selfishly held Chris's entire life and his heart hostage while you lived the life that you wanted."

"I think you'd better shut your mouth about my marriage to Christopher. You don't know a thing. You weren't there."

I wanted to rush to Claire's defense, but she didn't hesitate to do the same for me.

"No, I wasn't and thank God for that. I don't think I could've witnessed the emotional carnage. It would've made me sick."

Elise rolled her eyes. "Give me a fucking break. Christopher, you really picked a gem this time. She's lovely." She sneered, bitter disgust in her eyes. "I'm trying to figure out what the appeal is. It certainly isn't her charm or her beauty."

"That's enough—" I started.

Claire erupted. "You want to know what the appeal is? I'll tell you what the fucking appeal is." She stepped toe-to-toe with Elise. "I love him. I want him to be happy. I don't lie to him. I'm giving him the child he always wanted." Her body language—rigid shoulders and straight as a pin posture, told of her unfaltering determination, but her voice now wobbled with intensity. "If you want to know why he hasn't been nice or gracious to you, it's only because he has no reason to believe a word out of your mouth. The fact that he didn't have you escorted from the building as soon as he saw you, is testament to what a good person he is."

I reached for Claire's hand to pull her back to safety, even though after that little speech, I was certain she could've taken down Elise in the first round with the first punch. TKO.

Elise glared at Claire. "I'm leaving. It's clear this is going to have to happen some other time. Some time when she isn't around."

My hand was wrapped tightly around Claire's. "That time's not going to come."

"Remind me to piss you off every now and then." I followed Claire into our hotel room as she yanked on my arm. "If you'd told me that a pregnant cat fight was going to be so hot, I wouldn't have believed you." *So hot.* I wrestled my jacket from my arms. "I know Graham was turned on. He told me so."

"You know what? Maybe it's the hormones, but that felt really good." She dropped her purse to the floor then bent over, picking up a pile of paper items in the entry. "What's all this?"

Bugger. This was a familiar sight. "Oh, yeah. Some of the fans must've figured out this was my room and slipped some things under the door."

She sifted through the notecards and pieces of paper. "I love you, Christopher. You're so hot. Love, Debbie." She rolled her eyes. "Is this normal? There must be a dozen of these things." She held up a hotel key card in a paper sleeve. "A room key? Seriously?"

I plucked the pile of intrusive items from her hands and dropped them in the rubbish bin. "I've seen worse. Just ignore it. At least hotel security got rid of them before we got up to our room."

Her lips pressed into a thin line. "Not sure I like this."

"Think of it this way, darling." I pulled her into my arms and began kissing her neck. "All of those women and you're the only one I want. The only one."

"Good. Now stop talking." She rose up on to her toes and kissed me while both of her hands zipped under my t-shirt. Her lips grazed my jaw and the spot below my ear, prompting an uncomfortable snugness in my leather pants. "I don't want to think about groupies or pregnant cat fights. I want to think about you and me. Naked. In that bed." She pushed my shirt over my head.

Naked. Yes, please. "I love this whole pregnant randy thing." I kicked off my black leather shoes as Claire stepped out of her boots. Together, we hurried across the room, stopping next to the bed. My hands found her waist and I skimmed them north, gripping her ribcage. "It feels like I won the lottery." *The sex lottery.*

"What did I just say about talking?" She popped the button on my leather pants then dispatched the zipper.

"Always with the talking." I gathered her sweater in my hands and yanked it over her head as my pants dropped to the floor. Even with nothing more than moonlight in the room, the contrast of her creamy white skin against her lacy black bra showed that her remarkably full breasts could hardly be contained. *Man, I love pregnancy.* "Okay, sorry. I have to say one more thing." I reached behind and unhooked the garment, pulling it over her shoulders. "Your breasts are unbelievable right now." They begged to be touched and my palms were hungry for the opportunity, cupping them while I caressed her taut nipples with my thumbs. *So incredible.*

Claire rolled her head to the side as if she was a rag doll. "Oh, God, Chris. That feels so good."

I loved having that response from her, utter pleasure and surrender. Dropping to my knees, I unbuttoned her jeans, shimmied them and her panties past her hips. *That's better.* My fingers traced up and down the backs of her thighs as I kissed her stomach, reveling in the velvety touch of her skin against my lips and cheek. A breathy sigh escaped her as her fingers traced the contours of my shoulders.

I skimmed my mouth back up her torso and sought her breasts, but the angle with both of us standing was all wrong. In a movement sparked by the ferocity of my erection, I scooped her into my arms, dropped my knee onto the bed and laid her out below me. With no hesitation, I descended upon her, drawing a nipple into my mouth and swirling it with my tongue. Her skin was sweet and sticky. *Perfect.*

Claire arched and I grabbed on to her, flipping to my back and taking her along with me. She planted her hands on the bed next to my shoulders, straddling me and grinding, which caused my hips to buck off the bed. My hands roved to her ass, squeezing the extra flesh that had appeared once her body began nurturing new life. She likely had no idea that I now took every chance imaginable to look at her luscious rear end. *Bloody spectacular.*

Every part of her was ripe and full—a twenty-four/seven invitation to lock the door, take off her clothes and send her over the edge again and again. I could've spent the entire night exploring every exquisite peak and valley, every sumptuous curve, with my hands and mouth, knowing she would love every minute of it.

She dropped against my chest and dug her hands into my hair, kissing me intensely as her hips continued to ride forward and back, building heat with the aid of the slickness between our bodies. Her lips wandered to my jaw, then my neck, and continued, quicker now, down the length of chest and past my waist. She settled herself between my legs, her knees wedged against my inner thighs. Anticipation brewed in my belly.

Without use of her hands, she took me into her warm and supple mouth. I groaned, relief and need warring inside me. Sinking into the bed, I caressed her scalp with one hand, tucking the other behind my head. Her lips gripped. Her tongue played. Silky hair brushed my stomach and thighs. *Oh God.* Pleasurable hums delivered in her lilt, floated through the air. The notion that she enjoyed giving something so impossibly good flooded me with warmth. My shoulders rose, pleasure building, rising to the surface of my skin.

She slowed her motions and lazily looped her tongue in

dizzying fashion. Slowly, she released me and kissed my stomach. "Mmm," she hummed. She rose and collapsed her weight on me, pressing her breasts to my chest, her lips to mine.

"I love it when you do that," I muttered between our mouths. Although I was breaking my code of silence, that performance demanded praise.

"Good." I felt her smile as her lips came away from mine. "Because I love doing it to you."

"And I love doing this to you." I rolled her to her back.

She spread her legs wider and wiggled her hips from side to side. I did my damndest to employ patience with the first stroke. My eyes clamped shut as her impossibly hot body molded around me, welcoming, holding me firmly in her clutches.

She wrapped her legs loosely around me. Our hips rocked in opposition. Every time my legs met the inside of her thighs I felt as if I was about to explode. *Hold on.* I extended my arm, raising my torso, slipping my other hand between our bodies. I knew I'd hit the mark when she gasped. Quick, tiny circles and her breaths became short. Torn. Ragged.

She put more force behind each rock of her hips. I matched her, pulling out as far as I could with every stroke, before sinking back into her. My mind grappled with the onslaught of heady sensations, but it was too much to think about. *Just hold on.*

I focused on her reactions, pressing harder with my thumb when her moans became more insistent. If I'd concentrated on my own, I'd have given in long ago. Her body squeezed mine, telling me she was close to the brink, which only made it that much more difficult to contain the pressure inside me. *Come on, darling.*

"I'm so close," she said with desperation.

I lowered myself, leaving my body weight to steel the efforts of my thumb. I kissed her breast, licking the tight peak. My pelvis gave everything it had, and then she cried out. Her hips slammed into mine and I finally allowed the damn to break. Waves of pure ecstasy coursed through me. Her body grabbed on to mine and let go, time and time again. Her breasts rubbed against my chest. Her lips found mine.

We both struggled to catch a breath. I rolled to my side, not wanting to crush her and knowing my arms had had all they could take. Claire hitched her leg over mine and pressed her forehead into the center of my chest. I pulled her closer, stroked her hair.

"Wow," I said, certainly not poetry.

"I know. My word exactly."

I grinned and kissed her cheek. "I love you, my darling."

"I love you, too. So much." She groaned. "And I have to pee."

"There goes the romance."

"Sorry, honey. Price of pregnancy." She scooted to the edge of the bed, tiptoeing into the bathroom.

I collapsed on to my back and sighed. *What a night.* I'll probably sleep for twelve hours after all of that excitement.

The rush of water in the sink came. Claire was back seconds later.

She laid out flat on her back next to me and I sat up, settling the side of my face on her smooth belly. There still wasn't a pronounced baby bump, although Claire insisted it was most definitely there. "I'm envious. I want to feel the baby move."

She raked her fingers into my hair. "It might be a few more weeks. The baby's still so small. There were a lot of gymnastics going on in there tonight. It must've been the music. Sam used to do that."

"Oh, yeah?"

"I think it has to be fairly loud to elicit a response. She had a particular love for David Bowie from a young age. Especially *Scary Monsters.*"

I kissed her stomach then spoke to it. "We've got a lot of music to go over, you and your mum and me, but I'm glad your first gig was a Banks show. It makes your old man happy." One more kiss and I flopped my head down onto the pillow next to Claire. "Don't mind me. I just like talking to the nipper. Makes it feel more real."

A bubbly laugh came out of her. "It's sweet." She curled into me and I pulled the covers up around us. "I'm sorry about everything tonight. I don't know what got into me. I blame hormones."

I grinned, my eyes closed as I stroked her bare back. "It was wonderful to see you assert yourself like that."

"You have to admit, she had it coming from the minute she called me cute."

I laughed and pulled her even closer. "It was great to know you have my back."

She trailed her fingers in a dizzying circle in the center of my chest. "Of course I do. We're a team."

A team. "Indeed we are."

Neither of us said a thing for several minutes. It was apparent that the gears were turning for both of us and how could they not be? It'd been a crazy night.

"Did it bother you to see Elise like that?" she asked. "You know. Pregnant."

This was a difficult question. I still hadn't sorted my feelings. Part of me thought I might never, most of me thought it best not to devote the time or energy to it. "At first it did. I guess only because of everything that happened. Obviously, that was a very unhappy time in my life and it brought a lot of that back."

"Of course. I'm sure that was hard."

"In some ways, yeah. In other ways, it was good to finally deal with her and end that chapter of my life." Perhaps it was the high of the show or post-sex bliss, but through what had once been fog, I could see the silver lining in the black cloud called Elise. "In the end, the main thing I am is happy."

"Happy? For her? That's awfully big of you."

"No, darling. Happy for us." I kissed the top of her head, inhaling the sweet smell of her hair. "If those terrible things hadn't happened, I never would've found you.

CHAPTER TWENTY-TWO

DRESSED for dinner in a warm sweater and the one pair of nice jeans I could still squeeze into, I rushed down the hall, hair still damp from my shower, only to be stopped by the sound of music from Sam's room. My shoulders dropped out of frustration. *Seriously?*

I knocked. No answer. I knocked again. "Sam? Honey? Are you going to set the table?"

The music stopped and there were heavy footfalls. She opened the door. "What?"

"The dinner table? I asked you to set it?"

She cast her eyes away. "I sorta hoped Grandpa would just decide to do it since he's such a busy body."

Take a breath. "He and Chris are watching TV. Come on. We can talk while I finish dinner." It was a miracle I hadn't snapped at her. I'd stopped just shy of it. *It's Thanksgiving. And this is what you wanted.*

She stormed past me and down the stairs. By the time I arrived in the kitchen, she'd put the four chocolate brown linen placemats into position atop the ivory tablecloth I'd ironed that morning.

I straightened one of the placemats and smiled. She didn't return the gesture. "Silverware next?"

She purposefully set down each piece of cutlery with a thud. First, the knives, around the table she plodded, head hung low. Then the forks in another skulking rotation, during which there was copious grumbling. Lastly, the spoons made their trip. "Am I done yet?"

She wants me to argue with her so she can be mad at me about Bryce. No way was I going to take the bait. "Water glasses and dinner plates, please."

She groaned. "Yes, ma'am."

Sam continued with her task, while I placed my mother's favorite candlesticks on the table. They weren't the most attractive things in the world—brown ceramic with splashes of brick orange and cobalt blue, from a vacation to Mexico she and my dad had taken when Julie and I were kids. My mother had always put out those candlesticks at Thanksgiving and I'd nearly come to blows with Julie to get them after Mom died. The whole thing was stupid sibling rivalry. Julie was a cut crystal kind of person.

Glasses and plates in place, Sam stood before me. Hand on hip, she glared.

I sighed. "Is this really how you're going to be all night? Because it's going to make Thanksgiving significantly less fun."

"I don't see any way I can have fun."

"Honey, we've been over this a dozen times." I set down a half-peeled potato and took a peek at the turkey, a perfect golden brown except for one frustrating pale area due to the cold spot in my decrepit old oven. "It's our first Thanksgiving with Chris. It's our last one in this house. We're moving in a week and you've spent every Thanksgiving of your entire life in this house. I wasn't willing to give up this holiday so you could spend it with your boyfriend."

She shot me an indignant stare. "His name is Bryce and I only wanted to spend it with him because his mom invited me. She likes me. A lot. She wants me to hang around at their house whenever possible."

I choked back a groan. "Of course I know his name. And I like him too. He's welcome anytime he wants to come over."

"Except on Thanksgiving."

"Well, don't you think his family wants him there? Just like I want you here?" Was it unforgivably selfish to want Sam all to myself on Thanksgiving? Perhaps, but it still seemed like the way it should be.

"I don't know. I never had a chance to ask him since you shot down the idea without even listening to me." She folded her arms across her chest, telling me that nothing I'd said had made any difference.

"Why don't you call Bryce and ask him if he wants to come over for pie later tonight? We can all watch a movie or play cards."

Her eyes softened, but I knew that stubborn streak of hers, the one she'd inherited from me, would never let me off the hook that easily. "I can call and ask. It might be too late." She glanced at the clock on the wall. "They're eating dinner right now. I'll have to try in a little bit."

Chris wandered into the kitchen from the living room, where he'd been indulging my dad's penchant for American football. "That was some good male bonding until he fell asleep. I can't imagine what he'll do after dinner. Probably slip into a coma."

Dad seemed to be sleeping a lot, although he often told us that he was simply "resting his eyes". He'd certainly been working hard at the studio, but perhaps it was time for me to admit that he was getting old.

Chris opened the fridge. "I need a snack."

"Dinner will be ready in an hour." I dropped half a stick of butter into a saucepan to start a roux for the gravy.

Sam elbowed her way in next to Chris. "I'm hungry too."

"Too bad your mum would never let us tuck into the pumpkin pie."

Sam giggled. "Tell me about it. What about chips and salsa?"

"Sold." Chris grabbed the jar of salsa and a bowl while Sam made a beeline to the pantry, returning quickly with the tortilla chips.

"Seriously, you two?"

The bag crinkled when Chris dug in. "Don't worry. I promise to properly stuff myself with turkey and mashed potatoes."

Potato peels flew into the trash as I worked. "Whatever. You two do whatever you want."

"She's mad." Sam scooped into the salsa with a chip.

"Don't be mad, Claire. It's Thanksgiving."

"Exactly." I cubed the potatoes, dropping them into simmering, salted water.

"Do you want a soda?" Sam asked Chris.

"I'm thinking another beer." He opened the refrigerator. "There's so much blooming food in here. It's impossible to get at anything."

"That's sort of the point with Thanksgiving, right?" I asked.

Chris straightened, victorious with beer in hand. "Remember, I didn't grow up with this tradition. In fact, one could argue that I should stage a protest since much of Thanksgiving is based on the Pilgrims being thankful for their freedom from so-called British oppression."

"You're ridiculous. You've lived in the United States for

over twenty years." I scanned the cooking schedule I'd written up that morning. With a tiny 50s-era stove, the orchestration of Thanksgiving dinner was a high-wire act. I looked forward to preparing this meal in a brand new kitchen next year, but I didn't have to admit that today. "Plus, if ever there was a holiday for you, it's Thanksgiving."

Sam crumpled the chip bag, stuffing it into the trash. "She's got you there, Chris."

"I do appreciate the celebration of eating." Chris cupped my shoulder. "What can I do?"

Sam took that as her cue to escape. "I'm going to text Bryce and see if he can come over later."

The next forty-five minutes were a blur—checking the temperature on the turkey, finding the counter space to let it rest, then a careful sequence of shuffling various dishes in and out of the oven. It involved yards of aluminum foil.

"I was going to tease you about your schedule, but now I can see it's the only way to do it," Chris said.

I blew my hair from my face, stirring the gravy. Steam rose from every pot on the stove. Taking a shower had been pointless. "Not every Type-A thing I do is a waste of time. There is a method to my madness."

Chris began rubbing my shoulders. "Are you okay, darling? You seem stressed." He kissed the spot on my neck right below my ear, which only sent my blood pressure through the roof.

"I'm fine. I just wish Sam was happier and I wish my dad was awake and I wish everything wasn't so complicated."

Chris turned me in his arms and held on to me tightly. I settled my head on his shoulder. "It's okay. Dinner will be great. We're together. It's all that matters."

I nodded. "I know. I know." Maybe the pregnancy hormones were getting the best of me today. "This is hard for me. I feel like I have a million different feelings going through my head. I'm excited about the new house and I'm sad about leaving this one."

"We're moving. It's stressful. That's why you need to let us help you."

"Sam doesn't want to help and my dad is asleep half of the time." There was a sudden flutter in my belly. It came again. "The baby," I whispered.

"Is everything okay?" Chris reared his head back, eyes full of worry.

"Yes, fine. The baby's moving."

Pure excitement rolled across his face as he placed both of his hands on my stomach. His eyes met mine, his moment of jubilation faded. "I don't feel anything."

I adjusted his hands, closer together and lower. "There? Do you feel that?"

He concentrated then shook his head. "No. Nothing."

The timer beeped. "The rolls." I turned to see the gravy bubbling away like crazy. "Oh, shit." I lurched for the knob on the stove and turned down the heat. "I'm sorry, honey. Maybe you'll be able to feel the baby tonight."

"That'd be amazing. Until then, let me help you."

In what seemed like a miracle, Chris and I, with a small amount of help from Sam, managed to have dinner served only fifteen minutes late.

My dad, groggy and yawning, took his place at the table. "It smells fantastic in here, Ladybug. Your mom would've been proud. You know how much she loved Thanksgiving. It was her favorite holiday."

Sam set a basket of rolls down on the table and took her seat. I brought a casserole dish filled my mom's scratch-made toasted bread stuffing and Chris followed with the platter of turkey.

"Her favorite holiday?" Sam asked. "Did she just really like turkey?"

We all began dishing mashed potatoes, green beans, turkey, and Brussels sprouts onto our plates, passing each dish on to the next person. The smell was indeed heavenly.

"Your grandmother loved Thanksgiving because it was about being together as a family. No gifts. Just sharing a meal. She loved having everyone gathered."

I watched as Sam listened. A tear collected in the corner of my eye. These moments sneaked up on me, the times when I was reminded how tragic it was that my mother and Samantha had never spent any time on earth together. They would have loved each other to pieces.

Chris raised his glass. "I'd like to propose a toast to Claire, who has made a wonderful meal." He dropped his chin and smiled. "To Samantha, who was a big help, and to Richard, who has educated me on the finer points of football." He leaned closer and touched my belly. "And lastly, to the nipper, who will be joining us for this festive occasion next year. I can't wait."

"Here, here." My dad wore a grin a mile wide, more openly enthusiastic about his new grandchild with each passing day. He'd even made passing mention of moving from Asheville to Chapel Hill, as Chris had predicted. "This is so good, Jellybean. You've outdone yourself."

"Thanks, Dad. I appreciate that."

Sam sighed. "It's good, Mom. Really good."

Chris patted my knee under the table. "It's a lovely meal, darling."

I smoothed out the napkin in my lap, admiring those ugly old candlesticks. My mom was there in my head, telling me I'd done a good job and reminding me that I shouldn't let my dad eat too much bread. She added one more thing before she faded into the darkness and I answered her silently. *I know, Mom. I miss you too.*

"I THOUGHT everyone went Christmas shopping on the morning after Thanksgiving." Chris bounced up and down on the sidewalk in front of the house, wearing his new, electric blue running shoes.

"They do, which is precisely why we are not shopping." I tugged on a thick stocking cap. "Ready?"

I jogged to the end of the driveway, Chris following me. It was cold enough to see our breath, so I'd put on a lightweight fleece pullover, long running pants, gloves, and my hat. Chris had insisted he'd be fine in shorts and a sweatshirt. I worried he might freeze his butt off, but I loved looking at his super-long legs and there wasn't much to do when a grown man had made up his mind.

"This will be good," Chris said. A block into it, he was already breathing a little heavy. "I need to get more exercise. Swimming at the YMCA is miserable. That pool is too bloody cold. It'll be so good once we're in the house and we can put in the pool."

"Yes, it will." We started down one of the steeper hills on our run and I picked up speed.

"This isn't too bad. I sort of like running." He fell behind for a moment, then caught up and patted me on the butt. "Especially when I get to run with my very hot soon-to-be wife."

I smiled. "Goof." We got to the bottom of the hill and took a corner, dodging a couple walking their dogs. "I brought some leftovers over to Rosie this morning."

"Before I got to take a crack at everything?"

"There's plenty of food left. Believe me." The adrenaline

began to course through my veins, the moment when I start to feel like I could run forever. "I hate that my dad made a stink about inviting her over for dinner last night. She's all by herself."

"It's sad. Such a sweet lady."

"He has it stuck in his head that Thanksgiving is for family only, which is silly." I realized what I'd said as soon as it came out of my mouth.

"Uh, isn't that what you said to Sam about Bryce?"

Fuck. "Yes. It is."

"So what gives?"

It wasn't that I hadn't thought about this topic, I'd spent tons of time mulling it over, especially after the rift with Sam. It was more that I hadn't come to any real conclusions. "It's a couple of things, I guess. His mom is one of the women from school who tried to be friendly with me after the magazine photos of you and me in St. Barts came out."

"Oh. I see."

"I know I shouldn't hold that against her. She's been nothing but nice. I guess she just rubs me the wrong way with her perfect car and perfect house and perfect husband."

"Ah, see, I've only met Bryce's dad. I thought he was perfect, too. Perfectly dull."

I laughed quietly. "True."

"You know, it may not have occurred to you, but perhaps she envies you."

"I doubt it."

"Why not? You have a brilliant career and an amazing daughter, when she has a house full of boys. And I may not be some big prize, but at least I'm not Mr. Perfectly Dull."

I grabbed his arm as we took a left on to a busier street. "Oh, stop. Of course you're a prize."

He laughed. "You don't hold your opinion of his mother against Bryce, do you?"

Damn. Do I do that? "It's just that Sam is always going on and on about how awesome she is. She makes cookies and loves having Sam around and I don't know." I shook my head at every stupid thing I said. Funny how the things in your head that make perfect sense have an entirely different ring when they're out in the open. "This is just jealousy, isn't it?"

"Sounds a bit like that, yes."

"I know I'm being selfish about Sam's time right now. I know I am. But I can't help it. And with all of the crazy stuff going on, it feels like I barely see her."

"And it's worse when she's over at Bryce's house all the time."

"Exactly."

"You know, there's a solution to all of this. You need to roll out the red carpet for Bryce. Make him feel as welcome and wanted as his mom has done for Sam."

Huh. "I've never been the milk and cookies mom, but I suppose I could be."

"I love cookies. This could benefit everyone."

It was my turn to laugh. We jogged in place at a corner, waiting for cars then crossed the street and headed up one of my favorite hills, the "butt-blaster". "I need to stop fighting and try a new approach."

"I probably need to do the same where your father and Rosie are concerned."

"I don't get why he's so weird about it." I took off my gloves and stuffed them in the kangaroo pocket of my jacket.

"We actually spoke about it the other day at the studio."

"What did he say?"

Chris was quiet for a moment, and I wondered if he was having a hard time keeping up with me on the hill. "First off, your dad is a very sweet man." He swallowed and nodded, but kept up. "He's got a heart as big as an ocean."

"I know."

"Honestly, I don't think he's over your mother. He's still in love with her, very much."

After last night's dinner, my mom was so present in my mind. Even that morning, although she wasn't talking, I could feel her all around me. Perhaps it was the holidays making me feel that way. Perhaps it was the momentous life changes ahead —new house, wedding, baby.

I sighed as we crested the hill. My cheeks were getting chapped from the cold. "It's sad, but I think you might be right."

"Maybe he doesn't want to find someone. Maybe he likes being alone. After all, he has you and Sam. I suppose he has me as well now. That might be all he ever wants."

"So we need to abandon plan Rosie."

"I think so."

I slowed my pace on a straightaway, to let Chris catch his breath. "I'm really glad that you and Dad have forged a friendship. He always wanted a son."

"As much as he sometimes makes me want to beat my head against a wall, I'm happy about it too. He's a stodgy old bastard, but I love him."

How things change. Mere months ago, they hated each other. "If you can find a way to wedge that into a conversation and not make it too uncomfortable, you should tell him. I'm sure he'd love to hear it."

Chris laughed then began to cough.

"You okay, Penman?" I slowed down, turning to jog backwards.

"Yes." He cleared his throat and brushed his floppy hair from his face. His cheeks were bright red, eyes bright and electric green. His eyebrows pinched together as he shooed me ahead. "I'm fine."

"If you say so." I turned to run forward. "I know you're not quite in top shape anymore."

"I think I can keep up with a pregnant woman." He dashed several yards ahead of me, looking back over his shoulder.

"Oh, really? Is that a challenge?" I sped up.

"Maybe—"

That was all I needed. I sprinted ahead, leaving him in the dust.

CHAPTER TWENTY-THREE

"EVEN WITH MOVERS, that was entirely too much work. I don't plan to move for a good eight hours." I kicked off my shoes and collapsed onto the mattress. "Maybe longer."

"But the bed isn't made yet." Claire dug her hands into her hair, scanning the piles of boxes in the room. "Of course, no telling where the sheets are."

"Sorry darling, the appeal of being horizontal was too much." I patted the empty spot on the bed next to me. "Come on. Give in. You know you want to."

She fell into a heap next to me. "Just think if we'd tried to do all of it ourselves."

"My body can't fathom such a thing right now." I closed my eyes. My legs and arms felt as if they weighed five hundred pounds. Each. Sleeping on the bare mattress sounded like a perfectly reasonable activity. "I hate to say this, but I'm too old for this."

"You and me both, Penman. You and me both."

I cracked open one eye to see the sun setting over the lake—streaks of pink and orange amid a gray December sky. This house would be magnificent once renovations were done and the new furniture found its place among the few pieces we'd moved from Claire's house. Otherwise, much of the stuff we'd taken had been books and records, clothing and kitchen gear, linens and mementos.

I turned to my side, facing Claire. This had been a hard day for her—physically and mentally. She looked completely worn out. "Are you feeling okay about everything? Now that it's done." I took her hand and toyed around with her fingers.

"I am. I think it would be different if we'd had to say goodbye to my house completely." She showed me a sweet smile as a few strands of her hair fell across her face.

So bloody beautiful. "I'm glad. I really am. I know this was a big change."

"It was, but you were right. We had to do it. And I'm excited we get to build a household together. Start fresh and make things the way we want them."

"I'm wondering how long it'll take to convince your dad to sell his house in Asheville and move into your house."

"We have to make him think it's his idea. The baby will be enough to get him to move, but Rosie next door will be an issue. You know he'll make a stink about that."

"Either that or he won't make a stink, he'll merely refuse and we'll have to pretend that isn't the reason."

We both rolled to our backs, now holding hands, peaceful, silent, motionless.

"Chris. We need to change clothes and brush our teeth and make the bed. I can't sleep like this."

"Sure you can. Close your eyes and the next thing you know, it'll be tomorrow morning."

She groaned and got up, then tugged on my arm. "Come on. Out."

"Usually, you're trying to get me in to bed."

"Very funny."

I blew out a breath. If she wasn't so damn adorable and pregnant, I might have staged a protest.

"Plus, you don't get to sleep on that side of the bed anymore anyway. We have to switch." She flipped on the annoyingly bright overhead light and began examining the labels on the boxes.

I sat up and swung my legs over the side of the bed. "What? Why?"

"Because. You're the man. You have to sleep closer to the door." She turned a box on top of a tall stack. "I think the new sheets are in here."

"Back up one minute." I got up and removed the box from the stack, tossing it onto the bed and pulling my car keys from my pocket to break the tape. "Why do I have to sleep closer to the door? I'm used to my side. I like my side. This is throwing off my entire sense of right and wrong."

Claire pulled sheets and towels out of the box. "What if someone breaks into the house? You should be the first thing they encounter."

"So this is how you plan to get rid of me."

"Oh, stop." She swatted me across the arm. "Help me make the bed."

"Yes, dear." I slid the box onto the floor.

She handed me one corner of what looked like an extra-thick sheet.

"What is this?"

"The mattress pad?"

"Oh. Huh."

"Chris. Do you seriously not know what a mattress pad is?"

I shrugged. "I do. It's just that Helena changes the sheets at the house in LA and I guess I never paid much attention." Much of the domestic stuff was still a mystery to me, but I'd done a decent job over the last few months of faking my way through it.

She tossed a sheet at me, hitting the center of my chest. "That's the fitted sheet."

If you say so. "I know full-well what this is." I tucked one corner around and walked to the next corner to do the same.

Claire was putting on the pillowcases. "My dad was smart. He made his bed this morning after we brought the first load over."

"Sam has us all beat. Spending the day at Leah's was even smarter." With the fitted sheet on, I spread out the flat sheet. The one thing I did know about bed linens was that I most certainly did not like the top sheet tucked under at the end. It made my feet feel as though they were being held hostage.

"I think the new comforter is in the corner." Claire pointed to a paper shopping bag leaning against the wall beneath the window.

I climbed over the obstacle course of boxes to fetch it, unfolding it after I removed it from the plastic. Claire and I spread it out together—a pretty, fluffy cover of gray and pale blue and white, an oversized print of branches and leaves.

"I'm going to miss my mom's quilt," Claire said wistfully.

"We still have it. We can put it at the end of the bed. Keep it for when you get cold." I dropped the overnight bag Claire had packed for us onto the bed. "I predict I'll be putting it on you every night."

"I don't know. Pregnancy is making me very hot."

I beamed, pointing at her splendid chest. "I noticed."

"Not that kind of hot." She shook her head and plucked her pajamas from the suitcase. "Time for bed."

"I thought you'd never ask."

I ambled into the bathroom to brush my teeth. I turned on the faucet, noticing how dingy it was. I'd had it in my head that this room was one of the few that didn't need much work, but now that we were here, I could see that I'd been looking through I-just-want-to-find-a-damn-house colored glasses.

Claire was splashing water on her face, her hair pulled back in a ponytail. It felt like the first true glimpse of what married life would be with her, in our own house, the two of us together, alone. I stepped closer, trailing my fingers the length of her spine, looking at her reflection in the mirror as she patted her face dry with a towel.

"Hi." She smiled.

"Hello, yourself." I grinned after seeing the flash of her deep blue eyes.

"Ready for bed? Breath all minty fresh?"

I eased behind her and wrapped my arms around her waist, which made her breasts appear even more impressive…and tempting in a tight-fitting tank top. "I am more than ready for bed." I pressed my lips to her neck.

She hummed and knocked her head to the side. "I thought you were exhausted."

"I can always muster the strength for love."

She giggled. "That might be the corniest thing you've ever said to me. Have you considered a second career in the greeting card business?"

"I haven't. Why don't I take you to bed and we can talk all about it?"

"Why do I have the feeling we'll do nothing of the sort?"

"Oh, there'll be talking, but not about greeting cards." I took her hand and led her to the bed, but I reflexively went to what had apparently only been my side temporarily. "Do I really have to switch to be closer to the door?"

"What if I tell you it'll make me happy?"

I threw back the comforter and climbed in on my new side. "That's all I need to hear. The alternative is unbearable."

Claire snuggled up to me immediately and kissed me softly, while my hand skimmed beneath her top, caressing her back. "Oh," she said.

I pressed a kiss to her cheek then nuzzled her ear. "You like that?"

"No. Wait—"

That word—no. "What's wrong?"

"Shhh." Her hand scrambled behind her back until she found mine. She grabbed it and slid it around to her belly.

Wait. There it was. A wiggle. The lightest of thumps against my palm. "Is that?"

"Just wait." She pressed against the back of my hand, much more forcefully than I ever would have.

Again, the wiggle. It was stronger now, a feeling that I could imagine would be like caging a butterfly in your hands. Except that it was our baby. "I finally felt it." *This is real now.*

"I know." Her voice had a new lightness. "Isn't it amazing?"

"It is." There in the dark, I shook my head. This might have been the best baby milestone yet and there was so much to come. *Hard to believe it's finally happening.*

"I think he or she has decided to go to sleep."

I pulled her into my arms. "Oh well, the nipper needs sleep, just like mum and dad."

Claire nestled her head in my armpit and I sensed that perhaps tonight wasn't the night for romance. Even after the excitement of feeling the baby move, every passing moment pushed my body closer to sleep. "We did well today. The move is done and out of the way. Big hurdle. I got to feel the baby move. Doesn't get much better than that."

"I'm glad that finally happened. Now we have a week to get everything in order so we can get married."

"We'd better get our sleep now, while we can."

CHAPTER TWENTY-FOUR

I HUNG up the phone and scanned my notes—pages and pages of notes. An hour on the phone with Laura Simmons and I now had more than fifty interview suggestions, twenty recurring feature ideas, and an array of freelancers to contact.

I'd bit my tongue dozens of times. *But Chris's family is coming in from England. I'm getting married in two days.* It was all to remain top secret. The wedding was at home for a reason—no photographers, no limelight, no microscope. It was bad enough that the tabloids had figured out that I was pregnant. We didn't want them to find out about the wedding. Therefore, I shut my trap as Laura drowned me with ideas and additional responsibilities. I said "no problem" when she made me promise her a complete update on January fifth, the first Monday back at work after the New Year.

I tossed the legal pad aside. *How in the hell am I going to do all of this?* I tried to reason with myself. *Maybe it only seems like too much to get done. You always get overwhelmed when someone heaps a pile of work on you at one time.*

The baby squirmed. *I know, honey, I'm hungry too.*

I made my way down to the kitchen from the new home

office, which Chris and I were sharing. I found an apple in the shiny new stainless steel fridge that seemed to be the same size as my first car. The clock on the double wall-ovens said two thirty-five. Chris would be back from picking up his mum and one of his two sisters, Kate, from the airport soon. One more thing to be insanely freaked out about. *What if his mom hates me? My dad hated Chris at first. Then what?*

I leaned against the counter, took a huge bite of the apple. There were only so many things my pregnant brain could handle and at that moment, the most pressing matter was food. Needing a snack was becoming an hourly occurrence, annoying and time-consuming for sure, but at least I better understood how Chris must feel all the time.

Another growl. Another kick. Only one thing could satisfy this all-encompassing hunger—peanut butter. The jar and spoon had been my frequent companion of late. Messing around with graham crackers seemed like a waste of time. It tasted so damn good I wanted to mainline the stuff.

I dug in and wandered into the living room. *Mmm. Sometimes I can't believe this stuff is legal.* I sat on one of the white wood folding chairs we'd rented for the ceremony. Everything had already been delivered, we just needed to set the rest of it up.

I gazed up at the vaulted living room ceiling. Chris, Sam, and my dad had spent hours the night before hanging up countless paper lanterns—all different sizes, swinging from varying heights, all white. Each one had a bundle of twinkle lights inside of it, an idea Sam had found online. My dad, always in need of a project, had carefully coordinated where the wires would go, so that they were bundled neatly and out of view. I'd been barred from the ladder due to my so-called delicate condition.

As I spooned the peanut butter from the jar and sucked the spoon clean, I felt anything but delicate. Thank goodness the wedding was happening now instead of a month or two from now. My belly grew rounder every day. *And for fuck's sake, please let my wedding dress fit.*

One more spoonful, and I closed my eyes, finally feeling my hunger abate. *How did I get here? I'm getting married tomorrow. To Chris.*

When Chris and I had first started our relationship, it took a concerted effort to separate what he was, the rock star, and who he was, the man who I most loved. Now it took almost no effort at all. Almost.

"There you are," he said.

I whipped around and the spoon went flying, skidding across the floor. *Oh shit.*

Chris laid his hand on my shoulder. "You okay, darling?" He pointed at a tiny wet spot on the front of my shirt.

Fabulous. I was drooling. "I guess I dozed off."

Two women I'd only seen in pictures stood behind him. His mother, with a pile of gray hair threatening to topple off her head, smiled skeptically. His sister, tall and statuesque like Chris, with a cascade of silken coppery light brown hair, bent over and picked up the peanut butter spoon with the tips of two fingers.

"You must be Claire," she said, with an air of superiority. "And I take it this is your spoon."

Chris took the dreaded utensil from her and put his arm around me. "Mum, Kate, this is Claire."

I extended my hand and shook Kate's, noticing that her eyes were nearly as green as Chris's. "I'm so happy to meet you both. Chris has told me so much about you. I'm sorry about the spoon and the…" My voice feathered away as I noticed the open jar of peanut butter on the floor next to my chair. "Pregnant." I rubbed my belly. "I get tired. And hungry."

Chris pecked me on the temple then strode over to dispatch the evidence. "Now she knows how I feel."

I turned to his mother and my brain got stuck again. *What do I call her?* "Mrs. Penman, it's very lovely to meet you."

Her eyebrows arched as she appraised me with her twinkly hazel eyes, lips held firmly in a straight line like a schoolmarm. I was half expecting her to tell Chris he'd made a terrible mistake, that I would never do, but then her expression softened, she cocked her head and smiled. "Dear. Please. Call me Harriet." She stepped closer and took my hand, giving off a distinct aroma of whiskey and White Shoulders. Her skin was crinkled and pale, the back of her hands dotted with liver spots. "Christopher's sister Alice is very sorry she couldn't make it. Her youngest has been ill and you'll learn soon enough. It's difficult for a mother to go anywhere when she has a sick child at home."

"Mum, Claire already has a daughter." Chris placed his hand on her shoulder. "Samantha. Remember? I've told you about her over the phone several times. She'll be home from school any minute now."

Harriet let go of my hand and clutched her purse to her waist. "I do my best to remember these things, but I occasionally forget." She cleared her throat.

"It's okay, Mum," Kate said. "There's a lot to remember." She eyed me, forcing a smile.

"I'd like to get rid of this spoon," Chris said. "You two must be thirsty. The kitchen is right in here."

I grabbed Chris's arm to get him to hang back. "I'm mortified."

"It wasn't your most graceful moment, but don't worry about it." He looked down at me so lovingly. It made my heart flutter. "She's half in the bag right now anyway. She's terrified of flying, so she self-medicates."

We joined them in the kitchen, where Harriet had taken a seat at the new table in the breakfast area. Kate stood.

"Spot of tea, ladies?" Chris asked. It was certainly the proper British thing to do, but I'd never once seen Chris make or drink tea. He was a coffee drinker through-and-through.

"That would be lovely, Christopher." Harriet began to rifle through her black leather purse.

"So, Claire," Kate said. "Is this your second marriage?"

Well, then. Let's get right to it.

Chris filled the teapot seemingly taking no note of the tone his sister had taken with me.

"No, this will be my first." I pulled a chair out from the kitchen table. "Please, why don't you have a seat?" I went to the cabinet and found a box of crispy brown-sugar cookies my father had bought.

Kate sat, eyes following my every move. "I see. So, what happened to your daughter's father?"

Chris took the box of cookies from me and arranged them on a plate, again not indicating that he was aware of any tension at all in the room.

She's vetting me. Chris told me his sisters hated Elise. She thinks I'm going to be just as bad. "We never married. It's been me and Samantha all these years."

"Until I came along and broke up the girls' party," Chris chimed in. He placed a cup of tea before his mum and returned to the counter for Kate's.

Kate perked up. "Just like at home, huh, Chrissy? You and the girls."

Chrissy?

Chris laughed. "Oh, now, don't go calling me that. I'll never live it down."

"Don't expect him to be much help, Claire," Kate said. "Alice and I did everything for him when he was growing up and the rock star thing didn't equip him to be any good at lulling babies to sleep or changing diapers."

I pursed my lips. *It's true he didn't know what a mattress pad was.*

"Now, now." Chris rubbed Kate's shoulders, smiling in a way that said she was just joking around as far as he was concerned. "I'm a grown up. I'm not completely helpless."

"Just don't count on too much, Claire." Kate looked up and smiled at Chris adoringly. "I'm sure he'll do his best."

———

My sister Julie and her husband Matt had arrived late that night, as well as Graham and Angie and the entire Banks Forest entourage, wives and girlfriends included. They all stayed up late, drinking, entertained mostly by Graham. My tee-totaling pregnant self went to bed early.

Julie was a little hung over the next day, definitely off her game.

"Ouch." My hand flew to the stinging nape of my neck, where she'd just burned me with the curling iron. "Jules, I'm getting married. How about you don't burn my skin off?"

"Stop moving around so much," she snipped.

She's still pissed that I didn't make her maid of honor. I watched Julie's reflection in the mirror as she wound another section of my hair around the curling iron barrel. Perhaps it was dehydration from drinking, but she seemed to be showing her age more now. We may have spent much of our lives at odds with each other, but I still didn't enjoy seeing her that way. "Catch me up on what's happening at home. Everything good with your job?"

"Things are fine with me. Matt is the one I'm worried about." She let the curling iron go and a mostly perfect spiral bounced into place on the side of my head. "They're announcing another round of layoffs in the next few weeks. He feels like he just barely squeaked through on the last one."

"Did you have a good time hanging out with dad this morning?" I'd been waiting for a report, but she hadn't yet offered one.

She shrugged. "Sure. Although, I have to tell you, I don't know what you're talking about with him being confused. He seemed sharp as a tack to me."

"Really?"

"Yep. Same old Dad."

You didn't see him eating out of Splenda packets. "It comes and goes. Some times he's fine and the next minute he's really forgetful."

She made eye contact with me in the mirror. "You got him to go to the doctor, right?"

I nodded. "Yes. Blood work and everything turned out just fine. The doctor said he was healthy."

"See? I'm sure he's fine. You worry too much. You always have."

Somebody has to worry, don't they? "I don't really see what's so bad about worrying."

"I'm sure that Dad's forgetfulness is probably nothing more than old age. He's in his seventies. At some point, we'll have to start talking about the long-term for him."

I couldn't see the long-term anything right now. The stuff going on ten feet in front of my face was plenty to deal with. "He's happy living here in Chapel Hill. I was thinking he should just sell the house in Asheville and move here. Then I wouldn't have to worry about him so much."

She placed her hand on her hip, this time looking me directly in the eye. "You want Dad to live here." She looped her finger in the air. "Close to you. When he drives you crazy."

I frowned. "He doesn't drive me that crazy. And we were thinking that he would live in my old house. We just have to persuade him to move back there."

"When he's convinced you're trying to set him up with the lady who lives next door?"

"He needs to get over that. Chris gave up on that weeks ago."

Julie combed through another section of my hair, returning to the task at hand, just as Samantha joined us. "Hey guys, you almost ready? Everybody's here."

"A few more minutes. Your mom's hair needs to be perfect." Julie sprung another curl from the grip of the curling iron.

Sam hopped up on to the bathroom vanity. The knee-length black dress she'd chosen was adorable as was the white flower she'd put in her hair. "You look amazing, Mom. Chris is going to love it." She kicked her feet, her black high-top-sneaker-wearing feet.

"So you went with the Converse after all." At least she'd skipped the knee socks.

"Yeah. All of my other black shoes are ugly." She stuck out her leg and turned her foot back and forth. "You can't deny that the Chuck Taylors are classics."

"Indeed. I can't."

"Sam," Julie started, "Are you getting excited for the baby? You're going to be a big sister. Pretty cool, huh?"

"Oh, yeah. Definitely." Sam nodded, looking around the room. It felt as though she would have paid anything to avoid looking at me. She was having all kinds of change foisted upon her. I couldn't expect her to meet it all with enthusiasm.

"I love babies, but they can be so much work," Julie said. "I don't know how you're going to be able to deal with the sleep deprivation at forty. It's going to be a lot different than when you were twenty-two, that's for sure. Oh, and the laundry, good

God, the laundry. How a tiny human can go through so many clothes always mystified me." She shook a can of hairspray and popped off the top. "Don't forget the dirty diapers and the crying. You'll be lucky if any of you are able to get any sleep."

As if Sam didn't have enough reasons to be unexcited about this. "I'll have Chris to help me. We'll do great. I'm excited."

"He says that now, but men aren't equipped to deal with all of that." Julie sniggered, spraying my hair and creating a cloud in the process.

"That enough hairspray," I said. "I probably shouldn't be breathing in all of that right now."

"Oh, sorry." Julie held her hands up in surrender.

Sam hopped off the counter and knelt to tie her shoe. "I haven't been around many babies, but I guess it'll be okay."

I reached out, placing a hand on her shoulder. "We may have a new baby coming, but you'll always be my first."

She looked up at me, sucking in the corner of her bottom lip. "Okay, Mom."

CHAPTER TWENTY-FIVE

GRAHAM HELPED me put on the jacket of my best suit—charcoal gray, Italian, custom made for me a year or two ago. I buttoned the top two of the three buttons. With the wedding at home, a tuxedo seemed like too much. Plus, I'd never liked the way I looked in them and this suit had cost a fortune. Best to get my money's worth.

He patted me on the shoulder firmly, smiling at my reflection in the mirror. "Now, don't be nervous. You can ask me whatever you want about the wedding night. You must have a lot of questions about sex."

I laughed and shook my head. "You're a bloody wanker. You know that, don't you?"

"Ah, you love me for it." He leaned against the wall of the nursery, which we were using as a dressing area.

I turned and looked into the eyes of my oldest friend, a pain in the ass who I loved to the ends of the earth. We were both starting to show our age and it wasn't surprising—we'd been through the war together. Granted, the war had been an unforgettable ride littered with limousines, recording sessions and

Dom Perignon. "You're really serious about getting the band back together?"

"Yes. Terence and Nigel will gladly talk your ear off about it later if you like. Or I can bring them upstairs now. Last minute band meeting?"

"Later. I have a few things on my mind right now." I hadn't expected nerves, but now that we were closer to go-time, my palms were starting to sweat. I tugged at the cuff of my shirt. "What's Nigel's new wife's name again?"

"Heather."

"I don't know why Terence said she was dumb. She seemed very intelligent." I combed my fingers through my hair, none too carefully. Claire had reminded me that morning that she preferred it messy.

"Oh, she's blooming brilliant. Turns out when Terence called her a rocket scientist, that she actually is a rocket scientist. It's a real job." Graham tossed his hands up in the air as if he couldn't possibly be more confounded.

"Wonder how long before she figures out who she married."

"He seems to have pulled the wool over her eyes pretty well."

"Did Terence bring his girlfriend? The one we're supposed to call Angela so we don't confuse her with Angie?"

"That one dumped him. He has a new one. Name's Michele. She's just as gorgeous, minus the Southern accent."

I glanced down and noticed a scuff on my black leather dress shoes. "Never a dull moment, is there?" I grabbed the towel I'd used after my shower and kneeled down to buff the mark from the toe.

"Yeah, meant to tell you. Claire's dad had to scare off some bloke with a camera who was lurking in the driveway."

Bloody hell. "Really?"

"No worries. He's gone. Richard has the police patrolling

the neighborhood. And I know you love it. The limelight. The attention."

"Not like that, I don't."

"You know what I mean. Being in the thick of it." He cleared his throat. "What do you say, man? You ready to write some new songs? Get into the studio? Find a new record label?"

I straightened and tossed the towel aside. "In theory, it sounds amazing. I'd be a fool to turn down the chance to make another run at it, especially after the high of the New York shows. But with the baby coming and Claire's new job, I'm not sure. I need more time to think about it before I make that sort of commitment."

Graham nodded and smiled, but I sensed he would have preferred a straight-out "yes" from me. "Absolutely. Just don't take too much time. We're chomping at the bit."

"Got it. Don't worry. I'll have an answer for you in a few weeks. Does that work?"

"I'd like it sooner, but I suppose so. Not much sense making a decision until after the holidays."

Richard poked his head into the room. "Everybody decent?"

"Richard. Didn't Chris tell you that I'm never decent?" Graham stood and shook Richard's hand so enthusiastically that Richard's shoulders bounced. "I'm really quite a pervert when it comes right down to it." He elbowed Richard in the stomach.

Pervert. Just what Richard needs to think of my best man. Never before had I had a desire to rescue Richard. I usually enjoyed watching him squirm, but Graham might have been a bit much. "All set downstairs?"

"We are. I just checked in with Sam and Claire is almost ready. We should take our places."

"Graham, do you mind if Richard and I have a minute together?"

"Yeah, of course. I'll be waiting at the bottom of the stairs." He clapped me on the back and strode out of the room.

"Everything okay, Chris? It's okay to have some jitters. I did like crazy the day I married Claire's mom."

"Oh yeah? Nervous?" Anytime Richard offered some sliver of his past, I was eager to have it, especially when he talked about Sara. It made me feel a little closer to the woman I would never know, the woman so monumentally important to Claire.

"Oh, good lord. The minister practically had to talk me off the ledge. I was shaking in my boots. Of course, I wasn't actually wearing boots."

I laughed. "So what made the difference?"

"Seeing her in that dress, walking up the aisle to me, the most beautiful smile on her face. She was a perfect angel. I knew then that I shouldn't be nervous about being the luckiest man on earth. I just needed to get her to say "I do" as quickly as possible before she realized what she was doing."

"You know, Richard, it means the world to me to have your blessing. Truly."

"I don't offer it lightly."

That's an understatement. "I realize that."

"Claire's lucky to have found you, Chris." He looked down at the floor, out the window, anywhere but at me. "I know I misjudged you when we first met. I can admit that now." He then did something I never expected. He hugged me. "I'm proud to have you for a son-in-law." His voice trembled, such an expression of emotion for a stodgy, closed-off man.

"I'm happy to have you for a father-in-law." He stepped out of the hug and I straightened the front of my jacket. "I'm glad we've had the time working on the studio together. It's been great fun. You know, I missed out on that sort of thing with my own dad. You're the closest thing I have to a father."

"I'm sure this is hard for you. I know it's hard for Claire to get married, knowing her mom can't be here. It's certainly difficult for me."

"All we can do is keep the love we have for the people who aren't here anymore and move forward."

With a flick of his wrist, he looked at his watch. "Speaking of moving forward, I believe you have a date with my daughter."

My hands again became clammy. "Do I ever." We walked down the hall, stopping outside the master bedroom.

"Move along, buster." Richard shooed me away with his hand, faking sternness. "No seeing the bride ahead of time."

"I know. I know."

Graham was waiting for me at the bottom of the stairs. "It's show time, P-man." He grabbed on to my shoulders, as if I was a fighter in the ring and he was my trainer.

"Hey. The jacket. Careful."

We stepped into the living room, where the chairs were lined up on either side of a white carpet runner. Angie had been put in charge of getting everyone to take their seats, and they were all there—Bryce, who had been sworn to secrecy, and had told his parents he was merely coming to our house for dinner. Rosie, who was now so openly annoyed by Richard's behavior that she insisted someone else give her a ride home after the ceremony. Claire's sister Julie's husband, Matt, Terence and his girlfriend Michele, Nigel and his new wife, Heather, the rocket scientist. My mum and Kate were in the front. Kate managed half a smile, which might be as much approval as I would ever get from her.

It wasn't the grandest gathering of people, but we had wanted it this way. If Claire had invited any of her writer friends or I had invited other musicians, word would've leaked out. Not a great way to meet your new neighbors after two weeks in the neighborhood by having photographers stake out the house. I felt badly that Angie was Claire's only girlfriend in attendance. I had a relatively big turnout, but perhaps that was part of being in a band. At least Claire had her sister.

Graham and I took our places at the end of the aisle, in the far corner of the living room. The municipal court judge we'd hired to marry us, stood waiting, in a black suit. He nodded, but that was as much emotion as he showed.

Angie disappeared down the hall and returned seconds later, flitting along in a dress of royal blue, with a big grin on her face. She looked straight away at Graham and gave him the high sign, then took her seat. He took his cue and pushed play on the iPod, starting Stevie Wonder's *Happier Than The Morning Sun*. It couldn't have been any more perfect…the sparse arrangement of guitar and layered vocals, lyrics that expressed exactly how I felt—happier than the morning sun.

Sam emerged from the hall and the smile on my face could not be suppressed. She marched, a bit faster than she'd been instructed, wearing a cheeky grin. I laughed quietly when I noticed the black high-tops, as did everyone in attendance.

Richard appeared and turned back toward the hall, holding out his arm. I held my breath as I watched him wait for Claire. I could see her in my head—striding down the hall, flowers in hand, on her way to her dad. In seemingly slow motion, she rounded the corner and I couldn't fully fathom the weight of the moment—her beauty, her very being, everything I'd ever wanted from another person. She hooked her arm in her dad's and he held on to her for dear life. I couldn't blame him. I wouldn't have wanted to let her go either.

As she approached, I was so taken aback by the smile in her eyes that I'd hardly noticed the dress or the flowers or the way she'd done her hair, the trappings that required so much planning. It was nothing more than a beautiful backdrop for my stunning prize—Claire.

She kissed her dad on the cheek and he sat next to Bryce as the final strains of the song wound their way through the room. With a single step, she was exactly where she belonged, next to me. I took her hand and leaned into her ear. "We have to stop meeting like this."

She elbowed me and giggled.

"Friends and family," the judge started. "We are gathered here today to witness the marriage of Claire Louise Abby and Christopher James Penman. Claire and Christopher have come together out of love and respect, choosing to live their lives together as husband and wife, expanding family ties and embarking on a grand human adventure. We are here to celebrate their love and commitment, which is about more than the joining of two lives, it is the union of two souls."

I squeezed her hand. She did the same in return.

"Claire and Christopher will exchange vows they themselves have written."

Claire handed her flowers to Samantha, who now appeared to be shedding more than a tear. Claire and I faced each other and held hands.

I cleared my throat, but there was an awfully big lump present as she looked up at me with her wide blue eyes. She'd been radiant the entire pregnancy, but today it was magnified.

"Claire, I thought I knew what life was all about until I met you. Then I realized that everything around me was empty because I didn't have you." I counted off a few heartbeats. It wasn't that I couldn't remember what I needed to say next. I only wanted her and everyone around us to understand how much I meant it. "You are my sunrise and sunset, the air I breathe, the quietest of moments, and the loudest of exclamations. Everything I do is for you and that will remain until I have nothing left on this earth to give."

Claire sniffled and a tear rolled down her cheek. "That was

beautiful," she whispered.

"Thanks." I choked back a tear. "Your turn." My heart sped up as she eased closer to me and turned her back to the crowd.

"Excuse me," she whispered to the judge, reaching into her cleavage for a piece of paper. He didn't seem the slightest bit shocked. "I didn't want to forget anything."

I let out a quiet, breathy laugh. *Always keeping me on my toes.*

She stood back and peeked at the paper before closing her hand around it. "Christopher, you make me feel like the luckiest woman in the whole world. Every day." The way she trembled when she took in a deep breath made me want to sweep her into my arms. "You are sweet and kind and patient, but most of all, I know that the love you give to me is always freely given. You have accepted my daughter without reservation, welcoming her into your life, and that has meant the world to me. You love me and accept my every flaw. I love you more than you will ever know, but I will do my best to show you every day for the rest of my life."

Wow. "Well done, darling."

"Now, we will exchange the rings," the judge said.

I turned to Graham, who handed me the Tiffany box with Claire's diamond band.

"Claire, you will go first," the judge said.

"I, Claire, give you Christopher, this ring as an eternal symbol of my love and commitment to you." She placed my dad's wonderfully scuffed wedding band on my finger. It fit perfectly. I glanced over at my mum, who was in a heap of tears, clutching a handkerchief. *If only Dad had been around for this.*

"I, Christopher, give you Claire, this ring as an eternal symbol of my love and commitment to you." Claire held out her hand and I slipped the diamond Tiffany band on to her slender finger.

"By the power vested in me by the state of North Carolina, I now pronounce you husband and wife. You may kiss the bride."

Finally. I wrapped my arms around her and tilted her back, planting the most important kiss of our lives as a couple against her supple lips. She kissed me back—and then some. Graham hooted and hollered. I swore I heard Richard mutter, "That's enough you two."

"I would like to present husband and wife, Christopher Penman and Claire Abby-Penman."

Everyone stood, erupting in applause.

Graham attacked me with a hug. "I'm so bloody happy for you, Chris. Really."

I hardly had time to turn away before Kate was there to hug me as well, then my mum, her face red and puffy. I grasped her elbow, looked into her sweet eyes. "Mum, thank you so much for being here. It wouldn't have felt right without you."

She shook her head, bawling like a baby. "I wouldn't have missed it for the world."

I pulled her into a snug embrace and watched as Claire and Sam clung to each other, rocking back and forth—what an emotional moment for the two of them. Hell, it was emotional for all of us.

The next several minutes were congratulatory hug and handshake after hug and handshake, when all I wanted was to find my bride. After she'd hugged Rosie, I lunged for her and grabbed her hand. "Come here. I'm not letting you go for the rest of the evening." I got a heady waft of her perfume as she pressed into me.

"Please don't let go."

Angie, Graham, Sam and Bryce were clearing the chairs to the sides of the room. Richard dimmed the lights and turned on the switch for the lanterns above, which transformed the room into a space suitable for a party, something I sensed we were all anxious to start as the room was abuzz with happy chatter and commotion. Graham and Angie strode over, hand in hand.

"I don't think the judge did it right," Graham said. "I kept waiting for the part where I object."

Angie swatted him on the arm. "It was lovely you two. Really."

CHAPTER TWENTY-SIX

I THOUGHT I'd seen Chris look irresistible in every way possible, but I was oh so wrong. He was particularly devastating as he slumped against our bedroom door on our wedding night—suit pants hanging loose around his waist, wrinkly shirt mostly unbuttoned, hair a wonderful mess, feet bare, toting a bottle and two stemmed glasses.

"They're gone. Finally. Everyone is out the bloody door." He sauntered into the room, nearly weaving across the floor out of exhaustion, stopping short of the bed and cocking his oh-my-god-get-over-here-right-now eyebrow.

"I can only have a tiny sip of champagne." The glow from the candles I'd set out around the room caught his cheekbones with flickers of gold.

"Sparkling cider, darling." He placed the bottle on his bedside table, set a knee on the mattress and flipped over to his back. "Mmm. You look comfortable."

"Do you like it?" I smiled, guessing the answer, as he didn't hesitate to rake his hand up my thigh. It might have been as close as I came to playing seductress—a low-cut ivory nightgown of lace and silk charmeuse, but I felt certain that it was right on the money for Chris.

He brushed my hair from my face. "You're so beautiful. I'm such a lucky bastard." His stunning eyes, the green that had indelibly marked my brain, gleamed in the candlelight. "I can't believe I get to have you all to myself. It feels like a dream."

Watching and hearing him say that, all while we were close enough that I could feel his heartbeat, was a dream in itself. "Today was amazing. You are so ridiculously handsome. Today made it that much more apparent." I dragged my finger down his chest to the sole remaining button, un-tucking his shirt. "I can't imagine being any happier."

He dug his hands into my hair, cupping the back of my head possessively as he kissed me. I eased to my back and his hand traveled to the strap on my nightgown, flicking it off my shoulder. His mouth found my neck, then my collarbone as he teased my breast through the silky fabric with the tips of his fingers.

I arched my back and wrapped my leg around his, rubbing the back of his calf with my ankle. "We need to get you out of these pants." I bucked against him as his thigh settled between my legs. "And the shirt. And whatever else it is that you're wearing."

He sat back on his knees and wrestled with his shirt, having to tug on the sleeves because he hadn't bothered to do undo the cuffs. In a flash, it went sailing over his shoulder.

I propped up on my elbows. "Well? Keep going."

He shook his head. "No. That's your job. On the wedding night, the bride takes off the groom's pants. It's a rule."

I chewed on my lower lip. "If I must."

"I insist."

I inched forward, one of my legs between his, as he remained kneeling. My focus was drawn to the narrow trail of hair below his belly button, the one that led beneath the waistband of his pants. I kissed him softly there as he dug one hand into my hair and slipped the other down the front of my nightgown, cupping my breast. The blood rushed beneath my skin, flooding it with warmth. "Like this?" I peered up at him as I unhooked the front tab of his trousers and undid the inner button. Slowly, I slid the zipper down.

"Exactly like that."

I pressed another kiss to his belly as I shimmied the pants down to his knees. "You're going to need to hop down, honey. So I can finish the job."

He leaned forward, kissing my forehead before easing off the bed and stepping out of his pants. I scooted to the edge of the bed and he stood between my legs. He took the hem of my nightgown into his hands, pulling it up as if the clocks had stopped and we had as much time as he cared to take. *He's killing me.* Inch by inch, the air cooled my skin, silk traveling the length of my body until I raised my arms and he dropped it in a puddle on the floor. His gray and white striped boxer shorts were the only thing standing between us and I made quick work of those. Everything else between us was standing at attention.

Oh my, Mr. Penman. I looked up at him again—he had a most smug look of pride on his face, as if he'd accomplished a grand feat, and who was I to do anything other than match his showing with one of my own?

My hands went to his waist and inched around to his back. I loved drawing my fingers up and down the long column of his spine, feeling those sexy dimples above his ass. I licked my lips and gently took him into my mouth. He groaned his approval as I caressed and cradled him with my tongue. His legs tensed, his back arched slightly. It wasn't my intent to take him all the way —I merely wanted to give him some of the undivided attention he deserved. The wedding had been too much about me. Plus, I knew how much he loved it.

I looped my tongue and increased the suction, an action that prompted a response beyond a grunt. "Oh my God, Claire." He combed his fingers into my hair, raking them past my ears and urging my chin up. "Darling, that feels so good and it just wouldn't be right on our wedding night if that was the first act." I carefully let him go and he dropped to one knee, holding both sides of my head. "I want to make love to my beautiful wife." He kissed me for only a moment, then his mouth traveled to my breast. He sucked and licked so delicately that it felt as if my soul was melting.

Being with him, like this, was so wonderfully freeing. After everything we'd been through, we were together. I didn't have to worry about whether or not I got to keep him. We were starting a life together, a real life, the kind that everyone wants, and I knew why—it was incredible.

I kissed him and wriggled my way back on the mattress. "Come here."

"I love it when you beckon me."

I smiled. "I'll try to beckon more often."

He climbed onto the bed and descended on me, with soft, tender kisses and a hand through my hair. I opened myself to him—in every way—I didn't even close my eyes. I wanted to look into that stunning face of his and see the man I was so lucky to have.

He drove inside purposefully. *Wow.* He really did have reason to feel proud. I clutched the sides of his face and our kisses became a torrent of love and passion and heat, all swirled into one. He pressed down on my pelvic bone and I lifted my knees higher to let him in as far as he would go and it felt so sublime, so satisfying. It took my breath away.

He rocked against me faster now and the pressure was building. He dropped his head and I kissed his forehead, feeling the heat radiate from his skin.

"Look at me," I whispered. In the faint candlelight, his eyes fluttered open, showing me a dark intensity rimmed by soft, feathery lashes. His lips, the mole on his left cheek, that absurdly angular jaw—it was all so perfect and all mine. It left my insides feeling soft and gooey.

"I love this. I don't think I could want anything else. Ever." He smoothed my hair back from my face and shifted his weight to an even more gratifying place. He read my cues as my breath hitched in my chest, taking longer, harder strokes.

"Oh God, Chris." I had to close my eyes. It was too overwhelming—the pleasure and his beauty, coupled, was an overdose of amazing things. "Yes."

"My favorite word out of your mouth." He raised his upper body and picked up his pace. His own breaths came fast and shallow, the tension in his body more apparent.

The pressure pushed against the dam, pulsing and ebbing closer until I couldn't take it anymore and I let go. Chris quickly followed. Waves crashed and washed away, only to be followed by new ones. Eventually, they became soft and fleeting, replaced by contentment.

He carefully lowered himself alongside me and I curled into him. "I love you so much, Chris."

He held me as if he'd never let me go. "I love you so much, Claire Abby-Penman."

I reared my head back. "That sounds better every time you say it."

"Just wait until perfect strangers start saying it. Then your mind will really be blown." A happy wiggle happened between us. "Is that?"

"It is. Somebody is apparently awake."

He lowered his head, kissing my stomach. "Hello, Nipper. Mum and Dad love you too."

CHAPTER TWENTY-SEVEN

NEVER BEFORE HAD I been grateful for turbulence. *One more jiggle and I might have to be the first man to induct a pregnant woman into the Mile-High Club.* The plane to St. Marten pitched, it dropped, it bounced. Claire grasped my arm with an iron grip, leaning into me and digging in her nails, hard—totally worth it.

"I hate it when it does that." She glanced nervously out the window. "It's not even stormy out."

"I don't know." I pressed a kiss to her cheek, staring down into her cleavage. "It doesn't bother me."

The black top she'd chosen for travel was everything I could have asked for—a V-neck just low enough to display the incredibly sexy swell of her breasts, especially from my perspective. It was nipped in at the waist, flaunting the curves that were more maddening every day. Never in a million years had I anticipated that my pregnant wife would be such non-stop temptation.

Thank goodness for three whole nights, just the two of us, in my villa in St. Barts. *Our* villa. I had to start remembering to call things "our" and not "my". I loved the sound of "our". Even better—"pregnant wife" had the most incredible ring to it.

Three nights wasn't as much time as I would've wanted to spend stark naked and in bed with Claire, but three was better than none, and with the crazy realities of life at home, we didn't have much choice. Christmas was in four days, so we had to be back for that. Claire had a major update due to Laura Simmons on January fifth.

Claire's black top tormented me even further on the short flight into St. Barts. The rickety old airplane never maintained any one altitude, and her breasts jiggled and jostled as she clung to my arm. It was a miracle I was able to walk off the plane without my pants broadcasting to the other passengers how much my wife was making me barmy.

Jean-Luc, the caretaker's son met us at the airport terminal. "Monsieur Penman, Madame Penman." It was apparent he knew that he was skating on thin ice with Claire as he would only look at her for a fleeting second. He'd taken her daughter's virginity the last time we were here, so there was good reason for staying under the radar. Still, he retained a professional air.

"I've told you dozens of times, Jean-Luc. Please, call me Chris." Even with my sunglasses on, I had to shield my face from the blazing afternoon sun. "We're on island time. No worrying about titles and formalities."

"Yes, of course. Chris." He grabbed one of our suitcases and hoisted it into the back of the car. "Would you like to drive or shall I?"

"I'll take it." I put my arm around Claire's shoulder. "Precious cargo."

He tossed me the keys and climbed into the backseat while I held the door for Claire.

A little bit of turbulence in a jet had nothing on bumpy, virtually unpaved St. Barts roads. *Eyes on the road, Penman.* I didn't even really have to look. Claire's jiggling cleavage occupied my periphery and it was stunning.

We got to the house and I was quick to dispatch Jean-Luc. "You don't need to worry about the bags. I've got it from here. You go enjoy your day."

"I haven't had a chance to make sure the new cook has stocked the kitchen." He pointed to the front door.

"We've got it. I'll call you if there are any problems." I keyed into the door. "Go ahead, darling, but don't go in our room yet."

Claire started down the white stucco steps to the villa courtyard.

"What time should I come by tomorrow to check on you?" Jean-Luc asked.

I realized then that Jean-Luc would only be cramping our style when I'd been waiting for one thing...time alone with Claire, with zero chance of interruptions. "You know, we're only here for three nights. I'll call you if I need anything."

"Are you sure? You pay me to take care of things."

"And I'll call you if we need anything. That goes for the new cook. She can come for dinner tomorrow night, but otherwise, tell her to stay away."

"Stay away?"

"Yes. Stay away. Mrs. Penman and I need our time alone. Completely alone."

A look of recognition finally washed over his face. "Ah, I see."

Nothing like being a little slow on the uptake. "Thank you for everything."

I hurried down the stairs with the suitcases. "Claire?"

"In here." She'd wandered into the living room off the kitchen and was looking out through the picture window down to the churning sea. "What should we do today? Beach?"

Not unless you want sand in some uncomfortable places. "No way. You and I aren't going anywhere."

She turned, frowning adorably. Then she seemed to catch

the look in my eye. "Oh really?" She gasped when I swept her into my arms.

"I couldn't do this upstairs. Carrying a pregnant woman down a flight of stairs seemed reckless at best."

"Please don't throw me in the pool." She clutched my neck and leaned into me.

"Maybe later. For now, I have to carry you over the threshold."

She giggled. "Really?"

"Yes. I didn't have a chance to do it at home." I strode across the courtyard and leaned with my knee into the wall for leverage as I opened the door. With as much drama as I could muster, I walked her over the threshold. "There we go. That's how you do it." I kissed her and placed her feet on the floor.

She gasped again when she looked into the room. "Chris. Oh my God. It's gorgeous."

I'd had two hundred white tulips flown in from a flower importer in St. Marten. In vases all over the room, it was as if we were at a flower show. I walked up behind her and wrapped my arms around her waist, none-too-subtly pushing up on her breasts with my arms. *The ocean view has nothing on this.*

I kissed her neck and she hummed. "That feels so good."

"This top you're wearing has been tormenting me all day long. Now it's time for me to get my reward for being a good boy." I pulled the garment up along her body and dropped it to the floor. The black bra she had on, lace that barely contained her stunning breasts, had everything below my waist hot, tight, and on alert.

"It has?" She turned and looked up at me with those big blue eyes, her chest nestled between us.

I need her right now. "Yes." My brain stopped working—my dick was on duty now. I took off my shirt and pants in record time. The boxer shorts went right with the pants. No use wasting time. I reached around and unhooked her bra. Breasts. Lovely, lovely breasts. *In my mouth. Now*. I gripped her ribcage and teased her nipple with the tip of my tongue. She moaned sweetly.

One hand slid to her waist and shimmied down the knit skirt she was wearing. One feel of her lace panties and I had to look. *Oh shit*. Those had to go, too. *Now*.

My lips tore into hers. It felt as if I would never kiss her hard enough. On autopilot, as if I wasn't myself, I walked her backward until we were up against the door. *Claim her*. I grasped her hand and put it behind my neck, then reached down and cupped her ass, hoisting her up and bracing her back.

Her legs clamped around my waist. "Ooh. This is a new one," she purred.

Wait. Door sex? What are you doing? My brain decided to step in. "Do you think this will be okay? You know, for the baby?"

She nodded. "I think it's fine. The baby is still so small. Just don't drop me."

"Never." The mid-afternoon light glinted off her collarbone. I steeled myself, praying for restraint. "I don't know. Something about this seems wrong." I grunted when she licked her lower lip. "And something about it is incredibly hot." I eased my head back to see it all—her full breasts within reach of my mouth, her ripe little mound of a belly. "If I didn't want you so badly, I wouldn't even suggest it." My eyes continued to rove over her. *So sexy*. I reached under her ass, finding her wet already.

She closed her eyes as I rubbed in tiny circles. She hummed. I kissed her. Enough foreplay.

I eased my way in, wanting to be as gentle as possible. She surprised me when her eyes flew open. "Oh." A huge smile spread across her face. "Wow. That's different."

"You're okay?"

Her eyes closed again. "I'm better than okay."

She molded around me—intense, clinging heat that made it feel as if I might detonate. I sucked in a deep breath, grappling with the sublime way it felt to have her body around me. *That's it.* The air was sticky and sweet, her blonde hair stuck to her shoulders in tendrils, even a few draped down on to her chest. My body felt as though it was on fire, the need for her so unquenched that it had to be doused. And it wasn't as though we hadn't just made love the night before or had a quickie that morning, it was the freedom of the moment, away from everything at home—phones, demands. Away, from everything, for now.

Her breasts bounced when I popped her up to get a better grip on her now-slippery and sweaty body. *Careful.* Animal urges battled inside me, which I had to fight off—I didn't want to drive us both to our destination—I wanted to go sailing off a cliff, but she needed gentle. I would be nothing but careful. I ground against her slowly with every forward motion. She bucked her hips into me, moaning and gasping. Our wet and eager mouths slid all over each other, as we had the first night we made love, in this room, after an interminable wait.

"Oh God, Chris." Her eyes flashed open.

Is something wrong?

She pitched forward and bit my shoulder, digging into my biceps with her fingers. "Oh God, yes. Do that."

Everything's right.

The pressure in my groin was unmistakable. I was a whisper from rocketing into space, but I had to keep going, take my time, for her. Her ankles locked harder around my waist. The urge to unleash the beast inside me was overwhelming and still, I kept it controlled. *Slow. Slow. Slow.* She was tightening around me, which made my head swim. *Hold on. Hold on to her.* With an abrupt wave of sweet mercy, she gave way, knocking her head back against the wall, arching into me with such force that I thought I might fall over.

Every part of her body that touched mine hung on for dear life, especially the parts engaged in the release, which contracted around me in deep and powerful pulses. She squeezed the peak out of me—it rushed from my body in waves, deeply satisfying waves.

We were both breathing harder than we do at the end of a run. Claire's chest was heaving. There was no ignoring it, even after I'd just had my needs met. Round two would be soon, perhaps after a snack.

"That was incredible." She dragged her finger down the center of my chest. "I think you earn major husband bonus points for not only accomplishing sex against a door, but sex against a door with a pregnant woman."

She loosened the grip of her legs around me and I gently lowered her to the floor. I took her hand and towed her to the bed, where I threw back the covers. "As long as that wasn't too much for you, I will take all of the husband bonus points I can get."

She climbed into bed and I drew back the curtains. The sky was a brilliant pink and orange now that the sun was starting to set. "Trust me. That wasn't too much. It was just right."

The sound of the ocean rushed in as I opened the glass door out on to the terrace and stacked back the accordion doors, leaving that one wall of the bedroom open to the sea air. "It's been so cold at home. I've been looking forward to sleeping with the windows open." I took my place next to her on the bed and kissed her tenderly. "Are you hungry?"

"I'm always hungry. You know that."

"How the tides have turned." I placed another kiss on her forehead and scooted to the edge of the bed. "I'll find us a snack and bring it back."

"No, I'll come with you. Let me grab a t-shirt."

"You realize you don't need to wear a thing."

She gleamed. "You know I don't really do a lot of nudist activities."

"I think we should try as much of that as possible while we're here. It might be our only chance."

"True. Very true."

"Come on." I took her hand and led her out of the bedroom to the kitchen. "Food. Then more sex."

CHAPTER TWENTY-EIGHT

THE MORNING SUN brought the realization that Chris had done something he'd never managed to do before, which was saying a lot—he'd worn me out. My whole body was sore, especially my legs.

I rolled to my side and watched him sleep, his mouth slack and kissable. He was so peaceful, and who wouldn't be peaceful after the night we'd had? Five times? Six? I'd lost count. It was more than an impressive showing for a man his age, it was *Ripley's Believe It Or Not*-worthy.

He opened one eye, closed it, and smiled. His hand dove under the blue and white blanket and caressed the bare skin of my hip. "Morning, Mrs. Penman."

The corners of my mouth turned up, the only logical response. "Good morning husband of mine." Echoes of the waves crashing against the rocks below swirled around us.

"I like the sound of that." He opened his eyes again, shocking me with electric green. "Husband."

"I love it. I love you." *I still can't believe we're married.* The shadow of stubble along his jaw was so inviting. It made me hungry for him, not breakfast, even when my stomach was growling so loudly that it was audible above the din of the ocean.

"Sounds like we need to get you and the nipper some breakfast."

"Is it okay if I wear clothes?"

He shook his head in dismay. "Party pooper."

"Hey. I don't really want to make scrambled eggs in the nude. Sorry if that doesn't do it for me."

He climbed out of bed and found his boxer shorts on the floor. "This is all I'm wearing and I feel as though you shouldn't wear much more."

I tiptoed to our suitcase, pulling out one of his t-shirts. "How about this?"

"No knickers. It'll just slow us down later."

"It'll be a miracle if I don't develop a significant limp by the time we leave the island."

We ate breakfast by the pool—eggs, toast, fruit, and of course, bacon. Lots and lots of bacon.

"There's something wonderfully hedonistic about pigging out on bacon with your pregnant wife. I should have my own court jester." Chris sat back in his chair and rubbed his belly.

I had to admit that it was fun for the second time in my life to not worry too much about what I ate, although after five pieces of bacon, I did have concern for my cholesterol levels. "What should we do today?"

He sat up and leaned closer, looping my hair behind my ear, which I instantly undid with a shake of my head. "We could play farmer and the milkmaid."

I snickered. "Rock star and groupie?"

"Too far-fetched." He folded his napkin and placed it on the table before picking up our plates. "We could go to the beach. Do a bit of snorkeling."

"You want to hike to Colombier again?"

"I think that's better kept for another time. It's not a good idea for you to be up on that steep incline. If anything happened, we'd be far away from help."

I followed him into the kitchen. "A nap after that?"

"Followed by a rousing game of nurse and brain surgeon."

"You get to be a brain surgeon?"

"Don't be so sexist, Claire." He kissed me on the nose and slid his hand up the back of the t-shirt, caressing my bare bottom. "I'm the nurse. You're the brain surgeon."

Sure enough, we didn't make it out of the villa for several hours. The temptation to enjoy our privacy was too great, so we left behind a sink of dirty dishes to go skinny-dipping, ultimately ending up in several compromising positions on a chaise lounge. Thank goodness for cushions.

We arrived at the beach known as Petit Cul de Sac around three, once the sun had started to abate. One thing I'd learned about being on the island was that the middle of the day wasn't good for much more than sleeping, eating, and hiding from the constant barrage of the sun.

Chris had snorkel gear, so we didn't have to worry about renting anything. We grabbed our things from the car and started in from the beach. Into the warm, calm sea, a few dozen yards from land, the fish became more plentiful. It was so serene, floating along with the occasional kick of my flippers, following Chris and watching the marine life with the measured sound of my breathing in my ears. At one point, a sea turtle passed within a few feet of us, diving down, and Chris followed him. I stayed on the surface and watched as he and the massive creature had a playful interaction before Chris headed back up for air with a swift kick.

Chris took the spot next to me when we were back on the beach, sprawling out on his stomach. He collected my hand and rubbed the tips of my fingers with his thumb. "It felt great to get back in the water. We need to meet with the pool people first thing in January. As soon as it's warm enough, I want to get that hole dug."

I smiled—anything to make him happy. "Sounds like a plan."

As recently as a few weeks ago, most mentions of the long list of remaining house projects stressed me out. Throwing together a wedding in a few short months had seemed like such a monumental hurdle, that one more thing on our shared to-do list was frustrating brain clutter. Now we could concentrate on things like a swimming pool while we waited for the arrival of the baby.

"Oh." I clutched my bare belly. "Baby's moving."

Chris's hand flew to my stomach. "Oh, wow." He pushed his silver aviators up onto his forehead watching my stomach in utter fascination, placing his hand in different places and reacting to virtually every kick. "So cool." He pressed a kiss to my stomach then gazed up at me. "Have I told you lately how happy I am?"

I nodded, finding it almost unnecessary to reply with words. I knew exactly how happy he was because I could feel it from him every day. It radiated from him, pure and true. "Me too. I've never been happier."

"And you feel good about everything with the baby?"

"Yes, of course." *Why would he ask that?* "I'm excited. I can't wait for that first time the three of us can snuggle in bed together." My eyes began to mist. "It'll be incredible."

"Do you think Sam is going to be okay with everything?"

"I do. She's old enough to appreciate the little things about a baby that are so cool."

"Like the first smile?" His face lit up.

"Yes, or the first laugh, the first word. There are a lot of firsts ahead of us." I twined my fingers with his. "The best part is we get to experience them together."

"As hard as it's been for me to wait to become a dad, the timing couldn't be any better. I wouldn't have wanted to be on the road, knowing that I was missing out on all of the fun at home."

"What about Graham's plans for the band? Touring is pretty much a given at this point, isn't it? How's that going to work?"

He sat up and faced me, sitting with his legs crossed at the ankle. "We would have to have to figure that out. Place a strict limit on it. That's if I agree to it in the first place."

"The clock is ticking."

"Tell me about it. He was all over me at the wedding. He wants a decision now." He dragged his hand through his hair. "Actually, he wants a yes now. He'll be gutted if I say no."

"What about recording?"

"If you ask me, we should be the first band to make a record at my studio. We're only three months or so from it being ready. It'll be perfect. I won't have to miss any time with you and the baby."

"Huh. I hadn't actually thought about that, but that could work. If you can convince the guys."

"I have a feeling that they'll find the price pretty damn appealing."

"Sounds to me like you have a yes in the works for Graham."

He nodded. "Only if you're okay with it."

The prospects were thrilling, even if it meant more for us to juggle. "Of course. As long as the touring thing doesn't get out of hand. I can't watch you walk out the door for months at a time."

"No worries. That's not going to happen." Chris looked out over the water. "Looks like we're in for a beautiful sunset."

I rubbed my stomach. "You're going to think I'm sounding

like a broken record, but I'm starving. What are we going to do for dinner?"

"I made arrangements with Jean-Luc. There should be some cold salads and a big meat and cheese plate waiting for us back at the house."

I scooted forward and went in for a kiss. "Seriously. You are the most perfect man ever."

"I try." He dug his hand into my hair and kissed me, pressing his forehead into mine when the kiss was over. "You are seriously rocking the pregnant in a bikini thing." His eyes traveled down to my chest. "Tomorrow we go for pregnant and topless."

I shook my head. *What a goof.* "Let's pack up the car, Penman. We can talk about pregnant and topless on the way home."

Bouncing over the rocky, dusty roads in the jeep, sun setting, wind in our hair, I couldn't imagine any more perfect a picture. I died a little on the inside when he turned to me and unleashed his electric smile before returning his sights to the road. *Please, somebody pinch me.*

Chris dropped the beach bag on the teak bench outside our room and we went inside to change and clean up a bit before dinner.

"We probably should've taken our phones."

"No way. We're on our honeymoon."

I plucked mine from the bureau. The display lit up. "I have two missed calls from Sam. I hope everything is okay." I pressed the button for voicemail and set it to speaker.

"Mom—" Panic tinged Samantha's voice. Fire bloomed in my stomach, becoming worse when Chris rushed to my side. *This is bad.* "I know you and Chris just got there, but something is wrong with Grandpa. He fainted or something." *Fainted?* In the background, there were voices and commotion. Chris wrapped his arm around my shoulders. "I don't really know what happened. Bryce and I just found him on the bathroom floor. We called an ambulance. We're at the hospital with him right now. Bryce's family is coming to be with us. Oh my God, Mom. I need you to call me back right now."

CHAPTER TWENTY-NINE

"HE'S GOING to be okay. He's going to be okay." Claire stared out the window on the car ride from the airport to the hospital. She reached for my hand. "Tell me he's going to be okay."

I didn't want to make assurances that might later prove untrue, but I hated seeing her suffer. "I'm sure they're taking great care of him." I should've said what I was thinking, that I wanted to think that it wasn't serious, but that at his age and with the way he'd been acting over the last several months, it could be anything and it could be serious.

The sum total of the reports we'd been able to get out of Sam was that Richard was awake, confused, and that the doctors were doing a lot of tests. She told Claire that they'd put him in "one of those big machines" and that the doctor said she would know more by the time we got there. Julie was on her way from Virginia.

Aside from my worries about Richard, my bigger concern was Claire and the baby. She was a ball of worry. The thought of that kind of stress and strain on her body and mind was unnerving. It had to have an effect on the baby.

I wrapped my arm around her as we walked across the

pedestrian bridge from the hospital parking deck into the main building. We'd come straight from the airport, both wearing flip-flops in December. Neither of us had had the presence of mind to pack anything else when we'd left on our trip, not that anyone ever anticipated it would be cut short by a trip to the hospital.

We took an escalator up one flight and got on an elevator up to the sixth floor. Two nurses took the ride with us, chattering away about prospects for college basketball. I listened, mostly because I'd developed a taste for the sport, partly because thinking about what might be waiting for us when the elevator doors slid open was too much.

We checked in at the nurse's station and they directed us to Richard's room. What condition would he be in? Tubes in his nose, half-coherent, hooked up to countless machines? Intense dread came over me as I followed Claire into the room. Silly, but it felt as if I should go first, somehow shield her from what was coming.

There he lay in a pale blue hospital gown, cheeks flushed, what little hair he had in disarray. My shoulders dropped from relief.

"Dad." Claire rushed to Richard's side, took his hand.

Sam bolted out of her seat next to the bed. Julie turned to us, perched on the opposite side of the bed.

Richard smiled at Claire. "Hello, Ladybug." He looked up at me and shook his head. He was hooked up to an IV of clear fluid and what looked to be a heart-rate monitor. "I am so sorry you two had to cut your honeymoon short. I feel like an old fool right now."

I stood next to Claire. "What are the doctors saying?"

"Dr. Lesley should be in soon to go over the test results," Julie said. "For right now, the official diagnosis is dehydration."

Dehydration? We jumped on a plane for dehydration?

"I'd been at the studio all day and I hadn't brought any

water with me. Hadn't had a thing to eat all day either. I was preoccupied and forgot about it."

Bugger. Once again, he was working too hard, on my project no less.

"What is Dr. Stevens saying? Did anyone call him?"

Just then the door opened. A petite woman in a long ponytail wearing a doctor's coat and holding a chart stood in the doorway, talking to a nurse. "I'll be there in a few minutes." She strode in with a second doctor, a tall man in his twenties. The door closed. "Hello, everyone. I'm Dr. Lesley. This is one of our residents, Dr. Taylor." She scanned the room and zeroed in on Claire, reaching out to shake her hand. "You must be the other daughter."

"Claire."

"And you must be the son-in-law." She shook my hand. "Richard certainly is fond of you. I heard all about the big recording studio you two are working on. Sounds exciting." She stepped closer to Richard and clasped her hands behind her. "How are you feeling, Richard?"

"Honestly? I feel fine."

"Good." She brought out the chart and again scanned the room. "I'm ready to talk about these test results. Would you prefer if it was just us?"

"This is my family. They can stay."

"Okay then. All of the blood work came back normal for the most part. Your cholesterol is elevated, especially your triglycerides. We need to take care of that." She took a deep breath. "The more concerning part is the result of the MRI." She flipped open the chart and showed it to him. Both Claire and Julie craned their necks to see. My height allowed me the perfect view of a series of brain images on a single page.

Dr. Lesley took out a pen and circled a large white spot in

the center of one of the images. She spoke, but I couldn't make sense of it or of the white spot.

Richard's face blanched, but he otherwise didn't react. He nodded, staring at the chart as the doctor talked.

"Cancer?" Claire asked in a whisper, her voice shaking.

"We don't know that. We'd have to do a biopsy to determine that. There's a good chance it's benign, but we won't know for sure until we get in there. Unfortunately, the surgeon who really needs to see this is away for the holidays, but I've already got a call into him. He'll be able to better guess whether we can safely get to where the mass is."

I squeezed Claire's shoulder and she shook beneath my touch. *What a bloody nightmare.*

"I guess it was a lucky thing that you collapsed Mr. Abby. Otherwise, we might not have found this."

Lucky.

"I don't want anyone to get too overly alarmed right now," the doctor continued. "He's in good hands and worrying doesn't accomplish anything."

"He's been tired a lot." Claire looked up at the doctor. "He sometimes gets confused or forgets things."

"Now, Claire—" Richard started.

"That's normal. The mass presses on certain areas of the brain, which can affect cognition or make someone unusually tired. Brain tumors are much more common in people over age sixty-five, but so are those very same symptoms. They don't always indicate a serious condition."

"So what now?" Julie asked.

"Since it's so close to Christmas, as long as he's feeling well, he can go home tomorrow. We'll discuss a course of action in a few days. My biggest concern right now is the location of the mass. A lot of key body functions are controlled by that area of the brain."

"I don't want to do that." Richard shook his head. "I don't like the idea of anybody going in there and messing around with all of that."

"Let's not get ahead of ourselves, Mr. Abby. Let's wait and see what the rest of the team says." She made a few notes in his chart and closed the folder.

The doctors left. A deadly quiet fell on the room.

Claire looked at me, so helpless, clearly holding back emotions that were too much to let go in front of her father. "I need to use the bathroom." She squeezed my hand before she stepped in and closed the door.

"Dad, are you okay?" Julie asked.

"I'm not going to say I'm not surprised. I certainly am. But the doctor didn't seem ready to sign my death certificate or anything. I'm sure it'll be fine, Pumpkin." He patted her hand.

Sam was standing in stunned silence, not looking at her grandfather.

"You okay?" I asked her.

She nodded. "Yeah. I guess I should call Bryce. Let him know what happened."

"When did his family go home?"

"They left a little while after Aunt Julie got here."

"Make sure they know how much your mother and I appreciate what they did. I'm sure that wasn't an easy situation for you or Bryce. You both did a great job."

"Thanks. I'll tell him. I'm going to go call him now." She stepped out into the hall.

Soon after, Claire emerged from the bathroom, looking even more worried than she had when she'd gone in there. *I should never leave her alone. All she does is stew.* "You okay, hon?"

"Uh, yeah. I guess." Our gazes connected, the sadness in her eyes was palpable, like a punch in the stomach. "Well, actually, no. I'm not okay."

Julie came up behind her. "What's going on?"

I took Claire's hand. "What's wrong?"

Claire closed her eyes and opened them again. "I hate to say this, but somebody needs to take me to Obstetrics. I'm bleeding."

CHAPTER THIRTY

I GOT UP TO PEE, second-guessing my body's signals. The baby had woken me with a few kicks. That was a great sign. No cramping, another good sign. I went to the bathroom and was relieved when the toilet paper wasn't the slightest bit pink. *Merry Christmas.*

I glanced at the clock on Chris's bedside table. Eight-fourteen. The house was as quiet as could be, completely unlike every December 25th when Sam had been little. Time for a little more sleep.

I climbed back into bed and snuggled up to Chris, who stirred. "Everything okay?" He put his arm around me and pulled me closer.

"Yes. Everything is fine."

"Good." He pressed a kiss to my temple and began to doze off again. He'd slept so fitfully the last two nights it was of no surprise that he was tired.

At least we'd been at the hospital when the spotting had started, but neither Chris nor I handled it very well. He'd made it appear as though he was calm—smiled, held my hand, reassured me that everything was fine, but I could tell that he was flat-out panicking. I alternated between saying that everything would be okay and crying.

We were both able to relax a little bit when the doctor used the Doppler and we heard that frantic bunny-hop of a heartbeat.

"The baby sounds perfect," the doctor had said.

"Thank God," Chris had buried his head in his hands, then leaned over and kissed me on the forehead.

Luckily, that one episode was light and only lasted for a few hours. The doctor said it could've been attributed to a number of things—travel, sex, stress. Perhaps a combination of them all, which led Chris to declare that we would be going nowhere, I would be sheltered from stress whenever possible, and we would not be having sex again until the baby arrived. I promised him a fight on that last point. Regardless of the cause, I was under strict instructions to spend as much time in bed or with my feet up as much as possible for the next week or two. Rest. Rest. Rest. Doctor's orders.

We were awoken by a gentle knock at our door around ten. "Yes?" I asked.

Sam poked her head in. "Are you guys awake?"

"Yeah, honey. Come in."

Sam took a seat at the end of the bed. "I checked on Grandpa. He's already dressed and read the newspaper."

Of course. I noted the aroma of coffee in the air. "Good. Glad to hear that. How did he seem this morning?"

"Happy. He's anxious to open Christmas gifts."

"He is?"

"I guess we'd better get up then." Chris sat up in bed and turned to me. "Unless you'd rather stay in bed. We could open gifts up here."

"Don't be silly." I threw back the covers. "I'm fine."

"You're sitting in the chair with the ottoman." Chris shuffled into the bathroom.

I rolled my eyes and grabbed a hoodie from the closet, a bit too snug when I zipped it. "Is Bryce coming over this afternoon? I thought we could make hot cocoa and popcorn? Maybe light a fire?"

"He'll be over around three." Sam smiled, but her overall demeanor was sad. "Thanks for including him. That was really nice."

"I don't know what we would have done if he and his parents hadn't been here to help you when Chris and I were away." I still felt rotten about the way I'd behaved about Bryce at Thanksgiving, not to mention my general attitude toward his parents. They'd come to the rescue at a time when Chris and I were not able. I was nothing but thankful.

"Bryce said they really liked the gift basket Chris sent over. He said they pigged out on it all day yesterday."

Chris came waltzing out of the bathroom. "Glad to hear it." He rubbed his hands together. "Let's go open gifts."

The entire downstairs looked incredible. Chris had purchased a tree and Bryce and Sam spent the morning decorating it the day my dad came home from the hospital. They'd put out my mom's old nativity scene and hung her 60s-era glittery plastic snowflakes in pale aqua, lime green, and pink in the windows overlooking the backyard. Still no white stuff on the ground, but that was usual for Christmas in North Carolina. No snow, just cold.

Chris had a throw blanket at the ready. "Claire?" He nodded at the sofa.

"Thanks." I took my seat. The invalid treatment wasn't my favorite, but keeping the baby healthy was paramount, and I didn't dare make a fuss about it.

My dad came in from the kitchen and gave a mug to Chris. "Merry Christmas everyone."

"Morning, Dad. How are you feeling this morning?"

"Never felt better." He took a seat in the armchair next to my end of the sectional. His color was indeed better than it'd been the day before.

"Have you had any water yet today?"

"Two glasses."

I smiled. "Good man."

"Speaking of water." Chris handed me a big glass. "Are you hungry yet?"

"I wouldn't say no to an English muffin."

"I love these pet names you give me, darling, but I was talking about breakfast." He winked. "Jam?"

"Yes, please."

"Sammy, you going to play Santa Claus this morning?" Dad leaned forward, rubbing his hands together. He'd loved this day when I was a kid, serving eggnog and putting on the Andy Williams Christmas album on the record player in the living room. Even better, he'd play Dean Martin and serenade my mother with *Baby It's Cold Outside*. It was one of the only days of the year he ever seemed to have fun.

Sam was thumbing away on her cellphone, which she tucked into her pocket. "Sure."

She began to hand out packages while dad reminded us that we were to open them one at a time, and only when it was our turn. Normally, this would have drawn ire from me. Today, I cherished it.

Chris brought my breakfast and took the seat next to me. "I can't wait to see what I got for everyone. I can never remember."

My dad looked at Chris quizzically then started to laugh. "You crack me up, young man."

"Young man? Is that my Christmas gift? Because nobody's called me a young man since the 80s."

I elbowed him and he kissed me on the top of my head.

Doing things my dad's way made opening gifts a process. In this case, it took nearly two hours. We admired each other's new belongings—a sweater and some country music CDs for my dad. It was quite sweet of Chris to bring himself to buy any music that he truly abhorred. Chris was thrilled with the vintage turntable I'd found for him and even more excited by the stash of vinyl LPs that Sam had spent weeks looking for in local record shops. My dad and Sam chipped in on a package of prenatal massages for me, which I couldn't wait to use. Sam was the recipient of many gift cards, her clearly stated preference.

Chris had apparently done some unsupervised shopping at Tiffany's, giving me a pair of diamond-studded platinum hoop earrings.

"They're so beautiful. Thank you." I craned my neck to kiss him on the cheek.

"Not as beautiful as you, but those poor chaps at Tiffany's can only do so much."

Sam made a noise. "Oh brother."

"Oh, shush now Samantha." Chris produced a small package from next to him on the couch. "You'd better open this last gift. It's from your mother and me."

She grabbed it from his hands and tore at the paper. "What is it?" Her eyes lit up when she removed the blue box nestled inside the plain cardboard box he'd wrapped. "You hid the Tiffany blue?"

"I did." Chris nodded. "I'm clever like that."

She pulled at the white ribbon and lifted the lid, which gave me goose bumps. "Oh my God. A bracelet. The same charm bracelet mom has." She jumped up from the floor, grasping the bracelet and giving Chris a hug. "Thank you so much. I love it."

She wedged herself between us on the couch, turning to me. "It's so cool. We match now."

"Here, let me help you put it on." I took the silver linked bracelet and looped it around her wrist, hooking the clasp, remembering how much it had meant when Chris had given me the very same piece of jewelry. "It looks lovely." It really did look lovely—I held my own arm out, and we compared them side-by-side.

"Mom, are you crying?" She dropped her head, looking me in the eye.

It wasn't full on sobbing, but I couldn't help but be choked up. I nodded, tears misting my vision as I looked at my dad.

Sam knocked her head against mine. "It's okay, Mom. It's just a bracelet."

Chris rubbed my back. My dad looked down into his lap, pretending to read the back of one of his new CDs.

"It's okay. I'll be okay." I took a deep breath and listened to my mom. *I know, Mom. You're right.* Although the future was uncertain, at least we had Christmas Day.

CHAPTER THIRTY-ONE

ON A CAREFULLY CONSTRUCTED mountain of pillows in our bed, Claire had her early January call with Laura Simmons. I didn't want to hover, but I wanted to be there if she needed me. Plus, we would be heading for our first ultrasound appointment after she was off the phone.

"Yeah. Okay. No problem," Claire said, forty-five minutes after the call had begun. At face value, the words were of a person who was totally on top of her game. The tone with which she said them made me realize how concerned she was with keeping Laura happy. She scribbled notes, nodded her head. "Sounds good. Okay. Yes. I'll get on that right away."

I sat on the edge of the bed and folded my arms across my chest. I could see the stress on her face. Hell, I could see it in the way she was holding the damn pen. The urge to take the phone out of her hand and beg her to quit was overwhelming. She wanted this—no way around it, but it was precisely what the doctor had told her to avoid—stress.

"Great. Thanks for everything, Laura. I'll get all of this to you next week." Claire neatly placed the phone on the bed when she hung up.

My inclination was to launch it across the room. "You realize this is what the doctor warned you about."

"I'm in bed, aren't I?" She rubbed her forehead, tossing her notes to the side. "It's fine. I just need to take a deep breath." She did that, exhaling loudly. "See? I feel better already."

"You aren't fooling me. I know exactly how much stress you're under and I don't like it. Not one bit." *Why does everything have to happen at the wrong time?* If only she'd been offered the job a year from now, when we could deal with it. "You need to tell her that you're under a doctor's orders to take it easy."

"Okay. I'll mention it."

"Why am I having a hard time believing you?"

"I'll do it. I just need to find the right time. I don't want to be the needy pregnant woman."

I inched closer and took her hand. "You aren't needy. You're growing our baby in your body. That's the most important thing right now, not a job."

Her lips formed a thin line. "That's easy for you to say. Your career doesn't depend on what your body is or isn't doing at a particular time."

So bloody stubborn. "True, but I can't do much about human biology at this point. This is the reality of the situation."

"You're right. I'll talk to her. And I'll do a better job of not getting quite so worked up about it."

I hated myself for the words that had formed on the tip of my tongue, so I swallowed them instead. *You should quit this job. You can get any job you want. Don't jeopardize our child for a stupid job.* "Ready to head up to the hospital?"

"Yep. I gotta pee first."

We were at the doctor's office with a minute to spare and they brought us back to the ultrasound room right away. Claire got comfortable on the bed in the dark room while Rhonda, the technician, tapped away at a keyboard on the ultrasound machine.

As much as this appointment was a big deal, having Claire leave the house worried me. Still, I'd waited a long time to carry around one of those photographs in my wallet—I was excited for that part.

"Okay, Mrs. Penman, if you could slide your top up and inch down those pants, we'll get a look at baby." She squeezed a liquid onto the ultrasound wand. "Just a little bit of gel. Sticky, but it shouldn't be cold." Carefully, she placed the instrument on Claire's belly, tapping away at the keyboard with her other hand and looking at the monitor. "Okay, then. Can you see, Dad?"

I scooted forward in my chair and squinted.

"There's a hand." She pointed to the screen and my throat tightened. Tiny fingers. A slender arm. The baby kicked. "Oh, goodness." Rhonda turned to Claire and smiled. "Somebody is active today."

We all laughed, but a tear rolled down my face. I'd never been particularly impressed by ultrasound pictures, but I realized then why the dads were always so thrilled to show them off. They'd seen their baby move.

"That was the leg, obviously," Rhonda said. "Do you want to know the baby's sex?"

"Can you tell?" I leaned forward, scanning the frame for some noticeable sign of...something...a tiny penis, I suppose.

"That wasn't the question, Dad." Rhonda shook her head in feigned admonishment.

Claire and I looked at each other. "No," we said in unison. A big part of me had wanted to say "yes", but that was the temptation of the moment, like standing in front of a bakery display case packed to the very limit with pastries and cakes. We'd agreed we would wait, and wait we would.

Rhonda nodded and smiled. "The old-fashioned way. I love it." She moved the paddle and you could see the baby's head, large sloping forehead, adorable button nose, the way he or she moved its neck and torso in its weightless world. "I need to take some measurements here. This will help us determine if we need to do any further genetic testing, especially with the advanced maternal age."

Good God. That phrase. I brought Claire's hand to my lips and kissed it.

She looked at me for an instant, then immediately turned back to watch the baby. "It's amazing, isn't it?"

"It is. It truly is."

"I mean, wow. We made a human." She pointed at the screen. "And look how cute the nipper is now. On a screen. Just imagine what it'll be like when he or she is finally here."

"I'm trying to wrap my head around it at this very moment."

She squeezed my hand so hard I thought I might lose a digit. "I was excited before, but now I can't wait." She turned back to me. "I wish the nipper were here now."

"That would be wonderful, but we'd be nothing but ill-prepared."

"True. We need to get the shopping done. This week." She turned back to the screen.

"Online shopping." *We're not leaving the house for that.*

"I need to read the reviews of the new car seats. And strollers. We're going to need to make a decision on a crib."

The warmth building inside me was beyond measure. I'd waited so long to do these things. The fact that I got to do them with Claire made it perfect. "If there's anything you and I can accomplish together, it's shopping."

The procedure continued—every instant was pure entertainment, endlessly fascinating. At times, the baby would go mostly still, but there was always something in motion, a little wiggle here or there. *Good thing I'm not the one who's pregnant. I'd be staring at my belly all day long. Oh, and the boobs. Yeah, the boobs. Those would be hard to leave alone.*

The baby yawned. Such a normal, mundane thing and yet Claire and I both laughed, tears forming in our eyes, beaming at each other in astonishment. My heart felt as though it was ten times its normal size, so full of joy and relief, it was impossible to quantify. *What a day. What a beautiful day.*

"I'll print out some pictures for you to take home. I know Dad wants some for his wallet. I can email you digital files, too, for you to keep on your phone."

"We'll take whatever you have to give us," I said.

"That's the spirit." Rhonda placed the ultrasound device back in its cradle. She handed Claire a few paper towels. "This is to wipe that gel off your belly."

I helped Claire with the cleanup, taking her hand to help her sit. The smile on her face was priceless. Surely mine couldn't have been worth any less.

"The doctor will call you with any concerns. Congratulations."

We walked out of the clinic, hand in hand. I felt as if I was walking on air. "That was so much fun."

"It was, wasn't it?" Claire knocked into me with her shoulder. Ahead of us, a man in a white doctor's coat was getting out of a steely blue car. "Dr. Stevens?" Claire asked.

The man removed his sunglasses and looked at her.

Claire held out her hand. "Dr. Stevens, I'm Claire Penman, I mean, Abby." She shook her head. "I called you in October about my dad, Richard. Remember? I was concerned he'd been so forgetful and tired and he didn't want me to come with him to his appointment."

"Claire. Oh, my. It's nice to see you." He then seemed to put two and two together. "Are you?" He pointed at me. "And?"

She laughed. "Yes, I got married. This is my husband Christopher. We're expecting in May."

"That is wonderful news." He shook my hand heartily. "So nice to meet you. Truly wonderful. How old is your daughter now?"

"Samantha's about to turn eighteen, if you can believe that. She's going to graduate from high school this year."

"Wow. Time sure does fly, doesn't it?"

"It does." Claire nodded. "You know, I wanted to thank you for seeing my dad. I was wondering if Dr. Lesley shared the information with you about his collapse and MRI a few weeks ago."

Dr. Stevens knocked his head to the side. "Claire, he cancelled the appointment."

She dropped my hand. "He what?"

"Your dad never came to see me."

CHAPTER THIRTY-TWO

I WANTED to be furious with my dad for blowing off his doctor's appointment, but Chris was quick to remind me that getting upset wouldn't do any good now. My mom sided with Chris, imploring me to cut my dad some slack.

I knocked on his bedroom door when we got back from the ultrasound. No answer. I knocked a second time. Again, no answer. Anger quickly changed to worry. I knocked a third time and poked my head in. There he was, flat out on the bed. My heart pounded. I stepped closer. *Is he? Oh my God.* He rolled on to his back and snorted before slipping back into sleep. *Fucking A.*

I tiptoed to his bed and sat on the edge. Aside from the slight bit of disruption from his nap, the bedclothes were in perfect order. His entire room was like a military barracks decorated by Old Mother Hubbard, everything tidy, shipshape, all of it from another time.

The bureau had a single black comb, the kind you get for free from the barber. His watch was there, a book about the Revolutionary War from the library, a man's handkerchief neatly folded. Atop one of my mom's doilies was a framed photo of my parents on their wedding day, standing at the altar of the Cathedral of St. Paul, St. Paul, MN. Newlywed Sara Abby clutched her bouquet. Richard Abby smiled like a little boy who couldn't have been more proud that he'd lost his first tooth.

It was getting late, close to dinnertime. If he didn't get up, he wouldn't be able to get back to sleep tonight.

I shook his arm. "Dad?"

He opened his eyes. At first, it seemed as though he didn't know who I was, which was deeply concerning, but then I noticed that he didn't have his glasses.

"I thought it best to wake you." I picked up his glasses from the bedside table and gave them to him. "Chris is ordering some take-out for dinner. I thought you might be hungry." I crossed my legs.

He blinked and slowly sat up. "Oh, okay. That sounds great. How did the ultrasound go?"

I rested my hand on my growing belly. "It went great, actually. We have some photos to show you."

"Good. I can't wait to see the little nipper." He carefully swung his legs off the bed and slipped his feet into his brown leather shoes. He bent over, his right hand shaking as he held the laces.

Fuck. I can't be mad at him. "Dad, let me help." I knelt down on the floor in front of him.

"You don't have to tie my shoes."

"And you don't need to wear shoes in the house at all if you don't want to." I took a deep breath. "I ran into Dr. Stevens at the clinic today."

"Oh."

"He told me you never came to see him." I sat back on my heels, looking up at him.

He avoided eye contact, brushing at his pant leg with his

good hand. "Oh. That. Well, you see, I was very busy at the studio that day and I just couldn't break away."

"You knew how much it meant to me that you get a check-up. I've been worried about you. And it turns out that I was right to worry."

"You know I don't like doctors. Didn't like them much when I was a boy and then when your mom got sick, well, I just avoid them like the plague. Those few days I spent in the hospital before Christmas were terrible."

"Dad, if you'd just gone to the doctor like I'd asked you to, you might not be facing this right now." I planted my hand on the bed to pull myself back to standing.

"I don't think you can say that. I seriously doubt Dr. Stevens would've done an MRI."

"And you don't know that."

"It wouldn't have changed the fact that I have a tumor." He picked at his fingernail. "Do you want the truth?"

"Of course."

He nodded in contrition. "I knew that I was sick."

I wasn't sure of what he'd said. "You what?"

"I knew that I was sick. I could feel it. Don't think I wasn't well aware of how erratic my behavior had become. I just didn't do anything about it."

"But why?"

"I told you. I hate doctors. I hate the thought of being sick." He shrugged. "I didn't want to face it. So, I didn't. Guess you could say I buried my head in the sand."

Talk about burying heads in the sand. I longed to do that very thing. "Wow. I can't even fathom that."

"It's the truth." He ambled to the bureau, pressing a finger to the top of the wedding picture and picking up the comb to neaten his hair.

"Dad, you realize you're going to have to get over your fear of doctors really quick. We need to talk about this biopsy. Maybe chemotherapy and radiation if it's cancer."

"I've been thinking and I've decided not to do it."

I narrowed my focus on his reflection in the mirror. "Not do what?"

"No biopsy. No anything. I don't want to become an invalid or lose the ability to speak. I don't want to become a burden. I certainly don't want to go through what your mother did with chemotherapy."

The burden speech was a given with my dad. He hated having to depend on anyone for anything. "Dad, they've made a lot of advances in cancer treatment in the last seventeen years, and we don't even know if it is cancer. It might be benign."

He turned. "I hear what you're saying, but it doesn't matter to me. It really doesn't. You know, part of me was relieved when we found out about the tumor."

"Relieved?"

He sighed. "At least I knew what was wrong."

"See? There you go." I threw up my hands. "The miracle of modern medicine. I'm telling you, Dad, they've made a lot of advancements in two decades. It doesn't have to be the same for you as it was for Mom."

"Hold on a minute." His eyes blazed with fiery conviction. "I'm not going to risk living out my days in a hospital. That's no way to go. You know, your mother told me dozens of times that if she could've had anything, it would've been to be able to just live what was left of her life. Stay busy. Have a purpose. Enjoy her family."

My heart pounded. Of course my mom hadn't been happy at the end, miserable in a hospital bed. It'd never occurred to me that she'd had a choice in any of it, and perhaps it hadn't occurred to her either until it was too late.

He sat next to me on the bed and patted my knee. "If there

was any good in your mother leaving us, it's that it gave me a better understanding of this situation." He shook his head. "More than anything, Jellybean, you need to understand that in my eyes, this isn't all bad. If nothing else, it takes me one step closer. I'm happy for that."

"Closer to what?"

"Closer to being with your mom again."

CHAPTER THIRTY-THREE

FEBRUARY CAME with a bitter wind and snow flurries, but I tried to remain positive. At least it wasn't January. January had been a crazy mess.

Not cold—in fact, January had been unseasonably warm, enough so that the backhoes were at the house starting the hole for the pool. I watched out the kitchen window above the sink, working on my third cup of coffee. Funny, but I thought I would've been nothing but excited about breaking ground, but with Claire on modified bed rest due to more spotting, and Richard living on borrowed time, the gray morning matched much of the immediate future.

I cycled through thoughts much as the yellow machinery dug away. The man operating the digger worked methodically, with purpose, knowing exactly what to do. I almost envied him, having a life where you show up for work, do exactly what is expected of you—in this case, dig a hole. At the end of the day, you have a perfectly serviceable spot for some wealthy bastard to put in a pool, and you go home to your wife and kids, put up your feet, have a pint, go to sleep and start it all over the next day.

The reality was that I'd never survive such an existence. As weary as the drama made me, there was always some part of me that craved the excitement of change, even uncertainty, although the kind of uncertainty hanging over us was the kind we all fear.

My phone buzzed with a text. I took another sip of coffee, peering down at my phone on the granite counter. *Any update?* I hit the power switch to blacken the screen. Graham. *It's bloody six in the morning on the West Coast. What is he doing up?*

Graham was becoming the thorn in my side, constantly niggling me about every last detail. I'd agreed that we should record a new album. *If* that went well and *if* we found a new record label, I had agreed that I would do some limited touring. Limited. Only the US for now, perhaps a European festival, and I'd need at least two days off a week to fly home to be with Claire and the baby.

But first, the recording—the band had agreed that doing it at my new studio was the best option. We wouldn't have to record on anyone's schedule but our own, on anyone's dime at all except perhaps mine, since I at least had to keep the lights on. The advantage for me was that I'd have something newsworthy around which to announce the new studio and I wouldn't have to be away from Claire.

The studio was yet to be completed and there was no strict timetable—not a situation Graham favored. Once he had his mind set on something, he wanted to know the what, why, where, and when as soon as possible. Preferably yesterday. With Richard noticeably declining while ignoring his physical state, I could give Graham and the rest of the band everything but a definite when. "We're very close to finishing," was the best I could offer.

"Up and at 'em, I see." Richard shuffled into the kitchen.

It's after nine. "I am." He'd always been the first one up in the morning, now it was me, mostly because I rarely slept. Imagine my dismay the first time I awoke to a perfectly quiet house and realized I did not yet know how to operate our new coffeemaker. "They're out there digging the hole." I nodded in the direction of the backyard.

"That's good news." Richard had taken a seat at the kitchen table and was scanning the newspaper headlines. The ruffling sound of the newsprint told me exactly how much his right hand was trembling. I didn't even have to look. "You need me to go out there? Make sure they're following those lines they marked in the dirt?"

I set my mug in the sink and got out a clean one for Richard. "They seem to have it well in hand, but I'll let you know if anything changes." I brought him his coffee and took a seat at the table. "We have a long day ahead of us. Are you sure you're up for this?"

The insult and surprise on his face was as if I'd asked if he remembered what his name was. "You and Claire act as if I'm incapable of doing things. I am fine. I feel great this morning."

"Okay." I studied his face as he returned to his reading. It was impossible to know what he was thinking half of the time. I was still shocked he'd refused to seek any treatment, and then again, I wasn't. There was unquestionably a dignity in living life on his terms. "I'll need to run back to the house a few times to check on Claire, bring her lunch."

"Not a problem. I can handle things on my own just fine."

That was the tricky part—as far as Richard was concerned, he was still in charge of the project, but at this point, it was too much for him to deal with. He got tired, sometimes confused. That meant I had to do his work and make him think that he was in charge, asking questions I already knew the answer to so that he could consult his clipboard and tell me what was what. He frequently gave me the wrong answer.

We arrived at the studio a half-hour later. The up-fit of the space was essentially finished. There was still some trim carpentry to do, but we had walls with paint—a light gray, and soundproofing. There were doors and lighting and carpet. The reception area was turning out remarkably well with the help of a local interior designer and the band lounge was even cooler—a ridiculously large flat-screen TV, massive black leather couches, plenty of places to put up your feet.

The first wave of equipment was on-site, with more to come today. I'd hired some local musicians to help me load in and install some of the more basic gear, and a local engineer would be coming tomorrow to assemble the guts of the mixing board, which had been delivered in about eighty different boxes. The main board unit alone was a behemoth, over twelve feet long, having arrived in the largest crate I'd ever seen. It also weighed a ton.

"We need to be careful here guys." Richard watched as two of the other guys and I proceeded with the massive crate atop two four-wheeled freight dollies. "This is a very expensive piece of equipment. Take that corner before you go down the hall very carefully." He may have been on the decline, but he had no problem barking orders.

I saw the problem the instant we turned the corner in the extra-wide, main hall. "Richard, there's no way this is going to make it through the door into the control room. The angle is all wrong."

He came up behind me, peering over the top of his glasses. "What in the world?" He scratched his head, flipped through the pages of the all-mighty clipboard.

"It's not going to fit." I slumped back against the wall. *Fuck.*

"This can't be right."

"Look on the specs. Where was the door supposed to go?" I

grabbed a metal tape measure from the floor, unrolled a few inches and handed the loose end to one of the guys.

"Six feet, six inches," Richard answered.

"I'm telling you, they put the door in the wrong place." I watched as my helper reached the doorway with the end of the tape measure, then looked down to read our fate. "Seven feet, six inches." My stomach sank as the metal tape recoiled.

"That's not possible." Richard took the loose end of the tape measure and walked backward to the door, as if the empirical data might change if he was handling things.

"I'm telling you. It's not going to fit." Again, the numbers told the story. "Seven feet, six inches."

"Darn it all." Richard let his end of the tape measure go and it snapped against my thumb, slicing into it.

"Fuck."

"Oh, good lord. Chris, I'm sorry."

"It's fine." The cut was a thin, pink line with some redness around it. "I think it's just a nick." Blood oozed. "Or not. I need a tissue or a paper towel or something." I clamped my mouth over the tender skin between my thumb and index finger.

"Get him some toilet paper," Richard snapped. He again flipped through the pages of the damn clipboard.

"I don't understand. The framers must have made a mistake when they roughed in the opening for the door."

My hand throbbed. "You were supposed to be double-checking their work. We talked about this one detail dozens of times."

"I know that, Chris. I thought we were good to go. I must've missed something." He scratched his temple, flipping back and forth between two pieces of paper. His hand shook, making the paper rattle.

One of the guys came rushing up with a roll of toilet paper, shoving it in my good hand.

"Thanks." I unrolled the tissue, pressing it against the cut, which stung like hell. *Shit.* "We can't send the board back. We waited three months for the thing. It's one of the best you can buy. We're going to have to tear out the door and move it a foot closer to the corner. Hell, move it two feet to be safe."

Richard slumped down into a folding chair. "I am so sorry."

"Guys," I said, to our helpers. "Why don't you knock off early for lunch?" I reached into my wallet with my good hand and pulled out a hundred-dollar bill. "Here, my treat. The place down the block has a great beer list." They started for the door. "Try to be back by one."

The room was dead quiet. Richard was visibly shaken.

I crouched down next to him and placed my hand on his knee. "Rich, look. It's not the end of the world. It's a problem. We fix it. End of story."

"This is going to delay us by at least a week. There's electrical in that wall. Then we have to get the framers, the drywall guys back out, the painters."

"Yep. And those guys all need the work. It's not a big deal. We'll get it done."

"You'll have to reschedule the engineer for the board assembly."

My to-do list was now officially a sore subject. "I'll talk to him. Don't worry."

"You've got your band mates waiting on you."

"They're big boys. They can wait." *Graham is going to give birth to a litter of kittens.*

"I really messed up. I can't believe I let this happen." Any light in his eyes was gone—the gross disappointment he held for himself was plain.

Bright side. Where's the bright side? "Think of it this way. It's more time for us to work on this project together. You know, going out to lunch, guy time. That's not all bad, is it?"

He smiled, only one corner of his mouth going up. "You're a hell of a guy, Chris." His lower lip trembled slightly. "You're like a son to me, you know."

I squeezed his knee and patted it, remembering what Claire had said to me when we went for our run on Thanksgiving Day. "I hope you know I love you like a dad."

CHAPTER THIRTY-FOUR

THE FRONT DOOR SLAMMED. Sam screamed.

Oh my God. "What's wrong?" My heart thundered as I craned to see where she was.

"I got in." She ran into the living room, waving a letter. "I got in. I actually got into NYU."

Shit. Okay, back to breathing. "That is so wonderful, honey. Congratulations." I was about to get up, but she fell to her knees in front of me, baby blues brimming with jubilation. *Wow. NYU. Good thing I have Chris around to help pay for this stuff.*

"I can't believe it." She shook her head, unfolding the letter and scanning it.

"I believe it. I totally believe it." Relief washed over me. *She's okay.* Even better—she'd gotten into her dream school and her dream program, studying dramatic writing in the school of Film & Television. Thankfully, she'd be spending the next four years in the same time zone, a short hour-long flight away. "You've worked so hard. You deserve it."

"And if Bryce gets into Harvard, I won't be that far from him."

"Uh huh." *That's a mighty big if.*

Chris strolled into the room, buttoning the cuff of his shirt. "What's all the excitement?"

"Sam got into NYU." I watched as the pair embraced.

"Wonderful." Chris patted her on the back. "We should order in some dinner after we get back from childbirth class."

Sam's eyes pled with me. "Mom. You don't still expect me to stay here with Grandpa."

"Sorry, honey. I know the timing isn't great."

Her shoulders drooped. "Even after I just got my big news?"

I closed my laptop and set it next to me on the couch. "I can't do anything about when the class is."

"But I want to call Bryce. Go out and celebrate." She bounced on her toes, bugging her eyes, as if that might help me understand how earth shattering it would be to miss time with Bryce.

She was back to spending unearthly amounts of time with him, always at his house, never at ours. I was fairly certain it wasn't because of Chris or me—we'd done our best to make Bryce feel welcome. I could only attribute it to an inability to cope with what was going on with her grandfather. They had once been chums, albeit with a shade of feigned reluctance on Sam's part. Now she hardly looked at him, avoided conversation.

"Then invite Bryce over here."

"I don't want to. I want to go to his house."

I shrugged. "What do you want me to do?" I glanced over my shoulder and lowered my voice. "I don't feel right about leaving him alone."

"Mom, it's my birthday tomorrow and everything. This doesn't seem fair."

"Somebody should stay in case something happens. It can't be me or Chris, so you're the only other choice."

She blew out an exasperated breath. "How long will you be gone?"

"The class is two hours."

"Aren't you supposed to be in bed?"

How she loves to turn this stuff back on me. "I have permission from the doctor."

Chris tapped his watch. "We should probably get going."

I looked at Sam. "We have to go."

"I can't believe I have to babysit Grandpa."

"Samantha Jane." I hated myself for busting out the middle name, but she was pushing a lot of buttons. "Don't let him hear you say that. And you know that I don't ask that much of you, but I need you to do this one thing."

"I suppose you're going to want me to babysit the real baby when it arrives too."

Chris's voice came from behind me. "Sam. Please don't talk to your mother like that. She can't handle the stress." It pleased me to hear Chris take a parental stance. Most of the time, he was putty in her hands. "It's only for a few hours and then you can take your mom's car for the rest of the day. I'll give you money for gas."

And we're back to being putty. My car was practically Sam's at this point anyway, since I wasn't supposed to go anywhere on my own. "Please, Sam. Just this one thing. For me."

She stared up at the ceiling and shook her head. "Yes, ma'am."

Great. Ma'am. Serves me right for going with Samantha Jane. "Thank you."

We arrived at the hospital's wellness center a few minutes late, and it took us a while to find the classroom in the maze of hallways on the second floor.

"Welcome," a woman in a flowing purple skirt and white

blouse said. "I'm Cathy. I take it you're here for the childbirth class?"

It was a reasonable assumption, considering that I was taking on the shape and size of a blimp. "Yes. Hi. I'm Claire. This is my husband, Chris."

"Wonderful. Here are a few handouts." She handed Chris a fat manila envelope. "You can go ahead and have a seat on the floor. Dad, if you'll sit with your back against the wall and your knees bent, we'll let Mom recline between your legs. We're going to start with some deep breathing exercises."

The room was a large rectangle, covered in low-pile office carpet, with no furniture except a table for Cathy's papers. Several couples were already there, sitting as we'd been instructed.

"For a minute there, I thought Cathy was suggesting a new sex position," Chris muttered in my ear. He eased himself on to the floor and scooted back to the wall. He held out his hand, inviting me to join him. "Ready, Mom? Be careful." His sweet smile was enough to help me set aside my annoyance with Sam.

I lowered myself to one knee, then the other, planting my hands on the floor and turning over to my butt.

"Lie back, darling," he whispered into the back of my head. He put his arms under mine, cradling the sides of my belly with both hands. "This is exciting. Another step closer."

The baby kicked and I smiled. Sure, it wasn't much fun when they got big and started stomping on your bladder, but it was a reminder that everything was A-Okay. Virtually nothing was A-Okay these days. At least the baby was happy.

Cathy clapped her hands and rubbed them together, stepping to the middle of the room. "So glad to have everyone here today. Before we get started, I'd like to go around the room and have everyone tell us their first names and the baby's due date."

There were about ten other couples, so this was a fairly

quick process and a fun one at that, since I liked hearing when people were set to deliver. Most people mentioned whether they were having a boy or a girl. Chris and I still felt good about our decision, even though it was torture to wait. I really wanted a boy. I was fairly certain Chris did too, although he held fast with his claim that he didn't care. He only wanted a healthy baby.

As our turn came closer, it struck me how much younger everyone else was—fresh-faced, devoid of wrinkles. The only exception was a stunning couple opposite us, Robert and Bobbi. They looked as though they were closer to our age bracket. At least we might not be the only ones in the advanced maternal age boat.

When our turn came, Chris took the lead. "I'm Chris, and this is my lovely bride, Claire."

I blushed and waved. "Hi. It's nice to meet everyone."

"Our baby is due May 27th," he continued. "We don't know what we're having, but we are one hundred percent certain it will either be a boy or a girl."

The entire class laughed, except Cathy, who merely smiled. *Yeah, she's probably heard that one before.*

"We're going to start with some relaxation techniques," she said. "For the moms, I want you to close your eyes and focus on tensing and then releasing your muscles as you travel the length of your body. Start with your feet, then your ankles, then your calves and so forth. With each relaxation, I want you to focus on sinking into your partner. Put your weight on them."

I closed my eyes. Despite this being my second time giving birth, I'd been so embarrassed after attending one childbirth class on my own that I'd never gone back. Much of this was new to me. After relaxation techniques, Cathy described the stages of labor, how to recognize when it was starting.

"Dads, your number one job during labor and delivery is to

remember what we're doing." Cathy paced around the room. "When she's going through contractions, it'll be difficult for her to recall the various breathing and relaxation methods. That is where you save the day. Everything we cover in class is in the handouts. Be sure you review them and take them with you to the hospital."

Chris seemed to hang on her every word and didn't even goof around when she talked about having sex to induce labor. I was proud of him, although I was waiting for the joke. It simply never came.

As much as I'd wanted to get out of the house, I was wiped out after class.

"We need to get that hospital bag packed." Chris turned into our neighborhood.

"We still have two months until my due date."

"You never know. The baby could come early."

I rounded my hands over my growing belly. "That's wishful thinking. Sam was ten days late."

"Ten days? Nobody around to have sex with you?"

I shook my head. "Weird, but I had a hard time picking up men when I was the size of a submarine."

"Fools. All of them." He reached over and squeezed my leg. "If I'd been around, I would've ravaged you."

I giggled. "Thanks. That makes me feel better." *And wow, that would've been weird.* My phone beeped with a text from Sam.

Are you guys almost done?

I grumbled. "It's Sam. She wants to know when we'll be home." *On our way.*

She replied quickly. *Can I head over to Bryce's now?*
You can't wait five minutes?
It's only five minutes.

"This is stupid. I'm calling her." I pushed the speed-dial for Sam's cell. "Sam, honey. What is the deal?"

"This is boring. I've been cooped up in this house all day long."

"Welcome to my world. I just don't understand what the big rush is. We're literally two minutes from home." I hung up the phone.

"Trouble in paradise?" Chris asked.

"I don't understand why she's being such a pain in the ass about being at home."

He pursed his lips. "Honestly? I think she likes going to Bryce's house because life is dull there. Dull, but stable."

I'd give my right arm for stable.

Chris pulled into the driveway, where Sam was climbing into my car.

I huffed. "She just can't wait to make her escape, can she?"

Chris put his truck in park. "I guess this is her way of dealing with it."

I opened my door to go after her.

Lightning fast, Chris grabbed my arm. "Don't, darling. We have to let her go."

CHAPTER THIRTY-FIVE

CLAIRE CRAMMED her cell phone under a pillow. "Remind me not to talk to my sister. Ever."

"Now what?" I finished buttoning my jeans and sat next to her on the bed.

"This stuff with my dad. I asked her to come down for a weekend and she won't do it."

I took her water bottle from the bedside table after noticing it was still quite full. "Here. You need to be drinking more."

"Sorry. I keep forgetting."

"Not surprised. You're on the phone all the time."

She took a sip and put the bottle back. "There's nothing else to do in this bed." She must've caught the stupid grin on my face. "Except that. And I'm the size of a Volkswagen. I doubt you really feel like doing that with me right now."

I frowned. "I feel like doing that with you all the time. It's just that we need to keep things a little quiet in that department until the nipper arrives." *And it's killing me.* I leaned closer and inched her top up to reveal her now-bulging stomach. A dark line had formed above and below her belly button, her skin stretched taut as a drum. "You're nurturing our child. Rest assured, you couldn't be any more beautiful to me right now." I pressed a gentle kiss to her bare skin—the baby pushed back against me. "Hello there." I blinked and eased back a few inches.

Claire peered down at her belly. "Look. A baby butt."

Bloody hell. Sure enough, there was the distinct outline of a wee bottom. "Wow," was as poignant a comment as I could muster.

"I think the same thing happened last night when I got up to pee. I could feel it, but I couldn't see it in the dark." The outline receded and Claire sighed, lowering her top. "I don't know what to do about Julie. I'm afraid he's going to die without her coming to say goodbye. It's so stupid. It's all because she's mad at him."

"Mad?" I shifted and sat next to her, propping myself up with what was left of the pillows.

"She thinks he's being selfish. She thinks he should've had the biopsy and undergone whatever treatment the doctors ordered."

"Hmmm." I took her hand. "I have to say, I admire your dad for the way he's handled this. He's a stubborn guy, but there's something to be said for going out on your own terms."

"I know." The corners of her mouth drew down. She gently rubbed my knuckles with her thumb. "I just wish it wasn't so hard to watch."

"Claire, darling." Dipping my head down, I forced her to look at me. "It was going to be difficult to watch either way. Either he's in the hospital or he's here. There's no getting around it."

"They might've been able to prolong his life."

I nodded. "Maybe. But that's a pretty big might. Frankly, I don't think any of us can question his rationale. We don't know what we would do in his shoes."

"Samantha isn't dealing with this very well."

"I'd prefer it if she wasn't avoiding him so much, but we all have our coping mechanisms. They've been very close and I'm sure this is scary and confusing to her."

She rolled to her side and placed her head on my chest. "I hate this, just so you know."

"Of course you do. What's to like? It's awful."

"This isn't the way it was supposed to be. He was supposed to be around for a lot longer than this."

I raked my fingers up and down her back. "Knowing your dad, he'll surprise us all and still be here five years from now."

With nothing left to say, I pulled her closer. It was surreal to live with a dying person. Claire and I were so eager for life to remain, as it was, that we mostly went on as we had before the doctors had found the tumor. Not much else to do, really—not very nice to say, "Oh, thank goodness you're still here" every morning over coffee.

A tear came to my eye when it hit me. This was how we all lived. *We're all dying.* Any day could be our last. It happened to my mum and dad—he was there one morning for breakfast, gone the next. No time to say goodbye because we'd had no idea he was leaving. *At least we can say goodbye to Richard. The question is whether we'll all get around to doing it.*

I cupped my hand around Claire's belly. *And that is why we celebrate new life.*

"I have to call Laura," Claire mumbled into my chest. "I really don't want to."

The mere mention of Laura made me want to climb the wall. Whenever Claire reminded her that she was on bed rest, Laura acknowledged it and went right on pushing for everything she wanted. "That's not a good sign if you're avoiding her."

"Oh, I'm being a wimp. She's great. It's just keeping me on my toes when I really feel like taking a nap."

"Maybe that's a sign that you need a nap." I slipped a finger under her chin and again forced her to look me in the eye. "You need to listen to your body right now, darling. I'm serious."

"I promise I'll take a nap after my phone call." She dug around under the pillow for her phone and took her laptop from the bedside table. "Yes, hello. It's Claire calling for Laura."

Under no circumstances was I about to leave the room. This was as close as I could come to protecting Claire and our baby from the number one hazard of Claire's new job—stress. I went to the closet, took a stack of rock t-shirts from a shelf and began re-folding them. Good thing I was out of sight, still able to hear what was going on. Claire never would've bought that I would take on the task voluntarily.

Nearly everything Claire said during the phone call irked me. *I'm working on it...I need more time...Okay, I'll get it done... That's really close to my due date.* That last one was enough to bring me back into the room.

I stood at the end of the bed and watched, arms folded squarely across my chest. *This time I'm really going to take the phone out of her hand. This has got to stop.* Claire's face was painted in worry and concern. My jaw tensed, my back grew tight. She was being pulled in two very different directions, so much so that I could feel it. Every inch of me, every last shred of protective dad and husband was at the boiling point.

"Claire, I need you. Can you please tell Laura you'll talk to her later?"

She gave me a look that could only be inferred as asking if I'd lost my fucking mind.

"I'm serious. Now."

She threw her hand up in the air. "I'm sorry, Laura. Chris was talking to me. What did you say?"

I could only think of Claire and the baby. I took the phone

out of Claire's hand. "Laura, hi, this is Christopher. I'm sorry to interrupt. How are you today, darling?"

There was a moment of silence on the other line that made me wonder if I'd accidentally hung up. "Christopher? Hi. I'm well. How are you?" Her voice took on a decidedly bubbly and girlish quality. "What a treat to talk to you."

If Claire's eyes had been laser beams, I would've no longer had a head.

"It's a treat for me to talk to you." I had to turn away to avoid the look of utter disgust and disappointment on Claire's face. "I'm so sorry to interrupt, but I think Claire forgot that she has a doctor's appointment and we're going to be late if we don't leave right now. You understand."

"Oh, uh, yes. Sure."

"You see, this has been a very difficult pregnancy and she's under a lot of stress right now. These appointments are of paramount importance. We must make sure that the baby is doing well."

"Of course. You can tell her we can talk tomorrow."

"I'll have to see if that works with her schedule. She'll send you an email. Does that work?"

"Whatever you say. It was wonderful to talk to you."

I rolled my eyes. "You too." I hung up and put Claire's phone on the dresser.

"I can't believe you just did that." Her mouth was agape, her finger pointing at the cell phone, which was now out of reach. "Seriously. What in the hell are you thinking?"

"I'm thinking that you and I need to have a serious heart-to-heart about this job. I can't sit idly by and be unconditionally supportive when it's so obvious that the amount of stress you are under right now is not good for you or the baby." I took a seat next to her. "You two are the most important things in the entire world to me. It's my job to keep you both safe."

"Chris, I'm a professional. I can deal with this. If you're asking me to quit my job, the answer is no. It's too good an opportunity. It's a lot right now, but that's just because of everything going on with my dad."

"No. This isn't worse because of your dad. It's worse because it's worse. This is a toxic situation. You think that because she gave you a title and said you'd have more control, but you're more stressed and worried about your work now than ever. It's too much. I really think it's too much."

"You never wanted me to take this job in the first place. Be honest. You didn't."

The little voice in my head nagged me. I hadn't wanted her to take the job. "Okay. Fair enough. I wasn't thrilled about it. Is that what you want me to say?"

She shook her head. "I knew it. I knew it from the first time I mentioned it. I can't believe you would be so selfish. My career is important to me. You should understand that as well as anyone."

"I know that very well. I want you to do whatever it is that you need to do to feel fulfilled. I just don't think this job is a good choice for our life right now and I don't think it's the only thing out there for you. There are lots of things you can do with your writing. I know it."

"What am I going to do? Go back to freelancing? Be at the mercy of stupid *Entertainment Weekly* or *Rolling Stone* or whoever decides to cut my story to bits? Spend my days hustling editors to get the good stories?"

"I'm not suggesting you go back to that. It doesn't sound like that's what you want to do."

"It isn't what I want to do. At all. I'm tired of it." She began to cry and I felt as though my heart was being torn out of my chest. "I'm tired of everything right now. I'm stuck in this bed and I can't do anything. I look like the broad side of a barn. I feel like a mother hen sitting on her eggs."

"I know it's hard. I really do."

"And everything with my dad." She buried her head in her hands. "I don't know what I'm going to do if he isn't able to hold on until the baby is born. I can't do that again."

"I know, I know." More than anything, I longed to tell her that her dad would be fine, that he'd be here to meet the baby and spend time with his new grandchild, but I was certain of no such thing. "The important thing is that whatever happens, we get through it together. It won't be the way it was when you lost your mum. I'll be here."

She looked up at me, lips pursed, tears welling in her eyes. "I'm going to lose him, aren't I? I'm going to lose him and that will be that. I never will have had the father-daughter relationship I wanted. It's too late, isn't it?"

"Come here." I climbed over her and leaned against the headboard, pulling her into my arms. Her shoulders quaked, she wept quietly. "You and your father have a good relationship, you really do. Don't get wrapped up in what you thought it was supposed to be like, or comparing yourself to your sister. The reality is that you're here for him right now and she isn't. I don't think you realize how important that is to him."

"You really think so?" Her voice was nothing more than an unsteady whisper. "I don't want to say goodbye."

"None of us wants to say goodbye. But at least you have the chance to."

CHAPTER THIRTY-SIX

"JELLYBEAN, does Chris know you're in here?"

Shit. My dad stood at the door to the nursery, looking in on me as I sat on a pillow on the floor, folding baby clothes. "You're home early." *Crap. They're home early.* Panicked, I pushed up from the floor, easier said than done. "Is he here?" I knew full well what Chris's opinion of me being out of bed would be. It wasn't like I'd been truly stupid and gone out for a run, but that would be no excuse. Chris saw to it that the bed rest order was carried out to the letter of the law, even if it'd been a while since I'd had any spotting.

"No, no. You're fine. He dropped me off and then he was going to take your car to the Volvo dealership. Sam said it was making a noise."

I eased back on to the pillow. "How is he going to get home?"

"He worked something out with Bryce."

"Oh. Okay. That was nice of Bryce." Being stuck in bed all day long, sometimes it felt as if I didn't know what was going on in my own house. My car acting up was news to me, but then again, I hadn't driven it in months. "Will you keep my secret? I can't sit in that bed all day long. It's making me nuts. I want to be able to do something to get ready for the baby."

"Tell you what. Let me help and I won't say a peep."

I smiled. We were both as feeble as the other—together, we made a great team. "Deal."

He toed off his shoes, which surprised me. My dad never took his shoes off in front of other people. It was probably too much like letting his guard down. He sat next to me on the floor. "Put me to work."

I scooted the laundry basket closer to him. "I'm just folding t-shirts and sleepers and baby socks."

"Show me how you want this done. I don't want to be the grandpa who messes this up."

I laid out one of the t-shirts and showed him my technique—sleeve, sleeve, fold. "One, two, three." I flipped it over. "Done. Baby t-shirt."

"I think I can manage that much." His hands shook as he worked, but he was able to do it almost as neatly as me. Not that I cared. At least we were having this time together.

I'd done everything I could not to stare at him lately, but it was difficult. Another pound lost, the hollows beneath his eyes darker, the shaking on his right side more pronounced. Oddly enough, the other striking feature was that he seemed to smile more. With everything facing him, he was markedly less grumpy than his normal self. *Who knew this is what it would take?* "How are you feeling today, Dad?"

"Pretty good. Headache was bad this morning, but it's a little better now. And I'm tired, but that's every day. I'm used to it."

"Those pain pills they gave you should take care of the headache."

"I don't like to take them unless I really need it. They make me groggy."

"Dad. There's no reason for you to suffer."

"I'm not. I'm fine." He shook it off as if it was a triviality, fishing a single, tiny white sock from the basket. "Now this is adorable." He sifted through the laundry until he found a match.

"I know. Right? So teeny tiny." I stuck out my lower lip as he folded the socks in on each other. "I forget how little everything is. It's been a while."

"It certainly has, hasn't it? I remember when Samantha was this small. She sure brought a ray of sunshine into our lives, didn't she?"

As if it had happened last week, I could see my dad sitting in the chair in the corner of my hospital room, holding an impossibly small and wrinkly Samantha, smiling at her through tears. He and I had both been so sad at that time, so torn up over losing my mom, that the pure joy of a baby seemed absurd, as if it wasn't meant for us. She bound us together. She healed us. She kept us strong when she wasn't even able to hold up her own head. "She really did."

"And she's all grown up now. Such a wonderful young lady." He nodded and kept folding, as if we were having the most weightless conversation imaginable. "I'm looking forward to her graduation very much. I will be a very proud man that day."

I had to fight back the tears, choke them down—Sam one step closer to leaving, my dad doing the same but in a very different way, all while the baby was getting bigger and stronger every day. Maybe that was why I was so tired, looking forward to each new day as it carried Chris and me closer to the baby's arrival, all while dreading where it was taking us with Sam and my dad.

"Are you doing okay with the fact that she hasn't been around the house as much lately?" I didn't necessarily want to go down this path, but we were beyond ignoring the elephant in the room, which was so refreshing. The first forty years of our father-daughter relationship had been built on the premise that we should talk about everything except what was truly important.

He nodded and looked at me. "I understand why she doesn't want to be around me anymore. I'm not the same Grandpa she loves. Frankly, I don't want her to remember me this way either."

He's so sweet. "So you know it's not just because she wants to spend more time with Bryce."

"I may be forgetful, but I think I have a pretty good handle on what's going on around here."

He's so strong. "I can't believe how calm you are about this. You've made peace with it, haven't you?"

"I have and I haven't. Don't think I don't think about it, wonder if I did the right thing by not seeking treatment."

"Are you regretting your decision?"

"I only regret it because it's made your sister not want to talk to me, but I can't live to make Julie happy." He arched his eyebrows and shrugged. "I tell you what, I look at that picture of me and your mom on our wedding day, the one in my room, and I know that this world isn't meant for me anymore. That life that I once had, the one that I loved so much, is gone."

It hit me—exactly what he'd lost the day my mom slipped away. "It makes me so sad to hear that."

"Don't be sad. I had seventeen years to try to get over losing your mother. That day never came." He reached over and patted my knee. "I need to know more than anything that you've made peace with this. I know this is difficult for you. I don't think there's any question that your mother's death may have hit you harder than any of us, and that includes me."

"How can you say that?" What he'd said seemed impossible.

"Let's just say the timing couldn't have been any worse for you. You were a young woman and had a little baby, all on your own. You needed your mom and she wasn't there. I know I was a poor substitute."

Tears streamed down my cheeks. "No, Dad, you weren't a poor substitute. Don't say that. I don't know what I would've done without you." I realized then that all of the years that I'd spent butting heads with him didn't mean we didn't get along. It was our dynamic. When it came down to it, we'd really needed each other. I took a deep breath. At least I could see this while he was still here. "Dad, this isn't right. This isn't the way it's supposed to be."

"Ladybug. Really." He shook his head, laughing quietly. "You've been like this since you were a little girl." He puffed out his chest. "You always had such a strong sense of right and wrong. You certainly never liked seeing the injustices in the world go by without a fight." He took another t-shirt out of the basket, folded it, and added it to the stack. "Life is the way it's supposed to be. We don't get to choose half of what happens, it just happens. It happens when it wants to and how it wants to. If we get hung up on the way things are supposed to be, we'll never be happy."

I gripped a bundle of the baby's socks in my lap. "I don't want you to go."

He nodded, seeming resigned. "I don't want to either, Ladybug, but I'm tired." He sighed. "Look, enough of this talk. I want you to do something for me."

"Anything. Anything you want." With the back of my hand, I wiped the tears from my cheeks.

"You know that I left everything to you and Julie, to split

down the middle. Promise me you'll keep the house in Asheville, at least for a little while. I'd like to know that you and Chris and the baby have a place to get away that's nearby. Maybe you and Julie can go up there together. Both families. That'd make me happy."

I nodded. "Sure. Of course."

"And after I'm gone, there's a box in the attic that I want you to have. Your sister has no business doing anything with it. It has a project that I started when you were a little girl and I never finished, although I tried very hard to. I think you're the right person to do something with it." He cocked his head to the side. "Finish it."

My forehead crinkled with confusion. "A project? What? Like woodworking?"

"No. Not woodworking."

A project? My mind scrambled for the sorts of things my dad liked to tackle—putting up shelves and fixing plumbing. "I don't understand. I'm not exactly handy."

"You're going to have to trust me on this one. It's a cardboard banker's box. It has my name on the side of it. You'll know it when you see it."

"Why don't you just tell me what it is?"

"I don't really like to talk about it. I was never very good at it, even though I really wanted to be." He took the remaining t-shirt from the basket. "Honestly, it's a little embarrassing. It's the only thing I've ever done in my life that I never finished. You know I always finish everything."

Some mystery hobby I never knew about? "Did Mom know about it?"

"She did. She kept pushing me, but I could never see my way through to the end. It's not an easy thing."

"This is all way too cloak and dagger, Dad."

"It is precisely that." He patted my knee. "You're the perfect person to finish it. You're the one with the ability and most importantly, you have the determination. It will take a lot of determination to get it done."

He's so damn stubborn. "I still don't know why you won't just tell me what it is."

"Trust me, Ladybug. You'll find out soon enough."

CHAPTER THIRTY-SEVEN

STAY IN YOUR LANE, Chris. *Stay awake.*

"North Carolina is pretty in the morning." Graham drummed along to the radio on the dash of my pick-up.

I blinked and yawned. The sun was just now coming up. "How can you be so bloody chipper after taking the red-eye? It destroys me."

"Unlike you, I have no problem sleeping on the plane. One little sleeping pill and I get my five hours." He finally stopped the incessant percussion lesson and sat back in his seat. "All I need."

Bastard. "Right now, all I need is coffee." We stopped at a local spot with great coffee and even better breakfast, sitting outside on the patio that although it overlooked the parking lot, was pleasant enough.

Graham tucked into his eggs with vigor. "So, we'll go back to the house and fetch Richard, then on to the studio?"

"Yeah. That's the plan." I crunched away at a piece of bacon. "He really wanted to go along. He's proud of it, which is very cool. He worked hard."

"It's nice that you two were able to work on it together." He slapped me gently on the arm. "Real father-son project, eh?"

"I'm very happy we had a chance to do this, especially after getting off to such a rough start."

"Hey, remember, you and I were mortal enemies when we met in primary school."

"Mortal enemies for a week, and that was only because you lied to Mrs. Hammel and told her that I'd thrown that spitball."

"I was just protecting myself. I seem to remember you got your revenge in the schoolyard the next day."

I grinned and nodded—more than thirty years later and I still felt a swell of pride at the moment I'd decked Graham. We were best mates two days later. "That I did, didn't I?"

"I've been trying to get even ever since." He took a sip of his coffee. "How's Richard doing, anyway?"

"He's hanging in there. It's Claire who's having a harder time with it. She's physically miserable, she and Sam are squabbling, and she's still struggling with her new job, which is making me barmy. I wish she'd just quit. It's not going to work, but she has a very hard time quitting anything."

"You have to admire that."

I blew out a breath. "I do."

The two women sitting at the next table had been looking at us off and on during breakfast, but now one of them had apparently become emboldened enough to ask the question. "Are you?" She pointed at Graham then at me. "Graham and Christopher? From Banks Forest?"

Luckily, in this scenario, Graham liked to take charge. "We are indeed, dear. Can I sign something for you?"

She scrounged in her purse, producing a crumpled piece of paper and a pen. "That would be so awesome. Thank you so much."

"What's your name?"

"Kim." She nodded, smiling, her long blonde curls reminding me of Sam.

Graham signed the paper, taking up the majority of the available space, then handed it to me. "We're going to be recording a new album very soon."

"You are? That's so amazing. I'd heard some people say that Christopher had moved here, but that sounded a little crazy."

"Crazier things have happened." I handed her the paper.

She held it up in victory. "Thank you so much."

Graham watched her walk away, then turned back to me. "So, do you think we'll be able to sit down and look at the calendar today? Now that the studio is done, I'd like to be able to block out our recording time. I'm having dinner with Terence in New York tomorrow night. Would be great if I could let him know what we're looking at."

The calendar. Here we were, less than six weeks until the baby was due. Crunch time. My inclination was to clear the decks for our new arrival, when Graham wanted me to do nothing but make plans. "Yeah, I don't see why not. I mean, I haven't done a damn thing to get things off the ground, hire a publicist so I can start bringing in some projects. I just haven't had the time. Banks has carte blanche right now as far as I'm concerned." I took another drink of my coffee. "You just need to remember that things are going to get crazy for me when the baby arrives."

"Chris. I'm a dad. I've done the baby routine. I get it." He reached over and patted me on the shoulder. "Don't worry. We'll make it work."

After breakfast, Graham and I headed back to the house. "Still pretty quiet," I said, when we walked in the front door. "Richard and Claire must both still be asleep." I looked at my watch. "Sam's already out the door for school."

"The place looks great with all of the new furniture." He

strolled into the kitchen as if he owned the place, which wasn't surprising since Graham acted like that wherever he went. "How's the pool coming along?" He pulled the sliding glass door to the back yard open, to the sound of the dozens of birds that had begun frequenting our back yard since Richard had put up a feeder.

"Almost done. They need to put in the patio and get the final inspection and we can fill her up with water. Just in time. I could really use the exercise."

Graham slapped my belly. "I didn't want to say anything, P-man, but you need to get back into fighting shape for when we go back on the road."

"If we go back on the road. A lot of things have to fall into place before that happens." I closed the door. "Suppose I should go see if Richard is up yet. We have a lot to squeeze in today."

Graham sat at the kitchen table. "Yeah, I'll check email on my phone, send Angie a text and let her know I've arrived."

I headed upstairs and down the hall to Richard's room, rapping quietly so as not to wake Claire. There was no answer, so I eased the door open. "Rich? You up yet?" I leaned against the doorframe when I saw that he was still asleep. "I hate to wake him," I muttered, twisting my lips. There wasn't much choice, we had a lot of things to accomplish with Graham in town for only one day and Richard had insisted on joining us when we went to the studio.

I walked over to the side of the bed. "Richard? It's about time to get up." I knew the instant I touched his shoulder. *Oh, no.* My entire body froze, a stillness unlike anything I'd never experienced before. My heartbeat pounded in my ears. *Good God, no.* I sat on the edge of the bed, tears rolling down my cheeks. "It was time to go then, was it?" My hand returned to his shoulder and I rubbed it. His body was cold. There was a heaviness to it. His face was drawn, skin pale and thin, mouth open, but he was finally at peace. No more pain. No more suffering.

I straightened the blanket that covered him, folded down the collar of his pajama shirt. He would never want to be seen unkempt, not even by a medic. With the most delicate touch I could muster, I swept back what little hair he had from his forehead. "There you go, old chap. Much better."

My shoulders drooped and I bent forward, resting my elbows on my knees. I wept for everything—Claire losing her dad, Sam losing her grandfather, the baby on the way who would never know him. Selfishly, I wept for me losing the closest thing I'd had to a father in a very long time. *He's gone. I love him and the stubborn old bastard is gone.*

CHAPTER THIRTY-EIGHT

AS IF IT was any other day, my dad strolled into the kitchen, poured a cup of coffee and sat at the table to read the newspaper. The only difference was that he didn't say, "good morning", he didn't look at me. He went about his business as if I didn't exist, humming some terrible modern country song he always turned up on the radio. He flipped through the pages of the paper, scanning the columns. His right hand was no longer shaking. He looked healthier, more color to this face. *Maybe he's getting better.* He turned the page again and placed his finger on a small photograph, now reading intently. I approached slowly, not wanting to disturb his reading. He turned to me when I reached the table. His eyes were soft and sweet. "Look, Ladybug. I'm in the newspaper." *Oh right. The obituaries.*

I woke to a damp pillow, just as I had every morning since my dad had died.

In the past six months I'd planned both a wedding and a funeral. *Didn't they make a movie about that?* I might have been a bit shy on the correct number of weddings and this one didn't star Hugh Grant, but it didn't change the fact that life right now was a drama, continually unfolding. Sometimes, it felt as though

I was sitting there and watching it all happen to me, every recent minute of it unbelievably sad. I only wished our movie had come with good popcorn and would ultimately have a happy ending.

My dad's memorial ceremony had been a sparsely attended affair—Chris, Sam, and I, plus my sister Julie, Matt, and her two kids, and my dad's friend Marty, the electrician. Rosie had stayed away. She wasn't a spiteful person, but my dad wasn't her favorite person after he'd been so brusque with her.

Julie and Matt didn't stay long, they had to turn around and drive back to Virginia. Matt's new job didn't allow him to be away for more than a day and Julie was a complete wreck. I'd told her she would regret not taking the time to say goodbye to him before he died and that was exactly what happened. Not that I took any consolation in being right. She was suffering enough for the both of us.

"Every time I get back in this stupid bed, I feel like I'm returning to the roost," I mumbled to Chris after returning from that morning's tenth trip to the bathroom. He helped me adjust the pillows, but I was well beyond the point of deriving comfort from Fiberfil or feathers. As far as I was concerned, the bed rest order was silly at this point. I hadn't had a spotting incident in more than two months. Unfortunately, the doctor had pulled out the dreaded advanced maternal age when I argued with her about it.

"I'm sorry. I know this isn't your preference, but we're so close now. Less than a month until your due date."

Twenty-seven days, but who's counting? "Yep. All that time to sit in this bed." I looked out the bedroom window. Such a beautiful spring day. It would've been so wonderful to work outside, till up that old vegetable garden, run out and shop for seeds—do anything productive. "Plenty of time to stew and get more and more fat and think about my dad."

"You aren't fat."

"You're sweet, but we both know I'm huge." I pushed up the sleeves of my dad's fuzzy gray cardigan, feeling like the hormonal love child of The Hindenberg and Mr. Rogers. I could remember him having the sweater forever, since I'd been in middle school. The man never threw anything away. I'd worn it every day since he'd died, to keep my arms warm when the air conditioning got to be too much and my heart pumping when the sadness got to be suffocating. "You know I have to call Laura." To say that I dreaded this would have suggested that I had strong feelings about my job, when the truth was that I was really only hoping that my passion for it would return once I had a better handle on having lost my dad.

"This is the last call until the baby arrives, right?"

"Yes. I told her email only until two weeks after delivery. She isn't happy about it though. She hates the inefficiency of email." I rolled my eyes. Chris merely shook his head. I pressed the speed dial for Laura, keenly aware that Chris would not leave the room during these conversations. As irked as I'd been by his decision to swipe the phone out of my hand that day, I loved the way he made me feel protected. He always had my back. "Hey Carolyn, it's Claire calling for Laura." I waited. Chris grabbed a magazine from his bedside table and sprawled out on the bed next to me.

"Claire, hi," Laura said. "Where are we at with the story about the casting controversy on the *Black Beauty* remake?"

Hello to you, too. "I should be able to finish the final edit today. I'm a little behind after everything with my dad." I scribbled down a note to remind myself to follow up with the pain-in-the-ass writer for that story, another task I'd been delaying.

"Don't you think we're cutting it a little close? The clock is ticking if you haven't noticed. We're close to launch and I don't have everything I need from you."

I took a deep breath. This conversation was doubly difficult—with Chris right next to me, I had to word my responses to Laura very carefully when I didn't have the energy. "I hear what you're saying. Don't worry. I'll get everything to you. The deadline for that hasn't officially passed yet." *Although it is coming up really fast.*

"You know I don't like working like this, Claire. I feel like I'm nagging you for every last thing. I understand that things have been busy for you, but you can't allow your personal life to get in the way of your job."

This time, I didn't think before I replied. "Personal life. Interesting way of putting it." *It's not my personal life, it's my life. Period. Chris. The baby. Sam. Dad.* "I'm sorry to hear you feel like that." What I'd really wanted to say was, "fuck off".

Chris perked up, rolling to his side and looking at me quizzically. He was so handsome in the ethereal morning light streaming through our bedroom window. "I love you," I mouthed to him, silently. *He is my rock.* If he hadn't been there, I would've been falling apart, completely. He kept my head above water, kept me from slipping below the surface, a place I readily sank to after my mom had died.

"We're both adults here, Claire. This isn't about how I feel and I'm not trying to be a hard ass. This is about facts. You need to do the job I hired you to do."

I listened, but Laura's voice was buzzing around somewhere in the back of my head. All I could do was look at Chris. I'd waited my entire life for him. My partner. My love. *I'm wasting time with this miserable job.*

"Claire, are you there?" The annoyance in Laura's voice was plain.

"I'm here."

"Are you going to say anything?"

I nodded. Tears welled in my eyes.

Chris sat up and placed his hand on my arm. "Are you okay?" he whispered.

"Yes, Laura. I am going to say something. I'm going to have to say that I quit."

Chris's eyes grew wide, but the relief and happiness on his face was unmistakable.

"You what?" Laura asked, her voice cold and hard. "You can't be serious. You're quitting? I'm launching a magazine in six weeks."

"I know. That kind of sucks, doesn't it? Sorry about that."

"It sucks? You're sorry?"

"Don't worry. I'll send you everything I have. You'll find somebody to get it all into shape."

"Do you realize how fucking unprofessional this is on your part?"

"Maybe." I shrugged. "Or maybe it's really fucking smart on my part. See, I have this thing. It's called a life. You should try it some time. It's awesome."

Chris leaned forward and kissed me on the forehead, lingering for a few seconds.

"Nice," Laura said. "Is this when you remind me that you're married to the hunky rock star?"

"Nope. This is when I remind you that I'm thankful for the opportunity and I'll email you everything I have. Good luck." I ended the call and held the phone high above my head by two fingers before allowing it to fall on to the mattress. "Wow. That felt really good."

"It may have been good for you, but it was spectacular for me."

"I like how you can make a normal conversation sound like sex talk."

"I'm brilliant at that." He scooted closer to me and took my hand. "Are you okay? Are you sure about this?"

My heart hadn't felt so untroubled in months. It felt like I was finally making room for everything important, even if some of what I'd made room for was quite sad. It felt right. I hadn't felt that way since I'd said "yes" to Chris's bathroom floor proposal. "I'm sure. It was coming. I knew deep-down that it wasn't going to work, I was just being stubborn."

"Imagine that."

"Funny." I squeezed his hand. "Of course, I have no idea what I'm going to do for a job anymore."

"You'll figure something out."

Huh. Or we could do that. "Actually, with the job thing out of the way, that means we can go to Asheville."

"Absolutely." He nodded. "A month or so after the baby is born."

"Nope. Before the baby is born. I want to go tomorrow."

Chris looked me as if I was nuts, but it made perfect sense to me. "No way. It's too much for you. We'll wait until the baby is here. Then we can take a weekend and it'll be a getaway."

"Penman, I just quit my damn job. I have to sit in this bed for another four weeks. I need something to do. You can't deny me that."

"I really don't think it's a good idea."

"You know I'll pester you about it until you give in." I grabbed my water bottle from the bedside table and took a long drink.

"Claire, come on."

"Look, I just quit my job. I think you need to do that husband thing where you smile and nod at me and say, "yes" even if I'm being ever so slightly irrational."

"That? I have to do that?"

"Yes. We need to go to Asheville."

"I'm not agreeing to any of this until we talk to the doctor."

"Fine, but I want to talk to her if she says no."

CHAPTER THIRTY-NINE

FIVE DAYS later than Claire would've liked, I unlocked the door to Richard's Asheville house and held it open for her. "After you, M' lady." I would never, ever, want to compare my wife to a duck or give in to bad stereotypes of pregnant women, but as I followed her inside, the reality stared me in the face. Claire waddled. Poor thing—she had a ten-pound watermelon strapped to her and by all reports, much of it rested squarely on her bladder.

She placed one hand on top of her belly, one hand beneath it. "If I could just put this baby down for half an hour, I would be so happy."

"And if I could make that happen, I would." I watched as she wandered into what was apparently the living room, past a blue and tan plaid couch and brown leather recliner to the back of the house and a pair of small, curtained windows overlooking a wooded lot.

"It's sort of weird to think about him puttering around here. I haven't been to this house in a while. He almost always came to visit us. Now it feels like a lifetime ago."

"Are you okay?"

"I'm a little sad. Stuff brings back memories." Her left hand swirled in a circle on her belly. Light glinted off her engagement ring and wedding band. "But, honestly, I thought it would upset me a lot more. Maybe I just needed to get out of the house." She walked over to the recliner, rubbing the back of the worn leather. A breathy laugh left her lips. "He's had this chair forever. I used to give him shit about never throwing things out, but now I'm glad he kept this old stuff."

There was a cluster of photos on the stark white wall, some in black and white, some in color. The frames were a mishmash—displaying a revolving cast of characters, a wide array of settings—her parents ice skating on a frozen pond, a family vacation to what looked the Grand Canyon, the girls and their mother outside on a summer day. "These are amazing."

She walked over in a bit of a daze, as if she was being drawn forth by some imaginary power the photographs contained. "They are, aren't they?" She shook her head and I watched her in profile as her lower lip began to tremble. "Me and Julie in the back yard. We were probably three and four in this picture. We used to run in the sprinkler with just shorts on. Look at my mom. What in the world is going on with her hair?" She shook her head. "She said I always sat on the sprinkler." She gasped for air, tears streaming down her face, smiling at the same time.

I pulled her into a hug, delivered from the side now that her belly otherwise got in the way. "Is this too much? Don't feel like we have to do this today just because we made the drive. We can get you some rest, try tomorrow."

She wiped her cheek on my shoulder. "No. It's okay. This is good. I have to let it out, right?" Her shoulders quaked. "I miss them both so much."

I rubbed her back, wishing I could make it all go away. Watching anyone you love cry is difficult. When it's the person you love the most on the entire planet, it's torture. "Yes, darling. Let it out."

Her hands grasped my back, the sobs became deeper and her body went limp. I didn't say a thing, I only held on to her, kept her up. Nothing I could say would ever fill the hole that resided in her right now. There was no way to make that better. I could only endure it with her.

Eventually, her body quieted and I sensed the relief that follows the release. I cupped the back of her head and kissed her cheek. "I love you. I promise you that this will all get better."

She turned her face into my neck. "I love you too. Thank you."

"You don't need to thank me. This is what I signed up for. I want to be here for you."

"I bet you got a lot more than you thought you would."

"You've gone through a lot for me, too. I'm only holding up my end of the bargain."

She eased back and wiped her cheek with the back of her hand. "I'm a total disaster right now, aren't I?"

I pecked the end of her puffy red nose. "You're perfect."

"I suppose we should go hunting for the box that holds the mysterious project."

We headed up a rickety flight of steps covered with linoleum. At the end of the hall, I found a wooden ceiling hatch and a pull-down ladder. "There's no way I'm letting you go up there eight months pregnant. I'm going to have to look for it and tell you what I see."

She frowned. "That's not very fun."

"Sorry. That's the way this has to happen. Plus, let's be honest." I pointed at the narrow passage up into the attic. "There's no way you're making it through there."

A disgruntled exhale escaped her lips. "Fine."

I started up the ladder, the air warm and stuffy at the top.

"Is there a light up here?" I squinted in the darkness. A few spare beams of sunlight came through a vent tucked up into the peak of the gable roof.

"I don't remember," she called. "The only time I was ever up there was when we moved my dad into this house. Sam was a baby. It was a long time ago."

As my eyes adjusted to the dark conditions, I spotted a single bulb a few feet ahead. "Never mind. Got it." I pulled the cord. "Shit, Richard. You could've gone for a little more wattage with that bulb."

"What?" Claire shouted.

"Nothing." I crawled ahead on my hands and knees. The clearance seemed like less than five feet. At six-foot-four, there was no way I'd be walking my way through this. The dozens of cardboard boxes were in neat and orderly stacks, not surprising coming from Richard. He'd been fastidious in everything he did, even when no one would ever see it. *Or maybe he'd anticipated this day. Knowing him, he probably did.* "Tell me again what I'm looking for."

"A cardboard banker's box. Like you would use for hanging files. His name should be on the side."

Sure enough, there was a stack of boxes meeting that description. It also happened to be in the farthest reaches of the attic, where the roof sloped down and there was virtually no room to maneuver.

"Did you find it?"

"I think so. Hold on a minute." I crawled ahead, past boxes labeled "Christmas" and "Taxes". Everything I saw was through the cloud of fine dust I kicked up as I shuffled along on my hands and knees. "I'm going to need a shower after this." My head was inches from the roof trusses when I reached my destination, my forehead dripping with perspiration. At the bottom of the stack, were two boxes with

Richard's name on them. *Of course.* "I think I've got it," I shouted.

"Cool. Hurry up."

Hurry up. In the cramped quarters, it was easier said than done to drag along two heavy boxes, but I eventually got them to the ladder. "I'm coming down." I took the first few rungs, then pulled one of the boxes to me and continued until I could plop it down on the hallway floor. "One more."

"One more? He only mentioned one."

"I'm just following instructions." I headed back up and did the same with the second box, collapsing on the floor next to Claire when I was done. "Shit. It's hot up there."

"I bet." She was immersed in sifting through the first box. "This is all a bunch of my dad's old work stuff. From the hardware company he used to work for." Confusion painted her face. Her shoulders slumped. "This can't be right."

"Then let's try door number two." I pulled the first box from her and slid the second into its place.

Inside, atop stacks of paper, were three or four notebooks, with black and white pebbly covers saying "Composition Book". Richard's name was on the front of each one. They seemed to be numbered.

Claire quickly found number one. She leaned against the wall and scanned the page, then began reading aloud. "Jonathan Mills slyly looked up from his newspaper as the train rolled into the station. He was three stops from his office and he knew exactly who was about to step on board. He knew those shapely legs the instant they came into view. The owner of those legs drove him mad with desire." Claire put the notebook in her lap and giggled. "Oh my God." She stared at me, bug-eyed. "What is this?"

I laughed. "Shut up and keep reading."

She shook her head and opened the notebook again, finding

her place. "This is kind of freaking me out, but okay." She cleared her throat. "The raven-haired beauty stepped into the car and took a seat across the aisle from him, taking his breath away at the same time. Her skin pale as alabaster, lips red and pouty, womanly curves that went on for days. It was a good thing that his top-secret CIA training had equipped him to appear as though he was fazed by nothing. She fazed him all right, but he appeared nothing but calm and collected on the exterior."

I squeezed Claire's knee. "Who knew your dad had such a sexy side to him?"

"I never even knew he could write."

She read quickly, revealing a somewhat formulaic but still compelling tale of international espionage and intrigue—an American James Bond of sorts, but with a very strong love story. Sometimes, the prose broke down into rambling sections in which Richard wrestled with where to take the story. Once Claire had gone through a good twenty pages, the tale had started to veer off into multiple sub-plots. "He had a good idea. He just couldn't figure out where to take it."

"Lots of people want to write a novel and don't finish it."

"And he thought I could?"

"Correction. He knew you could."

She looked up at me, blinking, her eyes filled with wonder and life. "I feel like I'm seeing a side of my dad that I never knew. There's some amazing stuff in here. There's some really kooky stuff in here, too." She flipped it open and ran her finger down the page. "I can't believe my dad wrote this."

"He was a complex guy, Claire. He just didn't always show it."

She closed the notebook again and peered into the box. "You know what our relationship was like. We spent most of the time butting heads. We never did a single project together. He certainly never let me help him with things around the house. All that time, we could've been talking about writing."

I watched her, relishing the light in her eyes that hadn't always been there over the last few months. *Richard. Stubborn bastard.* He'd probably been too proud to open up to his daughter about his creative endeavors, worried that whatever he'd done wasn't good enough. "He wanted to share it with you. Apparently, he just didn't think it was up to snuff."

"You know, when he told me that he never felt like he and I had much in common, I'd always seen it as some shortcoming on my part, that I'd never taken after him in anything." She furrowed her brow. "Now I almost wonder if it was the other way around."

"I know it was. He admired your writing, because I would hear him brag about it. He wouldn't have shared this with you and been so explicit about his wishes if he didn't think you could do it."

"And he thought he couldn't do it. He thought he wasn't good enough, but he had a cool idea. Pulpy. A little seedy. I like it." She stuck out her lower lip. "I don't know whether to be happy or sad about this."

"If there's a choice, I think we go with happy. We've had enough sad to last a lifetime."

CHAPTER FORTY

CHRIS'S PHONE buzzed in the cup holder.

"Do you want me to look?" I shifted in my seat, my back protesting the way I'd twisted my torso. *Ouch.* Sleeping on the bed at my dad's house the night before had left me with a dull backache.

"Sure. I'm guessing its Graham. He's the only one who pesters me much anymore."

I picked up the phone and read the text. "Yep. He says hello and asks how you're doing."

"Sweet, but that's really his way of asking if things have settled down enough for me to finally commit to the recording schedule."

Recording. I might've been more excited than anyone about the prospect of Banks Forest returning to the studio. The chance to be around for some of the recording, sit in the studio and listen to the tracks as they developed and became full-fledged songs? Forget about it. Way too thrilling to even think about.

It was the touring that had me decidedly less enthusiastic. I was not eager for Chris to leave the baby and me at home, especially when Sam would be gone by the time they got around to going on the road.

"What do you want me to tell him?"

"Tell him the truth, that we're driving back to Chapel Hill and I'll call him when I get home."

I tapped away at his phone and hit send. I went to place it in the cup holder, but that didn't happen. *Ouch*. Pain came again, but this time from a different place, and an entirely different sensation. I cramped, lurching forward as far as my stomach allowed. I dropped his phone in the process.

"Are you okay?" Chris asked.

The cramp tightened, the muscle turning in on itself. "Uh, I—" Words wouldn't come. My brain and mouth felt disconnected. A long list of expletives sat on my tongue, waiting, but they stayed put. With a deep breath, my lower abdomen relaxed and I was able to straighten. I exhaled, my shoulders dropping. "I think the baby must've pressed on a nerve. I'm fine." I gently rubbed my belly. *Unless that was something else*.

"Okay. If you say so."

I knocked my head back on the headrest and remembered his phone was sitting on the floor. One attempt at bending forward and I realized there was no way. I was too big. "I don't think I can get your phone."

"Leave it." He turned the radio back up a bit and switched between different satellite radio stations, ultimately turning it off. "No radio. Let's talk. What are you thinking you're going to do with your dad's notebooks?"

I'd laid in the dark for much of the previous night, wondering that very thing. "I need to go through and read everything, but it's obvious that he meant for me to turn it into a book. Don't you—" The cramp came again. *Fuck*. This time, my spine and legs stiffened, so much so that my butt lifted off the seat.

"Claire? Are you okay?" Chris's voice was pure panic, but I was in the throes of something else. "I'm pulling over."

"No." I shook my head, wincing then relaxing as the tightening slowly let go. *This can't be...no...no way...there are three weeks until my due date.* "Keep driving. We need to get home." I shifted slightly to my side. *Maybe a change of position will help.*

"You're really worrying me. Do you think you're going into labor?"

"I'm fine. Truly. I think it's just Braxton-Hicks contractions. False labor." *False, my ass. These hurt like hell.*

He looked at the clock on the dash. "It's nine-fifteen. We're going to keep track of how far apart they are."

"Okay. I really don't think they're anything. It's probably just from sitting in the car."

"We have another two and a half hours ahead of us. We can always stop."

"No. Keep going. If it's not false labor, we have to get home."

Chris's eyes darted to my face and then back to the road. "So you do think it might be real."

"It might. Keep driving."

Sure enough, the contractions were coming regularly. Ten minutes apart. I was doing an okay job breathing through them, but I was far from comfortable and they were becoming more intense.

"Claire, maybe we need to pull over and find a hospital."

"No way. If this is real, and it still might not be, Sam has to be there. I'm not having this baby without her there."

"You may not have a choice."

"How much longer until we're there?"

"At the speed I'm driving, an hour tops."

Another contraction started. I closed my eyes and tried to relax, to "embrace the pain" as the childbirth instruction had told us, to "sink into the bed", or the car seat, as it happened to be.

"Another one?" Chris asked.

I nodded, concentrating, reminding myself to think of this as a "good pain". It only got me so far.

"Eight minutes apart."

It began to ebb and I blew out a long breath. "Distract me. Let's talk about something other than this."

Chris sat up straighter, leaning into the steering wheel as if that might make the car go faster. "Yes. Let's talk." He held up his finger. "Oh, I know. Baby names."

"Yes. Good. Baby names. We're set on boy names, right?"

"You really want to name him Christopher?"

"I do. I think it's sweet and old-fashioned. Plus, I love your name."

"What about the middle name? I'm not sure Alastair works."

"As nice as it would be to give him your dad's name, I agree. Christopher Alastair doesn't exactly have a ring to it."

"Honestly? It sounds like some pompous community theater actor's name."

I snickered. "Okay." I thought for a moment, wondering what he would say to my idea. "What about Graham?"

"So you want to go the pompous rock star route instead?"

I laughed, which felt good considering that my abdomen was again starting to do its thing. "Christopher Graham Penman. It sounds nice."

He kept his eyes on the road. "Let's put that one on the back burner. We'll see what happens."

"Fair enough." I wrapped my hand around my lower belly. "One sec." I held up my finger, asking for quiet in Chris's preferred way. The contractions were becoming more intense. I concentrated on relaxing when everything in my body told me to curl into a ball.

"Breathe, Claire." Chris gently placed his hand on mine. "Just like in class."

The pain subsided and I blew out a breath. "I'm good."

"You sure?"

"Whatever these are, they're still pretty short. I'll live." *I think.*

"You're sure you're okay."

"Yes. What about girl names?"

"I thought we'd sewn that up."

"I don't want to force you to name our baby after my mom."

"It was my suggestion, wasn't it?"

"Yes, I guess it was. But are you okay with it? We had some other cute ideas. I like Avery."

"If we have a girl, we're naming her Sara. It seems silly to name her anything else."

"Why don't we wait and see what she looks like? Maybe she won't look like a Sara."

I didn't have to see Chris's face to know that he'd rolled his eyes. "Sure. We'll wait. But if we're having a girl, I'm sure Sara will suit her perfectly."

My belly began to coil, this time with surprising ferocity. I braced for the pain as it held me firmly in its clutches. "Chris." I grabbed at the seat. *Oh shit.* "Find my phone. Tell Sam to meet us at the hospital."

CHAPTER FORTY-ONE

"NINE CENTIMETERS. We're very close to pushing." Dr. Thorp, the attending OB, snapped off his gloves and pushed back on his rolling stool. "I'm going to check on a few other patients and I'll be back. It won't be long now."

My heart skipped several beats. *Won't be long. Good. I've been waiting a long time.*

"No. No. I can't push yet. Sam isn't here." Claire shook her head vehemently.

"We might not have much choice," I said. "I even called Bryce and she hasn't called back."

"Please, call her again," Claire begged.

Margo, the nurse who'd been with us through much of labor, wiped Claire's brow with a washcloth. "Go ahead and make the call, Dad. Nothing will happen while you're gone."

I marched out into the hall and called Samantha. For the fourth time, I got her voicemail. "Sam, it's Chris. You'd better hurry down here, honey. Your mom will be really disappointed if you aren't here for this." I shoved my phone back into my pocket and returned to the room. "Voicemail. I left another message."

Claire closed her eyes. "She has to be here. I'm not doing this without her."

Margo had been watching the fetal monitor that told her when the next contraction would come. "Another one's coming, Claire."

I stepped into position and held Claire's hand, looking intently into her eyes. "Focus." I nodded, wishing I could take away at least some of her pain. She wrung my hand as if it was a wet dishrag. *Okay, I guess I'm feeling some of her pain now.* "Breathe. Hee hee hoo. Hee hee hoo."

She winced and crinkled her forehead, eventually just closing her eyes, losing her breathing pattern at the very end.

"Contraction's ending," Margo said.

I looked down at Claire. "How are you feeling?"

"The epidural feels like it isn't doing anything anymore."

"You'll be able to push more effectively," Margo said. "And trust me, you aren't feeling everything. It just might seem that way."

Claire closed her eyes. "I just want the baby to get here." When she opened them again, the blue was intense as midnight. "Sam isn't coming, is she? She's trying to get me back for all of that stuff with Bryce, isn't she? I'm so stupid. Why did I do that? I should've let him come to Thanksgiving. I can't have the baby without her here."

"Claire, darling. Thanksgiving was a lifetime ago." *Dammit, Samantha.* "I'm sure she's on her way."

"Then why hasn't she called?"

Excellent point. "I'm not sure."

"Will you try her again?"

"Sure. I'll be right back." I ducked out into the hall, grumbling to myself as I fished my phone from my back pocket. "Just answer your damn phone." I dialed Sam's number. Incessant ring after incessant ring came. Voicemail. *Bugger.* I blew out an exasperated breath. "Samantha, I don't know what else I have to do to get you down here. I'm begging you." My voice began to quake, but I was too bloody tired and pumped up on adrenaline, simultaneously excited and terrified, to care anymore. "This baby cannot come without you being here. You have to be here. For your mom and for me." I dug my hand into my hair, staring down at the speckled tile floor. *Just let it out.* "I love you, Sam. As far as I'm concerned, you are my daughter, and I am your dad. You have to be here when your brother or sister arrives. It can't happen any other way. So, stop driving your father crazy and get your ass down to this hospital now."

Sam and Bryce burst through the doors into the Obstetrics wing.

I dropped my head back, looking up at the ceiling. *Shit. Finally.*

"Chris. Oh my God. I'm so sorry. I turned my phone off and then you left that message for Bryce. We got in the car right away. Where is she?"

A nurse came out from behind the nurse's station. "Is this family? Only family for the delivery."

Not this. The last thing I was equipped to do was argue with the nurse. "Yes."

"Yes. I'm his daughter," Sam blurted. She whipped around, her blonde curls going everywhere, and pointed at Bryce. "This is his nephew. From England. He just flew in."

Fuck. Nothing like a complicated lie, Sam.

Bryce's face turned crimson and he instantly shook his head "no". He grabbed Sam and kissed her on the forehead. "I'll be in the waiting room." He gave me the high sign and retreated to the exit.

"Come on. She's ready to push." I stopped when I opened the door, pulling Sam into a hug. "I'm glad you made it. We couldn't do this without you."

"That means a lot to me. It really does." She gestured with a nod of her head. "Hurry up."

The nurses were tending to Claire, Margo holding her hand and looking directly into her eyes, breathing with her. Another nurse stood positioned between the stirrups.

That's good. I suppose somebody should be there to catch the baby.

"The doctor is on his way, Dad," Margo said.

Claire turned, starting to cry as soon as she saw Sam. "You're here."

Sam rushed to her side. "Oh my God, Mom. Are you feeling okay?"

Claire nodded intently, tears streaming down her face. "Where were you?"

"I was swimming with Bryce and my phone was dying so I turned it off. We got in the car as soon as Bryce got the message. I'm so sorry."

"You could've called." Claire's face scrunched up. "Oh, shit. I need to push."

I took Claire's hand, Sam by my side, clutching my arm. "It's okay, darling. You've got this. Just look at me and focus."

Doctor Thorp strolled in to the room. "Are we ready to have this baby?" His demeanor was in stark contrast to the tension of the moment.

Margo looked at the monitor. "We're starting a contraction."

The doctor nodded and snapped on rubber gloves. "Let's push."

Claire squeezed so hard that it felt as though my hand was in a vise. I couldn't fathom what her body was going through. This was her way of showing me. She rolled her head forward, the exertion turning her face red. Moments ticked by, Claire's groans becoming more pained and insistent. She collapsed back on the pillow, her chest heaving.

"Nice job, Claire. The baby is crowning. It shouldn't take too many pushes. Dad, do you want to come and see?"

This was one of those questions they'd told us to think about in childbirth class. I'd thought I had another three weeks to think it through. *I don't know if I can watch.* "I'm going to stay up here with Claire. I'll see the baby soon enough."

Claire appeared in a daze, almost as if she was slipping in and out of consciousness.

"Time to push again."

Margo and I helped Claire sit up, held her legs. My hand felt the force with which she was pushing as her back muscles tensed. "Come on, darling. You can do it."

"Man, you are strong, Mom. We are so close," Dr. Thorp said from the foot of the bed. "Do you have another push in you?"

Claire collapsed back on the pillow again. She took three deep breaths. "Let's do this." She crunched up again, this time with even more determination on her face. "I. Just. Want. This. Baby. Ahh." Her head dropped forward and she screamed, "Owwwwwttttttt."

An abrupt and loud squishy sound came.

The other nurse quickly handed the doctor a metal instrument. He mumbled.

What?

Claire's head bobbed up and down with every breath, her body still in crunch position.

Margo stepped to the end of the bed.

My eyes darted between Claire and Doctor Thorp.

He worked furiously.

What? My heart pounded.

Sam leaned into me. "Is that it?"

"It's a girl," Doctor Thorp said.

What? A girl? "I don't hear—"

And then it came. Our baby's cry. Sara's beautiful cry filled the room.

Doctor Thorp cradled her tiny squiggling body in a blue paper pad. Sara arched her back and sucked in another breath before letting loose again.

"What do you say, Dad? Do you want to cut the cord?"

I leaned down and pressed my quivering lips to Claire's forehead, tears rolling down my face. "It's a girl." *It's a girl. She's here. She's finally here.*

CHAPTER FORTY-TWO
─────────────

CHRIS STUMBLED INTO THE OFFICE, wearing only his gray striped pajama pants, rubbing his eyes, hair a wreck. "Here you are. Why don't you go back to bed? I'll take Sara."

I looked down at her tiny face, peaceful and sweet as I cradled her in one arm while sitting at my desk. I'd pretty well mastered the art of one-handed typing and the click-clack didn't seem to bother her one bit. The very corner of her mouth turned up. "She's actually asleep."

"Then why aren't you doing the same?" He reached down and took her into his arms. There was profound adoration on his face every time he looked at her, even when she was crying or fussing.

I smiled as he swayed back and forth. She looked especially small and precious when he held her against his comparatively massive frame. The two of them together was so beautiful, it made my heart swell and ache at the same time.

"I got sucked into writing and she was happy." I leaned against the desk top, realizing how sleep-deprived I really was. "I don't know. I guess I got carried away."

"I've noticed. I'd love to tell you that you need to get some rest, but I know how it goes when you're on a roll. It's hard to stop." He eased into the other desk chair, cradling Sara like the seasoned dad he'd so quickly become. He'd taken to it like a fish to water, changing diapers and teaching her to take breast milk from a bottle, although that job was more than he'd anticipated. She still wasn't a fan.

"I'm glad you understand what it's like."

"Remember when I told you about writing the second solo record after my divorce?" He rocked slowly in the chair. "I have a feeling it's a similar situation."

"Is that part of why you're being so overly amazing with Sara? I mean, I know you're excited to finally be a dad, but you're being almost superhuman with your efforts."

He pulled Sara close and kissed her forehead. She shook her small head and curled in to his chest. "Maybe." He looked at me and smiled. "Or maybe it's just that for the first time in my life, I'm having fun sitting back and letting other people be more important than myself. It feels good."

"Oh, come on. You're so sweet and generous. I wouldn't have married you if you were self-absorbed."

"I know. It still feels good to be selfless for once." He tucked the blanket around Sara more snugly. "I was thinking about it the other day, you know, your dad was a pretty selfless guy. As controlling as he was, everything he did was for the people he loved. He helped me a lot in those last few months of his life."

"It was his way of telling you that he loved you."

He nodded. "Indeed. It was. And I'm thankful for it. I only wish he was here to see this little peanut." He rose from the chair and ambled over to me. "I'm taking Jellybean back to bed. Don't stay up too much longer."

I stood to give him a kiss, clasping his shoulders, up on my tiptoes, Sara between us. "I'll come up now. I can get in some more writing this afternoon."

Sara got up for a little while around two, but settled in after nursing, and the three of us went back to sleep.

I woke when Chris jostled the bed. "Is she up again?" I watched him, perched on the edge of the bed peering down into the bassinet.

"No," he whispered. "She's still sleeping." Chris was so fascinated by watching Sara sleep that I was prepared to declare it his new hobby.

"What time is it?" I asked. Faint light peeked between the blackout shades and the window frame.

"Half five." He leaned back and kissed me on the forehead, pulling the covers up to my shoulder and settling in next to me. "Go back to sleep. She's just fine."

I smiled and closed my eyes, inhaling his heavenly scent. Sleep deprivation had been much easier to handle the second time around. Having a husband willing to get up in the middle of the night, bring me a hungry baby, sing *Blackbird* to us while she was nursing, then change her and rock her to sleep? If ever I'd needed someone to pinch me over the miracle of being married to Chris, it was now.

"You amaze me," I mumbled, eyes still closed.

"I thought you were getting more sleep."

"And you amaze me." I inched closer to him and he wrapped his arm around me. My face settled against his bare chest.

"Tell me, why do I amaze you?" His voice was deep and soft, so intoxicating. One more week until we could have sex again. *Thank God.* I never expected to feel that way the second time, either. After Sam was born, I didn't want a penis, regardless of owner, within fifty yards of me. Of course, Chris was the exception to nearly every rule, that one especially.

"How do you help me with Sara and never complain once? Julie said Matt would never get up with the kids in the middle of the night. And she's not the only one. Every mom I know says the same thing. Their other half gets up the first few nights and that's it. You're going on a month."

"It's easy. If you wait for something long enough, you're so excited to have it that sleep is secondary."

Chris's superhuman help was such a gift. Ever since I'd started the grand attempt at turning my dad's notebooks into a novel, my days were filled to the brim. Baby time. Chris time. Sam time. Writing time. The woman who became overwhelmed when her plate got too full, was happy even now that the plate was overflowing.

Chris started to snore, and I made a more concerted effort to get back to sleep, but my brain was awake and ready to play, eager to get back to writing. This was something I'd never before experienced. I'd always loved to write, had spent countless hours tapping away at the computer, banging away at the Smith-Corona or scrawling in a notebook when I was younger. It had been an escape, some projects better than others, an outlet for the things in the world that I took in and couldn't let go. Now that I was working on the novel, I was a bit obsessed—new ideas hit me all the time. Post-it notes covered the desk in the home office.

At first, my plan had been to write twenty pages. I knew I had that much in me and I at least had my dad's ideas as a seed, although I'd already strayed from them. I was concerned I would get stuck after those first twenty pages, unsure of where to take it next, uneasy about tampering with my dad's characters and settings.

Instead, my dad took residence in my head, leaving my mom to sit by and quietly listen. He and I riffed off each other for hours. He liked my ideas, would say that he should've thought of a certain plot point, would tell me that he knew he'd done the right thing by handing this all over to me. As I worked through the pages of those notebooks, plotted, wrote, and brainstormed, I grew closer to him every day.

I was still sad about my dad, but I tried to let that fuel the book. Chris and Sam had both found me in the office sobbing my eyes out, but that catharsis was exactly what I needed. I felt like myself at the end of the day, not some half-awake shell of a broken human, which was the way I'd felt after my mom had passed away. Perhaps it would've been different if I'd had an outlet like this when I lost her. It certainly would have changed the game if I'd had Chris. At least this time, I had a way through the depths of grief—a course through a wall of tears, at sea on a vessel called a work-in-progress. And Chris was the one paddling me to shore.

CHAPTER FORTY-THREE

WHY AM I not surprised Graham would continue to concoct his schemes? I set my phone aside and tended to the chicken sizzling away on the grill. The tempting smell permeated the warm June air. *It's not a bad idea. Guess I'll have to talk to Claire about this one.*

I took a long drink of beer, surveying the back yard. Now that the landscaping was in and the pool filled, things had taken shape. Bryce and Sam had spent the afternoon lounging poolside, reveling in their newfound freedom after graduation.

I was astounded that Claire and I made it through the commencement the day before, however proud we were of them both. Between the jubilation of Sam's achievement and Richard's very noticeable absence, calling it bittersweet would have been an understatement.

Now Bryce and Sam sat a few feet from me, playing with six-week-old Sara, who was nestled in her baby seat atop the outdoor dining table. The game they were playing, if you could even call it that, was a competition to see who could make her smile. This had become Sam's favorite activity since Sara had started to grin more regularly, a few days before.

"She likes me best. I'm telling you," Sam said.

Bryce put his arm around Sam, leaning into her. "I don't know. I think its just gas."

She shook her head back and forth. Sara smiled. "See. I told you."

I laughed quietly. *Poor Bryce. He never stood a chance.*

"Check this out." Sam performed her newest trick, a pretend sneeze with a high-pitched, "Ah-choo". Sara responded with another smile. Sam reached out and touched her nose with the tip of her finger. "Who's a good girl?"

"You are way too in love with this baby." Bryce took a swig of his Coke. "You're kind of freaking me out."

"She's adorable. How can you not be in love with her?"

Indeed.

Claire came through the patio doors with a large salad bowl. "How's the chicken coming?"

I lifted the lid on the grill and gave the meat a poke with tongs. "I'm going to give it another minute, then it needs to rest."

"Perfect. I'll get the bread." She watched as Sam fawned over Sara, smiling as only a mother can smile. "Sam, honey, do you mind changing her before we eat?"

"No problem." She carefully unbuckled the strap around Sara's waist and lifted her from the chair, cradling her in her arms, expertly supporting her head. "We'll be right back."

The turning point between Sam and Sara had come a few weeks earlier, when Sam became the first person to cajole Sara into taking a bottle. This took immense pressure off Claire and gave Sam sole ownership of her big sister role, a part she'd been unsure of at first.

Sam returned a minute later, holding Sara over her shoulder, patting her back. She turned so I could see Sara's face. "Look. It's Daddy."

Sara lifted her head for a moment then dropped back onto

Sam's shoulder. She tried again, watching me the entire time. "Hello, Jellybean. Sam is taking such good care of you. You're a very lucky girl." Everything about her was perfect—wide blue eyes like Claire's, tiny chin, button nose. She was our little bird, our Jellybean. I cradled the back of her fuzzy nearly-bald head, pressing a gentle kiss to it, inhaling her wonderful scent, something Claire had dubbed a baby's superpower. It was true. I was Jell-O in its presence.

Claire came outside and Sam put Sara in her seat, which she left on the table.

"Bryce, we're ready to eat," Claire said. "Sam, don't you think we should put Sara down while we're eating?"

"Where? Like on the ground?"

"It's not really the ground, it's a patio. She's still in her comfy seat."

Sam seemed unconvinced. "There's plenty of room for her on the table."

Claire looked at me, arching her eyebrows. "Fair enough. Big sister knows best."

"Damn straight." Sam plopped down in the chair closest to Sara.

"Sam. Language," Claire said.

"What? I said damn. I'm eighteen." She shrugged and took the salad bowl when Claire passed it to her. "And I might miss Grandpa, but I don't miss the profanity police."

We all missed Richard, much more than I had imagined. Just as Claire was coming to terms with it by working on her book, I had poured time into new music. For me, this was an important time to reflect on both Sara and Richard, new life and a life left behind, as well as the path ahead for Claire and I.

This burst of creative output was different than the times when major life events had sent me into a self-imposed creative exile. Now I had learned to be prolific while taking time to breathe, to enjoy each day as it came, bounce a baby on my knee, take my wife out for a coffee or join her for a run. Claire, Sara, and Sam—my girls, made that balance possible.

Of course, the timing was remarkable. Graham and the rest of the band would likely be ecstatic that I had so much new material to bring to the party when we started recording in a week.

"I do wish Dad could've been here yesterday." Claire looked at Sam with a familiar wistfulness. "He was very proud of you, Sam. Of how hard you've worked and your smarts and getting into NYU, of course."

Sam straightened in her chair. "Thanks. It would've been nice to have him here. That's for sure."

"He really liked you a lot, Bryce," Claire said. "I'm sorry you didn't have the chance to get to know him better."

Bryce had taken an enormous bite of chicken and was nodding while trying to chew. Finally, he got it down. "I know. Me too. He seemed like a cool guy. But thanks, Mrs. Penman. I appreciate your saying that."

"Hey, come on now. No Mr. and Mrs. Penman." I took a slice of bread and slathered it with butter, in honor of Richard. "It's Chris and Claire. Please. You're a university man now. No need for unnecessary formalities."

"Got it. Thanks." Bryce grinned and tucked back into his dinner.

"Have you two talked about how next year is going to go?" I asked.

Claire furrowed her brow, flashing me the "Where are you going with this, Penman?" look.

I shrugged in response. I wasn't sure where I was going with it. I was merely making conversation. "You two won't be far from each other. Boston is only a train ride from New York." Claire and I both knew that Sam and Bryce's romance likely wouldn't survive Freshman year, but we'd decided that it never worked to caution Sam about anything. Best to let her learn this one on her own. She could cry on Claire's shoulder when the time came.

Sam nodded. "Yeah. I think we'll just play it by ear." She and Bryce made eye contact that suggested that on some level, they also knew things might not work out, long term. "I mean, we're both going to be in a dorm, so we'll have to figure out how that will work."

"Smart," Claire said. "Get to school and go from there. You guys will probably be texting all day long anyway."

"We figured we could Skype every few days," Bryce added.

Sam's eyes grew wide. "Oh. Mom. Skype."

"Yes?" Claire took a sip of her wine.

"I can Skype with you guys and then I'll get to see Sara." Sam peered into the chair, where the baby had fallen asleep. "She's going to change so much when I'm at school. I don't want to miss too much of it."

"That'd be wonderful." Claire smiled. "I know I'd enjoy it immensely. Might help to make the house feel less empty."

This might be as good a time as any. "Actually, Sam, your mom and I might be bringing Sara up to New York some time in the fall."

Claire looked at me, perplexed. "Really?"

I set down my fork. "We would be coming through Boston as well if I can get everything sorted."

"What in the world are you talking about?" Claire set down her fork, telling me I'd better be forthcoming with an explanation, pronto.

"Graham called when I was putting on the chicken. He has a proposition for me. Well, let me put it this way, he has a proposition for us."

CHAPTER FORTY-FOUR

TWENTY-FOUR HOURS LATER, I was still trying to wrap my head around it. *I'm going on tour. With the baby. And Chris. Pinch me.*

Chris reached across the table and grasped my hand. The candles in the restaurant flickered, casting a flattering light. It somehow made Chris exponentially more handsome when he already had a distinct advantage over most mortals. *So unfair.*

"Date night, darling," he said, rubbing my fingers with his thumb. "It's exciting."

"I know. It is." I glanced at my phone as inconspicuously as possible.

He flipped the phone, screen down. "Sam will be just fine with Sara. Those two are probably sitting on the couch watching *Pretty In Pink* and eating popcorn."

"Popcorn?"

"You know what I mean. Sam's eating popcorn and Sara will have her bottle of mum's milk when she wants it." He dropped his head lower, his gaze connecting with mine. "Trust me. It's fine."

I sucked in a deep breath. "I know. You're right. I shouldn't worry."

"Right. It's my job to worry." He slid my glass of wine closer to me. "It's your job to drink more. I'm hoping to get lucky tonight."

"Oh yeah?" I succumbed to his persistent flirtation with a smile and took a sip of Sauvignon Blanc. "Who's the girl? Anyone I know?"

"Blonde I've known for a while now. Real saucy trollop. Bit of a handful."

"Saucy trollop?"

"Or a mother of two. I get the terms confused."

I laughed. "Don't worry. You won't have any problems with your saucy blonde."

The waiter brought our appetizer, jalapeño cheddar hushpuppies. As proper as the restaurant was, with crisp white tablecloths and impeccable service, the cuisine was down-home, exactly the food for which Chris had developed a strong preference. He dunked one in the dish of cocktail sauce and downed it at once.

"You know those are really hot, don't you?" I took a tentative bite of mine, and steam rose from the center.

He waved his hand in front of his mouth. "I'm learning that," he mumbled. He gulped down half a glass of water.

"What do we need to do to get ready for the band coming next week?" I asked. Graham and Angie, Terence and his new girlfriend Chelsea, Nigel and his wife Heather, were set to arrive Tuesday. Graham and Angie would be staying in our guest room. The rest of the band and female counterparts would be living in my old house.

"The cleaning crew I hired will take care of things at your place on Monday. Otherwise, I don't know. Buy a bunch of beer?"

"I just want to make sure everyone feels welcome."

"Everyone will feel plenty welcome. We're all just itching to get back into the studio."

I had to smile at his pure enthusiasm. *This is what he's meant to do.* Surely, it would feel good to get back to it. "I can't wait to hear what a new Banks Forest record is going to sound like."

"You and me both." He sat back as the waiter cleared the appetizer platter and refilled our waters. "How are you feeling about the tour, love? I don't want you to feel like I'm steamrollering you." He again leaned forward and took my hand, this time fiddling with my wedding band and engagement ring.

I'd been mulling it over since Chris had sprung it on me at dinner the night before. After recording a new record this summer, the band would do two-dozen small club gigs across the U.S., creating an intense demand for tickets. The hope was that the buzz would create record label interest and if not, the band planned to release the new record independently. This was the advantage of the band managing themselves, "lean and mean" as Chris liked to call it. They could embrace the unconventional, turn on a dime, head in whichever direction they chose.

"I think it sounds like fun, but I'm still trying to envision it."

"Oh, it'll be a little crazy, but we'll make it work. The three of us will just be living out of a tour bus for five weeks instead of the house."

"I did have a fantasy about going on tour with Banks Forest. Granted, I was seventeen at the time." *Funny how things work out.*

"It'll be wonderful, I promise. Our grand family adventure. There's so much bloody downtime on the road anyway. It'll give me as much time as possible with you and Jellybean. I don't want to miss a thing with her. Not one second." The waiter brought our entrees and Chris immediately dug into his plate of shrimp and grits. "You can write on the bus. I bet you finish the draft of your novel by the time we get home."

"You think so?"

"Definitely."

"I meant to tell you, I read something interesting online this morning. Do you remember Amanda Carlton's publicist, Valerie?"

"Sure. I met her the day you interviewed Amanda."

"Right. Well, she just took a job as an acquisitions editor at one of the big publishers. It turns out her background is in publishing."

"Now that is interesting." He cocked an eyebrow. "I believe she owes you a favor."

"A big favor."

"Even better."

"Of course, the book has to be good and I have to actually finish it." The prospect was both terrifying and inspiring. "Easier said than done."

"Claire, darling, you can do anything." He reached for my hand and raised it to his lips. "Hell, you've made me a happy man and everyone said that was impossible."

After dinner and a stunning piece of buttermilk pie, we made the short block-long walk to the studio, so Chris could finally show it off to me. When we stepped inside and he flipped on the light, I made an audible gasp.

"Wow." I turned in the stunningly decorated lobby area, a mix of modern and 60s vintage, gray and black and white, exactly the way Chris wanted everything. "This is unreal. Never in a million years did I think this ratty old building could look like this."

"Just wait. This is nothing." Chris led the tour, through a large rehearsal space, recording isolation rooms, an administrative office, a band lounge, and finally to the control room. There were comfortable leather couches, a beautiful wood floor, and the expanse of glass looking into the main recording room, buttons and dials as far as the eye could see.

"Is it normal for this room to be so dimly lit?"

"There are brighter settings. This is mood lighting."

"That mixing board is unreal. How did you even get it in here?"

He laughed. "That's a story for the ages, but it was a big mess. I didn't tell you because I didn't want you to worry."

I ran my hand along the very edge of it. "Well, however much work it was, I'd say that the results were worth it."

He turned in a slow circle, nodding. His pride in his accomplishment was unmistakable. "I wish your dad could be here next week. He would've gotten such a kick out of seeing the studio up and running." He knocked his head to the side. "Of course, eventually he would've complained that the music was too loud and I would've had to send him home."

I smiled, and it felt so good that I could think about him now without breaking down. I knew there were still rough days ahead, but I felt strong enough to handle it, Chris at my side. "There's a lot I wish he could've been around for."

"I know darling, but I promise you he's here in spirit. I know it. Your dad's mark is all over this project. And then of course, there's you." He drew closer, took my hand. "If there'd never been a Richard, there never would've been a you, and that would've meant a miserable existence for me."

"I'm sure you would've muddled along."

"But I've never once wanted to muddle." The back of his hand brushed my cheek. "I want to feel alive. You make me feel that way."

He combed his fingers through the hair at my nape, tilting my head back to kiss me. I melted the instant his lips touched mine, impatient and craving. I became a certifiable puddle when his tongue not-so-subtly tangled with mine. He sent ribbons of electricity through me when he possessively pulled my body against his. I arched into him, rose onto my tiptoes to get closer. A familiar bulge grew harder against my leg.

"Chris, honey," I said breathlessly into his neck. "Shouldn't we, you know, do this at home?"

His eyes were dark and intense, the most primal version of the look I'd ever seen. "It's been weeks. I'm beginning to detest the sight of my own hand."

I snickered. "I'm sorry, but I'm not having sex on that couch."

"Why not? It's brand new. I don't think anyone other than me and the engineer have even sat on it yet."

The engineer? Yuck. I shook my head. "No way. I won't be able to think about anything else whenever I come into this room."

"I know. Me neither. It'll be perfect." He kissed me sweetly and tucked my hair behind my ear. "Come on, what better way to test the studio's soundproofing than with some really noisy sex?"

I giggled. "Make sure you got your money's worth?"

"If the police show up, we'll know I got ripped off."

"No police. We've had enough excitement for a while."

He smirked at me. "Okay, darling. We'll do the respectable husband-and-wife version of this at home." He shut off the lights and hurried me out of the building. A frustrated groan came out of him when he put on his seatbelt in the truck. "I hope you know how much I love you. I don't drive around with a stiffy for just anyone."

It was a miracle that Chris didn't get pulled over on the way home. He took liberties with more than one stop sign, as well as the speed limit.

Sam was watching TV downstairs when we arrived, but Chris didn't feel comfortable chatting with her when certain parts of his anatomy were so animated. "Five minutes. If you aren't upstairs in five minutes, I'm starting without you."

"Don't worry. I'll be there." I gave him a quick kiss and walked into the living room. "Hey honey," I said to Sam. "How'd Sara do?"

She hit the mute on the TV remote. "She was so awesome, Mom. I love being with her." She smiled wide. "It might sound dorky, but we had the best time. I'm going to be so sad when I go to school. I'm really going to miss her."

She's so sweet. I bit my lip, fighting back the emotion. "She's going to miss you, too. We all will. That's why we have to see each other as much as possible."

She looked up at the TV. "Oh, my show's back on. Are you going up to bed? Chris must've been tired."

"You have no idea."

She handed me the baby monitor and returned to her show. "Sara's asleep in her crib. You're back on baby duty."

"Got it."

I tiptoed upstairs, praying I wouldn't wake up Sara.

Chris was waiting for me in our bed, as ready as he'd been twenty minutes earlier. "Took you long enough." He hopped out of bed and his talented eyebrows hopped up and down. "Now get over here."

I placed the baby monitor on the bedside table, kicked off my shoes and threw my arms around him. "It's been way too long."

"Far too long." He frantically unbuttoned my blouse and pushed it off my shoulders, zeroing in on my breasts, kissing along the edge of my bra and gripping my ribcage. "I love our daughter, but I'd be lying if I said I wasn't jealous that she gets to spend so much time with the girls."

Blood and heat flooded my skin when he dispatched my bra. I was thankful I'd pumped before we'd left the house. Hopefully I could make it through whatever came next without things getting messy. *Best to be quick about it.*

I shucked my jeans, hopped out of my panties. We were still standing, a difficult proposition when he regularly distracted me with his mouth and hands, gliding, grabbing, and caressing my entire body. *Oh my God. This has been way too long.*

He was breathing heavily already, nearly grunting. "Remember when I said we were doing this the proper husband-wife way?"

"What?" *Stop talking already.*

"I lied."

"Let me guess. Against the door? Not pregnant this time?"

"You are so smart." His eyes became even fiercer. "But, it's going to have to be the bathroom door. Otherwise, Sam might hear."

"Whatever. I'll do it against a garage door at this point."

He scooped me up, grabbing my butt as I wrapped my legs around him. In a flash, my back met the bathroom door, he came inside, and everything shifted became a whirlwind—unguarded thrusts, gasps and moans. When he lowered me to the floor, my chest heaving, I couldn't help but think back to the glorious memory of the shag rug in LA.

He kissed me, cupping the side of my face. "I love you so much, Claire. So much."

"I love you too." I watched as he swept his messy, sexy hair back from his forehead. "You crazy, crazy man."

"Come on. Let's go back to being proper." He led me to the bed and we climbed in, seeking each other's touch as soon as we were both under the covers. He put his arm around me and I settled my head against his chest.

"I feel so much better now."

"Amazing how much better you feel after a little roll in the hay, huh?"

"Or a roll against the door."

"If that suits your fancy."

I laughed. "We might as well do that while we still can."

"My sentiments exactly." He cleared his throat. "Speaking of doing things while we can..." His voice had a very familiar tone to it. Too familiar. "I've been thinking."

I rolled to my side and flipped on the lamp. "What? Bungee jumping in the Amazon? Dog sled racing in Antarctica?"

"Why are you looking at me like that?" His forehead was creased with feigned seriousness—he looked as if he was containing fits of laughter.

"I'm just trying to figure out what in the hell you're about to say. Like I said earlier, we've had plenty of excitement and there's no end to it. The band's making a record, we're going on tour. I'm trying to finish my book."

"Right. It's called life. We're living it. Remember?" He threaded his fingers through my hair. "Living our amazing life. Together."

I took a deep breath. He was right, so right. And I wouldn't have wanted it any other way. "Okay. I'm sorry. Tell me what you were going to say."

Sara started to fuss in the baby monitor.

"Sounds like somebody's up." Chris pulled back the covers. "I'll get her."

"Wait." I grasped his arm and he looked back at me with those heavenly green eyes. "Tell me first."

"I was just going to say that we should have another baby. No big deal." He kissed me on the forehead and leaned down to pick up his boxers.

"Another baby?" I couldn't quite believe the pitch of the high note I'd hit on "baby". *Another baby?*

He shrugged. "Yeah, sure. Two can't be that much more work than one and we're doing such an amazing job with the one we already have." He unleashed his electric smile, the one he surely knew turned me to putty.

Nice. Like that's fair at a time like this. "I guess."

"No worries. I'll get Sara." He reached for the door. "You think about it."

THE END

WANT MORE FROM KAREN BOOTH? Read the excerpt of *Secrets of a (Somewhat) Sunny Girl that follows.*

"Tender and touching, hot and heartfelt, Karen Booth's Secrets of a (Somewhat) Sunny Girl is a joy to read. Once I started, I couldn't stop."-Tiffany Reisz, USA Today Bestselling Author

EXCERPT: SECRETS OF A (SOMEWHAT) SUNNY GIRL

As sisters, they tell each other all their secrets. Except one.

Chapter One

My sister Amy and I had more than twenty ex-boyfriends between us, a zillion stories about awkward first dates, and miraculously enough, only one declined proposal. Nobody was under the impression the Fuller sisters were saving themselves for marriage. Not even close. But I'd sort of thought we might be saving ourselves *from* it.

"Engaged? To be married?" I practically had to shout over the Midtown Diner noontime rush— waitresses barking at bus boys, dishes clattering, customers yammering.

Amy worked her way out of her charcoal gray suit jacket, draping it neatly over her purse on the seat next to her. "What other kind of engaged is there?" She loved to answer a question with a question. If it was possible to be a born litigation attorney, that was my sister.

"I know. I know. I'm just..." I couldn't say more without my stomach lurching, which made me second guess my lunch order. Matzoh ball soup might kill me. Or, in the absence of wine, maybe chicken broth could help wash down the realization that the secret club I'd thought my sister and I had chartered was a sham. How long had she been planning her escape?

"I'm glad it's not just me. I'm speechless too." Amy beamed at her new platinum and diamond prize like she'd given birth to it. She tucked her neat, blonde bob behind one ear. I'd always envied her high cheekbones, but today they were straight out of a Technicolor film, blushed with every gorgeous shade of a ripe Georgia peach. She got the cheekbones, and the blush, from Mom.

"Speechless. Yes. That's the perfect word."

Patty, the waitress with the spiky persimmon-orange hair, slid white diner plates ringed in cobalt blue onto our table, putting my forthcoming paper-thin spiel about love and good news on pause, thank God.

"I still can't believe it. It's exciting, right?" Amy's voice reached a pitch like air squeaking out of a pin hole in a balloon. She picked up half of her Pastrami sandwich with one hand, leaving the other one—the bejeweled one—on display in the center of the table. It was no small feat. The diner served some of the fattest sandwiches in Manhattan.

"It is." I nodded, as if that might make my lackluster performance more convincing. I sucked flat diet soda through a straw, stalling again. If only I'd had time to prepare some remarks. If only she'd given me some sign that she and Luke were this serious. I'd assumed she was sleeping at his place most nights because the sex was halfway decent. "I'm just..."

"You're just what, Katherine?" She was losing her patience for my lack of gushing, even while her ocean-blue eyes flickered with optimism as she gazed at the behemoth rock on her left ring finger. Diamonds were beyond crazy if you thought about it—a nugget of dirty black carbon subjected to unbearable pressure and unthinkable temperatures until it had no choice but to turn into something sparkly and precious. Someone optimistic might call it a beautiful metaphor—even the ugliest thing could get better.

It just might take a few billion years.

"I'm wondering..." I innocently slurped my soup. *Don't say it.* "Did you know you were going to go back on our pact? Like all along?" *You are such a miserable excuse for a sister.*

She jerked her hand away. "The pact? Are you serious right now? You're supposed to be happy for me."

"I *am* happy for you." It came out as a plea to the universe. *Please let me be happy. Is that too much to ask?* "I'm ecstatic." I was going to have to lie until I could get on board with happy. I couldn't tell her how terrified I was. It pained me to think about her getting hurt and if anyone was going to hurt her, it was some dude she'd known for less than a year. Plus, Luke was a little too perfect—clearly spent a lot of time at the gym, had at least a dozen pet names for her, and was always celebrating tiny milestones. *Oh, honey. Guess what? This will be the tenth time we've gone out for Chinese food.* He had to be hiding something.

Then there was the not-small fact that our family tree had divorces hanging from every branch. The Fullers did not do well with the sanctity of marriage, and that led to divorce, which then led to heartbreak, for everybody, even the bystanders. If Amy's heart was going to get broken, who would pick up the pieces? Me. And I was terrible at picking up pieces. I could never figure out how to glue them back together.

"That was almost nine years ago." Amy lowered her chin, forcing me to look at her. "It was your idea, and you were drunk when you said it. Remember? Cinco de Mayo?"

"Hey. We had fun that night."

"And you had five Margaritas."

"You weren't far behind me."

"Exactly why this is a stupid conversation. I only said yes to the idea that we should never get married and stay roommates forever, so you'd shut up and get in your own bed."

It all came back to me. My head hurt just thinking about the hangover that came on May 6th that year. I didn't end up feeling right until June. "God. I got in your bed that night, didn't I? I'm sorry. I should never drink tequila. Ever."

"Exactly." She punctuated her statement by pointing at me with a french fry.

"You know, I kept the pact when Jason proposed."

"And you have very big balls to turn down a guy in front of his whole family."

Jason was the one declined proposal. He'd invited me to dinner at his parents' house in Brooklyn, a lovely old Brownstone—it was like something out of a romantic comedy. They were Italian and vocal, nothing like my family, Scandinavian and choking on every slightly impolite thing. I hadn't even taken off my coat before his mom put him on the spot. *Look at her. She's beautiful, with the blonde hair and the blue eyes. She looks like a milkmaid. You'll make such pretty babies.*

It didn't stop during dinner. *Your brother is already married and he's younger. He's going to have children before you. It's not right. You should marry Katherine. She's a keeper. I can tell.* After the Tiramisu was proudly presented for dessert, her mother's mother's recipe, she'd dragged Jason into the other room. I'd sat at the table with his dad and younger sister while we heard every word and could only exchange tortured smiles. I'd twisted the cloth napkin in my lap so tightly that I was embarrassed to give it back.

Ma, we're not ready to get married.

Just give her your grandmother's ring. You'll lose her if you don't.

My brain sputtered. *A ring? Oh, shit.*
What if she says no?
She won't say no.

The next thing I knew, Jason skulked into the dining room, followed by his grinning mother. He sank down to one knee and delivered the most dispassionate proposal a man had ever given. *Katherine, will you marry me?*

His mother gasped.

I wanted to cry.

And then I'd said what I had to. *No. I'm sorry.*

I was almost proud when I went home that night and told Amy, like I'd fought off the evil empire, even if I'd crushed a guy's pride in the process. The truth was that Jason and I were not in love, and the pact meant something to me. I wasn't meant to be married. I was too screwed up. Too much messy baggage, and my sister carried around a lot of the same stuff. I'd only been within spitting distance of love once, with an Irish hottie my sister knew very little about. That guy, the sexy heartbreaker, had been too much to hold onto.

"Look, Katherine. I'm not you. I can't spend every waking minute being pessimistic. I get enough of that at work. Please don't fault me for finding a guy and falling in love."

My shoulders dropped. "You're right. You're absolutely right. I want what you want. I've spent my whole life wanting you to be happy." That much was true. That part I didn't have to fake. I'd woken up every morning for the last thirty-two years hoping she'd have a good day, even before she'd been born. It was like this thing in the very center of my brain, a drive planted at my conception. Had that ambition come from Mom? Was it God's way of keeping my sister safe? He had to have known our mom wasn't going to be around to do it herself.

"Thank you. I appreciate it."

"Now can we please order some pie? We're supposed to be

celebrating, but I can't be late getting back to work." I flagged Patty, who nodded at me as she poured an old guy a cup of coffee and swiped a stack of empty plastic creamer cups from his table. "When are you going to tell Dad?"

"I'll call him tonight. He'll just start stressing about when the wedding is going to be and who's going to pay for it and where he should go for a tux. He'll probably book his train ticket as soon as we get off the phone."

Dad was always planning. He never wanted to be caught off guard. I could relate—Amy had inherited supermodel cheekbones, I got a hatred of surprises. "Don't give him a hard time about any of it, okay? I'm sure it'll be emotional for him. You're getting married. It'll probably bring up stuff. You know. About Mom."

"Yeah. I know. I need to psych myself up for that."

"Ladies?" Patty asked. "More ketchup?"

I grasped Amy's hand and held it up for Patty to see. "Look at what happened. My little sister. Engaged." There it was—my happiness. I guess I could muster it if I focused my attention outward. Note to self: stop thinking so much.

The sweetest off-balance smile you'd ever seen broke across Patty's face. She knocked my sister on the shoulder with her knuckle. "Look at you. Getting married. Is it the banker? The one with the tight tush?"

Crimson flushed Amy's face. "Yes. Luke. He asked last night. It was our eight-month anniversary."

"Which is why we're celebrating with pie." I was determined to hold on to this flash of happiness. I wanted to love it, give it a name, and keep it in my purse for later. "What do you want, Ames? Chocolate cream? Banana?" I looked up at Patty. "You know me. I'll have coconut."

Amy dabbed at the corners of her mouth with a paper napkin. "I don't know. I'm going to have to start thinking about fitting into a dress. Maybe french fries and a sandwich the size of my head is enough indulgence for one day."

Patty rolled her eyes. She didn't have much patience for healthy pursuits in her place of employment.

"She'll have the chocolate," I said.

"Got it. On the house. It's a big day." Patty sidled off.

"Hey, if you're worried about the apartment, don't," Amy said, pushing her plate aside. "Luke and I already talked about it and we'll pay my half of the rent through the end of the lease."

It hurt to know they'd already talked about my place in their new life, and that I would apparently be playing the role of difficult older sister. I needed to get used to no longer being consulted about things that involved me.

"You guys don't have to do that. I make good money." Better than good, actually. My job at the North American Color Institute paid great, not only because I was a model employee, but because I had a genetic gift, a one-in-a-billion anomaly called tetrachromacy. Most people saw a red rose as two or three shades of that single color. I looked at that same rose and saw two or three hundred colors in a single glance. The differences between hues was even more pronounced when I saw something in the sunlight.

"It was Luke's idea, actually."

"You guys should save your money. Go on an amazing honeymoon. I'll get a roommate if I need one."

"I know you. You won't get a roommate. We're paying my half of the rent. End of discussion."

It was sort of adorable when she ended an argument with an assertion, like dad used to when he was tired and grumpy and just wanted us to shut up so he could watch TV. Most of the time, Amy never wanted a disagreement to end. When we were little, Amy turned everything into a negotiation, some of which went on forever. Most of them had revolved around who got to be Barbie and who had to be Skipper, or who got to lick the beaters when we made brownies, but there had been big things we'd had to agree on, too. Like whether we should tell Dad that we were pretty sure Mom was cheating on him.

That topic had not been taken lightly, even though we were ten and eight and unable to fully comprehend infidelity. We only knew it was weird that she invited a man to stay at our house whenever Dad was on a work trip. Gordon. Gordon who stayed over. Gordon who once wore our dad's bathrobe.

Hours of discussion, over the course of months, went into the decision to tell him. We ultimately made a list of pros and cons, on a piece of the Hello Kitty stationery Grandma had given me for my tenth birthday. We'd been careful to consider every possible outcome. Well, almost every outcome. When you're a kid, and have a mostly happy heart, there were only so many horrible things you could imagine. We were much more inclined to believe that no matter what, everything would be okay.

To this day, I could recite every word Amy and I said to each other the final time we talked about it.

When do we tell him? When he gets back from his trip?

Yes. I'll tell him. I'm the oldest.

I could tell you what we were wearing that day—I had on a cherry red turtleneck and jeans, and Amy was wearing a celery green sweatshirt that said LOVE on it in rainbow letters. I could tell you what was playing on the radio, but not because I cherished the details. My mind refused to let go of that conversation and everything that happened over the forty-eight hours that followed. It liked to replay it all in my head, like a movie. With precision, it remembered every color.

Years later, when we were teenagers, I'd asked Amy if she remembered what we'd said to each other that day, our rationale, our thought process. Had I dreamed it? What had I overlooked?

"I was eight," she'd said. "I don't remember anything other than not wanting Mom to hear us."

I remembered that part, too.

Patty delivered our pie, two forks, and an extra stack of napkins.

"I won't live through the guilt," Amy said. "I can't give you a single reason to resent me for this."

"For what? Being happy?"

Amy scooped up a bite of whipped cream and chocolate shavings. "No. For leaving."

I stared down at the coconut cream pie, my absolute favorite dessert, and couldn't stomach the idea. This was really happening. Amy and I wouldn't be together anymore. Everything was going to change, and I hadn't seen it coming. "I think I'll take this to go."

"After you made such a big deal about ordering it?"

"Yeah. Sorry. I'm swamped at work."

Amy yanked back the sleeve of her white blouse and eyed her watch. "Shit. I have to get back, too."

I settled the bill with Patty, Amy ate only half of her pie, and I tried to turn my thinking around. My bond with my sister was too important to let my temporary shock get in the way. I needed time. That was all.

Amy and I said our goodbyes out on the street, over the steady hum of traffic and car horns. It was the most beautiful fall day—the air was crisp and dry, albeit perfumed with the aroma of the hot dog cart on the corner.

"You sure you're okay?" she asked.

The sun was shining right in my eyes, and even with my sunglasses on, I had to squint to see her. Something about that hint of warmth on my face, coming at me in a kaleidoscope of gold, made everything a little better. She looked like an angel in the sunlight, and in many ways, that was exactly what she was to me—a blessing. I grasped her by the shoulders, if only to underscore what I was about to say. "I am better than okay. The person I love most in this world is getting married. It's not possible for me to be more okay."

She smiled and stepped in for a hug. "Love you, Kat."

"Love you, too."

"I'll try to be home in time for *Jeopardy*."

"Perfect."

I turned back and started the walk down to my office, while Amy went in the opposite direction. All in all, I felt pretty good for someone who'd eaten a Matzoh ball for lunch. Sure, I'd just received life-changing news, and it would take some work to keep from slipping down into the depths of worry, which was my biggest downfall. But I had to focus on the good. Amy and I would always be close. Nothing would ever take that away from us, not even a man. We had an unbreakable bond—we'd made it through the obstacle course of our childhood, together. And even though Mom wasn't around to be a part of our adulthood, I wanted to believe that she watched over us every day, her heart full of a mother's love.

And hopefully some forgiveness for me.

Secrets of a (Somewhat) Sunny Girl **is now available.**

"Intelligent and sexy. Karen's prose sparks off the page."-Jenny Holiday, USA Today Bestselling Author

ACKNOWLEDGMENTS

Back Forever would not have been possible without the help of the following people.

My husband, Steve, the man who has learned to live with my particular brand of insanity. My children, Emily and Ryan, who always understand if Mom is grumpy because of writing. Sara Young, the woman who sleeps in her cheerleader uniform. Karen Stivali, my critique partner and unflinching sounding board. Heather Todd, my grace-under-pressure alpha-beta reader. Fellow authors who are always generous with advice and support: Sarah Dessen, Celia Rivenbark, Elisa Lorello, David Menconi, Bobbi Ruggiero, Piper Trace, Megan Frampton, Suzi Parker, Elisa Nader, Sam Stephenson, Tom Maxwell and Margaret Ethridge. Rhonda Rivera and Amanda Pustz from Daily Duranie for all-around awesomeness. The readers who went the extra mile from the very beginning, especially Val Skorup, Angela McAllister, Michelle Gaddis, Jill Noble, Kimberley Lowrey, Rob Lasher, Paula Langan, Patrece Pluck, Carolyn Boardman, Debbie Craggs, Sarah Tule, Lynn Capirsello, Cathy Cook-Ghesquire, and Cathy Junkin. Carolyn Boardman and Georgia Bowring for being my British dictionary on the fly. Mandy Pennington for jumping into the beta-reading fray. Everyone who took the time to tweet, send an email, call, or write me a letter about *Bring Me Back*. Those are the gestures that keep a writer writing. My prized and ever-growing circle of Duranie friends, especially the crazy ones on Twitter. You know who you are. The talented women of Turquoise Morning Press, my original publisher, especially Kim Jacobs, Shelley Rawe, Wendy Williams, and my unflappable editor, Suzanne Barrett. Michael Rank and John Plymale for musical knowledge that they both play off as "no big thing".

ABOUT THE AUTHOR

Karen Booth is a Midwestern girl transplanted in the South, raised on '80s music and too many readings of "Forever" by Judy Blume. An early preoccupation with rock 'n' roll led her to spend her twenties working her way from intern to executive in the music industry. Now she's a married mom of two and instead of staying up late in rock clubs, she gets up before dawn to write sexy contemporary romance.

Thank you for reading! If you enjoyed this book, please leave a review with your favorite online retailer or on Goodreads. Even if it's only a few words, it means so much!

Keep in touch!
karenbooth.net
karen@karenbooth.net

ALSO BY KAREN BOOTH

Hiding in the Spotlight

Save a Prayer, a prequel to Bring Me Back

Claire's Diary, a prequel to Bring Me Back

The KISS Principle

Rock Starred

Secrets of a (Somewhat) Sunny Girl

The Langford Family series:

That Night with the CEO

Pregnant by the Rival CEO

The Ten-Day Baby Takeover

The Locke Legacy series:

Pregnant by the Billionaire

Holiday Baby Bombshell

Between Marriage and Merger

Made in the USA
Middletown, DE
16 October 2020